REVIEWS O

### *I And You, And Me And Her*
"The story unfolds at a solid pace... very well-drawn and believable." (*Whistler Independent Book Awards*)

"Stories about men in love with women they can't have ... very detailed and vivid" (*BookLife Prize*)

### *Too Late The Hunter*
"An enjoyable and fascinating novel . . . the writing is lyrical and fresh; and, at times, completely brilliant." (*Whistler Independent Book Awards*)

"Psychological thriller... Grills writes masterful description! His phrases gave me goosebumps more than once... a bingeworthy novel!" (Marla J. Hayes, author of *Cassidy's Deadly Exit*)

"Lovely writing... naturally flowing narrative... *Too Late the Hunter* takes the reader to the heart of the human problem... [and] tackles the bigger job that real novels need to do, that is, to look at an enduring human issue... without prescribing a position that must be taken... integrating different perspectives over a wider and non-contiguous span of time... in a seemingly fluid manner that doesn't feel either contrived or clunky to the reader." (Ric de Meulles, author of *Junkshop Angel)*

### *Oblivion*
"The author writes well and is, like his protagonist, a good communicator... [with] tone and style." (*Whistler Independent Book Awards*)

### *Roadkill*
Shortlisted for the 2018 *Whistler Independent Book Awards*; Finalist for the 2018 *Next Generation Indie Book Awards*

"Set in a compelling dystopian future ... the story develops greater urgency as it progresses. Writing in fluid, lyrical sentences, Grills demonstrates a clear facility with language and tone ... alluring descriptions... striking prose and an enticing premise allow this novel to stand out within the larger category of dystopian fiction" (*BookLife Prize*)

"I absolutely loved *Roadkill*." (Donna Sinclair, author of *Saving The Future)*

"A thinking person's speculative fiction." (Erich Weingartner, editor of *A Journey of Faith Across a Turbulent Century: Memoirs of a Refugee Pastor*)

### Every Wolf's Howl
"Surprising, poignant, affectionate, and amusing memoir." (*Prairie Fire Review of Books*)

"An accomplished author of stories... Barry Grills... in his first memoir... [writes] a moving story of friendship and transformation, and anyone who has ever longed to companionate with wild creatures will be transfixed" (*Winnipeg Free Press)*

### Cock-Eyed Voice: Stories
The short story "A Game with Adonis" ... [is] "so successful the reader squirms in self-recognition" (*Books in Canada*)

"These stories are vintage gold... with a unique and pointed voice... A treat for readers." (Jennifer Rouse Barbeau, author of *Dying Hour*)

*To Tracey*

*Mum says Merry*
*Christmas*

*Best wishes*

*Barry* 25/11/23

# An
# Ecstasy

Barry Grills

Barry Grills

Books by Barry Grills

**Fiction**
*An Ecstasy* (Fluid Grouse Enterprises)
*The Last Light Spoken* (Fluid Grouse Enterprises)
*Cock-Eyed Voice: Stories* (Fluid Grouse Enterprises)
*Too Late The Hunter* (Fluid Grouse Enterprises)
*Oblivion* (Fluid Grouse Enterprises)
*I And You, And Me And Her* (Fluid Grouse Enterprises)
*Roadkill* (Fluid Grouse Enterprises)

**Non Fiction**
*Every Wolf's Howl* (Freehand Books)
*A New Day Dawns* (with Jim Brown) (Quarry Press)
*Falling Into You* (Quarry Press)
*Ironic* (Quarry Press)
*Snowbird* (Quarry Press)

# An
# Ecstasy

Barry Grills

FLUID
GROUSE
enterprises

Barry Grills

For information about permission to reprint, record, or perform sections of this book, write
**Fluid Grouse Press**, 635 Scollard Street, North Bay, Ontario, Canada P1B 5A2

This novel is a work of fiction; any resemblance to its characters by persons living or dead is
purely coincidental

**Library and Archives Canada Cataloguing in Publication**

Grills, Barry, 1948-   , author
An Ecstasy / Barry Grills

**Cover Design:** Jennifer Rouse Barbeau
**Cover Photo:** Isabelli Pontes (https://www.pexels.com/photo/forest-6992/)
**Author Photo:** Liz Lott

ISBN:
978-1-7780612-0-2

*In loving memory to my aunt and uncle, Muriel Ivy Parm and Richard Albert Parm; it was they who taught me the beauty, wonder and joys of cottage life.*

Barry Grills

**ONTARIO ARTS COUNCIL**
**CONSEIL DES ARTS DE L'ONTARIO**

an Ontario government agency
un organisme du gouvernement de l'Ontario

*We acknowledge funding support from the Ontario Arts Council, an agency of the Government of Ontario.*

## ACKNOWLEDGMENTS

This novel was written around the dates in which it is set. It is designed to form part of a thematically existentialist trilogy about romantic love. The other two novels in the trilogy include *Too Late The Hunter*, written in the mid 1970s, and *I And You, And Me And Her*, written after I moved north from Muskoka approximately twenty years ago. *An Ecstasy* was written near the end of the 1990s when I was living in Kingston, Ontario.

I mention these elements because *An Ecstasy* has gone through a great deal to get into print—which is just me apologizing to the novel as its author for my delays in finally delivering it into the world almost three decades late. The birthing room of novel writing is a very hectic place and sometimes "emergency" writings jump their place in line.

*An Ecstasy* was my first novel to receive an Ontario Arts Council Works-In-Progress Grant in 1998. I wish to express my gratitude to the Ontario Arts Council for this and other grants I have received since then for other novels. Without the Council's financial assistance, the writing of this book would have been virtually impossible for me to complete.

My deepest thanks to Jennifer Rouse Barbeau who painstakingly edited this book. She exercised patience, sensitivity and fairness relating to the historical period in which the novel is set— without rewriting history to match current cultural sensibilities. She also clarified female perception to me where male perception occasionally intruded.

As usual, the cover design is Jennifer's as well. My thanks to her for coming up with a cover that depicts the novel's theme and purpose in both vision and feeling.

Barry Grills

*And those who were seen dancing
were thought to be insane by those
who could not hear the music.*

– Friedrich Nietzsche

Barry Grills

Table of Contents

Barry Grills

# PART ONE: MAY 1996

## MATT

**Wednesday, May 1**

FIRST WRITING. LET'S SEE. The prodigal son has returned home to find everyone gone. Even the ghosts. It's just an empty cottage, hardly more than the occasional echo or creak, a cabal of lethargic shadows, a chill in the rooms the heat from the wood stove hasn't infiltrated yet. I expected to be alone, except for the ghosts of course. Maybe they're not coming, although it's awfully early to tell. I thought I'd be excited in a subdued way, looking forward with enthusiasm to the months lying ahead. Instead, I feel irritable and lost, confused my enthusiasm has disappeared now that this self-imposed exile, planned for so long, is finally underway. It's disappointing. I assumed I'd be in a better mood, feel crisp and expansive with so many beginnings ahead of me.

But there's nothing crisp about my state of bemused melancholy. It's a peculiar kind of sadness, fuzzy around the edges, like discovering a dusty bottle of Madeira at the back of the kitchen cupboards and consuming one or two drinks too many. Sadness, even when it's blurred and not very deep, is a dubious way to begin this journal, I think. It tends to vitiate the freshness in a new scribbler, a new pen, a new closet where I can hang my hat for a while. It's been a long time since I've fretted even slightly that I might not know what I am doing. Strange to consider doubts now. Doubts are such bushwhackers; they're always ambushing you just when you believe the road ahead is clear.

Perhaps it's time to consider, at the end of my first day at *The Crow's Nest*, that I have arrived here less because this is a place I need to be than because I have run out of patience with living *back there*. There, of course, is the new and improved Kingston of expanded boundaries and arbitrarily restructured services. Alas, politics goes with me everywhere. It's been this way forever. It's in the work that lies ahead. But it's also in the tediousness of the past. I've been battling the same old status quo since I first stood up on my own two legs. And these days the status quo is a mean little fucker. It's dirty laundry pretending to be clean, malice masquerading as practical wisdom, a series of falsehoods so brazen people believe they're true.

But this Kingston thing is more than that. Kingston and I are an old married couple and it's time we got divorced. We don't convey mystery any longer, on our own or within the relationship. Back there, I've discovered, I know everyone and everything a little too well. Worse yet, too many people know me. Almost invariably, when I have lived in a place a little too long, I come to realize I lose my required opaqueness, that altogether too much of me has become visible; there isn't much left unseen or unnoticed, right down to the bodily functions. Perhaps I should entitle this journal *Memoirs of a Transparent Man*. For some time now I have felt like one of those see-through anatomical models they use in biology class, the kind where you can examine the colored veins, arteries and organs through the clear plastic skin. It's not a state of being I endorse. Not only do you become a riddle resolved, a puzzle solved, a wrinkle ironed down to a crease, but it reduces you to a collage of colored bits and pieces displayed to explain their function, which is supposed to match someone else's function. Just because most people have two legs, it doesn't mean we all want to jog.

Huh! It appears Lynn Danby at *Bartlett & Strong* is going to get more than she bargained for by the end of the summer. The essays I've been contracted to write for her about the impact of current economic trends on the social fabric of Canada will have a bit of passion in them, if this journal entry is any indication.

She told me to ignore any temptation to be restrained. She said we'd worry about restraint later, but she may not know what I'm truly like when my political viewpoint is enflamed. Not to worry. It's just my mood tonight. Period of adjustment, I guess.

Still, it feels quite delicious to be this crabby. And it amuses me. I feel like I'm egging myself on. Because there's no harm in amusing myself with the richness of simply being pissed off. I feel a childish liberation in the notion of picking something up off the table—a fork full of twisted, congealed pasta or a salt shaker or a goblet of Valpolicella—and flinging it against the wall, just to get it out of my system, to stick my tongue out at gravity and mass, feeling a brief but heady rebellion in what I've done.

Except I've already cleared the table. There's nothing within reach but lined, three-holed paper and a binder so proud of the misspelling of *organiz-it* the corporate magpies have trademarked it. And I have this pen with which this very word is being written. If I toss the pen I'll be unable to write on this line what I did ultimately throw. Oh yes, a mug of coffee—that's a tempting rocket to launch from this tabletop Canaveral—except that it's good coffee with a tasty edible oil concoction miming Amaretto, now blonde inside the mixture. Besides, my practical side—I know I have one—wouldn't enjoy cleaning up the mess. So I'll hang onto my coffee, along with what remains of my smoldering cigarette, my Bic lighter and my package of duMaurier Special Milds. In truth, if I were really to throw anything at the wall at this moment, it would be the terrifying pronouncement on my cigarette package that smoking during pregnancy can harm my baby. To split a hair or two, if I was a sea horse, it really could. Sometimes I think I smoke only to irritate the nonsmoking zealots out there, although I admit it's an attitude I should have outgrown by now.

My favorite cigarette package warning, by the way, is "smoking can kill you," a capability smoking shares with runaway trucks, tornado-tossed tractors, even Wiley Coyote's anvil, not to mention the political trends of modern western civilization, the ones designed to make icons of greed, elect the free market God, and transform contempt for some poor bastard on welfare into a moral virtue. Yes, smoking will surely kill you if the typical capitalist cynic, economic think tank or bank doesn't do it first.

How festive I feel about my anger. Weeks from now when I turn back to these initial pages in my journal about my summer here, I will probably squirm at such whimsical self-indulgence. Somehow, upon this first writing, I expected I'd be more refined. I thought I'd report information, the weather perhaps, or at least a bittersweet acknowledgment of the ambivalence I feel at returning to this cottage after so many years' absence, especially knowing, when I leave again this fall, I will never be able to come back here again. But instead I'm having a party. Just limbering up, getting ready, shrugging out of my pack before I pitch camp. Yeah, that's a more palatable explanation. I'm not really pissed off, just recalcitrant. At my age, shit, I've got a right to be furious. It's been some time now since my youthful illusions departed the roof of my cave like a choir of rapping (kill whitey! kill whitey!) bats. You see, there it is. I'm not actually pissed off at all. I've just learned to live with the venom in my particular snake. I've moved a few degrees south of crotchety, while acknowledging everything I've been through in more than four decades. Life hasn't been dull. It's worth a grateful toast to admit that I wouldn't have had it any other way.

No wonder I'm glad to be briefly away from Kingston. I'm on the threshold of new times and circumstances. I'm in a place where I can't be on display because there is no one here to see. I have this work I'm commissioned to write—the book of essays—and perhaps some memories to say goodbye to. Beyond this, for the next four or five months it's just me and Canine Ben, my trusty sidekick and retriever, poised to embark on the next phase of our quietly promising lives together.

Besides, when the first nice summer's day hits, I want to be here. I don't want to go for a walk in Kingston or sit on my rented porch to be assailed by all those parading tourists in Bermuda shorts. Bermuda shorts leave me wondering whether maturity is a commodity, something you trade up to like a Lincoln Continental, but in exchange for a finer sensibility. You know, four units of good taste, good aesthetic taste, handed over for one unit of that ill-defined sense of arrival so many of us seem to desire. As if we're all trying to reach an age or a state of mind when we're too bland to care how tasteless anything looks any longer.

Here, at least, when that first really warm summer's day shows up, I won't have to put up with some rich, hometown Queen's University debutante down at my favorite park, the name of the school stencilled on the arse of her shorts, flirting with some guy majoring in frisbee trajectory, giving her some lessons in the backhand toss. I won't have to endure that careless good nature they exhibit, that sense that they are oh so happy with themselves and with each other, not to mention the fruits they can harvest from Daddy's corporate Mastercard. Here, on this island, I won't have to gaze at the passing traffic, mysteriously annoyed when *Eddy and the Cruisers* rumble by, their ball caps on backwards, their stereo system rocking the car's suspension, their sneers loitering at the edges of their collective upper lips, trying to ply a route through a moustache they aren't old enough to grow yet.

Or am I simply jealous? Is what I rail against at this moment nothing more than a jaundiced paean to my lost youth? Could it be that I am mysteriously crabby only because I cannot escape the determined truth that I am going to be forty-eight years old at the end of November? Is it returning here, to an important point of departure, which twists my emotions and gives birth to difficult questions? Will I next wonder if a life which feels essentially in focus—my life—has something missing in it, something which hides in the verdant grove around my history, immutable but hard to define, missed somehow when I was pursuing something else because I couldn't see it clearly?

I've come to believe we never truly know precisely what we are looking for. Because it won't stay still. It's there and not there like a bit of fluff trapped in the fluid at the corner of our eye, something we never catch up to or pull into focus no matter how hard we chase it, trying to really see it.

Mid-life crisis, Matt? Bullshit! You've outgrown even that. Even mid-life crisis is back there bobbing in the burbling wake of what's already transpired, waterlogged wreckage you've learned to be happier without.

Get a grip on yourself. You're not used to being home and, let's face it, this place is the closest manifestation of home you've ever known. Face it, Matt, this place, the whole thing— the cottage we named *The Crow's Nest*, the island we called *The*

*Island*, and Lake Ontario, known in the family as *The Big Lake*—is where you've put down roots. It's here that everything is embossed with gold: memories, profits and losses, diatribes, and, mysteriously, not infrequent outbursts of peace and tranquility so precious you've sometimes been tempted to weep over them.

It's my sadness that gives rise to my anger. This is my last chance to find solace here for a while, to enjoy it for what it once meant to me. Aunt Agnes is going to sell it. Now that Uncle Bart is gone, with no children between them to take over the upkeep, she's determined the cottage is too much to handle. Besides, she told me last Christmas, it's not the same without him. Bottom line, she doesn't want it any longer. I'd buy it myself except that being a full-time Canadian writer ensures that even the pot I piss in has its own two-dollar mortgage. So when Aunt Agnes sells the cottage at the end of the summer, plus the little piece of property underneath it, this sacred little last resort is going to fall permanently out of the family tree. The island too will become something irrevocably lost to me, gained by yet another careless stranger. All that will remain to me after this long, last summer will be a fading index of memories which, increasingly, will be difficult to recall.

It's disappointing as well to return here only to be confined by the cocoon of a tardy spring. Somehow, in my imagination, I foresaw the sensory embrace of summer whenever I conjured up this moment in my precognition. But it's too early in the year and spring's too late in arriving. If the Lake Ontario waves are even *shushing* onto the beach, I can't detect it with the windows closed so tightly to keep out the cold. I don't recall hearing any birds earlier today as I settled in. They must have been there but, if so, they didn't have much to say. A winter as long as this one has dampened even *their* enthusiasm. No wonder I feel so lost here. I'll forever associate this place with waves crashing against the shore, the sound of singing birds, and, yes, the smell of bacon sizzling in Uncle Bart's cast iron frying pan in the morning.

The persistently inclement weather is at least part of the reason Gord Mahaffey was barely civil today when I showed up to rent a boat and motor. Gord has owned the rickety marina, *The Inlet*, on the other side of the channel for as long as I can remember. He didn't even try to conceal that he thought I was crazy to be venturing out onto the lake this early in the season, especially with winter being so stubborn and harsh this year.

I'm the kind of man Gord doesn't approve of anyway. I think I remind him of what he would term "all that nonsense" which took place at the end of the Sixties. He wants to ask me why I haven't grown up yet. If Gord shaves, everyone should shave. If Gord can get through life without a pony tail and bits of leather hanging from his outfit, then I should too. Gord's a descendent of the family tree of rightness which was born the moment God invented convention and convention invented God. It's quite a pedigree; I'm a bastard by comparison. When Gord decides what is right and reasonable, he's got an army to back him up. That's the pedigree. Majority rules and Gord knows it.

"It's too early to be out on the lake," he lectured me this morning. "Ice has only been out of the channel a few days." He ran his tongue along the front of the upper deck of his false teeth, his way of conveying pensive wisdom. We stood on his main dock, gazing out over the channel, me Columbus, him Ferdinand of Spain. "Latest spring I can ever remember."

"That's why I called ahead," I offered, "to make sure you were open, that I could get across."

"Well, you'll have to watch for the ice. You lose the prop, you'll be in a fine mess."

"No problem," I said. "I'll keep my eyes peeled."

"And you'll have to veer wide around the point of the island. Ice'll still clog the bay there."

"Sure enough," I replied.

He stood there a moment or two in silence, his legs spread as if to prevent someone from knocking him down, his hands in his pockets, jingling keys or handfuls of change. Both of us wore our down-filled parkas but he was the one who shivered a couple of times, though I suspected he did so on purpose to stress that it was cold and, if he could really prevent it, he would abort this foolish plan of mine to go and live on the island so early in the year. Then he sighed as if free enterprise is sometimes too sacred a load to bear, bent to the gas can on the dock beside the fuel pump, twisted off the cap and began to pump my gas.

"You can still see the ice out there in the waves," he said

more or less to himself.

Yes, I could see the ice myself on the choppy lake surface. The sun kept going in and out, peek-a-booing with the stampeding clouds. When sunshine struck the bits of floating ice they sparkled in the dark water like gems.

"I thought your aunt had sold the place," said Mahaffey then.

"Not yet," I replied.

"Well, she won't want to delay too long. The prices are going down."

I didn't have anything to say to that. I simply watched in silence as he straightened up again and put the fuel nozzle back into its receptacle on the side of the pump.

I regarded his freckles and realized how incongruous they are on the face of a man well past sixty. They seemed unnatural to me, like something he had ordered on a binge one night from a tattoo parlor in town. Or was this observation only my tendency to associate freckles with elementary school bullies?

I realized then how persistent it is that men like Mahaffey make me unsure of myself. Although I continue to regret those times in my past when men such as these have caused me to explain myself too much, I still have to restrain the instinct to do so. Do I really believe that, but for people like me, the world would run as efficiently as a top? No, I do not. But that pedigree of conventional justice, it's hard to stare it down.

"I s'pose you'll be wanting the biggest boat I have," Mahaffey said at last.

"I had in mind one of those wide-bottomed ones," I replied.

"And you'll be wanting it for the whole summer."

I nodded. "Until the end of September or so."

"What are you going to do over there anyway?" he asked me then.

"I have some work to do."

"You mean getting the place ready to be sold?"

"That and some other work."

He didn't ask me the nature of my other work. Hear no subversion, see no subversion. "Well, I guess that'll be all right," he said instead.

He glanced over his shoulder then at my Escort jammed with groceries, luggage and other gear. I watched him lock gazes with Canine Ben who had positioned himself behind the wheel to watch what was going on, waiting for something new to happen.

"After you get the boat loaded," he said, "you can park over by those other boats in dry dock, being as you'll be here for the summer." Vaguely he gestured in the direction of a stand of boats, masts and tarpaulins. "You'll have to leave me an extra key in case I have to move it."

"Okay," I said.

After that, he bent down and lifted the fuel can, ignoring my halfhearted attempt to reach out and do so myself. Without another word, he stalked off towards the boat he had now determined I would be renting for the season.

After I paid him for the gas, the boat, and a fee he had concocted for the luxury of parking my car, Canine Ben and I departed, the aluminum craft bulging with our supplies. As we headed into open water, I glanced back at the marina and saw Mahaffey standing on the dock again, his legs spread the way they were before, sentry-like. Even at this distance I perceived the burden of responsibility he seemed to want to convey.

Mahaffey was right about one thing, however. It was a cold crossing, too cold at least for the first day of May, and those floating gems I'd seen from the dock made it treacherous. I kept the motor at half throttle and studiously watched for large, dangerous blocks of floating ice. My eyes watered bitterly and the throttle vibrated in my fist. I didn't relax until I gave the island a wide berth and cruised around the point. By then I was already disappointed in the depth of caution in my mood.

I had expected a pleasant anticipation in what I was doing, but as the cottage side of the island came into view, as the wind continued to slap nastily at my cheeks and the sun evaporated behind the now massing clouds above me, I felt strange, tired, unsure.

I perceived myself caught in some gridlock in time. It tended to reduce my size somehow, until I felt tiny in this small boat with Canine Ben. The present seemed miniscule too, while ahead and behind me incidents and possibilities loomed so large and overwhelming I might never cease shrinking. Normally a sense of wonder accompanies periods when I feel insignificant. This time, however, I felt a trepidation in my fragility, an undefined sense of loss. I felt betrayed by this feeling, in view of my fervent wish to look ahead in anticipation of the summer, the island, even the work I planned to accomplish. Perhaps it reflected a normal melancholy at returning here after so many years' absence. Certainly I felt the weight of incidents which had already happened to me here: losses, feelings, lessons learned, not to mention the constant harassment most of us feel when we are forced to remember we can never redesign our respective pasts in the better fashion we would prefer.

Eventually I rounded the point of the island and glimpsed *The Crow's Nest* from far out on the lake, familiar and strange at the same time. I slowed down to gaze at the shore over Canine Ben's cocked ears and sturdy shoulders, where he stood in the bow with his front feet up on the seat to permit him a better look. I slowed down to understand my feeling of being overwhelmed, though in the end I probably just prolonged it.

It was noon by then. The clouds had completed their gathering overhead and the sun was now obscured. The water had turned black in the gloom; the beach transformed from gold to white as the dark waves raced up onto the sand like blood. The trees along the shore at either end of the island, late with their budding, reminded me of witches or beggars, tattered and desolate. Even the island's two cottages—mine and the big one a half mile away, the one that has no name—seemed to draw even further apart as I approached, as if I had caught them in the salacious embrace they enjoy while they are alone. And they seemed set even further back from the beach than I remembered. The short climb over the rocks to reach *The Crow's Nest* appeared newly formidable. Yes, it all felt so strange yet so familiar, some collision of past and future with my marriage to the present crushed innocently in between. I believe I have come very far as a man, but earlier today, as I approached the island, it didn't seem far at all.

I beached the boat, struggled up the dunes with a couple of bags, then climbed the rocks to the sandy path which leads directly to the kitchen door, a route I've navigated a thousand times before. I unlocked the cottage, fumbling at first with the padlock, then entered its murky gloom. For several minutes I didn't know what to do next. Each idea seemed beyond implementation. I could only stand in the near-darkness and try to collect my thoughts. There was much to do to settle in. This, I hoped, would limber up my strangely flagging spirits.

It took more than a dozen trips to lug my supplies and luggage up the hill and into the cottage. After this, I got the wood stove going and put things away. I made coffee for lunch. It was all I could come up with in the mess all around me. I consumed another hour removing the plywood from the windows but the day was now so dreary it hardly made any difference. I had planned a walk with Canine Ben around the island, perhaps to establish our territorial imperative, but the rains came while I was uncovering the last window and I've put the journey off until tomorrow. I hope too that it will be warmer. Spring and summer seem hopelessly far away as winter lingers.

Now, hours later, safe in the dark, I feel like my present is walking through a narrow canyon between the future on my left and the past on my right. This sensation strikes me with such force because in recent years I've kept myself to the present, so much so that it was rare I contemplated what lay backwards or what might suddenly appear in front of me. Yet, today, I was pushed out into the traffic where past, present and future honk each other's horns as they jockey for position. I guess it's true that new and old, strange and familiar, are more than simply opposites: they are integral to one another.

I have underestimated the number of memories here for me. The ghosts are in residence after all. They're just shy because we've been so long apart. I have only now realized that this is the first time I've ever come here unaccompanied, with just my work to do and the scholastic silence that results when you're pleased to be alone. My shy ghosts probably don't recognize me now that I don't fret so much about what's missing in my life, at least in the way I cared so much before. I'm sure as well when we reacquaint ourselves—my ghosts and me—it will only presage our final goodbye when, come summer's end, I leave this place for good.

## NICOLE

COLLEAGUES FROM WORK BUY YOU LUNCH at your favorite delicatessen. You walk the block and a half from work, all four of you chattering comfortably with one another the way you usually do. Your heels clack in staccato ruckus on the concrete of the sidewalk. Brian Bannerman, the manager of *Pinnacle*'s adjustment section where all of you work, has given your friends an extra half hour for lunch. You have the entire afternoon off, this being your last day, maybe forever.

Still, everything today feels ambivalent. The sun is out but clouds keep darting across its face, interrupting the sunlight. It's spring in Toronto but it's cold, even wintry, especially for the first day of May.

"I wish it would warm up," Lorraine says as you approach your destination. "I feel the cold more than you guys do."

Cloris is wearing gloves, usually prepared for everything. But she's told you she saw several robins during the drive into work that day.

"Late springs," Barb says, "get everybody down."

*Freeman's Deli* has moved its seats, tables, window boxes and barricades out front in anticipation of setting up its patio but these items are still stacked against the building wall. It's too cold for patrons to sit comfortably outside.

You are regular customers, at least once a week—you, Barb, Cloris and Lorraine mostly, but sometimes a couple of other co-workers join you. Barb is just a couple of years younger than you, say, pushing thirty. Cloris is older, pushing forty. Lorraine is older still and what *she's* pushing is never really discussed. You've worked together for more than half a decade and this isn't the first hump day lunch you've shared at *Freeman's* or elsewhere over the years. Today Lorraine carries a wrapped package and you know it has your name on it. They've chipped in for a gift.

It strikes you that you're only *sort of* leaving *Pinnacle* for a while—this is part of the ambivalence you, and perhaps your friends, feel about the occasion.

Cloris finds a table for four, puts her coat on the back of a chair to stake ownership. Then she joins you and your other friends at the counter where all of you select something for lunch. No one is going to get fat, not even Lorraine who complains of a mature thickening of her waistline—all of you pick your lunch with care. No dessert, not even today when you're here to say goodbye.

YOU REITERATE UNNECESSARILY while you eat that your departure from *Pinnacle* is just a leave of absence. "I may be back before you know it," you remind them.

They have differing views of whether you really *will* or not, but these are exchanged good-naturedly, celebrating a measure of envy they feel about your immediate future.

"We got you a little something," Lorraine says, reaching for the gift leaning against the leg of her chair. She retrieves it and hands it to you. "To get those creative juices flowing," she adds.

"You guys are wonderful—you didn't need to do this." You slip the ribbon off, tear the paper away carelessly although you remark on the elegant choice, white flowers on a silver background.

Their gift is beautiful, a leather bound musical composition book. Your eyes well up.

"Don't you dare cry," says Barb. "We'll know then that it's permanent. We don't want to be seeing the last of you today!"

"That's right," puts in Cloris. "You can't cry when you're going to an island for five months to make a major life decision. That's a happy thing, isn't it?"

They all laugh. You laugh too. But an island on the cusp of a

major shift in direction may be a good time to cry after all.
"Islands and tears?" remarks Lorraine. "No way Jose."
But it's too late to stop the tears. You wipe your eyes and laugh. You stroke the velvety flesh of the brushed leather cover on the composition book. "I can't wait to have all that time to write some music."
"We're jealous, you know," says Barb. "All of us."

YOUR FRIENDS ALREADY KNOW what you plan to do, the choices you need to consider. They know about your family's large cottage on a small island in Lake Ontario. The Island, named Primrose Island for reasons that elude you, is so small, it isn't on most maps, as far as you know. Yet, it has a long beach, a large promontory of rocks at one end, and only two cottages some distance apart up from the same long section of beach. Your friends know you are going there because you're contemplating opening a music school in Kingston with your best friend and musical peer from university. They know you have a degree in music composition and that you're wondering if you should finally pursue the musical career that you have been missing. They know you're taking the cautious approach: a leave of absence that keeps the door open should you need to return to *Pinnacle* and the insurance adjustment business.

None of your colleagues has the courage to spend so much time alone on an island. They often come back to this topic, still clearly dismayed.

"Virtually half a year on an island alone—I'd be scared," Cloris remarks as the four of you prepare to bring the lunch to an end, glancing ritually at wristwatches. Your friends must get back to work; you are on your way home to finish packing.

"I won't be entirely alone," you tell them. "I'll have visitors. My parents are coming for a couple of visits. Karen, my friend from Kingston. Her husband, her daughter." You hesitate ever so slightly, long enough to be suspicious about the reasons why, then add, "Alan too, when he can."

This information too feels ambivalent, not just for you, but for your colleagues as well. They've been following your soap opera with Alan for months and you've told them the plot of just about every episode. There is a not unexpected unanimous exchange of glances.

"Mostly it'll be me, my piano, this lovely composition book, and the chance to figure things out," you say as a form of summing up while you all head outside. It helps moderate the atmosphere of excited ambivalence you continue to feel.

You hug your friends goodbye, then watch them walk down the street in the direction of the office, their heels clacking again in a receding cadence on the concrete. And life already feels very different, like it trembles underneath your feet.

## MATT

**Thursday, May 2**

I SETTLED DOWN TODAY to my various tasks. I realized more than yesterday that I've truly arrived to spend the summer with myself. That cryptic purgatory when I pined for what might be missing for me has been replaced by the probability that nothing is missing at all. I remember that discomfort—the scratchy hair-shirt restlessness crawling my skin back then— only vaguely now. Aging has its conveniences. One *forgets* before one even contemplates forgiveness or understanding.

I've decided to come up with a word of the day for the summer, two words if one doesn't quite cover it. I chose "practical productivity" this morning, although I was tempted by "masturbatory monkdom." I opted for the tasteful alternative because, as I have said, one ages, one loses one's adolescent edge.

I set up my work station on the dining room table. I hooked up my "Mac," set up the printer, turned on the microphone and recorded a new beep sound, in this case a stifled yawn. Then I unpacked all my research materials and stacked them on a corner. This is probably the last day these materials will exist in such a state of neatness. By the time I'm done they'll be scattered in untidy piles all over the room. At any rate, with all of this on the table, there's still enough room for me to eat. Thank goodness Canine Ben takes his meals on the floor.

After I was done with the computer setup I took him for the walk around the island I promised him yesterday. It was late morning by the time we got going. It takes time to inject myself with those first few fixes of caffeine and nicotine, and by the time I'd set up my "office" it was staggering inexorably towards noon. Nonetheless I'd decided during my morning endeavors that it was essential we circumnavigate our island. And I'd been thinking over coffee what it is about islands which attracts someone like me, especially at times of necessary introspection such as these.

Islands, I know, provide a kind of insular freedom which, to me, is the fodder for philosophical exploration. I have always wanted to reside on an island that I own, my version of birthing a colony. I enjoy toying with the sentiment that I can make my own laws, define my own realities, even conceive of my own icons, should I entertain the notion to do so. Never mind that to create our own variations of regulations is probably little more than removing ourselves from other laws, other realities, other icons. Still, I like my laws, my icons. These days there isn't much about theirs to appreciate.

Nor should one underestimate the satisfaction we feel in having to depend on our own ingenuity. There's no hospital on the island, no public works department, no convenience store down at the point. I like the idea, when some disaster transpires, be it large or small, I'm going to have to deal with it myself. I enjoy the deliberate risk in this. There's less chance I'll have to make a deal with someone to get something repaired. Money won't be exchanged. I won't have to politely nod while someone recites the free enterprise creed, turning something minor I need into an ideological conversion I *don't* need. There are no stockbrokers on the island, no bankers, no economic analysts, no town council Benito Mussolinis. There's just me, Canine Ben, my ingenuity, and my mission.

Oh, yes, and the storms nature plans to share with me over the next five months.

Strangely enough, I do not consider myself a recluse; I merely enjoy drawing back now and then to regain my perspective. It's not a case of disliking people either, one on one at least. The trouble begins, I think, when they clump together into clubs, societies and movements. When they clump in this way, their doors close. And when you look in their windows, you see nothing more than the opinion put forth by their particular clump. It's as if the characteristics making them truly unique have been handed in at the door, checked in on the way to the club's private function, as if none of us can bring our true selves to a gathering for fear it'll intrude on our association's mission statement.

Back in Kingston, when Mitch, my landlord, dropped by a couple of weeks ago to work on a leaky faucet, the conversation turned to politics after he learned about the book of essays I am writing. It became clear his view is contrary to mine. I wasn't surprised. Mitch is in his mid-twenties. As a business graduate, he makes his living in property management. And one day, several months ago, a magazine to which he subscribes showed up in my mail box. I don't remember what it was called, Success or The New Mafia or The New Fascist. I just remember that it billed itself as "the magazine for the entrepreneurial thinker." I stood there glancing at the cover, thinking what an oxymoron "entrepreneurial thinker" is; then I politely tucked it into his mail box which he rarely ever empties. But a few weeks ago, when we debated economics and politics, I didn't feel I was arguing with him, but with his association, his movement, the point of view he has felt compelled to embrace to belong to his particular club. Perhaps he felt the same way about me—I don't know. At any rate, I came to the conclusion there were two Mitches in my kitchen: one a uniquely interesting human being, the other a spokesman for the movement which would subvert his individuality in favor of his adherence to its political-economic creed.

So there it is. Sometimes I have to get away, not only from other people's associations but perhaps from the one trying to embrace *me*, the one with little patience for *my* individuality.

It's also why, for some time now, I've known myself to be retired from romantic partnership. In my experience, at least one of the factors in the failure of romantic partnership has been this clumping into a conventional association. I've partnered too many times in the past thirty years, then felt compromised by the association I inadvertently joined. Now I tend to think of society as a whirlpool tugging people away from themselves, from their instinct to make the most of a private life. In the past I've barely been able to keep my balance on the swaying tightrope between the need for lasting love and the seemingly inevitable failure brief periods of terminal intimacy has inspired. This sense of failure seems far behind me now because I am content in my retirement. I can do without the attention to self the goals of love seem to represent.

I ruminated on this subject for much of my walk around the island this morning with Canine Ben. Poor Ben! He thought I would change my mind again in view of the continued bad weather. Anticipating my demurral, he waited for me on the rug by the door, his nose between his paws, his eyes watching unblinkingly my ambivalence about venturing outside. I could see it was cold, that the clouds were thick and sullen. But at last I prepared to go. I needed to clear my head.

Outside I was glad of my winter coat and gloves. I hung Canine Ben's leash around my neck and let him explore the island unrestrained. We took the path I and other visitors have worn down over the years at the rear of the cottage and struck off into the fragile woods protecting *The Crow's Nest* from the north wind. As we set out, I felt again the peculiar dichotomy between familiar and strange which preoccupied me yesterday. I attributed at least some of the strangeness to the lateness of the season but, at the same time, I had to admit it was more likely the astonishing number of years that has passed since I last took this walk. Five years? Seven? In the end I realized it was more like eight or nine.

Yet this morning I recalled and remember even now my last walk here. There were four of us that day: Carolyn, of course, and her friends Sally and Luke from Alberta whom we had brought here as guests for the weekend while they were passing through Ontario. We were intent on showing them the island, its various personalities. It was a day then as gray as this one but warm and muggy, one of those July days whose every orifice seems patiently plugged by some kind of gauze.

Carolyn and I were still new to each other then. We would succumb every few minutes to the need to touch one another, still enthralled with the wonder of our physical *creatureliness.* Sally and Luke seemed a distant, rather irrelevant presence and we lost contact with them as soon as they returned home. But they were newlyweds that day on this path. They held hands as they strolled along behind us. Carolyn and I held hands too. Back then, as I recall it now, the world seemed to orbit on an ellipsis of hope and all neighboring planets displayed shimmering rings of possibility. All I had to do, I thought, was reach up and steal one to place it on my chosen direction's finger.

I have been foolish in my younger days and don't enjoy remembering it very much. It's astonishing to learn, as I get older, I remember embarrassment more clearly than I remember loss. Someday perhaps I'll know exactly why this is, what I end up hiding from.

I duplicated that past walk today, although not by design. The path leads only one way, through the woods at the rear of the cottage towards a large expanse of cliff on the north side of the island where, in a state of rugged exposure, the carved granite appears to trifle stubbornly with the persistent weather sculpting it. On pleasant days, I can gaze down into the channel; the water appears deeply green and turtles sun themselves on the rocks. But when the wind blows harshly, the green gives way to black and the water assaults the rocky shoreline with sprayed and harsh invective. Over the years, I have sat on this precipice in every kind of weather, fascinated by the area's moods.

After the cliffs, if one veers left instead of going back, one enters the inland dunes, cut off from the beach, yet sandy and fossilized, hot on the bare feet at the height of summer. As a child, I dubbed this area the petrified forest. Hardly a forest, I noticed today—the white trunks of dry, long dead trees sparse and forlorn. Still, they retained the eerie majesty they held for me when I was a child. Limbless, leaning out of the sand at awkward angles, they make music on windy days like giant flutes and oboes as the breeze passes over their knotholes. As a youngster, I studied this music for hours, never quite solving the mystery of the melody. Today the woodwinds were silent. Canine Ben and I kept moving between the stumps, like driftwood unable to find a place to settle.

When I came to the woods occupying the western end of the island I skirted them and made for the big lake shoreline. I saw no value in reliving that other walk with Carolyn any further. The contrast between then and now was too severe. We spread out a blanket that day on a dune among the dead trees, enjoying a light lunch I carried in my pack. Afterwards, while Sally and Luke dozed in the gloom, Carolyn and I strolled to the woods, wordlessly working our way deeper into the trees.

Carolyn wore her bikini but had covered it with a t-shirt and one of those long, wraparound skirts she favored then. I remember the skirt even now, gray and blue paisley. The bikini was turquoise. Deep in the cover of the trees, the wraparound skirt shielding our nakedness, we made love in guilty haste, then afterglowed illicitly with seconds we cheated from hospitality.

"You spoil me, Mia Caro," I said when we were done.

I was so grateful then for pleasure, for the times, astonishingly brief, when someone seemed to truly love me.

I think of myself as a fortunate man, I have been loved at times so well. But this conclusion occurs to me now like a courtroom summation delivered at the end of a lengthy trial, after all the witnesses have been called and the lies and admissibility have at last been sorted out. The gratitude I've come to now is felt entirely on its own, because I'm not surprised that I was loved. Back then, however, my thankfulness was just a silhouette of some indefinable guilt. "You spoil me, Mia Caro," not thanks so much as apology for something I might not have deserved.

I passed by those woods today a different kind of man. I do not apologize for embracing my change of heart about love. I have come this far at least in my state of romantic retirement.

After the dunes and the woodwind trees and the woods I did not enter, Canine Ben and I walked along the beach, our footprints faint and watery behind us. The lake whispered onto the sand, foam collecting milkily upon the beach's upper lip. We passed the other cottage, set back from the beach on the crest of the rocks. *The Crow's Nest* too perches on the top of the island but, for years, it has seemed a flimsier location compared to this larger cottage's apparent solidity. It must be four times the size of Uncle Bart's little retreat. And it seems cut right into the hill, with a lawn and garden walled into place in front, as if it has grown out of the earth itself. *The Crow's Nest,* on the other hand, teeters on the hilltop as if it arrived there during a violent wind and waits only for another storm to blow it away again.

I think, without ever admitting it, my family and I have always resented this other, much larger structure sharing the island with us. Its largeness. Its pretensions to permanence. But we're polite and we'd never make a deprecatory remark which might be construed as envy, not even to one another. The closest we ever came to criticism was the tone of voice we used whenever we reported to one another that it had changed hands again.

As I passed it earlier today I wondered briefly about its status. It was deserted, boarded up, waiting for summer to come. How many owners since I was a child? Half a dozen? This being my last opportunity to summer on this island, I finally gave in to my working class snobbery, my envy and contempt. Cottages, for some people, I reflected with chagrin, are hardly more than toys, like their boat or their trailer. I felt righteous indignation that for people like me, a cottage is more deeply loved because it reflects a way of life.

I stood on the beach forlornly and lamented anew the loss I felt because Aunt Agnes was going to give up *The Crow's Nest*. I gazed in spite at its larger antithesis, resentful because it looked like a feudal castle constructed to ensure I never forget I am only a peasant. Then I laughed at myself, feeling better in the laughter.

I considered how curious I am about the interior of this other cottage. I've never seen inside it. I imagine sunken hot tubs and exclusive works of art adorning the walls, sculptures on pedestals. Thinking these things, I laughed at myself again. I am proud of the contrast *The Crow's Nest* represents, right down to the crude little wooden joke signs Uncle Bart tacked on the walls, which still hang there even now, dusty and fading. These are linked forever to my childhood. I remember, for instance, puzzling my way through their corny folk wisdom. "Kwitchurbeliaken," still greets visitors from the opposite wall when one first enters the kitchen. Beside it, a question which intrigues me still: "Vy iz der zo miny more orziz azziz dan der iz orziz?"

At last, Canine Ben and I continued down the windless, whispering beach, strolling among the pieces of driftwood Uncle Bart gathered every spring and burned with great ceremony at the water's edge on the Victoria Day weekend—those pieces, that is, that Aunt Agnes didn't conscript for painting or for a favored place in her flower garden. And I made a mental note to check my calendar, to light a similar fire this year. I want to do it *all* this summer. Or at least as much as I can.

## NICOLE

YOU CALL KAREN ON THE CELLPHONE while Alan labours outside, removing the plywood sheets from the cottage windows. It's your first time on a cellular and it works fine. Karen's voice sounds strong and—you don't mean this unkindly—almost tediously happy.

"Nickie!" she gushes. "You're there."

"I'm here," you say. "We arrived about an hour ago."

"Alan's with you?"

"Yes. He's outside taking the plywood off the windows. And bitching about the rotten weather."

Karen laughs like tinkling wedding goblets. "Isn't it awful? The last thing you expect in May is a couple of inches of snow."

"It isn't what I pictured," you admit.

You stand, feeling as cordless as the telephone, in the middle of the cottage's living room floor. It's a brick colored terrazzo but it's turned a tragic brown in the shadows. You stand beside a pile of white sheets you've removed from the room's furniture. The sheets have that smell of cold dust: they ventriloquize an attic. There are no cobwebs but the impression of mustiness and time passing is so complete you can imagine them on your skin, clinging to your hair. You wish now you'd telephoned Karen from the bath, from the private womb of a bath. Alone.

"You have a phone," she is saying.

"Yes. Alan saw an excuse in me spending the summer here to buy himself a new one. So he gave me his old one. Alan shops. Any situation is resolved by consumerism."

"Oooh," says Karen. "You sound cranky."

"No," you hasten to assure her. "I'm just tired. I feel like there's so much to do."

You are aware now that you wanted to accomplish every bit of this arrival alone, that this summer is an important departure for you, that this first couple of days here you wanted to be self-reliant, in control of absolutely everything, not required to be grateful for any help or explain any whys or justify any decisions. But you mention none of this to Karen— now is not the time.

"The phone's a good idea, Nickie," Karen suggests at her end.

"Yes. He thought for emergencies, so he could check on me."

"And we can talk all summer," Karen adds brightly.

"Yes."

But you don't like the telephone, not really. Its usefulness is mitigated by its betrayal of your solitude. It feels like a leash. It suggests you've given in somehow, on a small point of debate, granted, but given in just the same.

"How's Liam?" you ask.

"Oh great. Upset about the snow. It was only a few days ago that he cut the lawn."

"And Cindy?"

"She's had a cold. Nothing serious. It's on the way out."

Just then Alan removes the first sheet of plywood from the first living room window. A sickly stream of light staggers dazedly into the room. And there's Alan peering in at you, six point eight on the intensity scale. It's as if he's lunged suddenly into the room. Between this illusory penetration and the sudden gray light, you nearly step backwards in retreat. The sensation of being caught doing something you shouldn't—though brief and irrational—is powerful. Alan stares at you a moment longer, at last severing the gaze with his grimace-grin, then moves out of sight, presumably to the next window and the next sheet of plywood.

"Nickie? Are you still there?"

"Yes," you say. "Sorry. Alan just startled me. The place seems a little spooky."

But this isn't true. It is dark and half asleep, but not spooky. A little white lie, you suppose, to explain the silence, a conditioned reflex like the cough button in a disc jockey's radio station panel. Fill all empty spaces, give every silence an excuse.

"Are you going to be all right, alone there for the whole summer?"

"Of course," you reply with a laugh. "Karen, I've been looking forward to this for months. I can hardly believe the time has finally come. It's important to me to be here. I'm happy."

"Okay," says Karen. "I want to say something, though. I have to, Nickie."

You wait.

"I want to tell you there's no pressure. Okay?"

"You told me already."

But Karen goes right on. "No pressure," she says. "If you decide to go back to *Pinnacle* in Toronto, that's okay. If you decide not to work with me in the school, that's okay. It's got nothing to do with us being friends."

"I know that, Karen."

"I just want to be sure. And I want you to be sure too."

"Okay. Enough already."

"Okay."

You tell her you brought your electric piano. "Alan lugged it up from the beach, swearing every five feet."

Karen laughs. "Oh no."

"Yes. But I figured I'd better get in some practice. It'll do me good to play again."

"Are you going to write some songs?"

"I hope so," you reply.

"That's great. I like the sound of this, Nickie."

Carmen, your spaniel, comes into the room, sniffs again at the pile of white sheets as if she's forgotten the story they told her last time, then disappears again, resuming an exploration of the rest of the cottage.

"Anyway," you say, "you and Liam and Cindy are coming to visit when the weather's better."

"Absolutely. We can't wait to see you. Say, you'd better give me your number."

You do as she asks. "Love you," you say afterwards.

"Love you too," says Karen. "We'll talk again soon."

Alan comes inside a few minutes later and loiters in a doorway. He looks cold and dishevelled and large somehow, although he is not a big man, barely an inch taller than you.

"Karen?" he asks after a moment.

"Yes. I wanted her to know I'm here safely. I gave her the number."

"Good."

Alan always wants to know who was on the phone. It rarely matters, but he feels it does, it could, it would; in his mind it should.

"How's it going?" you ask.

"Okay. Shitty day, though. Jesus. I mean it's May, you know?"

You nod.

"What about you?" he asks.

"More unpacking to do. And I have to set up the piano. I don't know where to put it yet."

"Well, I'm just about done with the windows. I'll give you a hand when you figure it out."

"Okay. Thanks."

His face displays that mysterious look usually preceding some worry or concern about your welfare. As you have so many times before, less from curiosity than obligatory ritual, you rise to the bait.

"What's wrong?"

He shrugs for dramatic effect. "I thought the island would be deserted, but the other cottage seems to be occupied. I saw him pull up in his boat. Some guy and a dog." Now his forehead writes itself some furrows.

"So?"

"I'd just feel better, Karen, if I knew who he was and what he's doing here."

"Oh, Alan. I'm sure he's harmless. That cottage has been on the island since long before this one. Besides, it's safer to have a neighbor, isn't it?"

He gazes at you, perplexed. "If you know he's trustworthy," he says finally.

To whom? you wonder. But you do not pose the question.

You simply stand there in silence.

"Well, I'd better finish up," Alan says then. "At least it's stopped snowing."

When he is gone you think about the snow that fell while you were speeding across the channel, the way it splattered on the boat's windshield, how it felt deliciously cold when, in a fit of exuberance, you raised yourself from the seat to feel it strike your face and catch in your eyelashes. Peripherally you noticed Alan remained down behind the windshield, not wanting to betray his frustration over the unseasonable weather.

"Be careful," he cried. "Jesus, Nickie."

But you just kept on driving the boat the way you always have, fast and sure and knowledgeably. Welcome to *my* world, you thought as you rocketed across the choppy lake. You whooped in excitement as you veered around the point of the island, not caring whether or not Alan heard you over the roar of the motor.

STILL, YOU ARE CONDITIONED TO BE APPREHENSIVE. When at last you get to be truly alone, during a long soak in the tub, the door closed tightly to keep Alan out ...

"Need me to do your back?" he called barely ten minutes into your bath.

"Alan, please. I just need some time to myself," you replied. "I'll be out in a while."

Followed by so much silence.

. . . You began to think about Alan's announcement that someone is staying at the other cottage. Some guy and a dog, he said. And you think about the apprehension you have been trained so well to feel. Everything from stern matriarchal lectures to movie thrillers; from incident-milking newspaper reports of rapes, assaults and crusty old sodomites to take back the night rallies; from solicitous, protective men so gallant and watchful on the surface yet smothering and possessive underneath; to living room conversations which begin, "You heard about that woman down on the Danforth." Until you are hardly yourself any longer. Until you are just a reflection of your violated sex, not the much-more-than-this you know yourself to be.

Alan plays this card frequently. He fastens himself to you

with the threat of other men. He slips inside your precautionary fortress by being your defender, a kind of well-intentioned Trojan Horse. Not even so well-intentioned actually. There are symbolic rapes, assaults and bondage on his agenda too. They're supposed to be appropriate because he's supposed to be tried, true and trustworthy. But nonetheless they're there inside his expectations of you, the things he takes for granted.

So he sows the seed of apprehension—"some guy and a dog." He knows you want to be alone during most of your long stay here on the island. He knows—or seemed to understand somewhat one night when you tried to explain it—that the only men you have strangely feared are those old and dying creatures from the nursing home you sometimes pass on your way to the No Frills store a couple of blocks from your apartment. You tried to tell Alan about their bloodshot eyes and yellow teeth, how they lurk on a porch behind a trellis exploding with ivy. You tried to explain how unsettling it is to be leered at by men with an oldness in their gaze. "Like lechery is forever," you said. "Like lechery never dies." On one level, Alan clearly understood. How many times, while you walked hand in hand along a Toronto street, had you felt his spine stiffen when an adversary went by and gazed appreciatively at you? How many times did you wonder if, at that moment, he blamed you for the leering stranger instead of blaming the leering stranger himself?

But that isn't it. That isn't the reason for the fear the old men inspire. After you pass these men sitting on their porch, you feel gnashed and bruised and wrinkled. It's that love's failure goes on forever, doesn't die; love's failure and love's leering survives until old age makes it all too late. Sometimes, when you accelerate by the paint-peeling porch, the burp, fart and mutter of this tragic truth about love seems so indisputable you're crushed by hopelessness. Your belief in love loses much of its voice, hardly able to manage a tired bleat.

"We're all going to be there someday," said Alan. "You just don't like that those men are so old."

And you knew he didn't truly understand. "No," you replied in a moment. "It's just that nothing's going to change except my faith in love, which is going to get old and tired and weak."

He sighed. "Jesus, Nickie. You're barely in your thirties."

You sighed too because you realized he would never

understand this part of your fear at all.

Now he taps gently on the bathroom door again. "Hey, are you all right in there?"

"I'm fine," you reply. "I'll be out in a few minutes."

Silence again while he considers this on the other side of the door. Then, at last, you hear the receding pad of his feet as he goes back to the living room.

You planned to watch the sun go down. You told everyone at work this was what you'd do at the end of your first day here. But the sky sulked with clouds as twilight arrived. And Alan kept working out details and instructions, telephone numbers which had to be written down, people he trusts. He kept grilling you about procedures, what to do when the power goes off, who to call if the boat breaks down. It felt suddenly like *his* island, not yours, and you reminded him of your experience here. At any rate, in the midst of all this babble, darkness came. There was no sunset. You simply noticed, somewhere during his parade of precautions, daylight had escaped.

"I think it's best I call you every night," said Alan, "to make sure everything's all right."

"If you do," you said, "I'll stop answering the phone."

"Oh, c'mon."

"Alan, I mean it. You start calling every night and I'll run away."

He laughed.

"I mean it," you said.

"Okay, okay." But he kept laughing even though it wasn't funny.

Now you get out of the bath, wipe the mirror with your towel, dry yourself, brush your teeth, put on your robe.

When you enter the living room in robe and slippers, you find him sitting in your father's favorite chair, the dark brown leather one facing out the patio doors over the garden and down to the lake. Alan is gazing into the darkness, although night gives him nothing to see. Doesn't this man ever read?

"I'm tired," you say. "I'm going to bed."

"I was going to make cocoa," he tells you. "It seems a cottagey thing to do."

"Not tonight, Honey. I'm tired."

"Okay," he says at last. "I'm tired too."

You let Carmen out for her bed-time pee, wait while she finds a spot, hold the door open to let her back in. You climb naked into bed. Flannel sheets in May, you think with a scornful *haruumph.*

When Alan gets into bed beside you, he sniffs at your cigarette, looks askance at the ashtray on the covers over your lap. "You aren't going to smoke in bed when you're here alone, are you?"

"Of course not," you reply. "But if you ask me that again, I'm going to butt this one on your pillow."

"Okay," he says with a bereaved little chuckle.

After you extinguish it and put the ashtray on the night table, he moves in close to you. He's partially aroused.

"Alan, I'm tired. I can't tonight."

"I won't be seeing you for *days,*" he says.

"There's always the morning," you tell him. "I can't keep my eyes open."

"Right," he says in the silence.

You blow out the candle he has placed on the night table to set the mood, then turn onto your side.

"Right," he says again from his side of the bed.

# MATT

**Saturday, May 11**

DIDN'T WORK TODAY. The crappy weather, I think. But not working has somehow made it all worse. When it snowed today it accumulated on my guilt. Guilt is soggy enough on its own without wet snow all over it.

Anyway, it seems unbelievable that the Victoria Day weekend gets underway in less than seven days. It looks more like March than May. Everything about spring is late—the trees are barely budded and what should be richly green remains a listless brown. And it's so cold. Whenever I go outdoors, no matter how briefly, I still have to put on my winter coat. It's beginning to wear me down. Each day, when I report to this journal, I must write how winter will not give way to a timid spring. Each day—and the deviation is rare—I write how the wind comes in off the lake, frowning in bitter malice; how the clouds obscure the sunshine; how the rain continues to fall.

All of this I've borne with the utmost patience, until this morning when, to my amazement, it snowed. Wet slop, but snow nonetheless, conjured up in a squall somewhere out on the lake. Standing at the window, I watched it fall and cling to the grass and trees, I nearly gave in to despair. As I'm sure many other people did today, I felt myself to be the weather's personal victim, especially after the long winter we've already endured, beginning as it did at the end of last October.

No wonder I didn't work. I'm sure, in the kind of angry snit I was in, I would have written nonsense. Certainly I felt an irrational temptation to believe the weather is yet another punishment engineered by our current corporate-political governments. Paranoia, I've heard, is just knowing something first, but blaming big business and the government for the weather is possibly pushing it a little too far.

I hear no news, of course, by my own design, and I remain grateful for it. Not only do I need a respite from new reasons to feel anger and disgust, but I do not want late breaking developments to intrude on the focus I need to complete my book of essays. So there is no radio here, no television. No newspaper arrives in the mailbox I do not have. I feel sometimes like I've dug a cave in the side of a mountain, that I hibernate in there like some scratchy, ancient grizzly. But I'm stubborn about this need to remain focused. When I'm done with the essays, I'm sure I'll resume my normal life and the awareness of current events it seems to require.

I think the snow today turned me a little crazy. By midmorning I was laid low with cabin fever. Feeling strangely compelled to rejoin society, at least for an hour or two, if for no other reason than to remind myself of what I have chosen to avoid for several months, I took Canine Ben into town with me, telling myself that I needed a few things. This kind of practical lie is merely one of those things a person says to himself so that he has something to go into town with. Not that you need an acceptable reason beyond just wanting a change in routine. I'm like everyone else, I guess, trying at times to wriggle into society's embrace so that I can pull away later and say I didn't need it after all. Socially we're all children, blinded by infantile delusion. I see it as backing into a room of venomous snakes and telling yourself they won't see you coming.

Of course, as I stumbled down to the boat this morning, I almost changed my mind. The thought of crossing the channel, then driving into town seemed fraught with discomfort. The wind drove the sleet into my face and the boat was filled with slush. I grew annoyed with myself that I hadn't thought to cover it with the tarpaulin I remember Uncle Bart keeps in the shed behind the cottage. I stood there for a few moments, too stubborn to go back up to *The Crow's Nest* for a towel. In the end I used the nylon sleeve of my coat to wipe the slush off the bench at the rear of the boat, but it didn't do much of a job. By the time I docked at *The Inlet* the ass of my jeans was soaked.

Canine Ben, being a dog, assumed that I was nuts. He kept glancing at me with that look animal comrades convey so well. I call it the "if brains were legs, you'd be walking on the cheeks of your arse" look. I ignored him and maneuvered the boat out into the swells, climbed aboard without getting my feet wet, then pushed myself into deeper water with an oar. And although I might have expected otherwise, the motor started on the first pull. I felt newly pleased with myself for my persistence as we made for the mainland.

It was snowing in town too and everyone there was disgusted. They drove their cars with a barely controlled fury and the pedestrians slouched into the wind like disenchanted robots. I discovered there have been changes in the years since I last was here. There is a new Tim Horton's complete with drive-thru, and several video stores have opened up. But new isn't so much of a problem if it leaves behind some of the necessary old. I was pleased to see Mom's Restaurant still open, along with the bowling alley next door, welcome blasts from the past.

In the A& P, there was a pervasive gloom at the end of every aisle. My memory of a Saturday in this store calls up the bustle of jostling tourists. Instead I found senior citizens, dressed in long coats and winter hats, standing perplexed in the middle of the aisles, holding tightly to their shopping carts, treating them like walkers. Nor was it merely the elderly; no, everyone seemed shaky, halfheartedly bailing a sinking ship. I noticed most people contemplated each purchase gravely. I sensed clearly today the palpable fear which vanishing security instills in many Canadians these days.

So I purchased a few hopeful things on purpose, with what felt like a measure of defiance. I bought some charcoal briquets and some barbecue starter fluid, both of which were on sale, no doubt because summer can still be officially cancelled. And I bought three of those foil-wrapped baking potatoes, a t-bone and some hickory flavoured barbecue sauce. This, I knew, was flying in the face of reason, but it felt good—no, even revolutionary and courageous—because I was not giving in to the disappointing weather.

Penny the cashier, so her name tag told me, was a short, stocky blonde in charge of the express lane; she apparently approved of my rebellion. She fixed me with a determined look as she wrestled the bag of briquets over the scanner until the cash register ingested the code. "Ray and me are barbecuing tomorrow no matter what the weather's like," she said.

"Good idea," I replied. "We'll force spring to arrive. We'll pretend winter is really gone."

"That's what Ray, my husband, says."

"Well I'm with Ray. Enough is enough."

Solemnly she nodded, then announced, "Sixteen thirty-two."

I paid her but winced as I did so.

"I know," said Penny the cashier.

She gave me my change and the cash register tape which, as usual, I held lamely in my hand, wondering what to do with it now that its function was complete.

"You have to bag your own at this register," said Penny then.

"Ah," I said, moving down to the end of the check out. I bagged the cash register tape first, although not quite in the same way it had bagged me. Confidently, I tossed in the steak, the potatoes, the barbecue sauce, everything but the briquets which I hoisted over my shoulder like a longshoreman would and left.

Strangely enough, outside in the waning sleet, I passed a jet black Camaro as I lugged my purchases back to my car through the parking lot. Its licence plate said, "*Ontario—PENRAY—Keep it Beautiful.*" At that moment, I don't know why exactly, I felt leaving the island had been a mistake. It felt like a pilgrimage to Delphi only to find the oracle away for the weekend or permanently shut down due to budget cuts.

I'd contemplated lunch at a cafe down the street, but now I just wanted to get back to *The Crow's Nest.* The ass of my jeans was still damp and I felt I'd returned to civilization prematurely. Somehow both of these observations seemed intimately entwined. So I climbed into the car, told Canine Ben we were going home and together we left, driving past the new Tim Horton's and Flicker's Videos (Adult Movies "Avilable"), past Mom's and the bowling alley and the Legion, then carefully out of the rest of town.

Later, coming in on the two cottages from out on the choppy lake, slowing the motor to glide in on the waves, I glanced at the other cottage and noticed the boards had been taken off a couple of the windows. I wondered when and how that had happened. Then I saw a guy come around the corner to stare in my direction. I would have waved convivially except that, for a moment or two, I felt intruded upon, as if I had been located unexpectedly by the posse on my tail. By the time I got over the sensation of being discovered, the man had turned away.

After we landed, Canine Ben leapt out of the boat to check out this now familiar section of beach. I watched him catch the scent of something he deemed important, sniff at it a while, then, without further ceremony, lift his leg and piss on it. I was tempted to do the same, confirming this was our territory, thinking in an irrational way that it would mean not having to kill all the lawyers after all, that banks would suddenly lend us money, that the sun would come out, that all the world's problems (especially as they applied to me) would evaporate in the indifferent clarity of my arcing yellow stream.

This, I think, was my last crazy thought. I have them now and then. I use them to silently giggle my way out of periods of frustration. They are my most closely guarded secret. Easier to admit to masturbation than nonsense inspired by moods of social ignominy.

I dragged the rowboat up on the beach, gazed at the sky to assess what it might have in store for me next, then remembered the tarpaulin again. As expected, I found it in the shed, neatly folded on a shelf to the right of the door. I was distracted then, in the dim light of the shed, by the forgotten footprints, hand prints and signatures I now encountered pressed into the concrete floor.

I stared at them a time, enduring a wealthy kind of heartache, then couldn't resist the urge to crouch down and position one of my hands over one of the prints in the cold cement. Each was less than half the size of my hand. Stephen and Greg, I remembered with a smile, so much smaller then, younger, pre-Pentacostal at that time in their lives, before they were "saved." Memories came flooding back and I saw them clearly in my mind's eye—fresh-faced children, wild with smiles, all high speed sprints and joyful voices along this very same stretch of beach. Stephen Bowman, July 21, 1984, the concrete said. Greg Bowman, July 21, 1984. Twelve years ago nearly. Steve was ten then and Greg was eight. They'd come here to stay with Uncle Bart and Aunt Agnes while Bart put in the concrete floor. They'd told me about this pressing in the concrete, then showed it to me the following year, one of the last times we'd come to the island to visit together.

I stood in the shed for several minutes, looking at the hieroglyphics in the concrete, feeling sad and hopeful and hopeless. I juggled regrets with ifs and buts, feeling overwhelmed at this moment by how much time had gone by, how long the history of our frequent separation had become. Except for one summer when they were teenagers, an alternating weekend schedule and two weeks most other summers when I was on vacation, I had not lived with them since Steve was three and Greg was only one. Nearly twenty years.

I had given up that time with them in exchange for various periods of wild, circuitous flight from this nest to that one, from one idea to the next, from one hopeful scheme to another, then back again. It amounted to all the missing years in which they had mysteriously grown up while, on the other hand, I had only grown older. I stood up to place my sneaker on top of one of their footprints but it was entirely lost under the size of my foot, so I pulled it back for fear of smothering it, overpowering something sacred.

Gradually, as it always does, my sadness began to ease. There is one truth in which I never cease to believe and I still share it with my sons, that regardless of obligation I cannot ignore the need to be gone when the reasons to stay have all drifted away. We don't talk about such things now. We each just go where we must go and return when we must come back. And when we perchance to meet, my respectable sons and disreputable me, we trade our stories well.

## THE MAN AND THE WOMAN

THERE IS ANOTHER WAY TO LOOK AT THIS—as an audience, as witnesses. Like bringing home a rented video, making some popcorn and settling comfortably on the couch in the dark to watch the man and the woman live out a fragment of their lives in angst and sorrow, or good nature and love. And afterwards, the video (rewound for the convenience of other witnesses) goes back to the store in time for the four o'clock deadline before the late charges are applied.

Yes, it's another way to ponder Matt and Nicole. From the perspective of a collective of witnesses or an audience, from the standpoint of smug superiority, one can verify that one is more quietly real, more authentic (perhaps tediously so) certainly less enticing, but, yes, more authentic than the world's performers are. And so . . .

. . . One notices at last the sun is out. Now and then a cloud staggers enthusiastically over its face, but the clouds are puppies today, playful and small, and soon scamper somewhere else across the rich blue of the sky, leaving the sun to warm the beach where the man exercises his dog. There's still an unseasonable chill in the air; it still feels like March, but the sun is warm when it shines, much more like May should be.

The man tosses a stick into the shallow waves at the edge of the shoreline and his retriever, blonde like Brigitte Bardot, plunges into the water after it. The waves break over the dog's fur. He shakes the water away and returns the stick to the man. "Atta boy, Ben," says the man each time the stick comes back.

But shortly the dog called Ben turns to gaze intently down the beach at the approach of another dog. At a distance of fifty yards or so, the dogs assume a stance of rigid attention, then they dash towards one another to meet, sniff, and wag their tails. The other dog is a spaniel, white with black spots, with long ears which dangle like rugs hung out on a line in the wind. Somewhat protectively, the woman who has been walking with the spaniel hurries toward her dog. Then, as the two animals run off to play together, she resumes her more casual pace.

"He's friendly," calls the man to further reassure her.

In acknowledgment, one witnesses that the woman waves her hand.

The man and the woman stroll slowly across the sand to a point five yards apart, then they turn in unison to watch their dogs frolic near the edge of the lake.

The wind is up today. Futilely, sometimes simultaneously, the man and woman lift their hands to rein in their blowing hair only to give in to what they cannot control. While it is out from behind a tiny cloud, the sun is extremely bright. Both man and woman wear sunglasses: black, opaque, mysterious.

"He's fixed," explains the man.

"She's spayed," replies the woman.

The dogs scamper along the beach, playing as hard as they can.

"How old?" asks the man as he watches the dogs.

"Carmen is three in August," the woman says.

"Still a pup, really."

"And yours?"

"Five." He turns to her and smiles. "In August."

One is now aware the woman likes his smile, that she catches herself liking it and must gaze down the beach at the dogs again because she has faintly betrayed herself. "A better day to be out," she says for something to say.

"That's for sure," the man agrees. "Yesterday was pretty disappointing."

"Wasn't it awful?"

"To tell you the truth, it ruined my whole day. It felt like the last straw."

"So are we ever going to get spring?"

"I hope so," he replies.

One sees that the man and the woman make sure they do not look at one another very often, except cautiously now and then, out of the corners of their eyes. The man has noticed the woman is beautiful. He likes to think this doesn't perturb him but one knows damn well it does. To the woman, though, the man is only intriguing and tall, notwithstanding his smile which she thought was warm, twinkly and kind. She has noticed a couple of other things too. He has a face which is lean for its age, swarthy but not weathered, set off by a closely trimmed beard. His hair is going gray and is tied back in a ponytail. When he lifts his arm to keep hair off his forehead, she sees a leather pouch tied to his wrist from which two leather thongs hang down. As if he is Crazy Horse, whom she has recently read about, we see her think out of the blue.

For the most part, though, they keep looking at their dogs. They believe they are making sure everything remains alright.

Some distance away on the beach, the dogs wrestle with one another, waving paws, panting mouths and wagging tails. They gambol into the big lake waves, then gambol out again, shaking off a cold, sharp spray before getting wet once more.

"You said you call her Carmen?" the man asks the woman at last.

"Yes. After the opera."

"I see."

"And your dog?"

"Canine Ben. Ben for short. Because I couldn't think of anything else."

"Ben's okay. Dogs don't care what we call them."

"No, I suppose not. It's such a tough life for them, you see." He smiles to make sure she recognizes his small irony, one notices.

She smiles too, feeling wry herself. "Yes, it's heartbreaking really."

Then they grin at one another, apparently satisfied with what they've said.

Over her shoulder, the man notices someone else coming toward them along the beach. The man he saw yesterday, he remembers after a moment.

"Had him long?" the woman is asking now.

"About four years. Rescued him from the Humane Society."

"Yeah, me too," says the woman.

They stand there a time in silence while the waves pound the shore in a loud rhythm. A few yards away, Canine Ben tries to mount a reticent Carmen, the way he sometimes does with other dogs he meets.

As usual, the man is deeply embarrassed. "C'mon, Ben," he calls at that point. "It's all in your head." Apologetically he turns to the woman. "Sorry," he says to her. "Every now and then I have to read him his guarantee, the one they gave me at the pound."

The woman laughs gently. Then she leans forward and extends her hand. "I'm Nicole Graham, by the way."

"Matt Bowman."

Clumsily they shake hands.

"Obviously," he says, "you're staying at the other cottage."

"Yes."

"Obviously," he adds, "I'm staying at that one." He gestures carelessly in *The Crow's Nest*'s direction as if to deny the working class pride he feels in the place.

Now the man who has been approaching along the beach is nearly upon them. This time, when Matt gazes over her shoulder to see him, he tentatively smiles. Noticing this, she turns.

"Oh, it's Alan," she remarks, though mostly to herself.

Nicole makes introductions in a casual way. "Matt, this is Alan Birken. Alan, this is Matt Bowman."

The two men shake hands, saying, "Pleased to meet you" and "It's a pleasure," although later Nicole will not remember which one said which. One doesn't care about such details when witnessing larger fish to fry.

"Pleasant day," says Matt.

"Still chilly, though," counters Alan. "It looked a lot warmer from inside the cottage."

"Have you had coffee?" Nicole asks him then.

"Yes. And I put on a fresh pot."

He wants them to go back soon, thinks Matt, not sure why he's cared to notice. He glances at Alan and imagines him behind the wheel of a BMW convertible. He imagines him late on his way to the brokerage, weaving in and out of traffic, his electric shaver—plugged into the car's battery via the cigarette lighter terminal—buzzing confidently through a weekend beard. He imagines a cashmere sweater and a martini after work. One knows these are the things that writers imagine.

"Here for the weekend?" Alan asks him then.

Behind her dark glasses, Nicole studiously watches the dogs.

"Oh, no," Matt replies. "For the summer. I arrived May first. I'll be staying until the end of September. Or thereabouts," he adds.

Nicole keeps to herself that she is staying the entire summer as well. She knows Alan believes she sometimes reveals too much. More comfortable drawing their attention to the dogs, she tells Alan what good friends Canine Ben and Carmen seem to be.

Alan nods as if he cares. "So what do you do, Matt?" he asks.

"Writer," murmurs Matt. "Actually that's why I'm here. I'm completing a book of essays I've been contracted to write. What about you?" he asks the other man before he can be asked what the essays are about.

"Real estate and property management," replies Alan by rote, as if he goes to too many parties.

One speculates Matt would like to say "how interesting!" but knows he no longer possesses the required energy to lie. He has learned to hide in silence instead. He sees himself as living outside the fringes of what the world respects. Alan lives inside it. Alan is flesh, he thinks at that point, while he is only blood. One senses him glancing at the woman and wondering, *which of these are you?*

Nicole comes up with her warmest smile. "Well," she says, glancing once at Alan. "I suppose we should be heading back." She turns to Matt again, extends her hand. "Nice to meet you, Matt," she says. "Good luck with your essays."

"Thank you," he says. "It's been a pleasure."

The two men shake hands and tell each other how nice it has been. Nicole whistles for Carmen through her teeth and Matt is impressed enough to smile. One knows, although he has tried it many times, he cannot whistle through his teeth; it just comes out like a hiss.

She and Alan turn away, Carmen trotting along behind, ears

flopping in the sand whenever she sniffs at something on the ground. Barely two yards from Matt, Alan takes Nicole's hand. Although she knows what he is doing—that the act is designed to convey ownership—one realizes she lets him hold it for a while because she is cornered by his gesture.

Matt watches them a moment, then turns to Canine Ben. "Whaddyuh think, Ben?" he says about nothing in particular that one knows might become everything soon enough.

Then he remembers how he had planned to gather some of the wood on the beach for the Victoria Day bonfire he intends to light. As he drags a few pieces further up on the beach, away from the waves, he discovers the wood is still heavy with the rain and snow which fell on it yesterday.

## NICOLE

KAREN CALLS BACK WHILE YOU STILL LOLLYGAG in the tub, building pensive mountains and excavating reflective lakes out of the white-capped suds of a rich and gently whispering bubble bath. You have been anticipating her call. The phone is nestled on a towel which, in turn, is folded on the toilet lid not far from the tub.

"Hi, Sweetie," says Karen. "I got your message. Is everything all right?"

"Everything's fine," you tell her. "I just wanted to talk some more. I couldn't really say very much last time. You know?"

"Is Alan still there?"

"No, he's gone back to Toronto."

And you picture him again, a memory already fading, standing beside his car at *The Inlet*, punching combination numbers into the door the way he always does, as if the numbers are misbehaving children or disgruntled tenants who require a finger-jabbing lecture. Then he stood there in the twilight, a lock of fair hair falling onto his forehead, left unkempt from when the wind tossed it about during the boat trip across the channel.

"I can come up this weekend for the holiday," he said.

"Okay," you replied.

He frowned. "Don't you want me to?"

"Sure." Then, as his lips moved closer to an expression of

THE LAST LIGHT SPOKEN

petulance, you added hastily, "Of course I do."

You kissed each other goodbye. It was one of those hip to hip kisses, with someone, you or him or maybe both of you, pulling away to be somewhere else.

Afterwards, though, this didn't bother you. Instead you were distracted by the anticipation of going back to the island, of being behind the wheel of the boat, careless in the near darkness, assured that you had made this trip alone so many times before. In fact, you felt released on bail—a subdued call of the wild, a sensation so subtly exquisite it defied analysis or explanation.

"So what are you doing?" asks Karen.

"I'm in the bath. I'm not getting out until I'm wrinkled. To be honest, Karen, a bath is only a bath when there's no one tapping on the door, asking if you're okay in there. Why do men *do* that anyway?"

"I don't know," says Karen.

"Does Liam?"

"Not since before we were married."

"Do you miss it?"

Karen laughs. "No. Liam and me, well, we know each other."

"I know."

"And we're happy about things."

"I know. I'm jealous."

But it's not of Karen and Liam you are jealous. No, it's the idea that two people can be contentedly close which fosters your envy. If two people can fall and stay in love, why is it you can't seem to find it the way that Karen did?

"So," says Karen then. "How's Alan taking all of this?"

"He's sulky. It's the way he gets when things aren't going the way he wants them to. He'll probably call Angie when he gets back to Toronto, cry on her shoulder. That's what ex-wives are for."

"*Oooh*," says Karen with a wicked chuckle.

"I think they should remarry, get back to making each other miserable."

"*Oooh*," says Karen again.

But you give it up at this point, feeling a little guilty. "I feel good, Karen," you tell your friend. "I feel strong and independent. I feel like me more than I usually do."

"Then all of this is working," says Karen, "regardless of what you decide."

"Yes."

"So has Alan talked about it much? I mean, if you decide to leave Toronto, what's it going to mean for him? What does he say about all of this?"

"He's being politically correct," you reply. "You know, 'it's your decision, Nickie' or 'I know you'll figure out what's best for you,' that kind of stuff."

"That's all?"

"Well, no. He mentioned during the drive up here that, down the road, if we were of a mind to, he could operate his Toronto business from Kingston, expand into the Kingston market. He said real estate's the shits in Kingston. But he said there was property management potential there, because of the university."

"So you mean, if you decide to work with me this fall and give up your job at *Pinnacle*, he might decide to move to Kingston?"

When you hear it put this way, you feel as bemused about the notion as Karen. Is that what you heard when Alan was talking, or just what you thought you heard? Is that what he really *meant?*

"Nickie?"

"Sounds like what he was driving at," you reply in a bit of a daze.

"Well how do you feel about that? I mean it's not like you asked him to."

"I don't know," you reply. "I've been through so much with Alan over the past two years. Angie and deception, half-truths, possessiveness. Most of the time I think we're finished and no one's gotten around to saying so. Other times, I wonder if we're just in a slump."

You hear Karen pause to phrase her next question carefully. "Can you make a decision, you know, about working with me, keeping him on the outside of it?"

"I have to," you reply with all the urgency of an oath. This is the one prerequisite in your decision you believe in completely.

"I think so too," offers Karen. "It is your decision. It's your life you have to be concerned about. But what about Brian Bannerman? When we talked last, well, the time before last, you were going to have lunch with him. How did that go?"

"Terrific. He was so understanding. I knew he would be. He understood completely that I need a change. He even admitted he gets tired of *Pinnacle* and the insurance business himself. He asked me to let him know by the end of the summer, though, so he can make arrangements to replace me. But he was wonderful about it. He said, in the interim, the claims and adjustment department could struggle on without me, that in the least I deserve an extended vacation. He was wonderful."

"Oh Nickie, that's great."

"Yup. So now it's all up to me."

"Absolutely."

"Karen, can you hang on a minute? I'm going to run some hot. The water's getting chilly."

You warm up the bath for a precious telephone minute, then turn off the tap. You round up the remaining suds and bubbles on the water's surface, covering your flesh with them, like cuddling into a baby blanket.

"I'm back," you say.

"So," says Karen. "Are you nervous there all by yourself?"

"Nah. Say! I have a neighbor here on the island."

You tell her about the man in the other cottage, about his dog, about how Carmen and Canine Ben became friends, how the man was "very nice," how he will be staying at the cottage for the next four and half months, writing a book of essays "or something."

"What does 'very nice' mean, Nickie?" Karen asks playfully after you are done.

More or less from habit—there can be no other reason—you grow defensive. "Nice," you say impatiently. "You know, friendly, polite, respectful."

"Oh," says Karen. "Attractive?"

"Karen," you say sternly, with rising exasperation. "He's older."

"Oh," says Karen again.

"He's a little different," you say thoughtfully. "I imagine he's an interesting man, once you get to know him. Alan thought he was stuck back in the sixties. He had a pony tail, a leather bracelet hanging from his wrist. Alan thought he was an oddball. But Alan thinks writers are all left-wing flakes anyway. But I thought he was very nice. Actually it makes me feel more secure knowing someone is down the beach and that he's okay."

"I suppose," says Karen. "I just wonder how he got his *Harley* across the channel."

It takes a second or two but both of you burst into laughter.

After this, you embark on the ceremony of bringing the conversation to a conclusion. You promise her you will call after the long weekend. You tell her you love her.

"Love you too, Kiddo," she says.

You disconnect.

Afterwards, however, something lonely and oppressive comes over the cottage as day admits it is done. The bath water grows cold again. You get out of the tub and go through the processes of restoring yourself and the bathroom to order. In the living room, you sit down in your father's leather chair with one of the several books you have brought with you to read this summer, holding it in your lap. It is now deep twilight outside the cottage windows. Night lurks beyond it like a scavenger. Carmen finds a place on the floor not far from your feet. You look at the cover of the book, a Tom Robbins novel, but still do not open it. Light from the lamp behind you ricochets over your left shoulder into a pool on the book's cover.

You consider what you said to Karen about Alan, about deceptions and half-truths, about whether or not the relationship is over and, if so, who will be the first to say so. You've been through romantic attrition before. It's like evaporation. The pool gradually dries up and yet you stumble around in the ensuing desert a while longer, vaguely waiting for something good to rain down on you. Is that what you and Alan are doing now? Or is the decision lying ahead of you—whether or not to change cities and occupations, whether or not to join Karen in her music school business—the downpour that will bring you back together?

Sometimes you cannot remember what attracted you to him in the first place. There was, in the beginning, a brief but intense excitement but it's been a long time since you felt even a flicker of anything similar to this remembered initial passion.

THE LAST LIGHT SPOKEN

You thought he was handsome at first; now he doesn't seem handsome at all. Each time you look at him, little betrayals step in front of your potentially appreciative line of sight, cutting it off. Yes, it's the betrayals. He was the one who brought up marriage, then gradually stopped talking about it. Even when his divorce came through and he claimed to be so relieved that the prolonged war he'd waged with his wife was finally over, he countered your reminder about marriage with a bemused silence which made you feel foolish for mentioning it. But you decided to move in together. You argued, complained and bickered. Angie, his ex-wife, would call, as sweet as treacle, sometimes twice a week, needing something from him, relegating you to second in line, transforming you into a churlish nag each time he acquiesced to one of her various requests.

Eventually you moved out, suggesting cohabitation was premature. You dated one another. Alan seemed to thrive on the circus of anxiety swirling around your relationship, sure of himself and everyone else only when you were quarrelling. He seemed used to misery, seemed even to need it. You just wanted it all to go away. Alan became, for you, the most recent in a line of bad romantic choices you believe you've made too often. And sometimes still, though not so frequently now, you wonder what is wrong with you, why you fall in love with scoundrels, with men who enjoy their pain so much they want to share it with you.

And now that you've arrived on the island to consider going into business with Karen, now that you might be slipping away from him, Alan is encroaching more deeply into your state of solitude, to keep you in his life. Part of you wishes he'd succeed; part of you prays he'll fail.

## MATT

**Sunday, May 12**
ANOTHER NIGHT HAS FALLEN; another day goes home to bed. I feel balanced tonight, buoyant, optimistic but reflective, vaguely compelled to look ahead, a little melancholy in looking back. This evening marks my first ten full days on the island. I feel like I'm going somewhere, some place inside my well-being. Maybe it's because spring is in the air. I cannot say for sure. Whatever the reason, I feel as settled tonight as I felt unsettled yesterday during that spiteful snowfall which came so late in the season.

Hmmm, maybe it's the weather that fills me with anticipation. Certainly, it's not so cold tonight. I've still got the woodstove on, but I've left it to die out. This seems enough to fill the cottage with comfort. I can't see the sky from here, whether the stars are out or not. All I can see is deep, dark night, that mysterious, enticing, intriguing void it represents.

I've been thinking about how *The Crow's Nest* feels like home to me. I suspect, come the end of September when I leave this place for the last time, I'll feel a profound sadness because it has meant so much to me. I feel a trace of that sadness now. It's like an expected death in the family. People say you can prepare yourself for loss. I'm not so sure, even if you've had lots of practice. It's not what you do before the loss that counts; it's what you do afterwards.

I believe this because I'm one of those people who doesn't

seem to hang onto very much, not like some people do. Our various losses, deeply felt when they occur, are ameliorated more quickly by what we conceive of doing next. This is what people like me do so well. I see the contest between grief and anticipation as two players who bat their tennis ball back and forth inside my soul. On the one hand, the mourning I feel over the loss of *The Crow's Nest* in a few months' time is legitimately felt. On the other, I have virtually settled on going to the mountains again and view the prospect with growing excitement. Once Lynn Danby has her book of essays, there will be nothing to prevent me from heading west again. It's been a few years since I explored the mountains and I *do believe* it's time I sought out a new milieu.

At any rate, there it is. People of my ilk recover quickly. When something is lost to us we don't waste much time replacing it with something else. I've only learned this about myself during the past few years. Or rather, I've learned to *forgive* this in myself. Prior to then, it seemed a hopeless, irresponsible, careless, even shameful way to be. No wonder I pursued so much commitment for myself. I think it was a means of dealing with the guilt I felt over wanting, most of all, to live an independent life. I now believe I failed at conventional marriage, at creating a conventional lifestyle because, in reality, I never truly wanted it. I would embark quite stubbornly on the conventional domestic adventure, sometimes even believing it made me happy. Then I'd discover myself standing at the window most days, looking out, anxious to be departing once more over the next hilltop, to see what kind of meadow might lie on the other side. I now accept that I'm destined to behave this way. At least now there's no one—no wife, no partner, no cohort—to be hurt by it. Just Canine Ben. But he goes where I go. Canine Ben has few expectations of me which makes him a perfect companion.

So I sit here on the edge of this deep, dark night, comfortable with my day.

I worked productively, I think. I am now half way through the first draft of the fourth essay. I don't resist the urge to write quickly, knowing full well the tough slogging will come later, during all of my many revisions. Ever has it been thus.

I suppose the only other happenstance demanding to be

recorded tonight is that it would appear I have a neighbor here on the island. I assumed, at first, only for the weekend. But I noticed her leave with her partner not long after dinner, then was surprised to see her return alone again as dusk was falling, piloting her boat in the twilight like a veteran. So it would appear she now resides alone on the island in much the same way I do. I didn't have an opportunity to ask her how long she is staying or why she is here so early in the season. Her companion came along while we were talking on the beach this morning and the ease with which the woman and I met was curtailed by his intrusion.

I didn't like him much, although I don't think it was personal. No, it was because he is of a type and his presence represented a missive from the *real* world, that implacable planet where right and wrong are so clearly defined. Everything about *him* suddenly seemed cosmically right. Everything about *me* was suddenly wrong. He had go-getter written all over him. The universe, in all its current decay and ethical rationalization, loves this kind of man; the woman, Nicole Graham, no doubt does too. He will not miss or even notice the fact that I find his kind of man fatuous.

As for the woman, it was Canine Ben that introduced us, racing up in his gregarious fashion to befriend her spaniel, Carmen. Never mind that later he made fools of both himself and his master—neutered, the two of us, although in different ways—by trying to hump her dog. Jesus, what is it about dogs and their love for Murphy's Law? Matt Bowman's axiom: on the only occasion your dog decides to tear the arse out of someone's pants, it will be a policeman.

I must admit Nicole Graham seemed more than pleasant. I found her warm and friendly, at least until the yuppie over-achiever showed up. Sense of humour too. It gave me pause to reflect how rarely I encounter warmth in people, so rarely in fact the chill has become, in my mind, an inherent human trait, like walking on two legs. Biped frostbite. Then again, it could be an indication of the harsh, dark times hovering all around us. Maybe we're simply afraid to reach out for fear someone will slap our hand. It's this kind of world now. To reach out is weakness and weakness is, at best, embarrassing; at worst, weakness invites exploitation.

She is, I should note, extremely attractive, young—perhaps not yet even thirty, bearing in mind that I am a notoriously poor judge of age. I didn't want to stare at her, so the sense that she was attractive came to me in a peripheral way, as information I absorbed, like venturing out and discovering it is a nice day. But what makes it nice is more pleasantly viewed as a cumulative mystery.

I remember, for instance, that she is quite tall, nearly my height, with long legs. And she has gorgeous hair, light brown, wavy, the kind that looks like she just tumbled out of bed. Beautiful smile. I'm sure some years ago, under the same circumstances, I would have been quite taken with her. Now I'm wise enough to know, purely on the basis of playful conjecture, that she is probably not my type. She is probably Mr. Go-getter's type. I doubt his type and my type could ever share the same tastes.

As a state, my romantic retirement satisfies me greatly. I am comforted to know my stupidity is at an end. I don't lose my head. I can meet a beautiful woman on the beach and derive satisfaction from the fact that I'm exactly who I am and feel no temptation to change myself in any way on the basis of even fleeting romantic interest. I feel happily beyond all of that. Most of all, I feel happily beyond all the stupidity that once characterized my past. I have reached, at last, the age of romantic safety. I no longer make any mistakes which can induce the grief, misery, disappointment and endless compromise which more or less defined love for me in the past. My time for that is over. I don't miss the brief periods of wonder and I certainly don't miss the protracted erosion of love which too much compromise inevitably creates.

I suppose all of this comes to mind because this island and *The Crow's Nest* are inextricably entwined with my romantic past. Here, most of all, I have felt the full gamut of sensations love usually inspires. Virtually all of the women with whom I partnered, whether briefly or for a period of years, came to this place to visit with me at some point. Even those who did not were carried here in my heart in some way, as if this place is where I once stored the components of my romantic nature.

My first intense romantic relationship took place when I was eleven years old. Her name was Winnifred, of all things, and she was pert and dainty. I loved to gaze at her face and writhed in joy and misery at everything I saw displayed there, apparently just for me. She never knew this island. But the summer I loved her so much I spent two weeks here with Uncle Bart and Aunt Agnes. In my state of endless yearning, Winnifred travelled everywhere with me here. I missed her desperately but suffered my pain in silence. Although I could never have explained it intelligently then, I knew instinctively that love for a child of eleven feels as crushing and important as it does for any adult, but to say so then would have presumed everyone believed this as I did when, in fact, I doubt they believe it at all. I admit I was a child. But where Winnifred was concerned, it would have hurt me deeply to be treated like one.

By the time I was fifteen love had become poetry for me—bad poetry granted, but poetry just the same. I wrote my first bad poems on this island, sitting on the dunes in the petrified forest, leaning against a long dead tree trunk, as tortured by unrequited love as the tree behind me was by the passage of time. Life during those days was a wondrous misery. I was intensely alive with it. I was as self-indulgent as only a love-struck writer of bad romantic poems can be. And lurking nearby was some large and shadowy feeling which never grew explicable enough to form a salient thought: simply, I wanted to be *everything*. To have such feelings is a state of emotional virginity I will never understand. These days I don't miss its humiliating innocence, although on rare occasion, I would like to visit the feeling like a tourist, even if only for a moment or two, to remember what it was like.

I lost this feeling forever when I was nineteen, the night Linda MacDonald and I, on a blanket at the edge of a fire we built on the point of the island, finally gave in to the lovemaking we'd been resisting for several weeks. It wasn't at all what I had anticipated. I didn't love her and she didn't love me and it was clumsy rather than fluid, and afterwards we both felt gooey and empty, deeply suspicious that everything we'd been led to believe about the pleasures of our respective futures was probably just another lie.

It's easy to remember things here. After ten days, the ghosts of this splendid island come calling less timidly. They remind me that the perpetuity I thought would be love, which I so clearly anticipated, has failed completely to be found. Still, I love this place for trying, for its consistent loyalty during the long period I spent learning my lessons. I am now a satisfied man, so much so that I'm glad each stage of my journey to this present took place in just the way it did.

## THE MAN AND THE WOMAN

WITNESSES KNOW PLACES LIKE *THE ROADHOUSE* very well. Although in some ways establishments such as these are often different from one another, one is aware they are also usually very much the same. Most towns of any size in Ontario have a restaurant-pub-bar like *The Roadhouse* situated somewhere along some downtown street.

They are born in older buildings to provide them with an intimate atmosphere which new buildings rarely achieve, looking as they do more like warehouses, no matter how hard they try not to. The attraction to older buildings is that they are contoured in ups, downs and arounds like small castles, small villas, even small caves. One deduces that the nooks add up to a kind of spelunking adventure through a twilight mystery one cannot find in the sprawl of modern warehouse eateries.

*The Roadhouse* restaurant pub is located in an old Victorian home on a primary artery in town, just around the corner from the main thoroughfare. There's a video store on its left and a Becker's with gas pumps on its right. When one walks around the corner to the right, one comes to the main shopping district anchored by a Zeller's store. Next to it are the office of The Gazette and a camera store with lawyer's offices on the second floor. Before one knows it, one is well ensconced on the main drag, heading quickly towards the Bel-Air Motel on the way to Mom's Restaurant and the bowling alley. And further up, perhaps half a mile away, that's where the new Tim Hortons has taken root.

Tonight is Friday night and it's busy at *The Roadhouse*. It's the beginning of the first long weekend of the summer, Queen Victoria's weekend, the *first* long weekend because Easter doesn't count. Easter doesn't count as a holiday in cottage country because it's mostly still winter when Good Friday comes along and everyone is out of patience with the season.

*The Roadhouse* is noisy tonight, not because of any unruliness in the crowd, but because the wooden chairs, porcelain plates and metal dinnerware all clatter at one another like tea party guests as they move back and forth from level to level in the large dining area. Voices rise in proportionate volume to scale the din of so much dinnertime activity.

It's dusk inside the restaurant. Lights dangle from the high ceilings at the ends of octopus-tentacled chandeliers that have been dimmed for atmosphere. Candles in glass vessels on everyone's table are as dull and sombre as accountants. One must also factor in the dark varnish on the walls. No wonder the lingering May daylight—still lustrous as evening begins and still filtering through high windows near the ceiling—can't quite breech the dark ambiance.

The local patrons are all sitting at the bar tonight, including those who are eating dinner. Most of them gaze up at TSN on a television screen on a shelf in the corner to their left. The sound has been turned off but they can't help glancing at the screen anyway, drawn by activity, statistical data and the intensity of broadcast delivery like moths to a flickering light.

As for the holiday crowd—the cottage owners and campers already in town for the weekend—these sit in booths or at tables located on the three levels of the restaurant. The upper deck on the right just inside the door is for non-smokers. The lower level, just inside the entrance, like the upper deck on the left, has been set aside for smokers. Most of *The Roadhouse* caters to smokers because smoking goes with eating out and drinking in public these days the way venereal disease goes with sex. The few children here with their parents have been taken to the non-smoking lower deck where the sound of their holiday excitement drifts into the rest of the restaurant.

This, then, is the scene one is aware of as a witness when

the woman comes in. One sees her glance down at then stand near a sign on a pedestal which says *please wait to be seated*. She waits as instructed, scanning the various tables and booths for the man she's supposed to meet. Some of the other men seated not far away, all of them strangers to her with companions of their own, turn to gaze at her in furtive admiration. She notices this in a careless way. One gathers she is used to tolerating the attention and the sneaky way it drifts in her direction when men are accompanied by their wives.

A pretty waitress with short, dark hair and a trio of studs and earrings in her left ear approaches and smiles professionally at her. "For one?" she asks.

"Two," the woman replies. "I'm expecting someone."

"Non-smoking?"

"Smoking, please."

The waitress nods and guides the woman up onto the upper deck on the left, then leads her to a table against the railing near the front of the restaurant. "How's this?" the waitress says.

"Fine."

The woman glances at the door, briefly considers which direction to face, then opts to sit with her back to the door. She orders a Blue Light.

When the beer comes, she lights a cigarette but leaves her beverage untouched in front of her while she watches the bubbles drifting to the top of the glass. Shortly though, she surveys the restaurant again, identifying as locals the personalities at the bar. She bets herself that they have names like Mickey and Carl and Vince. Then, enjoying the speculation, she picks out the tourists, names them John and Carol or Chuck and Daphne. At least some of the children, she decides, are called Jason or Sarah. The preschoolers are Caitlin or Kyle.

One can tell she likes the clatter of the restaurant, thinking that Alan won't. He'll claim it's hard on conversation and he'll want to leave early because there's too much noise, although in truth it's because he's a man who likes to get going even more than he likes to arrive.

While she sips at her beer, the woman begins to imagine a scenario here in which she tells Alan their relationship is over. She has no intention of doing so, not at this point anyway, but if she ever does, this is the kind of place where she would prefer to do it. And it would be on a busy night like this one too. Alan would be less likely to make a scene with so many people in close proximity. The woman, one realizes, toys with this notion for a few minutes, then guiltily becomes aware of what she is doing. So she tries to imagine something else, Alan admitting the error of his ways, for instance, coming to her in a state of conciliation to make appropriate amends. But this seems an even more unlikely fancy to her and she gives up on it quickly. In the end, she only wishes she would think about somebody else for a change.

At that moment, to her surprise, she notices the waitress with the short dark hair and the earrings guiding the unusual man from the other cottage onto the deck where she takes him to the opposite railing and seats him at a table there. One sees her recognize her neighbor right away despite having met him only once, despite the fact he is dressed differently than the man who was bundled up on the beach in his winter coat and dark sunglasses nearly a week ago. Tonight he wears a denim jacket and a bandanna, a long one that dangles down his back. One catches her wanting to smile, to wave and call out to him, but one knows she doesn't for fear of calling him Crazy Horse, the name she has bestowed on him since their first meeting days ago.

The man sits facing her but when his eyes glance in her direction, he does not recognize her. Again she is tempted to wave but again she does not. Instead she watches him as he converses with the waitress, ordering his beverage. He says something extra to the waitress, a twinkle in his eye she can see (or believes she can see) even at this distance. The waitress laughs and reaches out to touch the man's denim-clad upper arm, leaving her fingers there for a few flirtatious seconds.

The woman liked the waitress too but wonders now if she is too forward. Or do they all know him in this place?

Then Alan Birken shows up, right there at her table, as if he has risen like smoke from a genie's bottle on the floor in front of her. "Nickie?" he says in a voice climbing towards the last syllable, as if he too doesn't recognize her or fears she won't recognize him.

"Hi, Alan," she says, leaning forward a little to accept his kiss on her lips.

"Been waiting long?"

"No," she says as he sits down opposite her.

"You look good."

"Thank you," she replies a little stiffly. "You sound surprised."

"Well, you know, your first week alone and all that. Didn't know how you'd be taking it."

Bored with what Alan is saying, the woman glances at the man from the other cottage, one notices. He has put on a pair of stylish wire-rimmed glasses. Despite the lack of lighting, he's reading a hardcover book. His beer sits neglected on the other side of the book's cover. One sees her wonder what he reads, what his favorite subjects are.

Alan's sunglasses hang from his neck on a brilliant yellow cord. He hates to lose things so he ties them to his body. He turns in his chair to examine the rest of the restaurant, then turns back to her again. "Noisy, isn't it?" he says.

"How was your drive?" asks Nicole.

But the waitress arrives bearing two menus that she positions on the table in front of them. "Something to drink?" she directs at Alan.

"Mouton Cadet," he says. "Half litre. If you have it."

"We have it," the waitress replies.

"Sorry," says Alan after she departs.

"I asked how your drive was. Traffic must have been heavy."

"A little. It was the sun today, too bright, too intense. I thought I was courting a migraine but it turned out to be okay."

"Maybe you should have waited until tomorrow morning when you weren't so tired."

"No," he says, his face conveying disappointment that what he now must explain she should have figured out for herself. "I'd be going east, the sun would be right in my eyes."

"Maybe it would be cloudy."

He simply looks at her. "You're acting kind of strange," he accuses her at last.

"Strange? I'm fine."

The waitress brings the man from the other cottage his dinner. He thanks her and, when she is gone, admires it on the plate, an eight-ounce sirloin steak, rice pilaf and a small Caesar on the side. He glances up again at the sensational looking young woman at the opposite end of the deck, one notices. He does not conceive of recognizing her nor of wondering who she is. She is too young and he is too old. But he likes to look at her in an aesthetic way, the way he would a particularly pleasing painting or a chance encounter with a scenic vista. Still, he notices that her face has changed since her man sat down with her. Her expression has dropped a little, gone rigid, closed and tight. His own face has done that on occasion, one knows, although it was a few years ago now when he thought he had good reason.

"So," says Alan to Nickie. "What have you been up to?"

"Not much. Walks with Carmen. Doodling on the piano. Reading. I've come into town a couple of times to window shop."

"You sound bored already."

"I'm not bored," the woman says.

"Been working on your decision?"

"Alan, it's only been five days. I've got the entire summer."

"I know. But you're the kind of person who likes to make up her mind."

"No, I'm the kind of person people *wish* could make up her mind."

Alan smiles cryptically. The waitress comes to ask if they've decided. The woman orders the sirloin special with rice pilaf and a small Caesar on the side. Alan, muttering something to himself about not being able to get to the gym this week, orders the large Greek salad.

The woman glances at the man from the other cottage, one sees. She thinks he might have been looking at her, about to recognize her, but his eyes scurry away as he cuts into something on his plate. He's taken his glasses off. She decides he's far-sighted, his glasses are for reading. Matt Bowman is his name, she remembers at this moment. But without glasses he's Crazy Horse. With glasses, well, she doesn't know, or maybe he's Crazy Horse who reads. Maybe by the end of summer, they'll know each other better, well enough that she can tease him about being Crazy Horse.

"Nickie?" says Alan then. "I'm hoping we can talk this weekend."

"Sure," the woman says.

"I'm hoping we can clear up some things. I think they're important."

"Okay."

"I ..."

"... Not tonight, though," she says. "You just got here."

Alan nods, holding up his hand in a gesture of compliance.

The woman knows he plans his deep conversations in advance. With Alan, they never just happen. He likes to rehearse his point of view because it keeps him on track, one knows.

The waitress goes to Matt Bowman and asks him how his dinner is. The twinkle comes back and he says something funny because the waitress laughs and lingers. He must come here a lot, Nicole decides at that point.

"What about the guy in the other cottage?" asks Alan. "Have you run into him this week?"

The woman's eyes flick away from Crazy Horse. "No," she says in reply. "Haven't seen him."

"Probably keeps to himself," says Alan. "Kind of an oddball, probably a flake."

"Seen Angie?"

Alan sighs, the flood waters rising again and his sandbags running low. "We had lunch yesterday."

"How nice," the woman says.

"It's not what you think, you know."

"What is it then?" Nicole asks aridly.

"Trying to make peace now that everything's over."

She says nothing to this.

"Look, Nickie, there's nothing to be gained in Angie and me holding a grudge against one another. The fire's out. We're trying to build a positive friendship in the ashes."

One call tell that something in the flamboyance of his imagery makes the woman want to laugh. How long did he work on that one? From Bowmanville to Cobourg?

"It's one of the things I want to talk about," Alan is saying. "I want to systematically go through the whole mess—Angie, you and Karen's music school, our future together, everything."

The waitress delivers their meals.

"Not tonight," the woman says after the waitress goes.

"This weekend, though," he insists. "All of this is making me crazy."

They eat a time in silence.

"Heard from Karen?" Alan asks finally.

"No."

"Your mum?"

She nods. "They're coming to visit first weekend in June."

"Great."

The woman watches him pile into his salad and wonders suddenly if she'll be able to make love tonight. Alan will be unapologetically urgent because it's been more than a week, unless, of course, he boinked Angie under the restaurant table yesterday, midway through lunch, trying to build a positive friendship in the ashes of their marriage. Jesus!

Would Crazy Horse do that? But Crazy Horse, she discovers, has mysteriously departed. Evaporated. His table is being wiped and he's no longer there.

Was Alan talking again?

"Sorry," the woman says. "What did you say?"

"I said it's too damned noisy in here."

## MATT

**Saturday, May 18**

I MUST WRITE THIS EVENING about a disturbing event which took place this morning, leaving me unnerved and embarrassed ever since. It's a personal and private embarrassment, granted, but this fact doesn't soften the heat in the blush. There's even a side of me at this moment that doesn't want to write about what happened for fear of giving it too much credence. Yet, in the spirit of biting the bullet and hoping what shows up in black and white ameliorates my foolishness, I suppose I should report it as best I can remember it.

Now that I think about it, it's been a good long time since I felt this disconcerted. And the fact I must shoulder my foolishness alone only emphasizes the need to write everything down and deal with what comes up as a result. Cringe, Bowman, cringe, I keep telling myself. Address your duality. Salute what it is in you that feels like two people, one of whom has been shamed by the silliness of the other.

To begin on a positive note, I want to stress, for the record, that most of the time—indeed virtually *all* of the time—I know exactly what I am doing. I know where I am going and even approximately when. I bat temptation and compromise out of my ballpark like a *Louisville slugger*. Except today. Whatever it was in destiny's alignment, something unexpected crept inside my certainty so suddenly and so subtly that even now, hours later, I'm still shaken by the experience.

You see, I met my neighbor from the other cottage, Nicole Graham, again this morning, just like the first time nearly a week ago. We were on the beach. Our dogs rushed up to one another like long lost siblings. No attempted humpings on the part of Canine Ben this time, thank God, but lots of running in and out of the water, the usual doggy fun and games.

At the edge of all this activity stood their masters, discussing, for wont of anything else, how the weather's turned so chilly again. We talked about this too much really, wearing the subject down like an old bald tire as we watched our dogs at play. I thought the woman looked tired and cranky this morning, which, when you get down to it, was fairly nervy of me, being as I have virtually no basis for comparison. Still, Matt Bowman is my name, speculation is my game. Obviously I didn't say anything about it, I've only met her once before. Besides, who knows what tragedies lurk in the hearts of beautiful women?

We were pretty awkward together after we exhausted our mutual lament about the weather. Long silences developed, seemed to fall out of the sky in fact. Normally gregarious, I felt responsible for this somehow, like a tongue-tied Chicken Little. I had no idea why I was so uncomfortable. Finally, though, I came up with a harmless gambit and seized it like the proverbial, drowning man.

"So," I said, "are you all settled in?" Even then the "you all" sounded touristy, like I hailed from Alabama, so I was definitely off my stroke, adrift in a sea of ineptitude.

"Oh sure," she replied, glancing at me neutrally. "Everything in its place, a place for everything."

I had noticed by then that she wasn't wearing sunglasses this morning. Nicole Graham, I discovered with some appreciation, has the most beautiful blue eyes I have ever seen. I remember thinking some young bastard—probably Mr. Go-getter from last weekend—is a very lucky man. And I felt a new pang of grief over my now departed youth.

Still, with all of that, we fell silent yet again.

Then, quite unexpectedly, she said, " I saw you at *The Roadhouse* last night. Or else you have a twin."

"No, that was me," I told her, recovering from my surprise.

"I'm just wondering how I didn't see *you*."

"I wondered too," she said with some amusement. "I was sitting opposite you on the upper deck, you know, at the other end. I wasn't that far away."

"In the smoking section?"

She nodded.

I remembered her then, of course, the young woman I'd admired a couple of times from my vantage point several feet away. I just hadn't made the connection. I gazed at her now to figure out why, finally concluding that, seated, she hadn't looked as recognizably tall last night, nor was she as formally made up this morning.

"I feel kind of foolish," I said. "I hope you didn't think I was rude or unfriendly. Normally I have more presence of mind. I may have to acknowledge my advancing years, my approaching senility."

I suppose I was trying to be humorous, concluding my formal parade of stammering excuses in this way, but as soon as that last bit was out of my mouth, I wished I hadn't said it. A self-inflicted kick in the ass, even with a bare and well-intentioned foot, is still a kick in the ass.

"I was going to say hello," she mused at any rate.

"Next time, I guess," I said.

"I will," she promised pensively. "Do you eat there often? You seemed to know everyone."

"No, that was my first time actually."

"Oh," she said, nodding thoughtfully.

It was at that moment what I now think of as the first disturbing incident took place. It was personal, as I've said, but entirely unexpected. Just then a gust of wind came up and, by reflex, she tugged hair away from her cheek. To my dismay, it was such an enticing gesture, I felt it spin, quite literally and inexplicably, inside my belly. The sensation was warm, pleasantly exciting, surprising and unexpected. It was also uncomfortably familiar. In its wake I felt like an adolescent at his first school dance. I swallowed. I worried, should I speak, my voice would come out in a state of male change again, riding two or three simultaneous octaves, transforming me once again into a juvenile yodeller. I felt stupid and exposed and glanced around for any distraction.

Fortunately, my neighbor on the beach seemed unaware of this. Together we watched our dogs still playing along the shoreline. I took a deep breath and tried to regroup.

"Ben?" I called firmly. "Make biggies, will you?"

My neighbor stared at me, a smile on her lips.

Feeling I had returned to safety, I grinned back at her. "Another word for doo-doo," I explained redundantly.

"I thought as much," she said.

It was then that I remembered why I shouldn't tarry on the beach. And I felt relieved that I had good reason to escape. It was possible I would be saved from future awkwardness by the banana muffins I had put in the oven before bringing Ben down to the beach. I told Nicole Graham what I was baking.

"They'll be burned," she said, concerned.

"I have them on low," I replied. "But Ben should do his business. Even on low . . ." and my voice trailed off like the smoke that would begin to drift out of the oven door if I did not return to the cottage soon.

Not long afterwards, though, Ben cooperated, even inspired Carmen to do the same. Nicole and I bagged the respective produce, then lamely held the containers in our hands, just standing there, not sure now what we should be doing next. The dogs had resumed their play and showed no signs of letting up.

"Your muffins," she reminded me.

I nodded and called to Ben who promptly ignored me. As we stood there looking foolish, the way dogs sometimes seem to intend—Carmen wasn't interested in going home either—I grew awkward again.

"Time for sterner measures," I suggested at that point.

Together we advanced on our dogs and grabbed them by their collars. It was then, in the midst of the ensuing struggle to disentangle our dogs, that a disturbing incident of precognition came barging into my consciousness. While the animals kept wrestling, my neighbor and I bent down to restrain them. For a moment our arms became entangled and we nearly bumped heads.

I know we were both embarrassed. No wonder we laughed and complained, both at the same time, as we struggled to part the misbehaving canines.

In real terms, all of this probably lasted hardly more than a few seconds, but it seemed much longer than that, especially for me, before we tugged them a few yards apart, panting and apologizing. Because it was during this entanglement that I suffered my powerful delusion.

Suddenly, for no apparent reason, I was convinced I knew Nicole Graham much better than I actually do, that we were and are not strangers. At that moment, she was entirely *familiar* to me. Not only had we seemingly untangled our dogs before, but I sensed and even glimpsed an assortment of other events we had either shared in some distant past or might share at some vague time in the future. These mirages cascaded in and out of my memory with a clarity I still hesitate to acknowledge. I sensed I remembered walks along this very beach, dinners eaten together on outdoor patios, even hills climbed together, walking hand-in-hand. I say I *sensed* I remembered these things. This is because each memory, each scene, entered my recollection in a hazy way, then grew gradually clearer before dissolving again to give way to its sequential replacement. It was like counting beads on a string. Each memory took its turn.

But it wasn't just the memories themselves I found so disturbing. It was the way they combined to suggest that there is a prior intimate connection between this young woman and me. Worse yet, while I was caught in the maelstrom of this astonishing sensation of memory, I heard a giddy inner voice proclaiming that this woman on the beach was *her.* I felt myself divide in two. While a part of me was aware of how lame this conclusion actually was—that she was *her*—another part of me defended the sensation, wanting to acknowledge it as true. In this case, the *her* part of it all seemed plausible indeed, especially because the entire deja vu incident literally drooled with metaphysical predestination.

I shudder now at such foolishness. Indeed, I know it for what it actually is, a recurrence of the perpetually juvenile and sanguine ambition we humans tend to sustain: that somewhere out there in the cruel beyond there is a particular someone who is absolutely *right* for us. Although I know why we need to feel this the way we do—the way I also know how it has no basis in fact—I was nonetheless staggered by its arrival in my particular consciousness at this time. It's been many years since I have suffered such a powerful hallucination.

Shortly, of course, it drifted entirely away. In its wake, I felt flustered and weak. More or less to compose myself, I glanced at my companion still pulling her dog away from mine, to see if she had noticed anything in my behaviour which visibly betrayed what had happened to me. I concluded that she had not. Strangely enough, even then, I felt two conflicting sensations at once: relief of course, but something else more troubling, a kind of hushed disappointment.

We parted then with hastily called-out *see yuh laters*. On the verge of a subdued hysteria, I wanted somehow to laugh. But I gained control of myself. As I walked Canine Ben back up to our cottage, I glanced over my shoulder down the overcast beach at the woman and her dog, going back the way they had come. It was then that I felt the last gentle tug of regret that what had happened to me just moments before had happened to me alone.

Silliness, really. The regret, I mean. Now, of course, I'm glad things worked out the way they did. Feeling foolish is a mission best flown solo, away from a mocking audience. Better I be alone to wrestle with this strange little secret of what happened to me this morning in an attempt to sort out what it might mean.

I tend to think of the incident now as a mysteriously powerful but terminal attraction, a kind of aberrant emotional chemical spill. It reminds me of a summer in Europe twenty-three years ago when I met a young woman in a cafe in Paris and thought I fell in love with her. Her name was Claudia and she was from England. She too was beautiful; come to think of it they always are. Nothing at all came of the prolonged sensation of attraction that day. There was merely a long mutual gaze punctuating several hours of stimulating conversation before, at last, we parted, forced by normal cruel logistics to get back to our separate lives.

Nonetheless, for years afterwards, I thought of her every day and wondered where she was. I imagined other encounters with her frequently and fancied running into her unexpectedly at some intersection, social gathering or otherwise innocuous appointment. Of course I was different then, young, a romantic, I suppose, Byronic from head to toe, devoted to my instinct in a way Rousseau and Lawrence would have admired.

Still, once red in tooth and claw or not, here it is in black and white, in words set down on paper. And I feel less foolish now, having captured the incident in this journal. I am resolved to maintain my perspective. Men my age have no business forgetting who they are. I'm comfortable accepting this.

So there it is. Two disturbing events enriched my day this morning, and left me troubled afterwards. But I have reported them—the strange sense of romantic familiarity, the deja vu, the fancy of predestination. And I have confessed to the other troubling incident as well, the one which, in its own way, was even more provocative, when my belly whirled at the attractive way Nicole Graham attempted to straighten her hair in the wind.

In my younger days I would have believed such a sweet twist of the knife in my guts presaged some kind of falling into romance. Certainly the feeling this morning reminded me of the first germ in the virus of the epidemic I have sometimes thought of as love. But with evening comes a more balanced reality, a knowledge that I'm done with such illusions because I understand them for what they are: namely a conjurer's trick, a prestidigitator's performance to the applause of foolish human myth.

Besides, I know this much about who I am: I no longer have the patience or the time to make a fool of myself. Those days are definitely behind me. I don't want them back again.

## NICOLE

IT IS THE SECOND DAY of the Victoria Day weekend now, the filling inside the holiday weekend sandwich: you nibble on the crust in a state of culinary ambivalence. On the one hand it's a sunny day and the breeze coming in off Lake Ontario this morning tends to be warm for a change—spring remains weeks later than usual but at least it seems to know it owes everyone an apology for being so tardy. You feel willing to forgive and forget. On the other hand? Alan Birken sulks around your setting like a disappointed child with nowhere else to go. A little contrition from *him* might be welcome

At this moment he waits for you down at the lower corner of the patio, sipping coffee from the mug he brought with him all the way from Toronto, the one with the roaring lion on the side underneath a bloodstained red astrological warning that he is, and will always be, a Leo. You know he intends to leave the mug here when he goes back to Toronto tomorrow night—his way of moving something he owns in with you for the summer, to encroach at least a little on this period in which you wish mostly to be alone. And tomorrow evening, at the moment of his departure, you will innocently say, "don't forget your mug," and he'll offhandedly reply, "I might as well leave it here for now, you know, for the summer," and you'll either have to make an issue out of it, feeling foolish for being so picky, or keep the damned thing in the cupboard, quietly annoyed about it for the rest of your stay. In bringing the mug, he cannot lose and he knows it. Unless, of course, you shatter the goddamned thing on his deliberately manipulative skull.

You consider these things—Alan and coming spring and the long overdue inspiration that might reveal what you should do about him—as you pour your own coffee into a plain mug which doesn't depict or say anything at all. Are we the mug from which we drink? you wonder. If so, this one is black from stem to stern, the color of your heart.

You and Alan have been essentially separate for most of the weekend, not saying much, drifting by one another, in this room or that room, waiting for something to happen. Even now you pour coffee inside while he waits outside, yards away.

He sits, you notice through the kitchen window, at the sunny edge of the terrace where, yesterday, to show his good intentions, he swept up an assortment of dead autumn leaves and oxblood pine needles, then burned them in the barbecue grate. He slouches at a patio table in white t-shirt, white shorts and expensive sandals, in a state of perpetual anticipation. He looks so Toronto, like he's parachuted into the wrong resort and is resolved to sue his travel agent. And it crosses your mind, before you can rein it in, that maybe things are worse between you and him than you thought a few days ago when you were happily living here alone. It occurs to you again, as it has so many times before, that you can't always remember what you once liked about him. Or maybe it's just the way that fucking mug tends to intrude on you by design.

So you try to get hold of yourself. What can you decide about love and dislike at this moment, especially when they sometimes resemble one another, dressed up in each other's emotional clothes?

It's your fault that he'll insist you talk this morning. You didn't feel like making love again last night. If you had, it might have helped to abort at least some of this big conversation he intends. Now he's got you. Something is clearly wrong with you and, accordingly, you simply must discuss it. It'll be for your own good, he'll tell you, because you need to release the pent up urgency in your hapless sexual juices.

Or some such version of horseshit.

So at last you take your coffee and depart for his office on the patio stones outside. You feel him watching you as you sit down across the table from him, as you tilt your head back to take in the gratifying rays of the sun. At last, when you are ready, you open your eyes and gaze back at him.

But he glances away for the moment in that familiar, coy way of his. He wants you to ask him what's wrong.

"You're so pale, so white," you tell him instead. "This sun will do you a lot of good."

"It's a nice day," he admits, uncharacteristically ignoring the criticism in your observation. "It's a lovely spot. I can see the merit in building a cottage here. I mean, look at the view."

"Yes," you say, taking in the rocky shelf on the other side of the patio wall, the beach sprawled out below, the blue expanse of the lake beyond. "I've missed the place."

"Nickie," he begins, toying with the nearly empty coffee mug, "we need to talk."

"You need to talk."

He gazes at you without a word. Anger flits across his features but he keeps it under control. He doesn't say anything.

"I'm not sure I need to talk. Not right now, at any rate," you add.

"All right," he says. "You're right. I'm the one who needs to talk. That's how I've been thinking about this business anyway. I want to say some things and then leave it with you. I have only one expectation, that you'll give me the chance to say my piece."

"Of course," you tell him then.

"I just need to explain how I feel."

"Okay."

He lifts the Leo mug to his lips, discovers his coffee is nearly gone and sighs in frustration. "I'm going for a refill first, all right?"

"Sure."

Then you remember your sunglasses are on the shelf just inside the kitchen door. You ask him to bring them back for you.

Shortly he returns, carrying his coffee and your sunglasses, wearing his own, the florescent cord startling as it dangles from his neck like the gallows in a psychedelic trip.

"Migraine?" you ask.

"Not yet," Alan replies.

Soberly you nod.

He clears his throat. "I've been thinking about us a lot, Nickie. Sometimes I can't think of anything else. I've been going over how much has gone on between us, how much is behind us now, how much I've learned from it. I want you to know that I have a lot of respect for what you're doing this summer, for the independent way you're approaching what to do about Karen's music school proposal. I think you're doing the right thing, regardless of what you decide, approaching it as an issue separate from you and me."

"Okay."

"But it's made me realize I've been taking you and me for granted. Not you, specifically—I'm not taking you for granted per se—but you and me? Absolutely and I'm sorry."

"Okay."

"Sometimes when it gets close to being too late, we realize what we've been doing wrong."

"That's true," you admit to avoid saying "okay" again.

"And I guess that's what I've been learning about myself." He takes another sip of coffee, slowly spins the mug, playing with it again in his fingers. "It's like thinking you have all the time in the world, that nothing's going to change. Then you discover it can and will change, that you've been holding back, procrastinating. Know what I mean?"

"Sure."

"Anyway," says Alan, "it's made me realize that I've been sort of confusing."

The baldness of his understatement makes you want to laugh. It's like an amputee casually asking if you can give him a hand. And, yes, of course you would if you could.

"The point is, Nickie, I don't want to be confusing anymore. I want to be clear about how I feel about you and me. The rest is up to you. I know your decision this summer is about other things too, but I hope there's some you and me in there too. And if there is, I want you to know clearly how I feel, what I think about our future together."

"That makes sense," you tell him, somewhat encouraged—or at least trying to be—by what he is seeking to say. If Alan is simply manipulating you this morning, then at least his approach is unusually inspired.

He gets up now and strolls the few feet to the edge of the

terrace. There he turns and gazes at you for a time, as if in profound study. "I want to get back what we had, Nickie," he says at last. "I miss it. I miss you. I miss your love."

You're aware that this moment should be touching but you can't quite feel it that way. Not yet, at any rate. Instead you feel strangely embarrassed and hardly know what to say. Do you believe him or is it too late to believe?

He is embarrassed too. Clearly he expected something more accommodating than your silence. "I guess I need to know if you're willing to try to get it back," he says, summing it up at last.

"I don't know, Alan."

Birds twitter in the ensuing silence. He stands there at the edge of the patio; you sit at the table. You sip the dregs of your coffee. A delinquent coffee ground gets caught in your teeth. You dislodge it with your tongue.

"Jesus, Nickie," he says at last. "We talked about getting married. We moved in together once." As his voice adopts a pleading tone, it sounds like a droning bee.

"Yes," you reply with rising anger. "You and me and Angie."

He sighs deeply, considers this a moment.

"Did you talk this over with her?"

"Yes."

"Oh good," you murmur drily. "And what did you say?"

"I told her I love you."

"I'll bet *that* made her day."

"She told me she knows I do."

You snort. It just comes out—dry, thank goodness—but a snort just the same.

"I understand about the Angie thing," Alan says then. "It's one of the issues I have to deal with once and for all. But that isn't the point right now. The point right now is do you think we can get back what we once had? Don't answer me now. What I mean is I want you to consider it, think it over while you're here. That's all. And I want you to know I think you and I have a future. I want us to have a life together. Okay?"

"Okay, Alan," you say. "That's fair enough."

And you suppose it actually is, for the time being at least. Time is what you need. If he's willing to give you time, well you'll accept it gratefully.

He comes over to you, leans down, kisses you on the lips. As he pulls away, you smile and ruffle his hair.

"More coffee?" he asks.

"If you don't mind," you reply, handing him your mug.

## THE MAN AND THE WOMAN

ONE WATCHES AS THE INITIAL WHOOSH of the large bonfire tears into the black fabric of night, then drips gold as it scalds the darkness around the edge of the lake and nearby length of beach. What results is the kind of pyrotechnical display which, as a special effect, inspires an audience to forget its innate reserve long enough to gasp briefly in appreciation.

Even the man who has constructed the large pile of driftwood, doused it with starter fluid, then tossed in a match, is startled for a moment by the ferocity in the fire's early enthusiasm. He steps back a couple of yards, soundless in the sand. But his caution doesn't last; it's quickly replaced by the admiration he feels for his handiwork. His mood is celebratory anyway. He's gratified with himself for going ahead with this ceremonial tribute acknowledging important events he cherishes about his past.

After a moment he moves a rickety chaise lounge a few feet further back from the fire, then reaches down for a beer he has already opened, then tucked into a drift in the sand. "Here's to you, Uncle Bart," one hears him say aloud before lifting the bottle to take a deep swallow.

For a few minutes he watches the fire settle into a steady burn. Then he turns and gazes over the rocks to the crest of the hill where his cottage perches in the distance, lights twinkling in its windows. To his surprise, unexpectedly, his eyes mist up as he considers the relentless approach of the end of summer and his stay here on the island, this period destined to be his last. Finally he turns back to the large bonfire again, drawn by its urgent life, mesmerized by the jitterbugging flames, the crackling spit of the burning wood.

The fire reaches out to illuminate a confined perimeter in the darkness. But the darkness grows denser beyond the edge of the light. In this way, the light delicately hints at the simple props in the set of his ceremony. It hints of the black lake beyond the fire, the black sand at the edge of the stage and the lounge near which the man's dog lies down to watch what happens next. The dancing light partially outlines a cluster of capped beer bottles at the foot of the lounge and, not far away, a hibachi still warm with dying coals where, a couple of hours ago, one watched the man cooking his evening meal.

He is dressed in denim from head to foot and wearing scuffed white sneakers. To ward off the night's chill, he's wrapped in a Hudson's Bay blanket and, pulling out the tails of a long bandanna at the back of his neck, he snuggles into the blanket. While he stands before the fire, one fist holds the blanket closed at his throat, the other holds his beer. He stares into the blistering flames, recalling bonfires in his youth, the traditions of his past.

Bart Maddox, his favorite uncle, was a storyteller, a shaman of the tale. A bonfire in the darkness was his storytelling loom. One remembers when the man was only a child, his uncle would sit at the edge of the flames and spin clearly fictional yarns that widened his nephew's eyes. Neither of them expected the stories to be believed. Instead the tales were designed to encourage the universe of their rich imaginations. Bart Maddox, the World War One pilot who narrowly escaped after a dogfight with the Red Baron. Bart Maddox, frontiersman and scout, mountain man and trapper. Bart Maddox, private detective, who caught a ring of truck hijackers, single-handedly bringing them to justice.

Remembering the stories and the bonfires around which they were told, the man smiles warmly into the tunnel of his recollection. But it's a sad smile too, one notices. Matt muses that Bart's Victoria Day bonfires must have been strangely melancholic affairs like this one now after Matt grew up and away. No audience to hear the telling and escape the real, less romantic world for a while.

And so it goes for several minutes. The man sips his beer, remembering his uncle and addressing the melancholy occasioned by what the simple passing of time has taken from him. His reverie is so deep he is startled when the woman's voice bursts out of the darkness some distance from the fire.

"Hello," she calls from the blackness.

"Hello," he replies at last, realizing who it is.

In a moment, one sees her step out of the darkness, as through a curtain, Alan Birken at her side. They move closer to the fire.

When she sees the man at that moment, she realizes how much like the real Crazy Horse he actually is, much more so tonight than he has been previously.

"Wow," she is saying at the edge of the flames. "I saw your pile of wood this morning. I wondered what it was for."

"A family tradition," he explains. "Victoria Day bonfire."

"I wondered if we might have to call the fire department," Alan Birken says.

"The fire department?" The other man turns to him, briefly bemused. "There is no fire department."

Oh, Alan, thinks the woman, clearly embarrassed for him then.

But Matt Bowman comes to his rescue. "I'm sorry if I startled you," he says. "I never thought. I should have warned you in advance what I'd be doing."

"Oh that's okay," the woman says. "Alan's only kidding."

They stand in silence in the glow of the fire. One notices they are briefly awkward at what she has said. All three of them are keenly aware that Alan never kids.

The man wrapped in the blanket sips from his bottle, then remembers his manners. "Can I offer you guys a beer? In honor of Bart Maddox's traditional Victoria Day bonfire?"

"Oh, that's okay," the woman says. "Thanks anyway."

"Yes," adds her companion. "We should be getting back."

"I've got lots," Matt says. "You'll ensure that I don't get drunk."

The woman laughs. "Okay," she says. "Thanks."

"Alan?"

"Sure, okay, if you two are having one."

"No glasses, I'm afraid. But glasses would violate the Victoria Day bonfire tradition anyway."

"No problem," the woman says.

Crazy Horse takes off his blanket to twist the caps off two bottles of beer before handing them out.

"To Uncle Bart," he says, tilting the neck of his bottle at his guests. "And old Queen Vic. Long may she reign."

All three of them drink.

"Where's Carmen?" the man asks. He glances at Canine Ben, as if Canine Ben might want to know, but Ben just lies by the lounge entirely unconcerned.

"Up at the cottage," the woman replies. "We only came out for a few minutes. . ."

". . . to see about the fire," Alan Birken finishes.

"I see," says Crazy Horse. He reaches down to the lounge, retrieves his blanket, wraps himself in it, resumes holding it together at his throat. "Chilly night," he says.

Alan and Nicole agree. Both of them wear nylon parkas and turtleneck sweaters.

"Still," Crazy Horse is saying, "it was so fine out today. That's why I lit the fire tonight. I thought it might not be so pleasant tomorrow and I'd miss my opportunity. Can't count on the weather this year."

The woman smiles at him, apparently grateful again that he seems to be so nice, that in some vague way she hasn't previously misjudged him.

He smiles back at her, then remembers to include her companion. He also begins to remember his deja vu experience yesterday morning, what he wrote in his journal last night. Feeling renewed embarrassment, he resolves, no matter what, to avoid thinking of the incident again.

"So," the woman wants to know then. "What tradition are we helping you celebrate? More than Queen Victoria I'd expect."

"Oh yes," says Matt Bowman. "Queen Vic is just an excuse. My late Uncle Bart, when I was a kid, used to build a bonfire here every Victoria Day weekend. We'd come down, my aunt and me, and he'd regale us with tall tales. Then, when my own sons were growing up, he'd bring *them* here too. So the fire tonight is more a tribute to him than anything else." His voice grows reflective and sombre. "My aunt intends to sell the cottage at the end of the year. This fire is the last Victoria Day bonfire, at least in *my* family. So you'll have a new neighbor next year, I guess."

"That's sad," Nicole says.

One can tell the poignancy of the situation touches her deeply, much more than mere empathy would. She wonders about this and how, just then, the man who has built this fire seems so much a part of this particular place.

"In a way," adds Crazy Horse, "I'm here this summer to say goodbye to everything."

Nicole swallows.

"Why don't you buy the cottage yourself?" asks Alan.

"I'm afraid not," the other man replies. "I just don't have the money."

"Not even with a mortgage?"

"Nope." He isn't tempted to elaborate.

The woman notices that his one-word answer dangles between them, mysterious, immutable, even tragic. One catches her wondering what it means, what secret it reflects.

And Matt is faintly embarrassed. "To tell you the truth," he confesses then, "I intend to move out west next year."

"Oh," says Nicole. "Of course, if you bought the cottage, you wouldn't be able to go."

"No."

"The trouble with an island," adds Alan then, "is that it's not practical in the winter."

"No."

But it could be done, thinks Nicole. If you really wanted to do it, it could be done. Frustrated with Matt's view, she somehow wants to argue with Alan, so that the man in the blanket can hear the alternative at the edges of the debate. In the end she keeps silent. Some other time, perhaps.

"Anyway," says Matt, embarrassed by the serious turn the conversation has taken, "this is supposed to be an upbeat occasion. *Wakan Tanka* moves in mysterious ways. I guess I'm supposed to go west."

"*Wakan Tanka?*" echoes Nicole.

"The Great Spirit."

Crazy Horse is smiling, as if at their private joke. When she glances at him, Nicole wonders if he has read her mind at some point, that he is now aware she calls him Crazy Horse when he invades her private thoughts. Rather foolishly she wants to blush, even knowing it isn't really justified. One shares her relief that a blush would disappear inside the reflection of the flickering flames on her face.

"Are you native?" Alan asks the other man.

"No," replies Crazy Horse. "Only in my heart."

"It's trendy," observes Alan.

"Yes, that's true," agrees Matt. "But most of my life I've never felt very white. Not greedy enough, I guess. Next we'll be talking about cultural appropriation." He grins, one notices, mostly at the woman. "Only my ancestors know for sure.

In the ensuing silence, they stand transfixed in front of the flames. The fire has burned down somewhat already, as if it too is party to the vague melancholy the occasion has inspired.

"So will your sons be visiting this summer?" the woman asks.

"I've invited them. I hope they want to come to say goodbye too."

"How old are they?"

"All grown up," says Crazy Horse with a sigh of resignation. "Twenty-two and twenty."

"Busy with their own lives," says Alan.

"I'll say," admits Matt. "What about you guys? Are children part of your plans?"

"It's been talked about," replies Alan.

One catches Nicole glancing at him in dismay, grateful when her astonishment doesn't show. Alan has *never* discussed children with her, not even once. One can see she feels pierced by the sharpness of his lie and the presumption existing inside it.

No one says anything else for a time.

Until Crazy Horse offers them another beer.

Alan declines for the two of them because "we really must be going."

"Thanks for the beer, Matt," says Nicole.

"My pleasure."

"Maybe you can join us for a drink soon."

"Thanks. I'll look forward to it." He does not believe it will happen; she is only being polite.

He watches the younger couple depart. The woman turns once and smiles. He waves with the dregs of his bottle of beer. Then he gazes into the steadily dying fire, feeling strangely morose, more personally a victim of his casual victim*hood.*

One notices Nicole turn again to see him standing at the edge of the light, growing faint as they walk away, turning into the apparition he sometimes seems to be.

"He's a nice man," she mentions to Alan to make the apparition real.

"Yeah, he's okay," offers Alan grudgingly.

But then Alan has already lied about wanting to have children. And the trouble with Alan, she remembers, is that he believes his lies himself.

Barry Grills

## PART TWO: JUNE 1996

### NICOLE

AS SOON AS YOUR FATHER COMES INTO VIEW, walking casually up the beach, your mother gets up from where she has been sitting with you at the patio table and departs for the kitchen to put some waiting croissants into the oven.

"There's your father, Dear," she says in routine exasperation.

"I see him," you reply, unwittingly caught up in your mother's impatience.

This too is routine, her assumption that you have been as impatient as she was.

"Do you need any help?" you ask before she leaves the terrace.

"No, that's all right, Dear," she replies over her shoulder as she hurries away.

In truth, everything but the croissants is ready. The patio table has been set and the umbrella raised to shield the family from the first hot sun of the year. The orange juice has been poured and the jams, marmalades and spreads have been placed in serving dishes here on the table. Even a fresh pot of coffee waits in the carafe in the kitchen.

Your mother craves normalcy. Normalcy is derived from a variety of scheduled ceremonies including breakfast, lunch and dinner. When the first ceremony of the day, breakfast, is at last underway, she can stop fretting for the time being about having so much time to spend without any apparent function. For as long as you can remember, your mother has measured out her days with required errands and obligations. Any gaps in between have been a source of quiet concern. In this way you are different from one another. Even when you lived with Alan, you resisted the call of similar domestic ritual whenever either one of you was tempted by its pattern.

Yet ritual is somehow part of the affection between your parents. It's a kind of dispassionate lovemaking they have shared for years. Both pretend not to enjoy it; both would be lost without it. Your father claims not to enjoy the fussing but actually he does. Your mother claims he needs her many reminders though, in fact, he doesn't.

"Don't be long, Sid," she cautioned him this morning when he announced he was taking Carmen for her walk along the beach.

"I won't be," he replied. "Just need a bit of a constitutional."

But "Oh, that man," she said to the world at large before he was even out of sight.

No reason to be concerned about him really; he's healthy, vital and independent. It's just forty years of amiable habit. Although you sometimes find this way of caring vaguely tiresome to watch, you tend to envy its longevity, its solidity. It contrasts wearily with the incessant disappointment love has represented in *your* life so far.

It's Saturday morning now; your parents arrived last night. They will stay over until early Monday morning before heading back to Toronto, remaining the extra night to avoid the Sunday evening traffic. A function of their ages, perhaps. Alan, on the other hand, leaves on Sunday nights, enjoying the war that the weekend traffic represents. The prolonged skirmish behind the wheel of his car seems to get something out of his system. Or fills him up somehow.

At any rate, for this weekend at least, the cottage is no longer yours. It belongs to your parents again. In a disconcerting fashion some of your odds and ends—books, notes to yourself, colored stones you've been gathering on the beach, a sweater tossed on the arm of a chair—have been disappearing from where you left them to reappear in the large guest room where you've been sleeping the past couple of weeks. You feel like a visitor again, time-warped back to childhood, tidied after to the point where you've lost any possession of the place you established shortly after your arrival. It doesn't really bother you—there's no malice in your mother's fidgeting. You've just noticed its pervasiveness and you are wryly amused by it.

As they draw nearer the cottage, your father waves while Carmen races up the rocky pathway and greets you, then lies down under your chair where you gently scratch behind her ears.

When he reaches the terrace, puffing a little from the climb, your father lifts his cap and runs a hand through his thinning, silver hair. "Going to be a hot one," he says.

"About time," you reply. "The weather's been rotten so far."

"Where's your mum?" your father asks as he approaches the table.

"Getting breakfast into the oven. Your tardiness has been noted."

He grins at you and winks, and you smile back conspiratorially. Your father knows you share the knowledge that your mother is his best friend.

Betty Graham comes out of the cottage at that moment to underline the truth in your conclusion. "And where have *you* been? Did you walk around the entire island?"

"Good heavens, woman," he replies with a snort. "Actually I ran into the fellow from the other cottage, down on the beach."

"Matt Bowman," you tell him knowingly.

"Yes. He has a dog too, a friend of Carmen's, I gather. Calls him . . .

" . . . Canine Ben."

"Yes, Canine Ben. Unusual name. Unusual man, actually."

Thoughtfully, you nod.

"Well, we got to talking."

"Breakfast is late."

"Oh hell," he says pleasantly enough. "It's the weekend."

"I'm burning the croissants," his wife cries, turning to go again.

"Hell," he mutters when his wife is out of earshot. "She never burned a croissant in her life."

And you have to laugh.

"Kind of a shame," your father adds later as the three of you sit at the table, enjoying the perfect croissants. "The fellow down the beach . . ."

". . . Matt Bowman . . ."

". . . Matt Bowman, tells me his aunt is selling their property at the end of the summer. Sounds like a lot of happy memories are going to go with it."

You nod. "I think, secretly, he's pretty upset about it."

"I told him he should buy it, you know, to keep it in the family. He just said he wished he could."

"Matt doesn't have any money, I'm afraid," you explain. "And he wants to go out west next year."

"Ah," your father says.

"Sounds like you two know each other fairly well," your mother remarks with some surprise.

"A little bit," you reply. "Carmen and Ben are close. So we often meet on the beach to let them play together. We've had coffee a couple of times and talked."

"Oh," your mother says, digesting this bit of news.

You say nothing more about it. The coffees, which began after the Victoria Day weekend, have become long and interesting affairs. You talk easily with one another. Matt has become a friend. Although sometimes you tend to regret afterwards the ease with which you relate to him—you fret you've said too much to him, about Alan, about yourself, about life, about love—there's no denying Matt Bowman is comfortable to be with, a little like the island itself. Sometimes you wonder how he does it, how he carries so much of this place inside him, a sense of familiarity so powerful you frequently forget you haven't known him long.

"Has Alan met him, Dear?" your mother wants to know.

"Of course. But Alan doesn't approve of him. Alan thinks he's weird."

"Weird?"

"He needs a haircut," your father explains.

The way he says it makes you smile.

"Well, how old is he?"

"Forty-seven," you reply.

"Oh, I hate long hair on men old enough to know better."

"Maybe I should buy the place," your father muses at that point, mostly to annoy his wife.

"Oh, Sid. Whatever for?"

"Well, we'd own both places on the island. We could use it as a guest house or something."

"We don't need it, Sid."

But your father just grins at you and winks again.

"Oh, Sid," your mother says, in deference to the wink.

"Well, I liked him," your father says. "He was very pleasant to talk to. Actually, Nick, he said you were a nice young woman."

You're tempted to blush at this revelation but manage to avoid it. The recognizable paternalism in Matt's remark is what saves you from embarrassment. You can almost hear him saying it. Oh yeah, you would say in reply, and you're so *old*. He talks about growing old often, not complaining exactly, but as if he's bemused by the fact, only just having considered it. Don't you believe it, you've said once or twice. Age is just a state of mind.

"Maybe we should have him over for dinner tonight," your father is suggesting. "It can't be much fun staying alone down there all summer long. I thought I'd barbecue a few steaks tonight. He might enjoy the company."

"Really, Sid, are you serious?"

But your father turns to you. "Whaddyuh think, Nick? Would that be okay with you?"

"Sure. Matt's very sociable. I can invite him and see what he says."

"He's an interesting man. Betty, you love to entertain."

"I suppose," admits his wife. "I'm just a little surprised, that's all. You only just met him."

"When we're done breakfast, I'll walk down and ask him," you say. "*I* haven't only just met him."

"We can talk politics," your father says, a twinkle in his eye.

Which elicits another spousal warning. "No arguments, Sid."

"Aah," replies your father. "Who argues about politics?"

"You do!" both you and your mother cry in unison.

MATT AGREES TO COME TO DINNER although he's shy about accepting. Your mother goes along with the plan but lets you know she's not too pleased about entertaining a strange man whose relationship to you is ill-defined.

"Ill-defined?" you say. "He's just a man I know."

But that afternoon she asks you about Alan, while the two of you are alone—your father puttering around somewhere out of sight—as if understanding how things are going with Alan will somehow clear both matters up.

"Has Alan visited you much?" she asks while the two of you sit on lounges on the terrace, enjoying this luxury of warm sun.

"Every weekend but this one," you reply. "Frankly I'm glad for the break."

"I see."

"I feel like he's in my face too much."

"He probably misses you, Dear."

"More likely he's afraid I'll decide to live my own life. Despite what he says to the contrary."

Your mother considers this, falls back on platitude. "Well, I suppose it's a little threatening to have you move so far from Toronto."

"Hmm," is all you say.

You've never talked about Alan much even though he's been in your life for a couple of years. His fault perhaps; yours too, you guess. Your parents know him, of course; there've been a couple of social engagements. No doubt assumptions have been made about the permanence of the relationship, but the assumptions are never discussed. To try to explain how manipulative he can be, the ambivalence you've felt about him in recent months, and the need you feel to get on with your own life seems like too much to embark upon now, especially since, traditionally, you keep your personal life to yourself and your parents rarely offer unsolicited opinions. They want you to be happy—you know this fact to be true. Beyond this, they tend to leave you to flounder in your own romantic whirlpool.

"You've always been independent," your mother is saying now.

"Not as independent as I intend to be."

"Your father and I want things to work out for you."

"I know you do."

"I think about you here all by yourself. Don't you get lonely? Don't you miss Toronto?"

"No. I love it here. I've been playing a lot of piano. I've written some music. I've been doing a lot of thinking. I think, by the end of the summer, I'll know exactly where I'm going with myself."

"You mean this music school business?"

"Yes. Besides, there are things to look forward to. Karen and Liam are coming for a visit in a couple of weeks. And Alan wants to have a party, closer to the end of June. It's not like I'm stuck here all by myself."

"That's good."

"I'm glad I have some choices, Mum. It feels good to have a choice."

"Well," says your mother then. "Things are different now, compared to when I was young. It's a good time to be independent, to have choices you can make. Women didn't feel we had so many options when I was your age."

You reach out and squeeze her hand. Your mother squeezes yours in return.

"Everything's going to be fine," you say, "regardless of what I decide."

LATER THAT SAME AFTERNOON, you meander down to the beach where your father is tinkering with the motor on the boat. The day remains warm and nearly windless, so much so the lake hardly expresses a ripple as it inches forward to meet the beach. The cowling is up on the motor but your father isn't doing anything with the innards. Instead he sits not far away in one of the boat's seats, gazing distractedly at and beyond the array of metal bits and pieces that make the motor work. As you approach, you recognize his reflective pose and consider how long it's been since you've seen it—at least a couple of years, you think.

You feel a brief yearning for your childhood, then let it go again. Time is only mysterious when you look backwards into the past. Back then your father smoked a pipe and your senses associate the habit with his periods of reflection. Even now you recall the aroma of drifting *Blue Amphora*, hear again the hiss of air and spit along the pipe's worn stem. He's been a nonsmoker for a few years now but at this moment the pipe is noticeably missing, as if he lost it somewhere rather than gave it up.

He hears you approach the boat, even though you're barefoot, your toes gliding in the sand. So he calmly turns and smiles. "Hello, Sunshine," he says. "Isn't it a day?"

"Yes," you have to agree. You lean against the side of the boat, not far from the water's edge. The sand here is wet and cold, reminding you it's only the beginning of June. "Everything all right?" you ask.

"The motor? It's fine. I'm not sure I could fix it if it wasn't. To tell you the truth, I just like to lift the cover and take a look inside, so the world thinks I know what I'm doing."

"This is the first time you've ever admitted it," you tell him with a smile.

He nods. "I'm getting too old to be sowing illusions. You reach a point in life where you stop faking even the little things."

"How's the construction business this summer, Dad?"

"Slow," he replied. "I should sell out. Can't, though, wouldn't get anything for it. The only people with any money are the banks. Government's gone too far with this cutback business. Too many people cut off at the knees. They can't afford to spend any money, especially on a house they'll get less for in five years. I didn't think things would go this far."

You don't comment. Your father's view resembles Matt's, on the surface at least, although it's more terse and simplified. Matt thinks the entire money system has "gone for a shit" and his reasoning is complicated. He thinks the poor should storm the Bastille once and for all, that all the rules should be changed. If they get to talking politics, your father will dismiss him as a radical.

"What's your mum up to?"

"Making that German potato salad she promised us last night."

Your father nods his approval. It's a favorite summer dish, bad for the cholesterol but, in his mind, definitely worth the risk.

"I'm supposed to tell you, though, that you should come up soon and get ready for dinner. She's worried that Matt'll show up and you'll still be down here puttering around."

"She still upset we're having company?"

You nod. "She thinks you've adopted another orphan. There's a lot of sighing and tsking going on."

A gull breaks into a loud squawk overhead, then dives towards the lake several yards away. Both of you watch the bird a moment, though with an interest that quickly wanes. It's been like this for hours; the day is too perfect somehow for any kind of focus on the details. Even Carmen, who's followed you down to the beach, cares less about the gull than she normally would.

"What about you?" your father asks. "How are things with you?"

"Pretty good."

"Your mum says you and Alan are . . . ." and he waggles his hand in a sympathetic tribute to your ambivalence.

"Yeah," you murmur truthfully. "I'm not sure it's going to work out."

"Better you sort out your answers now, Nick, before you take a serious step."

"That's what I'm doing," you say.

"You know," your father adds thoughtfully, "I've always thought of you as someone who's her own person. Sometimes I think I remember it better than you do."

"I forget myself sometimes," you admit with a gentle shrug. "Forget where I thought I was going."

"Sure. There are a lot of people to try to please. I used to say to your mum, 'our Nick is going to be different, she's going to go in her own direction.' I think that's what you're doing now. Trouble is, people sometimes want you to do something else. The trick is to know your own mind and stick to it."

"That makes sense."

"And if people aren't happy with who we are or what we need to do, sometimes we're better off without them."

"That ever happen to you, Dad?"

"Yup. A long time ago. I'll tell you about it some time, when we don't have company coming for dinner."

"Okay."

"Stick to who you are, Nick," he says. "That's the person you have to live with the rest of your life."

You nod and smile. "I miss your pipe, Dad, at these philosophical moments."

"That makes two of us."

"Maybe I should take a long trip around the world," you tell him with a grin, the idea a new one, a distraction, a fancy.

"I always thought you would. It's not too late, you know."

"Maybe you're right. Get ready for dinner, okay?"

"Tell her I'm on my way," he says.

You turn away believing the day remains too lazy for anything but serious conversation. The spectacular weather assumes a tranquil command, insisting on shared wisdom. The lake pretends to go on forever. The sky has no limit to its cloudlessness. The water whispers against the sand. The gulls squawk from their ritual parliament just down the beach. The sand smells mossy and sweet. You sigh in pleasure, serenely loving this place at this moment, feeling a now rare comfort inside yourself inside this island setting. Carmen leads you happily back up to the cottage, her ears dangling in the sand.

## MATT
**Saturday, June 1**
IT'S LATE, MUCH LATER THAN I THOUGHT IT WAS. Once again
the inner clock I count on to tell me the time misplaced an hour
or so while I wasn't paying attention. As I walked down the
beach from the Graham cottage, feeling a little fidgety and high, I
decided to brew myself a last mug or two of coffee and sit down
at this journal to record what feels like, in retrospect, an
unusual day. It wasn't until after I prepared the coffee and
opened this scribbler at the dining room table that I conceived
of checking the time. To my chagrin, it was eleven-thirty and,
accordingly, I should have considered going to bed. I had
previously assumed it was closer to ten o'clock.

My restless spirits, I suppose. It appears my dinner with
Nicole and her parents over-stimulated me, all that
conversation, the social waltzing to which I'm no longer
accustomed. So, at this moment, quite literally having lost track
of time, I am faced with the prospect of writing into the wee
hours. And I wouldn't want to waste all that coffee.

One of these days I'll probably succumb to the temptation
of wearing a wristwatch again. It's been three years. In the
intervening time I've transformed not wearing a watch into an
epiphany, as if releasing my wrist from the bondage of
measured time represents a spiritual awakening. But to truly
believe this is to shower myself in an accolade I don't actually

deserve.

I believe most epiphanies enter our house through the back door anyway. They arrive, for example, as a rundown wristwatch battery one doesn't get around to replacing. Then, as time passes, these oversights insinuate themselves inside our perceptions in the guise of spiritual calling. The wristwatch I no longer wear resembles the life I no longer lead; a battery ran down and, after I didn't immediately replace it, I learned to go on without it. Eventually I convinced myself this state of doing without represented spiritual choice.

But in the end, all of it—or at least most of it—boils down to attrition. Epiphanous attrition, let's call it. I know what I'm talking about. I've got an assortment of batteryless wristwatches locked away in a drawer somewhere to prove it. And as long as they're there I cannot be truly certain that I'll always walk by the battery display in a local store without purchasing one in a moment of weakness. What then will I call an epiphany that has reversed itself? *Anti-epiphany?*

I know what makes me think these things these days. It's the harmless little crush I have on Nicole Graham. To push the wristwatch metaphor to the limit, she is my favorite battery rack. Sometimes, when I stand before her enticing display, I feel a powerful compulsion to purchase something. Perturbed by this, I eventually jam my hands into my pockets and resolve instead to go home and throw out my wristwatches, just to be sure I don't betray my personal commitment to leave wristwatches, time, and love alone.

None of this private inner debate worries me. There's something rather human about the foolishness of a crush. I am a sensible man, but being still capable of romantic feelings makes me see myself as a little more endearing. It's an innocent enough distraction. I'm in no danger of behaving stupidly and I'm too old and experienced to be found out. So what can be the harm?

Still, I squirmed like an astonished schoolboy when Nicole showed up at my doorstep today, bearing an invitation to dinner. I told her I wouldn't dream of intruding on a family weekend.

"It's not an intrusion," she countered, stressing the point in no uncertain terms. "It was my father's idea. He enjoyed meeting you on the beach this morning."

"Well I enjoyed meeting *him*," I replied.

"So come to dinner. You like to socialize."

Briefly I wondered if her observation was true but, nonetheless, I told her I'd be delighted.

She smiled and squeezed my arm with her fingers.

I kept my hands jammed into my pockets, making sure I didn't reveal how much her touch meant to me.

Actually her father and I had quite a pleasant time down on the beach this morning. After Canine Ben and Carmen got up to their usual lake shore shenanigans and I explained how well the two animals know one another, we introduced ourselves and began to talk about our respective island histories.

Sid Graham is a gregarious but reflective man. I liked him, so much so that I forgave him those wretched Bermuda shorts he was wearing. I'm sure he forgave me my ponytail and the way my beard needed a trim—the trim I gave it in fact before I sauntered down the beach for dinner this evening, out of deference to Nicole's mother who is reputed to be sternly old-fashioned.

Sid seemed impressed that my family has been in possession of our cottage for so many years, going back to before I entered school. I asked him how long he's owned *his* place. To his surprise, he had to think about it for a moment or two before he could answer me.

"Twelve years," he replied at last. "Doesn't seem like that long at all."

I told him this cottage is to be sold. He suggested right away that I buy it from my aunt. I told him I couldn't, although I didn't elaborate about the economics.

I imagined at that moment, as we stood chatting on the beach, that he makes in one year what I struggle to survive on in ten. I've encountered this disparity numerous times in recent years. It isn't the number of dollars exactly that creates the current gap between those with nothing and those with a great deal. No, it's what the dollars—their plenitude on the one hand and scarcity on the other—permit or prevent.

For example, when he drives downtown in his Lincoln or Cadillac and parks at a meter, he dashes to his destination without putting in a quarter. If he gets a ticket, he mutters an invective under this breath and decides, this time, he didn't beat the odds. On the other hand, before I take my Escort downtown to park at a meter, I figure out if my last few quarters are enough to give me the time required to do my errand. I have to be this cautious because the parking ticket I might receive would reflect a serious financial loss. I'm sure I take more economic precautions on any given day than Nicole's father would in two or three months.

But I enjoyed talking to him just the same, not only this morning on the beach but also earlier tonight while I was their guest at dinner. This evening we shared a beer while I watched him fire up the barbecue on the terrace. Elsewhere Nicole helped her mother set the patio table where her mother announced we were going to eat.

I felt less comfortable with Betty than I do with Sid. She was politely hospitable but I sensed my presence was an imposition and she resented that the dinner invitation had been sprung on her without warning. I thanked her for the invitation but felt my gratitude only acknowledged in her mind that we both knew I was putting her out. And I suppose it's true—when you're imposing on someone you're imposing; there's nothing (or everything) moot about it.

Sid's quite the barbecue chef. Betty brought down a large aluminum pan with an assortment of vegetables in it—carrots, green beans, cauliflower—and he shook up a jar of broth which he poured over them. Then he covered the mixture with aluminum foil and put the whole works on the grill, carefully adjusting the propane so that it could simmer. I could see they entertain often this way. There's a visible fluidity in the partnership around a dinner's preparation. It must take years of practice, years of happily sharing the same goals.

It was too early for the steaks. Sid had seasoned them and they waited on a large table with wheels not far from the barbecue. Carmen had no interest in them. I told Sid, had Canine Ben been present we'd have to beat him off with a stick. He just grinned. "I'm with Canine Ben," he said. But while we waited for the vegetables to cook—periodically he used the handle of the pan to jostle them under the aluminum foil—we began to talk again. We covered most of the man-to-man stuff, our respective work, politics, what the world is coming to. The Jays.

He was mystified to learn that writing is such a low paid profession, at least for most of us. I explained how I'd come to full-time writing by circumstance, how I was no longer married, how my sons were grown, how I was trying to make the most of a particularly malicious economic political environment in which to pursue writing—at my age the only viable employment available to me.

"Making the most of the freedom in adversity," he said.

"That's about the size of it," I admitted. "If the government wants me to be poor, then I might just as well be poor doing something I've always wanted to do."

"You don't really think the government wants you to be poor, do you?"

"Yes, I do," I replied. "Not directly, mind you. Not personally. But if my poverty is the price to be paid to prop up the rich—we're governed by business lobby, not by the wishes of the people—then that's the price they'll exact."

He just looked at me. Perhaps he thought I was nuts. But Nicole came along to see how we were getting on, and when she caught wind of the political tenor of the conversation, she soon put a stop to it.

"Dad, you promised no politics."

"I promised no such thing," he retorted with a grin.

"My fault, Nicole," I confessed. "You're dad's getting a bum wrap."

"Well, you too, Matt," she said. "No politics."

"Okay."

She grinned and squeezed my arm again.

In a dazed fashion I wished she wouldn't touch me that way. While it implies that I am safe and trustworthy, it makes me feel treacherous because this is only partly true. And although I like the notion I'm safe, there's a component to my character that finds it rather dismissive.

Still, Sid and I managed to stay away from the subject of politics and I suppose it provided for a more pleasant evening. Instead we talked about times on the island, our appreciation for the sense of peace this place conveys. I regaled them as well with anecdotes about storms here, about adventures and mysteries the island has always inspired. In turn, they responded with tales about Nicole's high speed hijinks in their boat, some water skiing parties that nearly got out of hand. Nicole, of course, blushed and pleaded exaggeration.

It turns out that both Sid and Betty like to fish on occasion and they take to the usually calm waters of the channel around dusk. "It's the peace and tranquility we're after," Sid said. He reported, though, there are bass to be had not far from the eastern point of the island. I admitted I haven't fished in years but the tranquility sounded appealing.

It struck me tonight, while all of this was being discussed, that Alan Birken was noticeably absent. I paused at one point to wonder why. I didn't miss him, of course; he seems like such a prat. But I wondered, in view of Nicole's admitted ambivalence about him, what he would have thought of my presence there with the Grahams for dinner. And I wondered, if he'd been there, whether I still would have been invited. Probably not.

Nicole looked beautiful. I was aware of that fact all evening long in a way in which only a  man with a crush can be. But I know it didn't show.

I'm glad I'm not a younger man where my attraction to Nicole is concerned. I'd probably fall in love with her, then, step by step, make most of my habitual mistakes all over again. For me, at least, love and compromise tend to blend so completely together one becomes the other. I must always remember, from a precautionary point of view, that I've embarked on three potentially permanent relationships—on three separate occasions I've carelessly approached the brink of disaster while pursuing some hapless notion of permanent romantic love.

It's not the concept of permanent romantic partnership which is at fault of course. Nicole's parents are evidence of that. No, the fault lies in me specifically and in other people much like me. A relationship with romantic permanence requires a relatively willing acceptance of convention, I believe. I've come to know I'm not that kind of person. I don't see myself making a priority of cutting the lawn or repairing the vacuum cleaner anymore, of transporting children here and there most nights of the week, to ballet class or a Cub-Scout meeting.

Years ago I honored these kinds of obligations but it was a lifestyle which eventually made me feel trapped and injured. I felt caught, a frog in a jar. Aggravating this loss of personal freedom was a powerful sense of self-disgust. While I enjoyed

# THE LAST LIGHT SPOKEN

everyone's approval for what I was doing, I failed to approve of myself. I blamed myself for failing to live a more rewarding creative life. And for failing to sustain my interest in this conventional alternative. It's an existential purgatory not everyone faces. For a man like me there are only two choices. He must have the good fortune to encounter and love a woman as committed to an authentic life as he is or, failing that, he must accept and learn to enjoy the fruits of his solitude. These days it seems clear solitude is my best self-preserving option.

As Nicole and I have become friendly, spending more time together, I have alluded to the unfortunate errors in my past, but I have not been very specific. I don't want to look like a fool, especially now that I've learned my lesson. I don't want to have to justify being reformed while explaining why I've fallen off the wagon of romantic coupledom so many times. Better to just know what I know on my own. So I don't bother saying very much. I am what I am today because I was what I was back then.

Nicole knows little about Gwen, the first woman I married and the mother of my children. I haven't explained that I was only twenty-two years old when we married, or how (although I was quite candid before the wedding about ambitions to travel and write), Gwen guided us (in a domineering fashion) into home ownership, parenthood and a powerful burden of conventional obligation soon after marriage. Gwen simply changed her mind about the acceptability of my creative ambitions and dug in, applying a stubborn inertia to my pleas that we escape. She thought my view was childish whimsy. Childish was *her* word but I soon took it for my own. I told myself to grow up, to accept more responsibility, conventional or not.

But good intentions don't always ease the resentment that occurs. I felt trapped and betrayed by Gwen's change of heart, condemned to a life of conventional domestic frustration and boredom. It's hard to explain to people who haven't felt it quite this way. I can say, though, that my heart was broken three times—at the loss of myself, of my hopes for my marriage, and of daily life with my two young sons.

Nor have I detailed to Nicole much about Esther and my second marriage. I haven't told her about how, out of a fear of solitude, I embarked again on a conventional marriage which

115

concluded in a similar way as the first. This time there was even more for me to rationalize—Easther's violent temper and paranoia, the scratches, bruises and injured dignity I tried to endure. Her middle class ambition too, her need to be upwardly mobile. There's no place in a relationship like this for a man with my sensibilities, although I didn't know this then. When I remember that period now I recall only a state of perpetual inner conflict. I see myself standing by our swimming pool (or one of the pools owned by others in our social circle), discussing with ridiculous gravity the ph levels of the treated water. It took me a number of years to admit these people and that ultra-conventional me bored me to tears.

After that, of course, there was Carolyn. Although we didn't marry, I accepted manipulative stepchildren and the nagging intuition that once again I was shelving my personal goals. I martyred myself on the altar of responsibility. With a sad nobility, I stumbled on, trying to be acceptable to a world that didn't care. This time I collapsed. I repeatedly developed blood clots in my lungs and spent several months in hospital over the space of two long years. I was subjected to numerous tests but in the end all I learned was that I was exhausted and psychologically spent.

During my period of recovery, it became apparent to me that my physical health depended on at last coming to grips with my stubborn pattern of compromise. Perhaps Carolyn saw the writing on the wall. Certainly my ill health provided her with the means of *her* escape. When it became clear my usefulness was at an end, she and her children moved on.

That was more than three years ago. Now I'm a different man, grateful for my independence and my friendship with my sons. If I feel any regret, it's based only on my failure to pursue much earlier than I did an authentic life that supported who I am and was. Now my health has returned to normal. I've learned to live in a state of redeeming acceptance of myself. Poverty is the fee that I have paid for my personal and creative freedom. I doubt I've ever been happier than I am now. The less that I possess, the less possesses me. This seems a fair and just arrangement.

So is this an epiphany? Not entirely, I suppose. Even this brief review of my past mistakes contains evidence of attrition.

That is, when the batteries energizing my former life ran down, I didn't get around to replacing them. But I like the ideal of epiphany. It implies that something insightful and deliberate happened to give me the opportunity to control my own life more than I actually do.

As for Nicole, she teases me about being a rebel purely for the sake of it. I forgive her this point of view because of how little she knows about me and how much I refuse to explain. But if I was a younger man, if there was any true romantic potential between us, perhaps I would have to explain the things I've learned about myself. As there's no denying the gap in our ages and the harmless nature of my attraction, I'm convinced it's best to be guarded. Once summer runs its course, Nicole and I will no doubt go our separate ways; I do not look forward to that transmigration of souls we call "losing touch."

For now, the crush is rich and sensory, an added personal joy enhancing my bittersweet return to this island for the last time. Life, even for someone like me—primarily a watcher—is capable of unexpected pleasure. Nicole is one of these and I'm grateful she is here. When this summer comes to an end, I'll look back on her friendship fondly.

## THE MAN AND THE WOMAN

THE STORM ARRIVES AT DUSK. It rumbles in over the southeastern edge of the island, drawing its breath from the broad surface of the turbulent lake. The wind begins to build. The rain festers quickly into an angry gusher and the clouds cluster and blacken as they approach the exposed and lonely island. Thunderheads occupy the sky, elbowing out of the way the day's blue tranquility. The light fails quickly, a kind of deeper, meaner dusk that arrives too early.

In the distance the storm lets loose its colicky bitterness. By the time the first harsh bolt of lightning explodes across the horizon, followed in a few seconds by the cannonfire of thunder, a quasi-night has fallen so deeply the man imagines he's tumbled down a well. By then, though, his mood has become electric. One realizes the awe he feels for an island storm now fills him with delight.

He has anticipated the disturbance for more than an hour, detecting it first at the ends of his nostrils, a fresh, tingling bouquet rich with the moist scent of impending rain. He noticed the brewing storm while he was barbecuing his dinner on the rocks in front of the cottage. When he turned towards the lake he saw the thickening clouds in the distance confirming its approach. He has witnessed this sight on many occasions before. He began to take note of the storm's stages of development, ticking them off one by one on his fingers. It was all so deliciously familiar, the way the rising wind began to slap his cheeks with gradually increasing spite and how the sound grew muffled and thick inside the clamour of the darkening sky.

One can see why he loves a good storm on the island: that he feels spiritually revived when he's made insignificant by the ferocious power of nature. His transformation is a celebration, from bully to bullied, from modern to primordial. Island storms, he believes, are good for his perspective, illuminate the purpose in his purposelessness. Storms marry him to the elements, interrupt his foolish arrogance, remind him that he cannot sever his connection to nature after all, a nature so colossal and mighty his various human projects shrink by comparison. Storms remind him that the rigours of his life are created by his fellow man or by mistakes he makes himself. A storm is nature as the universe, relegating him to an orbiting moon among so many other insignificant moons. For a brief exalted time—while the storm demonstrates its startling fury—he remembers that it is nature's electricity that pulses through his veins, not the adolescent tribulations concocted by his society. While the storm gives vent to its temper, he is ecstatically alive, free of the bane of his conventional wisdom and its conventional applications. The storm leaves him with his instincts so that he can be private, lonely and wondrous.

All of this is what he feels as he battens down the hatches. It's part of his ceremony of awe. As he retrieves the tarpaulin from the shed, pulls the boat higher up onto the beach, ties the tarpaulin around it, gathers chairs and other flimsy objects inside the cottage, he feels like a sailor readying himself for his first ocean squall. Inside the cottage he closes all the windows and secures the screen doors. Then, his preparations completed, he moves to the windows to watch the storm approach.

The lake is now swollen with angry whitecaps, like eyebrows dancing on the black face of the water. In the distance he can see an oncoming curtain of heavy rain. Moments later, the first silver droplets of the downpour splash against the glass and the first real boom of thunder explodes across the sky.

In the other cottage, the woman is caught by surprise. Hoping to retire early, she has been enjoying the first few minutes of a bath. While she reads in the tub she hears the initial grunts of distant thunder. Feeling an excitement of her own, she abbreviates her bath, climbs out, dries herself off and hurries to put on her robe.

At first she doesn't succumb so completely to the sensations of awe the man feels in the other cottage. She's too annoyed by the storm's interruption and what it demands of her. She cries an invective when—on the terrace where she gathers the lounges, cushions and leftover coffee mugs—the wind comes up beaded with icy rain and blows her robe undone. The fabric flaps noisily in the gale, leaving her flesh briefly naked. The lounges fall with a clatter on the patio stones while she refastens the billowing garment.

She stows the lounges inside and races to snatch an assortment of towels from a small clothesline at the rear of the cottage. Her mother doesn't believe, for some reason or other, that an electric dryer is appropriate to roughing it on the island. This opinion is worth another invective as she bends to retrieve small puddles of clothing on the ground where the wind has tossed them. She closes and locks all the windows; then, like the man in the other cottage, she stands facing the simmering lake as the rain begins to pour. A bolt of lightning nearly blinds her and the ensuing explosion of thunder shakes the cottage.

But it is then that she succumbs to the magnetic beauty in the growing tempest.

In his cottage, the man wonders how she is faring in the squall. He wonders if she's frightened, alone in the noisy cacophony of thunder and wind, rain and lightning.

The woman wonders what the man is doing too. One gathers that they watch the disturbance from nearly identical vantage points, sharing a similar awe for the temper of the storm.

The man and woman watch the same sights in the storm, hear and smell its natural wrath. Often storms here come and go in minutes and this one is no exception. There's the sound and smell of the pelting rain, the black of the crushing clouds, lightning like nuclear debacle, thunder that sounds like war. And the wind cuts through the groaning trees like a stranger stampeding through a crowd. All of this passes quickly over the island on its way across the channel. The storm drags its tail of heavy rain over the roofs of the trembling cottages. Then the winds begin to die down. The lightning grows dim and the thunder softens in the distance.

The power goes off.

AFTERWARDS, AS HE SITS IN CANDLELIGHT, the man weighs the pros and cons of walking down the beach to make sure the woman is alright.

The woman, knowing by this time that he has a gallant streak, wonders about that time if he might venture out to check on her. She carries one of her candles to the battery clock on the kitchen wall and discovers it's only ten o'clock. She debates going to bed early again and walks to her bedroom illuminated by a kerosene lamp. But the storm has charged her battery; she's not tired any longer. She feels a sense of anticipation she doesn't fully understand. It's just the electricity of the storm; she knows that much at least. It makes her restless now to have something—anything—happen that hasn't happened before.

She'd like to talk to Matt about the storm and its aftermath. Maybe he'll come to see if she's survived it. He'll ask her if she's okay. She'll say she's just fine, thank you for asking. And maybe that'll be enough to make her sleepy again.

But the man is thinking things over. What will be conveyed to the woman about his feelings, his intentions, if he stumbles through the darkness to her cottage to see if she's alright? Will it imply he cares for her beyond the appropriate concern of a neighbor or friend? Will she begin to suspect he has a bit of a crush on her? Worse, will it appear he's exploiting an opportunity provided by the storm and the deep black night it's left behind? Will she not then wonder if his friendship is nothing more than a patient variation of attempted seduction? God, how complicated it gets even when the initial premise begins so simply.

Still, soon he prepares to go. His fears cannot measure up to the legitimacy of his concern. He doubts she's actually afraid. But as a friend he should make sure.

A deep chill has come over the night now that the storm has departed. He puts on a favorite sweater underneath his nylon jacket. Uneasily, his dog stands a yard away, watching him intently. "I'll be right back, Ben," he says, patting him on the head to comfort him. "I'll just be a few minutes."

He takes down a lantern, gives it a shake to see if it has any fuel. Then, satisfied, he retrieves one of the long matches he keeps in a kitchen drawer. He slips outside, the screen door slamming shut behind him, the sound a startling rent in the new hush of the night. Ben stands at the screen, imploring him to take him along. For now, Matt strikes the match on the zipper of his jeans and lights the powerful lantern.

"Okay, Ben," the man says, reaching for the door, feeling happy to relent. "You can come too. But stay close, okay?"

Then they move into the wet darkness along the path leading across the top of the ridge behind both cottages.

Less than half a mile away, the woman begins to wonder if Matt is on his way. She has questions of her own. If Matt shows up, should she be dressed instead of naked under her robe? But if she gets dressed and there's no knock at the door, will she feel foolish for having dressed? And why should she feel foolish at all? Why, most of all, is she asking herself so many silly questions?

"Go to bed," she says out loud, slowly heading towards the bedroom.

But halfway there, she hears a gentle knock at the kitchen door.

"Nicole? It's Matt Bowman."

She goes to the door and opens it.

He stands on the stoop, on the other side of the screen, holding a lamp so bright the glare hurts her eyes.

"Come in," she says, stepping aside. Her right hand clutches the top of her robe to keep it closed tightly over her breasts.

He puts down the lamp on the stoop and steps inside. The light shines so brightly behind him, it embraces each crevice of his body, dressing him in a dazzling aura.

"Just thought I should check on you," he explains. "The storm, I mean."

"Wasn't it a dandy?"

"A beauty," he agrees.

"I'm fine," she tells him then.

"Okay. Just thought I should check."

Her hair is a wonderful tangle in the moisture of the night.

His hair too is a nest of tightening coils gone shiny in the dampness. If she were to touch it, her fingers would come away moist. "No," she says out loud about nothing in particular. Then she quickly adds, "I'd decided to go to bed."

"I didn't get you up, did I?"

"Oh no. I was just on my way when you knocked."

"Okay. Well I'll be going then. You have candles?"

"Yes. And a kerosene lamp."

"Okay. Just wanted to make sure everything was all right. With the power off."

"When do you think it'll come back on?"

"Soon, I hope. By morning anyway. If not, and if you're desperate for morning coffee, come over. I have a Coleman stove and a percolator I use for camping. I can do without anything but my morning coffee." He grins.

"Okay," she says with a smile.

"I'll be going now," he says. He opens the screen door, steps outside, picks up his brilliant, hissing lantern.

"Thanks for checking," the woman says.

"No problem," the man replies. "Good night," he says as he turns away.

"Good night, Matt."

The man walks back to his cottage, the lamp swinging brightly in his right hand, his dog scouting the route ahead of him. He is relieved that Nicole is okay, that he decided to check on her. He is relieved there has been no confusion about what his intentions were. These feelings predominate even later as he opens his journal to report on the storm, to set down in words how he felt about its fury. He feels strangely comforted that he got away with something, with caring when it isn't allowed—a crime he has learned over time can carry the harshest of sentences. No wonder he feels so relieved. Condemned by the isolation of his secret caring, he still believes himself to be mostly an innocent man.

Shortly, as she reads by the light of her kerosene lamp, the woman feels gratefully comfortable, even a little pleased with herself, although she isn't exactly sure why. Whether it has something to do with how considerate it was of Matt to come all this way to check on her, she wouldn't want to say for sure. Some moods are just hard to explain.

## NICOLE

EACH TIME YOU'RE REUNITED WITH KAREN, especially after a long gap between seeing one another, you're taken aback by how petite she is. It's as if she grows in your memory somehow or, in reality, shrinks with the passage of time. This incongruity is made all the more acute because her husband, Liam, remains so much the same each time, a big Irish bear with an unruly red beard and laugh wrinkles fissuring deeply around his eyes. As for their daughter, Cindy, she seems to have ducked all of her father's genes. Cindy is a mirror image of her mother when her mother was a child.

The day has begun cloudy and heavy, disappointing again for a Saturday. You rose this morning, leaving Alan to the unselfconscious nonsense he often mutters in his sleep. While you made coffee and took a quick bath, your frequent glances out the window filled you with trepidation. Contemplating the boat trip across the channel to pick up your friends, you not only feared it might rain but that bad weather would incarcerate all of you in the cottage for the weekend like so many trapped vermin. The Alan Birken factor, you were forced to admit, gave you cabin fever anxiety.

But as you prepared the boat for takeoff, the cloud cover began to break up and the sun finally forced its way out. By the time you and Carmen were halfway across the channel it had become surprisingly hot and oppressive. Carmen took to the bow, her long ears blowing backwards comically in the breeze. Due in part to the improvement in the weather, the morning's scene felt newly complete to you, this voyage across the water, just you, the planing boat and Carmen.

And you remembered that last night Alan had asked you to wake him, so that he could go along this morning. But you didn't want him to. "They'll have luggage," you said. "The boat will be too crowded." Both of you knew this wasn't exactly true but for once he didn't argue. You'd already clearly outlined your expectations for the weekend. You and Karen would need lots of time alone together, to catch up, to gossip. Liam, you said, habitually makes space for you to be close to Karen. Alan too, you explained, would have to learn to make space too.

He didn't argue about that either. Probably because you had sex with him last night, although, in truth, your heart wasn't in it. Sexual lesser of evils. Sometimes it's better to just give in than to default to your current tendency to say "no." So he was probably appeased enough not to argue about this morning's boat ride and your anticipated preoccupation with Karen. But while he felt sleepy and satisfied after lovemaking, you felt strangely soiled. It was as if you had betrayed yourself by giving in somehow.

And that's the thing about Alan and his anxiety and the way it maintains a hold over you. As you meander through its machinations—his worries, his attempts to control your lives together—you begin to feel mean or unfair. You begin to feel as manipulative as he seems to be. You treat *him* the way that he treats *you.* You dislike *your* manipulations as much as you dislike *his.* You forget how to be the better person you'd like to be.

You wait only twenty minutes at *The Inlet* before you spot Liam's green Cherokee driving down the long driveway sloping towards the marina. You've spent the time sitting on a dock piling not far from where you tied up, leaving Carmen leashed to the boat. From there, you watched the hectic morning activity that always belies and exaggerates the rundown pretensions of *The Inlet.* Two college kids, trying like blazes to appear nautical in white shorts and t-shirts and wearing boating shoes, one of them a young woman with blonde hair out of California mythology, the other a young man with skinny legs, crooked glasses and acne, pumped gas and cast off lines the entire time, their smiles chipped like pale gashes into the tanning granite of their faces. Meanwhile, out on the channel, boats slithered in and out of one another's wakes like lazy silver snakes.

It's been a year since you last visited in person and Karen is nearly out of the Jeep before the vehicle comes to a halt. In shorts and t-shirt, she hurries across the asphalt and hugs you at the end of the dock. In the background Liam simply grins.

"You look great, sweetie," says Karen.

"So do you," you reply.

Her dark brown hair is shorter now in her summer cut. It's tinged with red in the brilliance of the sun. She has delicate, perfect ears.

"No Alan," observes Karen right away.

"Back at the cottage. I thought the boat might be crowded."

Karen merely smiles and crinkles her nose, perfectly attuned to your need to greet her and her family on your own.

Then Liam shows up for *his* hug and, although your are tall yourself, you find his embrace as big as a room. You disappear inside it, like hiding behind a drape.

"How's it going, kiddo?" he says. No brogue. His name is old country but the family accent vanished two generations ago.

Cindy hugs you too but it's childlike and shy. When you were ten years old, adult hugs were vaguely uncomfortable too, some kind of gilded cage. They were like New Year's Eve; you didn't understand them.

In the awkward few seconds which seem to follow most warm greetings, you stand back from the O'Shaughnessys, gazing at them with an affection only mildly tinged with envy. As they beam at one another and at the bright sunshine of the day, anticipating this weekend at a cottage, you long for the bond they share. One day, you hope, the man you love will be standing beside you, part of this excitement. But the men for whom you've cared have been so much like Alan somehow. Eventually you leave them behind when you want to do something important, like picking up dear friends. You feel a pang of loss and guilt about this and—those weird machinations again—at least some of it is on behalf of Alan.

There's busy conversation as you load two suitcases and a trio of plastic grocery bags into the boat. Asparagus is in season and they've stopped along the way to pick up five pounds or so. And Liam is looking forward to his first swim of the season, although you tell him the water is cold this year, a result of spring's unusually late arrival.

"Well Cindy and me are going in," Liam says. "Even if we turn blue."

Relating how ambivalent the weather has been, you describe the electrical storm earlier in the week. "The power was off for hours," you explain, "all night, all the next morning, until mid-afternoon."

"Oh no," says Karen.

"Actually it was kind of fun," you admit. "Matt Bowman has a Coleman stove. He perked morning coffee, invited me over, then cooked up a homemade soup for lunch."

"Matt Bowman?"

"My neighbor in the other cottage. I've told you about him."

"Oh yes. Yes, you have."

But if Karen is going to tease you about this, and no doubt she will, she decides to wait until later. Distracted by Cindy's excitement and the fact you have cast off, she tells her daughter to sit down. "Your Aunt Nicole likes to drive fast," she announces. "Find a seat and hold on tight."

With a reputation to maintain, you rocket away from the dock, your fist raised in a fierce hosanna.

All the way across the channel, around the point of the island and along the island's shore, the four of you shout at one another over the cry of the engine, festive conversation that's blessed with anticipation. As you ease the boat towards land, Alan emerges from inside the cottage and moseys slowly down to the beach as you bring the boat to shore. You are dismayed that your heart sinks a little.

"There's Alan," you say redundantly, embarrassed by the disingenuousness of his swagger.

After this, both your voice and the powerful motor slip safely into neutral.

STILL, EVERYTHING GOES ALL RIGHT, for the most part anyway. As well as can be expected. Alan and Liam shake hands, although they're not each other's kind of man. On the one occasion in the past they tried talking to one another seriously, it was only to learn they come at life from different corners of the ring. Karen offers her cheek for a kiss when Alan holds her by both shoulders. Cindy, standing off by herself, says "hi," then ignores with a child's innocent wisdom the vacuum in the dazzle of his smile. There is, thank goodness, so much to do, so many distractions. Lunch comes first. Alan fires up your father's barbecue, grills hot dogs and Oktoberfest sausage—too few hot dogs and too many sausages at first, something you cautioned him about yesterday. Alan will never truly understand a cottage: it's a way of life too subtly working class for him. It's hot dogs and beer, not sausage and champagne. It's a culture he wants to outshine as if his version has more merit.

Conversation is nothing more than chitchat before, during and after lunch. It's politely interested and interesting, like reading the "B" section of the dictionary, and as impossible to retain. Alan politely re-invites Liam and Karen to the party he plans with you here towards the end of the month, knowing already that they can't come. Rather tiredly, Karen must explain her regrets all over again, the way she has to you already the last time you talked with her on the phone. "We're hoping to visit again in July," she says. "We just can't get away until then."

"That's too bad," says Alan.

You hope you're the only one to feel the disingenuousness in his remark.

Liam suggests a swim. "Alan?" he says.

"No thanks. Too cold for me."

"Take Cindy," says Karen. "Nickie and I'll do the dishes."

"Alan, you be the lifeguard," you suggest just in case he doesn't realize you and Karen need to be alone.

"Now *there's* an idea," he replies with a stiff little nod.

"I'm sorry we can't make your party," says Karen in the kitchen a few minutes later.

"That's okay," you tell her. "It's more or less Alan's party. Most of the people coming are actually *his* friends. I've invited Matt Bowman, though."

"That name keeps popping up," Karen says coyly, gazing into the sink.

"He's been a good friend to me. I like him."

"Does Alan?"

"Not a chance. He groaned when I told him I'd invited Matt to the party. He said he wouldn't fit in."

"Nice," murmurs Karen.

"I want you to meet him," you say. "I thought, tomorrow morning, when I take Carmen down to play with his dog, Canine Ben, you could come with me."

Karen places the last dish in the rack, pulls the sink plug, dries her hands. "Wouldn't miss the opportunity," she says, looking straight at you, unblinking. "Your voice changes when you talk about him. I must admit, though, the picture of him I conjured up is getting hazier."

"What picture?"

"Your neighbor in the other cottage. I had pictured an old relic with a paunch and a *Harley-Davidson*."

"No paunch," you say with a grin. "No *Harley*. Does that clear things up for you?"

"It's beginning to," says Karen, suddenly flicking you smartly with her tea towel.

You laugh and embrace her. "I love you, Karen, you know."

"I love you too," she says.

You look like Mutt and Jeff, you know, and you always have. In some ways, you really are.

When you rejoin the others down on the beach, the sun is even hotter, although the water is very cold. Cindy is shivering and Liam admits the swim was a bit of a test. Still, you suggest a little water-skiing and everyone assents.

Liam drives the boat, maintaining he's too heavy to get up on skis. With Carmen a furry, windblown hood ornament standing on the bow, he pulls you, then Karen around the island edge of the lake. Cindy stands on the shore, applauding everyone's prowess. You feast on the afternoon sunshine as you clatter across the lake's choppiness. Alan has to be talked into a turn but, to your surprise, he finally gives in.

"Just stay in the wake," you tell him. "If you feel yourself falling, let go of the rope. That's important. And when the boat is pulling you out of the water, you know, at first, keep the skis together."

With you, Karen and Cindy now on shore to allow the boat more speed to lift his weight, he nods, gasping because the water's so cold. But he's grown stubborn about succeeding. He

Barry Grills

signals to Liam that he's ready.

He gets up on the skis first try and, for most of his ride, respects your advice to remain inside the wake, But wanting to impress, he leaves the wake inevitably during a wide turn some distance from shore. When he begins to fall, he forgets to let go of the rope. His body meets the surface of the water the way a fly collides with the windshield of a car.

You see it all from the beach, your concern modified by an equally undeniable urge to laugh. After Liam collects him from the lake and brings the boat back to shore, you discover Alan's nose is bleeding.

"I know, I know," he says, one hand holding his nose, the other held up in supplication. "I forgot to let go of the rope."

"You'll be all right," you tell him.

"Of course I will," he says.

One more thing happens while you are taking your final turn at skiing. When you pass Matt Bowman's *Crow's Nest*, his boat is nowhere in sight. You wonder if he's decided to go away for the weekend and feel surprised at your disappointment.

But he returns that evening around dusk; You hear his boat arriving as you and your guests, mostly for Cindy's benefit, are sitting down for a game of *Rumoli* you suggested during dinner. No one else pays any attention to the drone of Matt's outboard motor. You feel an intriguing pleasure in your secret relief that he's returned.

"What time tomorrow morning?" whispers Karen as you meet in the kitchen just before retiring.

"Huh?"

"You know. Carmen's walk. Matt Bowman?"

"Oh. Around nine-thirty."

"You guys arranged a time?"

"Of course not," you reply. "I know what time he's there."

WITH WHAT HAS BECOME RIGID MORNING RITUAL, Carmen dashes up the beach, feints a turn in Canine Ben's direction, then resumes her headlong dash along the beach, encouraging her retriever playmate to give chase. As usual, he goes along with her familiar gambit and, in an explosion of silver spray, they gallop through the shallows together a few feet from the shore.

As you stroll along with Karen, you realize you are trying to

130

perceive Matt Bowman the way that she will. Perhaps her view of him will reveal something extra to you that you have somehow missed. Are you hoping for an endorsement perhaps? Or maybe Karen's sense that Matt has something special you don't know yet that you need? But even through Karen's imagined perception, to you he's the same old Matt approaching. Jeans, denim shirt, brown feet sprouting from his sandals. Brown-skinned because his skin has tanned with disconcerting speed. Things dangle from his wrist and hang from his neck. He's Crazy Horse to you each time, like he's in the business of being mystical. Oh yes, no paunch, no *Harley-Davidson*, not a relic in any way. He's just travelled longer along this beach and knows the dunes a little more intimately.

Karen reads your mind. "Well," she murmurs beside you, her voice a playful elbow in your ribs, "toss out the relic part."

Matt waves then, without waiting for a response, bends down to fuss with the frolicking dogs as Carmen comes up for her greeting, dragging a happily possessive Canine Ben along behind her. After the dogs dart off again, he comes forward, halving the distance between you. His trousers are wet and sandy where the dogs have brushed up against him.

You make introductions, surprised at how rewarding this ceremony is. When you ask yourself which makes you happier—Matt meeting Karen or Karen meeting Matt—it's hard to make the call. You are so dismayed by this new revelation, for the moment you cannot speak.

But Matt is telling Karen that he's heard so much about her.

Karen laughs and suggests not much of it can be good.

"That's true," Matt says with a grin, "but I'm sworn to secrecy."

The conversation meanders along a predictable course—how fine the weather is, how it's the perfect few days to come to the island for a stay. And you review for him the weekend's activities so far: *Rumoli* the previous evening, water skiing yesterday afternoon. You tell Matt about Alan's fall during his first time on water skis, his bloody nose, how he looked like Rudolph the Red-nosed Reindeer by the end of the night last night.

"Uh-oh," comments Matt, but he let's it go at that.

"Has Nickie had you out in the boat yet?" asks Karen.

"My insurance broker advises against it."

Karen remarks that you have told her Matt is here for the entire summer.

"Until the end of September," he explains.

"I noticed you weren't here yesterday," you tell him.

"No. Went into town for supplies. Stayed in town for dinner. But I have some big news. I called Greg, my younger son, and he said his brother is coming back from Europe in a few days. So we set up a visit."

"They're coming here?"

"Yes. For a couple of days. I guess you'll get to meet them."

Although you've heard so much of the meat in the conversation before—how Matt's cottage is being sold, how this is his last summer here after more than four decades of summer visits, how he lives in Kingston and doesn't want to any longer, how well Karen's music school is doing and the nature of its fresh approach to teaching, your ensuing opportunity to change careers, Matt's book of political essays and, of course, all the spontaneous quips driven like spikes into the pauses in between—it still seems fresh and new to you. Karen's presence has given each subject extra substance, made it that much more real.

Soon this recess on the beach begins to run out of time. Karen is ready to go back to her husband and daughter, and the dogs are both played out. You've asked Matt what he plans for the day; he's mentioned he's going to work. There doesn't seem more to take place that would require that you tarry.

Still, "I'm brewing fresh coffee," he says. "You're welcome to have a cup."

But you and Karen decline with thanks.

"Alan and Liam are making brunch," explains Karen. "We'll be needed for damage control."

"Of course," says Matt. And he smiles something cryptic at you, or at least that's the way it seems.

Then it's done. Karen has met Matt; Matt has met Karen. Something feels complete for you. After the usual "pleased-to-meet-yous," you walk back along the shore with Karen, Carmen trotting a few yards ahead of you. Strangely, it feels like you've stumbled over a warp in time, that the last several minutes have happened to another you. No wonder you manage only at the last moment to prevent yourself from turning around, to glance back in Matt's direction to make certain he's really there. The notion is absurd—of course he is. And the glance might be misconstrued. Karen might wonder what you're doing, the way you're beginning to wonder yourself.

Pointless caution, as it turns out. Because Karen says, hardly a moment later, "we have to talk."

"We do?"

"Yes. We'll do the brunch thing with the others, then go for a walk, to that place on the other side of the island."

"The rocks?"

"The rocks. I love it there."

"Me too. Okay, we'll slip away for some private time."

Enigmatically Karen nods.

"What's wrong?" you ask.

"You're vibrating," she replies in good-natured diagnosis.

"I'm what?"

"You're vibrating. This beach feels like the San Andreas Fault."

THAT AFTERNOON YOU AND KAREN slowly arrive at whatever has to be said, the way you always do. Information updates come first. Karen's mother has been seeing the doctor; the veins in her legs are clogging up. Her brother, Gary, is about to be let go as his firm completes a restructuring. ("Restructuring," Matt told you one morning over coffee, "is just a euphemism for your average workplace massacre.") Her father is fine, normal at least, still bemused by his recent retirement, gratified, says Karen, that he made it that far safely, economically inviolate.

Mostly you listen. There isn't much for you to relate about your parents. The last phone call covered it anyway. Liam? Liam, says Karen, is worried. He's a carpenter and work has been increasingly sporadic. He believes it's going to get worse. Housing starts are down drastically. You tell her that's what your father says. And so it goes for several minutes, your variation of *and now the news*, as you make your way along the path at the top of the ridge behind your cottage.

The sky is blue but crumpled-paper clouds scurry over the pastel expanse as if pretending to have a destination. There's a bit of a breeze up here, originating out of the north, and it's successfully prodded the morning's warm haze south over the lake. By the time you reach the rocky cliffs which peer out over the channel, the mainland is sharply defined in the distance. The air feels solid and clear, crisp. If you were to reach out to touch it, it might crackle in your fingers. Immediately below you, the water is green and translucent. You are mesmerized for several minutes by the vegetation beneath the surface, shimmer-dancing to the endless music in the current.

Karen sighs in appreciation of her favorite island view as she makes a seat out of a cleft in the rocks. You find a similar spot just across from her. Nearby, like a scrawny mountain man, a tenacious cedar clings to this barren summit, its roots scrabbling frantically for purchase in the rock.

As the two of you sit there in silence, taking in this summer's day, you consider again how well the friendship has prospered in the fourteen years since you first met. Piano class. Conservatory stuff. That first day, while you stood outside on the stone balustrade in the rain, awaiting separate rides, hugging the school wall to keep dry under the protruding soffit, you thought Karen was a little too droll. You found out later she dismissed you as a bit of a shapely siren, a potential cliché of self-absorption. "I thought you were going to be one of those bimbo pains in the ass," she confessed once you were safely friends. But friends you were and friends you have remained, seeking out each other's advice, sometimes heeding it, sometimes not.

You were her maid of honor when she married Liam at barely twenty-one. You thought she was too young to marry, although by standards strictly your own. Liam was great, though. Somehow you knew it was going to work out. Nor was her marriage the only indication of Karen's head start into life. Scant months later, she announced happily that she was pregnant. Cindy was born two days before her first wedding anniversary. Although you were thrilled for her and knew she was probably content, you felt lapped in the racetrack oval of life, already aware that your engine was sputtering, that your carburetor suffered an unhappy cough.

There's been an inequity of happenstance in the friendship from the beginning. It's been so insistent, become so constant, these days you hardly ever give it any thought, but the upshot of it is this: Karen makes few mistakes in her life while you seem to have made far too many. It's the Mutt and Jeff thing of which your height and her daintiness is but some kind of physical manifestation. In life, you've decided, you stumble and fall and stagger, even careen clumsily around dangerous corners. But Karen seems to discorporate with magical ease. She glides through life's walls and razor wire like a ghost, with hardly a scratch to mark the journey.

Over the years, on your bad days, you've gently resented this. She seems like the knowing, compassionate psychiatrist while you assume the role of persistently hapless patient. On good days, though, this ritual unfairness in your contrasting voyages seems something else much kinder, a state of obligatory balance. Besides, where your friendship with Karen is concerned, your bad days are exceedingly rare while the good days stretch out in front of you like some pristine, golden highway.

Thinking these things, you smile warmly when she catches your eye.

"I've been thinking," she says. "You and Alan? I don't know, Nickie."

"Me neither," you admit.

"I mean, do you want this guy around? You don't seem close. When you pass one another in the same room, you give him this great, wide berth. Like he's got something you might catch."

"I know." You say this with resignation. "It's true that I don't feel close to him anymore. When I first came here, to the island, I just thought we were having difficulties, that I just needed time to work things out for myself. I thought being here would give me perspective. And maybe it has in a way. I just wish I'd stop thinking it's something wrong with me."

"Yeah," says Karen drily. "That gets to be a bad habit."

"To be honest, I wonder if Alan encourages that feeling. It keeps him in control somehow. I'm easier to deal with when I think I'm at fault, that there's something wrong with me. But since I've been on the island—oh, Karen, this is going to sound so awful—I think I've begun to dislike him."

Now that you've begun to confess, you want to let it gush. "I mean stupid, little things," you add. "I find myself hating the way he walks, the way he says things, looks he gets on his face. I don't like the way he combs his hair in front of the mirror—he kind of spins and peers and primps it this way and that. Ugh! You know, Karen, I hardly let him touch me unless I prepare myself for it in advance. The idea of feeling close to him again seems impossible. It's like, to be close to him, I have to put part of myself away, put it to sleep or something, and, afterwards, I hate myself for it."

"You have to break up with him." Karen looks at you sadly.

You shrug. "I would if I was sure I'm not the one who's being unfair."

This dismays Karen. "Shit, Nickie, you're supposed to feel comfortable with the man you love. You're not supposed to hate the way he walks and talks and combs his hair. You're not supposed to be questioning your fairness all the time."

"But what if I'm just being grumpy and critical? What if it gets better?"

"Him or your feelings?"

"Both, I guess."

"Well," says Karen brusquely, "*he's* not showing any impetus to change. As for your feelings..."

A gull cries loudly above your heads. Startled, as if caught planning a conspiracy, both of you glance up. The gull squawks again, then tails off further out over the channel.

Karen grins. You grin back halfheartedly.

"You know," you say after a time, "I've gotten pretty cynical about romantic relationships in the past little while. I'm probably doomed from the start, because of the cynicism, I mean. I think you and Liam are the exception, that there are more people out there like me, people who should stop kidding themselves about finding forever-after love. I mean, look at my history, Karen."

"Yeah, yeah," says Karen with a dismissive wave of her hand. "Nicole Graham, romantic felon."

"I've been thinking," you tell her anyway, "that people like me should set a time for a relationship right from the beginning. Like a 'best before' date or something. Like on a carton of milk."

"Huh?"

"You pick a date at the very beginning, based on your past experience. Then, when that date comes, like a carton of milk that's going to go sour, you pour it down the sink. Then you go get yourself a fresh new carton of milk."

Karen is aghast. "Shit, Nickie, love isn't milk. No one knows what it is anyway, where it's going, how it'll end up. We don't know any of that. We just know what it isn't, I guess."

"What isn't it?"

"It isn't milk, for God's sake."

Both of you chuckle at her exasperation.

"What about you, Karen? What's love to you?"

"Wow," says Karen with a smile, simply shrugging her shoulders. "What a question."

"I guess I really mean, how does it feel when you've felt it as long as you have?"

Thoughtfully she gazes out over the channel. "Comfortable, I guess," she replies at last.

"Like safe?"

"No, comfortable. Comfortable is beyond safe. You know? You don't worry about being safe anymore. It's not even part of the equation. Safe doesn't seem a worthwhile ambition, the way unsafe wasn't either back in the early days."

"Does it stay passionate? I wouldn't want that to go away."

"Sure. But the passionate part can be comfortable too. You know something, Nickie? I can't even remember the anxiety that used to be connected to love, that state of vulnerability."

"I don't know anything about that kind of love," you admit sadly. "I don't think I've ever felt it, you know, comfortable passion. It's all been anxious and vulnerable."

"Well I didn't set out to find this state of calm," says Karen. "I guess it just evolves. One day I looked up and that was what I felt."

You nod.

"But for me I guess that's it—love feels comfortable. I guess that's what my answer is. The friendship is comfortable, the routine is comfortable, even the changes in routine are comfortable. The passion is comfortable. The sense of sharing is comfortable. Making love is comfortable. The not feeling I'm missing anything is comfortable."

"Freedom? Independence?"

"Comfortable," says Karen.

"Then maybe it's me after all. Maybe I just spoil things for myself."

"Nah," counters Karen. "You just haven't found the right person."

"I'm thirty-two."

"Talk to me when you're eighty-two."

"I probably will," you say with a snort. "And it's a pretty frightening prospect. We'll creak down here to the rocks, all blue rinsed and wrinkled, and then I ask you the same questions. I hope not."

"No way," says Karen to the notion. "If fifty years from now, you keep asking me what's wrong with you, I'll murder you. Then you won't have to worry about it anymore."

"I hear you," you reply.

"So," says Karen then. "On a not entirely unrelated topic, you neglected to mention that Matt Bowman is attractive in a craggy sort of way."

"You think so?"

"Yup."

"Well I guess he's such a good friend, I didn't notice."

"Didn't notice?"

"You know, took it for granted, didn't think of it that way, as important or anything."

A smile with a different excuse forms on Karen's face. "Nickie, sometimes you are so full of shit."

You cannot help but laugh.

"That guy on the beach this morning wasn't what I expected at all. I expected a paunch that could block a doorway, in spite of what you said. I thought there'd be a bottle of *Geritol* sticking out of his back pocket. Okay, some of it was accurate. I mean you told me about the dangly stuff, the sixties stuff, the grey in the beard, that sort of thing. But when you said 'older,' I thought you meant old. How old is he anyway?"

"Forty-seven."

"Shit, Nickie, that's not old, that's young. It'd better not be old when I get there, anyway."

"Well it's not as young as thirty-two."

"You're splitting hairs with a hammer."

What she's said sounds funny and you laugh. But it's more than that. It's enjoyable to be talking about Matt. You nearly tell her this, but can't quite come up with the courage. It'll only confirm what she already understands. The ease between you and Matt. The way it's safe and undemanding. You're not ready to admit this to yourself.

"We're friends, Karen," you say at last. "Matt and I are only friends."

"Who says friends can't be attracted to one another? That's part of what comfortable is. I'd rather have the hots for a friend than for someone I don't know very well. Maybe comfortable is realizing that friendship and passion aren't mutually exclusive."

"Karen, please."

She just continues to grin. "I felt tremors down there on the beach this morning."

"So you said."

"I did. And they weren't all coming from him, sweetie."

"We're just friends."

"We've covered that," retorts Karen. "I love you, Nickie, but I know an impression of the queen of denial when I see one."

The silence which ensues is a long one. In the absence of further conversation, the sounds of your natural setting there on the island's summit come to urgent life again. You hear another gull, at a greater distance this time, and the water splashing rhythmically against the rocks below you. You even become aware of the sound the breeze makes as it blows stiffly by your ears.

"Something else about Matt," you say at last. "Or any other man, for that matter. The last thing I need right now is a further complication."

Karen doesn't seem to hear you. "I guess we should get back," she says, rising to her feet.

You get up too, prepared to accept that Karen has had enough.

But then she adds, "Nickie, you don't get to pick all of this out. That's an aspect of comfortable too. You don't get to slot situations or people into your appointment book of life. You don't get to give people a role, keep them performing it, define their function so narrowly that it's trespassing if the relationship grows or changes. There's nothing convenient about the way things happen."

"Okay," you reply, although the appointment book analogy seems a little harsh. Now *you* want to end the conversation, feeling foolish and more than vaguely threatened by all the things your conclusions are going to mean and how you will have to face them.

"God, I hope you move to Kingston," Karen says with an impish grin. "I'm going to love working with you more often."

"You mean psychologically?"

"Not in any serious way," Karen explains.

"Matt lives in Kingston." You meant this remark to be light but it comes out of your mouth with too much intensity. Perhaps because you are annoyed, you are a little hurt. But at what, you're not entirely sure. Alan? Matt? Karen's well-intended confidence?

Overwhelmed by all that has been said, you simply stand there nodding your head at something unspoken.

Still, on the way back down to the cottage, you bring up one more thing. "If I break up with Alan, he won't take it very well. He doesn't like to let go. He has an obsessive streak."

Karen goes sober and stiff. "Tough shit for him," she says with a frown.

But it isn't Alan you're worried about.

## MATT

**Saturday, June 22**

NEARLY TWENTY MINUTES PAST MIDNIGHT. Deep night. From my vantage point at the table, the darkness is as thick as tar. Even night's sounds—the gentle arrival of the lake at the distant shoreline and a polite smattering of applause from the twitching leaves behind the cottage—reach my ears muffled and shy. And something else too. My sons, the boys, sharing the other bedroom during their brief stay here, whisper unintelligibly behind the sliding door. I wonder what good Christian brothers say to one another just before sleep; how proper are the jokes that inspire their frequent laughter? They've always been the closest of siblings. It's impossible that one could be saved and not the other.

A few feet away something buzzes around the light still burning in the kitchen, but I can't quite make it out—a moth perhaps. Entomology has never been my strong suit. Come to think of it, I don't even know what you call those little insects that slip through the screens during July and August, making frantically for the light shining over the dining room table. I only remember them as tragic. When they reach their destination, they fall flamelessly and pointlessly to the table where they shortly die.

When I was young, Uncle Bart told me these delicate creatures only live one day. I pitied them then for the brevity of their lives, unwilling or unable to understand that lives and time itself share an inescapable relativity. Back then my pity transformed me into a mercy killer. As they danced crazily across the plastic table cloth, rocking and rolling to the beat of their imminent deaths, I would squash them quickly with fingers or thumbs, hoping I was abbreviating their suffering. Their crazy, end of life celebration seemed painful to me. And after they spent all day preparing to reach our light, I thought it unfair that they should fall uselessly to the table afterwards instead of burning up like a fighter plane or flaming out like a meteorite.

I suppose I enjoy keeping this journal because, when I sit down to begin, I never quite know what I'm going to say beyond my report of the day's events. This is especially true tonight. None of what I've written so far is what I would have expected on the day of a reunion with my sons. But then, what should pensive people write after a day like this one? It felt so heavy and light, so thick and thin, much and less, big and little. The hours in this day took turns with themselves in just such a fashion. I felt like the day's valet, responsible for and at the mercy of its various changes of outfit.

No wonder, in the end, I resort to a day's chronology. Humans are only good at describing happenstance exactly the way it went. Perhaps we're merely larger versions of those tiny day-long insects that die to reach the light.

I've asked Nicole to dinner tomorrow so that she can meet Stephen and Greg, and she's agreed to come. When I asked her this morning the invitation seemed spontaneous, a logical consequence of her interest in their visit. She asked me what time they were arriving and I told her around noon, that I'd be leaving to get them in about an hour. Then she asked me if I was excited. I said that I thought I was. It was easy at that point to suggest dinner at *The Crow's Nest* some time during their stay.

Yet, to be honest, I now believe the invitation was a premeditated act. She'd already mentioned at some point days ago that Alan would not be on the island this weekend, busy instead with one of those boozy get-togethers with male friends she tells me he enjoys. This one is at a cottage near Peterborough.

I've imagined a few times in the recent past the four of us

together around my dinner table, Greg and Stephen and Nicole and me. It's a prospect I find inviting. If Birken had been staying at her cottage, I would have turned down the opportunity. I can't imagine him being part of a scenario I've imagined so well without him.

This raises the question of why I find the idea of Nicole meeting my sons so inviting. Could it be that I believe my sons put me in some kind of more respectable light, especially now that they're adults, having grown up healthy, independent and emotionally undamaged? Is it because my sons tend to modify the unconventional side of my nature? But, if so, why do I enjoy the prospects of appearing a little more respectable? Am I not committed to going my own way without a hostile world's approval? I've never expected my sons to share my views of life or duplicate the direction I have taken. Why then would I be tempted to use them as a bridge to a potentially more conventional lifestyle? Does it reflect an ambivalence I haven't truly overcome? What is it that I want Nicole to see and why do I seem to need her to see it at all?

Perhaps I make too much of this. I know how cautious I can be. Whenever I detect an apparent weakening in my resolve to lead an authentic and private life, I snap to militant attention and double the sentries around my isolation. Then, like a reformed alcoholic, I berate myself for briefly forgetting that the conniving attractions of the secular world are never entirely outside my interest. I remind myself that now that I have chosen a private life, I must never forget how unrelenting the act of maintaining it can be. Independence is as flimsy, let's say, as democracy. If you don't defend it *constantly*, someone can and will successfully erode it away.

The complication surrounding my monastic view is that I truly believe it reflects my personal balance; only a conventional world could ever perceive it as radical. Although I'm gratified whenever I dabble in a small social honeycomb perceived to be more traditional, what I really strive for is moderation. As I've noted before, it isn't what people do on their own which can aggravate my view of life—it's what they do when they swarm in blind allegiance to the rigid edicts of their particular hive. I feel outside these kinds of edicts, although I tend to enjoy their distraction from time to time.

At any rate, I want my sons to meet my favorite friend. I want my favorite friend to meet my sons. There is no confusion surrounding this.

The guys, I think, have gone to sleep. At least the whispering has stopped. By mutual agreement, we blew the whistle on conversation precisely at midnight. We plan to explore the island tomorrow so that Stephen and Greg can say their goodbyes to the place. And we want to take our time. After that, as they always have, they'll watch me prepare dinner. They are great boosters of my culinary talents and I want this meal to be particularly special.

I was pleased when they informed me—when I called them last weekend to make arrangements—that they can stay over until Monday, in view of the opportunity it provided to invite Nicole over Sunday evening. Apparently Greg, who is working for a student painting firm for the summer, was able to take Monday off because he has to work on Canada Day. As for Stephen, he's on vacation for four weeks. His time is his own until he returns to Slovenia where he is on missionary placement to teach English, part of his four years at university.

The boys showed up at *The Inlet* a few minutes after noon, came rolling down the hill in Gwen's husband's second car, what they refer to as The Corolla. Stephen was driving, making up for not having the opportunity to do so in Europe. I've travelled with each of them—a few times anyway—always a little bemused that they're grown up enough to drive. I wasn't around for the driver's licence rite of passage itself; it was one of the things I missed during my absences in periods of their growing up. Greg is placid, a conservative, competent driver. Stephen is more erratic. I wouldn't consider him careless or reckless, but he privately debates universal questions while he's at the wheel. Sometimes he has to be reminded about an approaching stop sign if, at that moment, his mind is piloting some distant metaphysical galaxy composed of the fibres of a grand scheme he would like to reduce to understandable workings.

Stephen seems so completely unchanged by the several months he's spent in Europe. He sauntered over to embrace me as if it'd only been a month or two. He's my height but always seems taller when I try to put my arms around him. It's the reaching up, I guess.

"Hi, Dad. How's it going?"

"Great. You look terrific, Steve."

"Thanks. Nice to be back for a visit. It's been a while."

Where North America is concerned, he's so far committed to being an expatriate. He has a youthfully broad definition of "irrelevance," and he maintains that North America is its symbol. After Slovenia, he wants to work in Japan. After Japan, he's looking at Argentina. After Argentina, he wants to teach as a missionary somewhere in Africa.

As for Greg, the reach upwards to embrace *him* is even more arduous. Greg is six foot three and thicker. Stephen and I feel small by comparison. "How did my younger brother get taller than me?" he asked me a few years ago while the three of us were making fun of one another. I gazed at him with my resigned-to-fatherhood expression and replied, "*He* ate all his veggies."

On the way across the channel they asked about my summer here alone on the island. So I told them about the weather, the tardy spring, the changeable June, the bad storm nearly two weeks ago, my work. I didn't mention Nicole, not wanting them to perceive that I have a crush on a younger woman. There will be time to discuss her later, when and if it doesn't intrude on this long overdue reunion.

Then again, it's probably more than that. Embarrassment, I guess. My sons have witnessed the romantic folly of my past. Their mother, then Esther, then Carolyn. Although my sons have never expressed even a modicum of disapproval, I've managed to be ashamed entirely on my own. I consider myself a failure as an example of romantic longevity. I'm not the best example of a fidelity which never falters. When they meet Nicole tomorrow night, they must regard her as a dear friend, which in fact is what she is. They must not recognize that, for now at least, I care romantically for her. I don't want her to appear to be the most recent passing float in a parade of romantic vehicles.

After we landed on the beach, carted their barely adequate gear up to the cottage and fussed with an excited Canine Ben, I put the kettle on to boil and made them tea, brewing coffee for myself. Then we took our steaming mugs outside, down to the beach so that Ben could run in and out of the lake and chase the sticks they threw. Afterwards, in a subdued and moody sunlight diminished by gauzy clouds, we sat on the beach and caught up with one another's voyages, sharing our various news. While we talked I kept looking at them in shameless admiration, almost afraid they might turn out to be someone else's sons.

They've grown up to be handsome fellows and I'm father enough to feel a pride in this. Yet they don't resemble one another very much. Gwen and I counted out the genes of our propagation as rigidly as an accountant tallies figures. So Stephen, physically, is *her* son while Greg belongs to me. Stephen looks Mediterranean—brown-skinned with black hair. All of his features come from the pool of traits confined to *her* family's history. Greg is Bowman through and through—blue-eyed, barrel-chested, dark rather than black-haired.

What makes this strict delineation even more pronounced is the way inherited character traits have duplicated this rigidity, though in a precisely opposite way. With respect to inherited personality, Stephen is considered *my* son. Greg is Gwen's. Greg is quiet and calm but possessed of a powerful will. Stephen is intellectual and intense, resisting what he perceives the world would have him do. Stephen is loved or enviously hated; Greg is mostly loved.

After their mother and I parted, especially while the boys were very young, I protected them from my relationships with women until I believed there was a future in the arrangement. Often several months went by before I thought it was safe for the parties to meet. Some of this caution was designed to shield them from my giddy commitment to failure. Nonetheless they came face to face with failures just the same. Esther in particular. I shouldn't have married Esther. She despised Stephen, seemed to fear his prodigious quirkiness. She favored Greg, although I think it was just because his placidness cast such a large shadow she could hide her fury inside it. Even then, he possessed this gift of peace, of tranquility. Between bouts of insane rage, she could milk my son of some of his calm. As for Stephen, so much like his father in many ways, she could sidle up to his pump and fuel still more of her endless anger.

And Carolyn? My sons were older then, wise enough by that time to see the ending for what it was: her astonishing capacity for betrayal at my most fragile moments.

I kept meandering in and out of these thoughts as the boys

THE LAST LIGHT SPOKEN

and I conversed happily on the beach. Greg's news didn't take very long. He's working. He'll be able to afford next year's tuition at Bible College. Everything is fine. Life is calm. Not long ago, Greg told me he doesn't worry. In fact he cannot remember having experienced worry at all. I tend to believe he was telling me the truth.

Stephen's stories were less a matter of news than a verbal travelogue, spiced with linguistic information. We toured his Slovenia together, sampled its contrasts in food, translated the language of life and despair into terms the Slovenes would use.

Still, as pleasant as it was, I kept slipping into the past. I couldn't help myself. Although I don't wish to escape what happened while they were growing up, I still feel compelled at times to occupy a position of self-defense. I cling to the idea that I've done my sons no lasting harm in choosing to leave them primarily in their mother's care—with regular visits from me—while I protected my sense of self. I'm a father of divorce, to some therefore hardly a father at all. Although I think my secret thoughts, wishing I'd done better than I did, this is merely a judgment perpetrated by conventional society and I no longer actively defend myself. I know, where my sons are concerned, I do not need to and I hope my example of authenticity inspires *their* authenticity. As for everyone else? Well, they can go fuck themselves.

I know this much, that I never divorced my sons. I know, for the first four years after I left their mother and—on the surface of it—seemed to leave them behind as well, that on the drive to return them home to their mother (fifty miles or so each way on the weekend designated as mine) I would ache my way along the highway after I dropped them off. I wept each mile of the MacDonald-Cartier Freeway because they no longer lived with me and I was missing out on so much. It was perhaps the most honest weeping I have ever known. There was no regret that I was crying, no wish for it to end, no fraudulent enticement for it to begin. I simply wept every other weekend for that fifty miles of time, alone with my secret loss, broken down by a brutal longing for the companionship of my sons only I know ever existed.

I never divorced my sons even when, during their mid-teens, they found fundamentalist religion. I could conceive of no argument, no theological debate to counter their zeal. My own spiritual solitude, enjoyed intermittently while I wandered along lake shorelines, through woods or into mountains, has no congregation to make it mighty in its righteousness. And my "religion" is so solitary it tolerates entirely every other religious doctrine. I felt not even the slightest compulsion to argue with them over Christian ideology. To me it's simply another kind of faith. And I've always respected faith.

Still, there was one incident six or seven years ago, and sometimes I tell it like a story, to step back from what was said.

It was one of my weekends with the boys. Probably June. I was driving them through the last few streets of their community before I'd turn into the driveway where they lived. Stephen was in the back seat. It was Greg's turn to ride in front.

"Dad?" said Stephen behind me. "You're going to hell and it really upsets me."

Just for an instant I wondered if he was teasing me. Then I remembered, during the past few months, Stephen had begun to carry his Bible everywhere. I even knew, at the moment of his remark, that it sat on the seat beside him, unopened in the darkness.

"Why am I going to hell, Stephen?"

"Because you haven't publicly acknowledged Jesus Christ as your lord and saviour."

Some sentences, originating from the mouths of babes, explode like a neutron bomb when they come in contact with the air. This was one of those statements. I noticed the ground shake, heard the concussion, saw the nuclear particles approaching, threatening me with imminent vapourization.

So I turned on the signal light. Then I turned into their mother's driveway. Then I glanced cautiously at Greg who rewarded me only with a stubborn profile gazing awkwardly through the windshield.

I decided I didn't have stomach for this now. The silence wore on, worsened after I shut off the car's engine.

"Stephen," I said at last, "we'll talk. Two weeks from now, we'll talk. Okay?"

"Okay."

Everything seemed the same that night even while it was becoming so painfully different. We performed our parting rituals. I opened the trunk and they reached in to remove their suitcases. We embraced at the rear of the car. Although everything was the same, everything was now altered. I felt far away somehow, as if, while caught in the box this moment represented, I was slipping through its molecules.

Ultimately, in fact right on schedule, Stephen and I met to have our talk. Theologically, of course, it accomplished nothing. And, after all, how could it? But we had drawn closer by the end of our conversation. God, we decided after a couple of hours of explanation—his, mine, his church's—would be left to sort out the good and the bad, and, where father and son were concerned, we would leave Him alone to make His decision.

But the incident was some time ago now and it no longer seems to matter. The definition of our respective beliefs is constructed with different materials. But the structure comes out the same, an edifice called spiritual faith.

Still I am a fallible father and, as such, dream of perfect times when I can explain myself. Perfect words of explanation and the perfect moment to spit them out. I don't want to apologize, not really, but I want to be understood. It's the most provocatively appealing fantasy I can imagine.

Inevitably, though, I accept what I have with them. I realize that I'd rather live my life than understand it all that well. Rather live it than have it understood. My history of error and failure remains back there in time, waiting to be sorted, perhaps even to be judged and sentenced. That sorting isn't my sons' role nor is it mine. And that's just fine with me.

## NICOLE

YOU SLEEP LATE, WAKING AT NEARLY NOON. You've had one of those nights when you felt tossed into a hole and crawling out of the black took almost too much effort. As you emerge from your slumber, muscles aching, skin soiled and chilled by sweat, you drag the chains of an extravagant and quietly terrifying dream behind you. You struggle through some viscous plastic barrier separating night from day. Steam seems to rise from the sheets. Everything is wrinkled and knotted—the bedding, your flesh, your focus.

The dream has already begun to break up, of course, jogging backwards into time, taking your memory of its events along with it. Relieved, you let the dream go at first because it contained a vivid and frightening garden of painted, looming faces. But when at last you feel sure that it can't come back, you let yourself remember it and wonder what it might mean.

Clowns. Gaudy, silken outfits and faces painted black and white, yellow and red. White smiles, yellowed teeth, red grimaces and orange quizzical bars in places where their mouths should have been. Runny paint at the edges of their features, dyed tears set against bleached cheeks. The clowns swayed, leaned and staggered, stumbled like movie ghouls in the throes of a death caught somewhere between malevolence and hilarity. You couldn't see yourself inside the dungeon of this dream. Instead you existed on its fringes, part of its thick stone wall, so that the dream of gaudy cloudscape lunged forward at you, wanting, it seemed, to be rid of you as much as you wished to be rid of it.

You noticed your hand, though, as it reached out to the nearest clown, the one the others pushed forward like a delegate, the one who had no eyes, the one who began to loom. You recognized your fingers, even the turquoise and silver detail of the ring your wear on your right hand. The jewellery danced as you clawed at the paint of this nearest clown, discovering that his face was rubberized so that you could easily tear it away.

It was Alan Birken beneath the mask. His eyes, now released from bondage, were familiar. His expression, as it was revealed, grew sad and kind and flushed with relief. It was clear you'd now liberated him from some burden greater than his mask, a prison you could not define. You felt the intensity of his gratitude—it was visible on his face. But at the moment of his greater release, you suddenly woke up.

You realized then you can never free him of his mask: that is not a romantic partner's job. Whatever Alan has to do, he must learn to do himself.

Still, even as you let go of the dream, you feel distressed by its memory. It remains difficult to claw yourself into wakefulness. As you lie there, you want to call your mother into the room, tell her you had a bad dream, hear one more time what she always told you as a child, that it must have been something you ate. Several minutes meander by. You remain in bed inside your tangled morning. You have to get up to turn on the coffee maker but you can't quite summon up the required motivation. You wish someone would bring you coffee just the way you like it, with a teaspoonful of sugar and just a smidgen more, with lots of two percent so that it takes on the color you prefer, rather than a tired, muddy brown.

But no one brings you coffee. Come to think of it, no one ever has. "Coffee's down," a man or two has announced from behind a Sunday newspaper on mornings in your past. "I guess I should have made coffee," still another has testified after you staggered out of your bedroom and gazed at him in a state of resigned surprise. "Coffee in bed gives me indigestion," is Alan's version of why he hasn't performed this service, as if your appetite must resemble his appetite for you to have any appetite at all.

*Whatever Alan has to do he must learn to do himself.*

At last you find the will to rise out of the stream of your sluggish daze. You count to three to rise. For a moment the sheets hold you back as fiercely as The Gordion Knot. Your right leg is tied to the mattress by a corner of the sheet locked stubbornly under your back. One full breast, looking larger this morning than ever, is free to start its day; the other is caught underneath somewhere and doesn't spill free until you liberate your leg by tugging the knots from under your back with an exhausted, audible grunt. Finally you extricate yourself from your bed, slip into your robe, chase down and snare the left hand end of the belt so that you can knot it closed. Somehow you reach the kitchen and the "on" button of the coffee maker. Then, as the phlegmy gasp of the coffee maker begins, you glance out the window and bestow admittance on the day.

It's subdued again outside. Not cloudy exactly. The sun is there—there are subtle shadows everywhere—but it comes through the haze sickly as if ashamed that its normal brilliance might be construed as vulgar. Still, when the coffee's ready, you take a mug outside to the terrace, letting Carmen dash through the door ahead of you. There you claim a seat among a quartet of empty chairs and collapse into its mesh to let yourself repair. It's muggy and warm, and you soon collect the day's clammy moisture in secret little pockets of flesh inside your robe. So you part the garment a little to release your shoulders. And you hike it up a bit to let a gentle breeze blow up your legs.

Nearly noon and you feel a ritual guilt. As you sip your coffee, you regret the dishes you didn't wash last night. You won't want to wash them this afternoon either, and it's doubtful you'll be home early enough tonight to want to do them then. Tomorrow morning perhaps, except. . . And not tomorrow afternoon which might be too nice a day to labour in the kitchen. And by tomorrow night, notwithstanding being at Matt's for dinner tonight, the dishes will have risen a little higher and stickier like some porcelain mountain range.

But the coffee has begun to work its magic. You light a cigarette from a package you don't remember bringing down to the patio with you. Life begins to hold, if not new meaning, at least the same meaning it possessed last night just before you fell asleep. Strange about the tobacco addiction, you reflect in delicate condemnation. You know you're hooked when the package of cigarettes follows you around like a puppy, when you can't even remember picking them up or carrying them to your destination, unnoticed in your hand.

You know you must be a picture, slouching the way you do in your chair, the coffee mug held in both hands in desperation, the cigarette caught between two fingers so that it juts up and out hopelessly, like a falling antenna, your naked body leaking out of a barely cinched up robe so that you can be fondled in clammy places by the breath of an obsequious June. No wonder, a moment later, when you see Matt Bowman and his sons trudging slowly along the beach, back towards his cottage, you hurriedly cover yourself. They enter the realm of your point of view, specks in the right hand corner, and they can't see you very well in the distance, if they're looking up at you at all, but you continue to cover yourself by reflex, relieved to have the time to resume a less pagan pose.

You watch them meander along this stretch of beach marked out by the rim of your coffee mug. Matt is in the middle, a son on either side. Canine Ben saunters just ahead of them, fatigued, you conjecture, by their walk around the island. It occurs to you to go inside in case they see you here and decide to come up for introductions. But you know this isn't necessary and you remain where you are. Matt will wait until dinner to let you meet his sons. Sometimes you know what he will do much more certainly than *why* you know.

Just before they pass directly in front of the cottage, although still at a distance down at the water's edge, they notice you on the terrace. Matt waves. You wave back. Canine Ben, no doubt remembering Carmen and other coffee-guzzled mornings on this terrace, veers up the hill towards you. But when Matt and his sons keep going, the dog reluctantly turns around and catches up with them.

Matt's sons are larger than you thought they'd be and you realize that unconsciously you pictured them younger, even knowing they have embarked on their early twenties. You imagine Matt younger too, or yourself older in some chronological state of parity your friendship seems to inspire.

Now that you're on the subject, Matt has brought you coffee just the way you like it in the tiny dining room of his cottage. But it's not the same thing as when someone brings it to you in bed. Of course you'd have to be lovers for that. And to be lovers, you have to have married those restless bits of your hidden, secret flesh. To have married those places, those concert halls of lust, you have to both admit you've heard a similar music, a meaningful, inquisitive and melodious overture which will leave you no longer only comrades. Then one or both of you must leap across some formidable, cautious barrier into the dark chasm of risk beyond.

The Bowmans vanish from your view. You light another cigarette. You feel a trembling in your belly, connected to your thoughts. Karen's San Andreas Fault? Or just that kind of morning filled with uneasiness, when life seems much more difficult than it is supposed to be?

THE AFTERNOON EVOLVES LIKE A WATERY CONDIMENT spread over the broken cracker of the morning. You pass the time between events reflectively, dinner at Matt's still ahead of you, the residue of the past morning still clinging to your mood. You make yourself a sandwich but leave behind the crust. You turn on the electric piano, fidget idly over the keys, then turn it off again, afraid the piece you've written about the storm earlier this month will sound hopelessly complex, empty of the simpler substance you want it to convey. You shower. You do your nails, both fingers and toes, searching for some color to paint yourself inside.

It's not that you're unhappy—you look forward to this evening, wanting it to be fun. It's that you're feeling restless, on some *verge*. Or maybe your body, now that it's recovered from such a troubled sleep, celebrates being alive with just a little too much twitchy vivaciousness.

Then Alan calls from the stag at the cottage near Haliburton, sounding froggy with last night's drink. "Hi," he says. "It's me."

"Hi. Everything all right?"

"Hung over," he replies. "All of us."

"Good stag?"

"Yeah, the usual. Jason's sick. But he's got two weeks to

recover. I imagine he'll be all right."

Hard to be relieved about the groom-to-be but you don't know Jason very well. And the fact that they're all hung over does not endear Jason or any of his friends to you. The way you feel this afternoon, this phonecall comes from Mars. It's like this island is your fortress. Alan shouldn't be able to get in unless you want him to. You know this is unreasonable but you can't help yourself.

"What about you?" he asks.

"Lazy," you reply. "I overslept, had a bad dream. I can't seem to get going."

"Oh," is all he says.

It was safe to mention the dream. He doesn't like people to tell their dreams. He says people make too much of them. You've wondered more than once if he is just afraid to look inward the way dreams seem to do.

"Are you well enough to drive?"

"Sure. The party is breaking up. We'll all be heading out as soon as we clean things up."

"Okay."

"Bobby's sailing up from Toronto for *our* party."

"Huh?"

"*Our* party. He's not driving. He's bringing up *The Rook* instead. Most of the gang will be on board with him."

Next weekend's party has become Alan's passion; it's all he talks about. Bobby Gallagher is his favorite new friend, perhaps because Bobby is his wealthiest acquaintance. *The Rook* treads that thin line between large boat and yacht, as if being considered for an imminent promotion. Bobby calls it *The Rook* because it's his floating castle, the chess piece. But the first time you heard its name you conjured up a crow, a cawing, thieving bird. One of the complaints Alan has about you is that you don't trust his taste in friends. To you it's a broad stroke of the brush. People can't like *everybody*.

"It means," Alan is saying, "that your taxi function will be simpler. I've been counting heads and most people will be coming up with Bobby. So they can sleep on the boat. I think you can pick everyone else up from the mainland in just one load."

"Okay."

"Okay? Geez, Nickie, I thought you'd be relieved."

"I am. And I can tell Matt he doesn't have to pick up any people after all. He's volunteered to help me out."

"In a rowboat?"

"It has a motor, Alan," you protest impatiently.

He grunts, disapproval without words.

"Anyway," you add, trying to be more grateful, "fewer trips back and forth to the island helps out a lot. Matt won't have to bother and one trip across the channel to get guests certainly appeals to me. And we won't have people sleeping all over the floor. I wondered how we were going to swing a whole weekend with only three beds."

"Well, that's what *I* thought."

"As long as they don't arrive too early. Bobby's boat, I mean. It won't be much fun if everyone is passed out by nine o'clock. Sometimes the party gets underway too early, you know?"

Alan lets that one go by. "Did you get the stuff on our list?"

"Not yet. I thought tomorrow or Tuesday, whichever day is cloudy."

"Maybe I should do it," he says, sounding let down.

"No. You're working. I'm not. There's no need for worrying. When you get here Friday night, just about everything will be ready. The rest we can take care of then."

"It seems like a lot for you to do," says Alan distractedly.

"Tell you what," you counter, giving in at last to feeling bristly. He's forgetting that his party is going to be held at *your* family cottage. "Would you enjoy this more if I visit Mum and Dad so you can hold the party here yourself?"

A long silence ensues.

"Sorry, Nickie," he says at the end of it.

You cannot speak.

"Nickie?"

"I'm here," you reply at last.

"Anyway, I just wanted you to know about Bobby's boat. That's the big news."

"Where's he going to moor it?"

"Close to shore."

"Warn him it's shallow. He can't come in too close."

"He knows that," moans Alan. "He has some kind of large dingy on board."

Your conversation has strayed out of rhythm. It's not the first time but you seem unable to repair the damage. It even annoys you that it feels like it's up to you to find the beat.

"Lights?"

"Whaddyuh mean? 'Lights?'"

"Does he have lights?"

"Of course he has lights. Shit, Nickie."

"If he's parked out on the lake, there's a chance some boat will crash into him. I've worked in insurance for a decade; I don't want anything bad to happen at my family cottage. Look, I guess I'm getting cranky. I think it's because you're stressing out about this party again." It crosses your mind that you are actually annoyed that Alan has invaded your island privacy even though he's not really here, bringing his urgent worries to be seen as a good host with him.

"You want me to call you tonight when you're feeling better?"

"No," you say with a determined laugh. "Thank you, but please don't call me tonight. Tomorrow night, okay? I won't be crabby then. Tonight? I'm not so sure."

"Okay. Whatever you say."

"I'm glad you had a good stag. I hope your headache feels better soon. Take some aspirin, will you?"

"Done already."

"Talk to you tomorrow night. And, Alan, drive safely, okay?"

"Will do."

And you both hang up.

Strange, you think, staring at the cell phone in your hand, that this confusing muddy day should suddenly bestow such a clear resolution on your future. But there it is. Alan is not for you. At this moment the conclusion is so clear it's not even politely surprising. It's just a matter of where and when you let him know. You moved out once before. Shouldn't the decision to break up be easier this time?

Yet, you grow nervous. And angry that he can't see for himself how intrusive and demanding he has become. And, yes, you should have gone to town yesterday and purchased at least some of the supplies on his list. You could even have picked up a bottle of wine to take to Matt's tonight. Alan has all that wine he pulled from the trunk of his car the minute Liam's Jeep disappeared over the top of the hill last weekend. Like it had to be hidden from Karen and Liam. Like it couldn't have been replaced if the four of you sunk so low as to drink a bottle extra. Like next Saturday's party is his while Karen and Liam are yours, and the wine that flows between would be tainted if it mixed.

You stomp into the kitchen and—by Alan's petulant neck—grab a bottle of his red. Then you strut back into the dining room and set it trophy style, happily strangled in effigy, in the middle of the table. So you don't forget to take it with you when you walk down to Matt's cottage a few hours from now in the better mood that you hope is perching on your horizon.

*As for you, Matt Bowman,* you decide an instant later, *how come you won't give me an opinion when I thought you were my friend?* Which sends you down another path in the sanctuary of your private ambivalence. It occurs to you now that sometimes Matt's friendship tends to be incomplete where larger issues are concerned. Yes, there's the comfort in the companionship, the ease with which you talk, the way you volley your opinions easily back and forth. It's close. It's buddy like. Until you begin to ruminate on the decision you must make about moving to Kingston to work with Karen. Or until you confide in him about some of your reservations about Alan. These subjects tend to make him reserved. He resorts to listening well, barely making a comment. You want to ask him why but you know what he'll say—he doesn't feel comfortable intruding. The best that he can come up with is the admission that if he was to meet Alan now, knowing you as well as he does, he'd have noticed some points of incompatibility between you. Even mentioning this the other day inspired him to apologize for his observation.

Couldn't he see what you really wanted? Some support for your legitimate doubts? What's he afraid of anyway?

Karen's at fault too, you reflect. Good old Karen, pointing out the way she did that Matt is attractive, snorting contemptuously when you said his attractiveness is irrelevant to you. Karen's fault that she got you to notice, gave you the liberty, implied encouragement. Ever so gently too, like Cupid with rubber-tipped arrows. And, shit, it's true that he's attractive. He's tall and lean and so like Crazy Horse, and his face draws you into a place that's warm and pleasant. He takes your love for this island and places himself inside it until he seems to be everywhere.

You walk outside and gaze at the lake from the edge of the terrace. Alan, Karen, Matt. Dreams about clowns, thoughts about Cupids and medicine men. You weep a moment or two, overwhelmed by what you've been thinking. You didn't want to cry—the anguish just didn't seem worth it. But afterwards you feel cleansed. In the end weeping just feels good.

"DAD'S ALWAYS BEEN THE COOK," Matt's son Stephen tells you that evening while, nearby, his father nurses dinner.

"Really?" you reply.

Matt has already mentioned during some earlier conversation that none of the past women in his life enjoyed cooking very much. You felt a gentle glee at your advantage over them, ignoring the temptation to wonder why.

"Greg and I used to laugh when we talked about it with friends. Kind of hard to admit that your dad cooks better than your mum."

Greg laughs, encouraging his brother.

"Your friends are pretty conservative," you say. "Don't you think so?"

"Maybe," Stephen replies. "Traditional anyway." It's apparent, having said this, that he is proud of the fact and of his own traditional leanings.

"I like to cook too," you mention as an afterthought.

Matt glances up from what he is doing in the kitchen, grins at you where you sit at the dining room table.

The table is already set, although he hurried to put out three wineglasses—Greg doesn't drink—when you showed up with your bottle of red, one of Alan's favorites. Matt's stack of papers and his computer are now piled neatly by the cottage's second door, underneath one of his uncle's eccentric wooden signs. This one consists of a piece of string dangling from a tack. "String stiff, it's cold outside," it says among several other meteorological observations.

It's easy here in Matt's cottage. His sons are big and comfortable too, even the philosophical one, the zealot Matt has said often likes to think too much. The ambiance is naturally homey. Matt prepares a meal without that jittery panic you feel when you cook for guests (an insidious trepidation you inherited from your mother).

Greg sits in a corner, hardly saying a word except to respond to one of your questions that usually begins, "Greg, your father tells me . . ." But his reserve isn't the kind that makes you nervous. He isn't a gap to be filled. No, he's mostly a tranquil corner on the other side of the room.

Matt seems to know his sons well. He said that Greg exudes tranquility, that Stephen is more intense. Now you can see this for yourself. How did Matt put it? Colorfully, as usual. Stephen, he said, runs square dances like a professional caller just to see his ideas do-si-do around the dance hall floor. And Greg? Matt said he exudes that sleepy uncle feeling that everything'll be all right. Matt also mentioned that his sons are *Gentlemen's Quarterly*, preppy, fashionable, conservative. Greg certainly is. But Stephen not so much so. In fact, give him the right do-dads, chokers and bandannas, longer hair, a mandala on a necklace and he'd become his father, another medicine man.

When you first arrived at *The Crow's Nest*, as Matt made formal introductions, you wondered how he'd defined you to his sons beforehand. A friend? A neighbor? An attractive woman? And did whatever he said match what they were seeing now? If not, what did they see instead? Did he explain you in some way that diminished your friendship? What did he tell them beyond what you've learned they know about—the dinner with your parents, the morning coffee klatch, the instant comradeship between your respective dogs?

Somehow, even amidst so much hospitality, you feel strangely disappointed. Something's diminished the caring existing between you and Matt. *If* it exists between you the way you think it might. Strange, a week ago, you would have been annoyed with yourself for pondering questions like these. But tonight—combined with a friendly glance into the kitchen again at Crazy Horse the cook, liking his face, his wink, his smile—your self-ruminations make sense. You sense you've begun to care for him as someone you could one day love. Well, maybe anyway.

Matt assumes a facilitator's function as you get to know his sons, dropping conversational pucks onto the ice to keep the three of you scrimmaging. By the time he serves dinner you've discussed all the appropriate subjects: the walk around the island, the goodbyes that took place this morning because the cottage is going to be sold, Stephen's life in Slovenia, Greg's plans to be a pastor, your own memories of cottage life here on the island, even some of the funnier moments in the friendship between Canine Ben and Carmen.

Stephen is impressed that you compose music. You want to pass it off as less than it really is but Matt embarks on a brief tirade about creativity, the art which results and the apathy he detects in society's definition of what in their world should be construed as quality. Even here his view is politically motivated and becomes an opportunity for him to pick on what he believes is an antagonistic status quo.

Seeming to agree with him, Stephen mentions that cynicism is the byproduct of a godless world.

A silence results. Stephen's point seems such a broad stroke of the brush, there's a hushed embarrassment afterwards, until the conversation retreats again to chitchat—boats (and your high speed reputation), motorcycles and the trouble with hamburgers in Slovenia.

Accolades for Matt's dinner.

"Dad, this is delicious," says Greg, large and calm and solid, a young man who loves his food.

"Great, Dad," says Stephen.

"Wonderful," you chime in.

He serves strawberry soup as an appetizer, chilled, refreshing. This he follows with a curried chicken dish packed with vegetables and nuts, accompanied by a toasted pita he's browned in a frying pan. The rice, you have to admit, is as perfect as any you've ever had. There's fruit sherbet for dessert to cut through the aftertaste of the curry.

You eat more than you normally do. No wonder he did the cooking all those years he didn't live alone. You give in to a brazen notion as tasty as the food: Matt cooks sensuously, his food tastes like lazy sex. Just your little secret considered here alone among so many unknowing men.

"Dad bakes too," Stephen is telling you now. "Pies, cakes."

He tells the story of a culinary tragedy, a family favorite apparently, about the day he turned twelve and his father baked

Grills

a chocolate mocha cake to celebrate the occasion. Called away while he was assembling it at the kitchen counter, he forgot to move it out of reach of their Irish setter Susy.

Matt takes over the story. "Susy was such a bandit. Anyway, when I got back to the kitchen to ice the cake, the cake and its filling were gone."

"The whole cake?"

"Three layers," he replies. "I was furious and I told her off, put her outside. But she was higher than a kite with all that chocolate, sugar and coffee. Her feelings were so hurt, she raced down the driveway and stood on the white line of the highway outside our house. Just stood there. Suicide attempt, I guess. Fortunately it was just a county road. But I had to go and rescue her."

Even Greg adds an epilogue. "Esther was so mad she wanted to take her to the pound."

"Huh," adds Stephen then. "Esther was always mad. It's a wonder we all weren't sent to the pound."

Over coffee and tea (Matt's sons spurn coffee), some terrible jokes are told. Then, as the groaning subsides, you notice twilight has arrived.

"Perhaps we should do the dishes," you suggest.

"Nah," says Matt. "We'll look after them later, the guys and me. Actually, if it's not too late, we were wondering if you play cards. Stephen has a game called Rook. He was hoping we could play."

You smile, thinking of Bobby Gallagher's boat. Floating castles, crows and cards. "I'll play a few hands," you say.

Although you're not a devotee of cards, you enjoy the evening very much. Matt's sons draw you quickly inside the game's rites of comradeship. Gentle insults fly. Remarks ricochet around the table. Even Greg is less reserved. Laughter is spontaneous and frequent. You toss a few barbs of your own, easily caught up in the spirit of the game. But soon, before you know it, it's nearly eleven-thirty.

"I should get going," you say.

"It's gotten to be that time," Matt admits.

Shortly, after you've expressed your thank-yous to Greg and Stephen, you leash Carmen and take her to the door. Matt reaches for his lantern and the long matches he uses to light it.

162

"Would you like me to walk you home?" he asks.

It comes out of his mouth more formally than he intended and it makes you want to laugh. "Okay. No point in me stumbling around in the dark."

Indeed, the night has thickened greatly. Its humidity has intensified, can be felt along your skin. Matt pumps the lantern, lights it, holds its whoosh about shoulder height.

"Can we go by way of the beach?" you ask. "Do you mind? It's such a beautiful night." This is an imposition—it's a much shorter route along the ridge from one cottage to the other.

"Why not?" says Matt with a smile.

You angle your way to the beach, Carmen at the end of the leash in your right hand, Matt on your left. He holds the lantern aloft in his left hand where it casts a brilliant glow. He slides his right hand into his pocket. Noticing this, you wonder what it would do to your friendship if he ever took your hand and held it for a while. So you say something, anything, to keep from wondering why he doesn't or whether or not he's considered doing so himself.

"I enjoyed myself," you say.

"All of us did," he replies.

"Your boys, what can I say?"

"They liked you a lot, Nickie."

"I'm glad."

"Stephen and Greg seem comfortable with the notion that you have a female friend."

"That's true, I guess."

"I suppose they're used to it," you add, hoping the remark wasn't as transparent as it sounded.

"I wouldn't say so," Matt replies. "Now that I think about it, I haven't had many female friends. You're one of the first."

"Really? You've never mentioned it, Matt."

"Didn't think of it, I guess."

On you trudge with him, your feet whispering over the sand, happily accompanied by your ticking mind. Moving as a unit, you imagine the two of you looking like a trolling vessel crossing this ocean of beach, Matt, you, Carmen, even the hissing lantern shining from your mast.

"How come?" you ask him then. "How come no female friends?"

He considers your question in silence. "You mean a female friend like a male friend. Platonic. Right?"

"Of course."

He goes silent again.

"So how come, Matt?"

"Well, I guess because something always happens."

*Something always happens.* Like what, Matt? you want to ask. But you don't, you can't, you won't. "I see," you say instead. "That's the way it goes sometimes."

"Yup."

And you continue on in silence.

Then, with almost spiteful haste, your cottage appears in front of you, lurching out of the gloom. You climb the last few yards of hill, sad to be nearly home.

"What about the rest of the weekend?" you ask. "You and the guys, how was it?"

"I enjoyed it," he replies. "We usually do. It was a little sad this morning for all of us, but even that, well, I guess we shared it as best we could."

"Saying goodbye to the island?"

"Yeah, the last tour of the sights. For some strange reason, it felt like my fault."

"Why do you say that?"

"I don't know. Economic failures, I guess. It just felt that way, like I was letting them down somehow."

"Oh, Matt," you say, wondering if you should give him the hug he deserves at this moment.

But you don't. It wouldn't work at all, too much room for misunderstanding. And rooms inside those rooms, and closets after that. So much emotional housecleaning, so vast a mansion to get to know.

When you gain your door, he stands there on the stoop, holding his silly lantern while you press down on the latch. In this light, with the gray in his beard, he suddenly looks old and sage, as if twenty years ago he got away from you, that even then it was too late. But it could be the artificial light, just more trickery after dark.

But you want to hurry inside to be alone with yourself. You want to explore on your own a new urge of restlessness. So you thank him for walking you home. And for dinner too, of course.

"I'm glad you could come, Nickie. It meant a lot to me to have you meet Stephen and Greg."

"Ah," is all you say as you lean forward to kiss him gently on the cheek.

Conventially, the kiss is technically perfect. Whether it accurately reflects your feelings—flawed, foolish, perverted little charlatans who won't quite come out and say who they really are—is another matter.

"Goodnight," says Matt, turning away.

"Goodnight," you answer back.

As he and his lantern bob deeper into the darkness, it occurs to you, watching them, that many situations in life never get to happen. Not here, not somewhere else, not anywhere. As a tragic incompletion, this truth is very sad. You feel it around you and out there in the distance, lying heavily on the night.

## NICOLE

FROM THE VERY BEGINNING OF THE WEEKEND of Alan's party—it is, by now, on the eve of the event, *his* party, can never be yours and his together—you note sign after weary sign of approaching apocalypse. Everything around you becomes fragile, slips out of kilter. Everywhere you turn, seemingly innocuous clues combine to announce some kind of impending disaster. As this catastrophe collects its mysterious parts together, component by component, you become more and more anxious, a process accelerated by your lonely awareness of what is happening. If only there was someone to share this knowledge with you, to verify it, more importantly to free you of your unwitting collusion in whatever the disaster is—namely your continued ambivalence about what to do about Alan and how he does or does not fit into your future plans with Karen in Kingston. Yes, this latter need most of all. If the choice you must make wasn't so convoluted, then perhaps you wouldn't feel such an accomplice to the debacle that seems to lie ahead.

The signs are everywhere that Alan's party may go wrong. At this moment, for instance, as you pilot your way across the channel towards *The Inlet* where you have arranged to meet Alan, the boat seems unusually sluggish in the choppy water. Although still blue in the waning afternoon light, the lake appears to gradually turn black, thickening into a molasses of heavy dread.

166

You tell yourself all of this foreshadowing is foolish. Your mind doesn't want to accept it. You are, after all, a sensible woman, even when you struggle inside yourself over what is real and what is likely only imagination. But your feelings all day long, building the framework of your mood, have tended to believe in signs and clues. They read then constantly review everything you've seen or sensed.

Even this morning down on the beach with Matt and your frolicking dogs, you noticed subtle indicators that the world now tilted strangely. Matt apparently couldn't see it. This private vision was, you now believe, a severe moment of the predatory whim of solitude.

You remarked on the shape of the clouds, superficially white and harmless against the blue sky, the same way they have presented themselves on so many other island mornings. But, "See how jagged they look?" you said. "Like their points are being sharpened."

He gazed at them a moment, then glanced at you in surprise. "I don't know," was all he said.

As usual there was a large convention of gulls meeting just down the beach from you. This time they stood perfectly still, as if carved out of wood, unwilling to interrupt their ethereal motionlessness to strut along the water's edge they way they usually do, harping at one another in head-cocked, open-beaked ill humour to protect their small slice of territory.

Matt seemed different this morning too, disrobed in some way of his usual magic. Some of the traits which make him Matt appeared imprisoned behind glass where they could not be touched. At least this was how it seemed. You wondered momentarily if it was you who'd moved behind the glass, perhaps because of your secret knowledge that something unpleasant was on the way.

"You know that dress is casual tomorrow night?" you mentioned at some point, trying to resume reality through some kind of harmless inconsequence.

He glanced at you a moment, then quickly looked away. "Casual is all I own," he said.

You felt you were trespassing on some past argument with another woman you would never know. "Oh, Matt . . . ," you began to stammer.

"I know," he murmured with a conciliatory nod as your voice trailed off in confusion.

Standing there alone, you interpreted yet another omen in this brief and unsatisfactory exchange. Omen seemed the only way to explain being on the verge of a lover's quarrel with a man who is your friend, not your lover.

Eventually he asked you up to *The Crow's Nest* for coffee, though.

But you declined. "Matt, I've got so much housework to do."

"Is there something I can help you with?"

"No," you said. "But thanks."

After this exchange there was little more than silence. And of course the motionless seagulls and the innocent but jagged clouds you imagined arming themselves with barbs. Your setting there on the beach was so still and threatening, you wanted to crawl inside Matt's pocket to be safe from future doubt, from noticing so much turbulence in what should have been a state of calm.

"Matt," you said at last, just before you parted. "The people tomorrow night..."

"... No problem," he said with a smile. "I know you'll look after me."

At his remark, you returned to normal, gently patting him on the arm. "And I *will* too," you said, smiling to make it so.

But the tranquility didn't last. Hardly a moment later, the uneasiness in your mood came over you again, that sense of apocalyptic vision you couldn't quite define.

Later that afternoon, after you'd cleaned up the cottage within an inch of its life, frequently cursing Alan while you were at it, despising his party and his friends, you went outside to the terrace to drink a glass of lemonade and smoke a cigarette. There the southern sky displayed several purplish hues the like of which you'd never seen. You thought you could see colorful particles pulsating against the sky's fabric, purple atoms so vivid in their restlessness their dance seemed a preliminary ceremony to some state of maniacal savagery.

Typically your mind tried again to leash your soul, one of its daylight functions. But the struggle became so fierce you felt like a battleground. Until your mind gave in with a ritually smarmy and oft-used diagnosis: "I'm having a nervous breakdown." But of course a breakdown wasn't likely, you made yourself decide. You tried to laugh at the idea but the bravado only felt false. Even your laugh seemed an ill-omen, sounding like broken glass as it reached your ears.

So all of these things are fresh in your mind as at last you reach *The Inlet.* There you tie up the boat and pay the attendant your docking fee. By the time she is returning with your change, Alan has climbed out of his car where he has been waiting for you. Now he approaches you on the dock, drily kissing your lips and asking you if you brought his list.

"Of course," you snap, resenting him for being so officious and preoccupied by the party.

The dock attendant gives you some coins. You give her a tip. "Have a nice night," she chirps, then, aware of the prickly posture you and Alan have assumed, wisely retreats.

"I thought we'd go out for a quick burger," Alan says, "then get to the grocery store."

"Whatever you need," you say.

"Are you okay?" he asks now that he must acknowledge something bleak in the sound of your voice.

"I'm tired. The cottage—I spent the day cleaning it."

"Shit, Nickie, why didn't you wait until tomorrow when I could have helped?"

This does not deserve a reply. Heifer dust grows up to be bullshit no matter who spreads it around. In all the time you've known Alan, you've never seen him dust or vaccuum, even during that brief time you lived together.

"Nickie?"

"I'm hungry," you complain. "We should get that burger you mentioned."

"Okay," mutters Alan, zipping it, knowing, this time at least, it is time to stop talking.

Although you've tied your boat securely, you turn and glance at it again. No reason, perhaps only out of habit. But the instant you turn, lightning flashes in the distance from within the pulsating, purple sky on the other side of the island. You hesitate a moment, waiting to see it repeat itself, but it does not flash again.

"You ready?" Alan asks behind you.

"I'm ready," you reply, turning your back on the torn seam

of the sky where you imagine catastrophe is being let out on probation.

WHILE SPENDING THE EVENING WITH ALAN you have less time for signs and portents. Alan is a bundle of nerves over his party and this defines the time you spend running errands in town. You dislike him for it and recognize the feeling from other occasions in the past. You feel comforted by this familiarity, regard it as evidence of your incongruity as a couple, a notion to which you cling like you would a storm-tossed raft. For one thing, he picks out a burger drive-through not far from the A & P. It offers only one picnic table at which a family of six have pitched their hungry tent. You are too weary to quibble about the fact you're going to have to eat in the car, that the parking lot is paved with dust. You would not have minded when you were younger, five years ago perhaps, or maybe in a state of forgiveness inspired by love or lust with someone similarly inclined. But here, with Alan, caught up in his commitment to haste and preparation for his party, you feel trapped inside the experience, in the wrong place with the wrong person, with the wrong next few days ahead of you.

As you wait at the drive-through window, ordering your food, you endure another one of those occasions when you can no longer remember what it as about him that brought you together in the first place. He wears white shorts and a white t-shirt, white sneakers without socks. The ass of his shorts is a little stained from some grime he sat on earlier in the day. You realize clearly, if not for the party tomorrow night, you'd break off the relationship tonight, simply to be done with it, to never go through anything with him like this again.

The food is okay. You eat it without spilling anything into your lap. Small comfort with all the misery lying ahead, which begins in the grocery store. In the produce section he fondles every cucumber, examines every head of lettuce, squeezes each tomato. You stand leaning on a shopping cart in a zone just far enough removed that passing shoppers cannot be sure if you belong with him or not. His passionate concern over his friends' gastronomic preferences makes him inordinately fussy about his purchases. It contrasts sharply with the haphazard approach he took to dinner when dinner was just with you. At the meat counter he's even worse. He sorts through bacon and steaks, chops and ground meat, ribs and chicken pieces, then tosses them bitterly aside.

"Don't they have those buttons here where you can buzz the meat department?" He addresses this question more to himself than the audience you represent. Nor does he glance at you in search of a reply. It would seem nothing can interrupt his frantic search for buttons to push with his thumb.

You cling wearily to the shopping cart. If you move to Kingston to work with Karen, is it likely you will miss this man? At this moment, it doesn't seem so.

"I should have done this part in Toronto," he says. "It's less expensive and there's a much wider selection."

Annoyed with this smug and not entirely accurate judgment, you grow annoyed with Toronto too. With the way it sometimes appoints itself the center of a shrivelling universe. Your resentment feels warm but this could be merely contrast as you stand in the deep chill of the store's merciless air conditioning.

Eventually, though, the ordeal withers to an end. You return to the boat, stock it with your purchases, then charge south across the channel. It's nearly dark now, except in the western skies. Ahead of you, just above the boat's windshield, you catch glimpses of frequent sheet lightning. Or is it the flash of murderous artillery in some battle beyond the horizon?

You decide to go to bed with a book shortly after returning to the cottage. Alan wants to consult with you on the menu, but you smoothly sidestep his invitation. "Tomorrow is soon enough, Alan. I think it can wait."

"I suppose," he murmurs back.

"I'm heading to bed," you tell him. "I've really done enough for one day."

In astonishment he glances at the groceries that have yet to be put away. But all you can think about instead of helping him is that he's going to sleep in your bed tonight, taking his place there for granted, expecting accommodation because it's existed there before. Yes, eventually he'll come into your bedroom, take off and fold his clothes, then climb naked under the sheets. He'll want to feel you up, more tomatoes to be squeezed, more melons to be fondled. God! No wonder you intend to be asleep by the time he comes to bed.

You read for a few minutes, although not calmly or with any concentration. Instead, most of your attention monitors the sounds in the rest of the cottage as Alan puts groceries away. By the time you hear him make coffee for the morning, your chest feels tight and anxious. You put your book aside. When you hear the toilet flush and know he is on his way, you turn off your reading light, roll over onto your side and embark on a rhythmic breathing that can pass itself off as sleep.

SOMETIME DURING THE NIGHT the clouds have rolled in and bunched up like sheep in a pen. When you awake and slip out of bed in the morning, they're still there, hovering and restless, now transformed from sheep into a group of waiting movie extras filling time on a Hollywood set. Alan has already risen and you're relieved he is gone. You know the disappointing skies will have angered him. "It had better be sunny Saturday," he warned the elements at large several times last night. Alan often threatens the weather like he would a misbehaving child.

After you pour your first cup of coffee, you notice him standing down on the beach. He gazes this way and that, up at the sky and down. Nonetheless, he divines the information that you are out of bed, the way—in your mind—a bully determines with malevolent precognition which route his victim takes home from school. He starts up the hill towards the cottage and you venture outside to meet him. You're generally eager to be outside with nature, no matter how imperfect it might be, yet you expect to come face to face with his agitation that the skies have let him down.

But he's much more cheerful than you expected. "There's a large patch of blue in the southeast," he reports. "I think it's going to be a nice day."

"That's good," you remark, relieved.

"No sign of *The Rook.*"

"Thank God," you say, trying to keep the day on an optimistic track. "We've still got all the cooking to do."

Distractedly he nods. "You sure fell asleep fast last night."

"I was exhausted," you reply.

He nods. "Well, the cottage looks good," he says.

"Thanks."

You feel a nervous safety in your lie about being asleep. It contains some of the same dangerous freedom a much more provocative infidelity would have achieved. In truth, Alan went to sleep last night long before you did. He even reached his state of trouble-mumbling while you were still awake. While he talked things over with his dreams, you lay in the darkness nearby, recalling your day of signs and portents (none so far this morning), then turned your thoughts to Matt, the party, Alan, back to Matt and a couple of variations entitled "what would Karen say?" Mostly Matt was on your mind. Relief that he would be at the party. You recalled you said you'd look after him but you realized at least some of the time he would be looking after *you*. You wondered if he was asleep while you were lying in bed awake. You remembered last night your exchange about casual dress. And you decided, yes indeed, it was a lover's disagreement, although Matt is not your lover. Disturbing at the time, that realization became a pleasant memory, an omen of a different kind, of approaching intimacy. Comfortably close to argument, it seemed comfortably close to love.

And what are you feeling, Matt?, you wondered last night. No answers were forthcoming, although you spent a great deal of time giving it consideration. You retraced the paths you've travelled upon, the dozens of times you've spent together, like a detective seeking clues at the various scenes of the crime. Now, remembering last night's sanguine solitude, you acknowledge Matt's ability to be mysterious. If he cares for you romantically, he keeps the feeling leashed. He's like the *Starship Enterprise*: his shields are up and holding.

"So when do you want to get started?"

"Huh?"

"Cooking, preparing the food."

Alan. He's been standing there beside you, sandalled on the patio stones, and, briefly startled by this, you pretend to be shrewdly contemplative to recover from your surprise.

"Soon," you say. "I've been thinking about that. But this is my first coffee. I need a cigarette."

For the moment, Alan only frowns. Then, "Maybe I'll go up and get the stuff out—you know—get it organized."

"Okay," you say cheerfully. "I'll be along."

After he's gone, your forced good nature evaporates.

Fretfully you glance towards the western edge of the lake, anticipating that any moment Bobby Gallagher's boat will invade your island outpost. It isn't there, of course, and you feel a profound relief. The thing about you and Alan's friends is that you've never drawn close to them. Now you feel more distant than ever. You haven't seen these people in months. Not only do they seem more alien, but you're a different person yourself from the one you were trying to be back then when you had more faith in a future with Alan.

Certainly you've never been comfortable with any of the men. They are politically correct with you and with their own wives or girlfriends but you've never found this consideration very sincere. You remember again that day the spring before last, when all of you gathered at Bobby Gallagher's Avenue Road home. Alan and Bobby, Greg Hinton and Derek Connors all sat on the deck at the back of the house, cold beers clutched in their hands. As you came around the corner, it was just in time to hear Derek say, "I love summer. I love to go downtown to watch the titties bounce." No wonder, as you suddenly appeared, unexpectedly, you stepped into oncoming laughter that swerved to a sudden halt.

No one apologized, not sure whether or not you'd heard. No one weighed the percentages of solidarity against the possibility that you felt victimized. But you kept right on walking, ashamed of these men and angry, not letting them know one way or the other whether they'd been caught being fools or not.

Derek has not sinned again since then. Yet each time you see him, you remember the incident clearly, so much so that it's the first thing you think about. Nor has he forgotten it either, although he pretends it never happened. Both of you arrange stubbornly never to be alone together, even for a moment. No doubt he doesn't want to learn that you heard what he said that day. And you don't want him to stop wondering, because the wondering is his punishment.

And the women? You like only the ebony-eyed Rachel who puts you in mind of Karen. She's bright, cutting and funny, the one you wished you'd been walking beside when Derek Connors made his stupid remark. Rachel's ensuing reaction would have strafed the entire group. You would have felt emboldened, able to reveal your scorn. Together you would have taken no prisoners, cared not a whit about collateral damage. But the others? Susan Gallagher, Linda and Em and Judy, the women connected to Alan Birken's group? You've never wanted to know them. They remind you of a grainy portrait of a listless women's auxiliary, a photograph best left in an attic trunk with the rest of some bygone age.

Today all of these opinions feel much worse. Your separateness runs too deep. When you all gather to celebrate summer tonight, you'll not only wonder who these people are and what they have to do with you, you'll wonder who they were back then—and who you were as well—when you thought you might relate. It's going to make for a long night with them, so locked in the past while you need everything to be new.

*THE ROOK* DOESN'T ARRIVE UNTIL SEVEN and by then you're ready to receive your guests. You and Alan have quietly exhausted your long list of preparations. The food has been prepared; the fridge is stocked with beer. Snacks and veggies with dip have been placed in strategic locations around the cottage. Appetizers are arranged on a table outside on the terrace, covered with napkins to keep the insects away.

While the best you can achieve is a bland neutrality that the evening has now begun, Alan gushes with relief when the large craft comes into view. You realize he has feared fresh water versions of collisions at sea, tidal waves and typhoons, angry reefs and the desolation he would feel if his friends had stood him up.

With the arrival of *The Rook,* the party moves inexorably closer, a looming tyrant camped on the borders of your preference for solitude. As something vital in your mood deflates, you realize you've been hoping all along that the party would fall through. Short of a dull regret that, yes, you agreed to perform the function of hostess, you retreat to a state of benumbed detachment somewhat like the final moment of acceptance before execution by firing squad. It seems inconceivable now that you once cared about Alan's party which has preoccupied him for weeks. Somehow, during this period of his rising anticipation and anxiety, you've become keenly aware of how far apart you've grown. Alan and his friends exist in a distant place from you. You don't want to care about them any longer.

You go back inside the cottage as *The Rook* drops anchor some distance from shore. Glancing at your watch, you realize there's still nearly an hour to go before you must travel to *The Inlet* to pick up the handful of guests who'll be arriving there by car. Staying behind inside the cottage, you can keep your distance, especially from Alan who hurries down to the water's edge to stand on the beach like a tragic mistress, forlorn and foolishly hopeful.

You watch all this wistfulness from a window, an audience of one. Alan's friends, from various vantage points on Bobby Gallagher's boat, wave at him with hands holding drinks and fluttering handkerchiefs. The antics are absurdly melodramatic, a scene from a B movie. It's worse because you're becoming aware that after tonight's party and its long tomorrow aftermath, you might never see these people again. If you sever yourself from Alan—and you've been avoiding the decision that you might—you'll be dismembered from his friends. You feel no regret in this, only an empty resignation that you must pass the several hours ahead in a convincing performance of hostess so realistically rendered not even Alan will suspect it is disingenuous.

You wander down to the beach when Bobby Gallagher's dinghy deposits the first group of guests on the shore. You're relieved that you'll get to leave early on your brief journey across the channel in case the other guests arrive there earlier than expected. But just before you go, you take part in the expected greetings on the shore—the kissed cheeks, the stiff hugs, the empty exclamations of comradeship.

"Good trip from Toronto?"

And then the insular anecdotes about the cruise to this island with meaning only for the participants.

Shortly you move towards your boat, explaining to all where you are going, that Alan is their host. Then you maneuver your boat into the lake with the help of a couple of the men, hurriedly reach full throttle and gratefully travel around the point of the island, satisfied to be alone again. Except for a brief glance at Matt's tiny cottage, you don't consider looking back. The crossing to the mainland is briefly euphoric. By noon the skies cleared and now evening is going down blue and crisp. Alan's bullying of the weather somehow worked for him. But the evening is so pleasant, the solitude of this crossing so comforting, you're preoccupied by a crazy yearning to fill the tank with gasoline and depart for parts unknown. Maybe Matt would go with you because he understands such yearnings to be gone and has talked about them a number of times. Still, you'd never do such a thing; you are a sensible woman. But the feeling that you could run away, that you might, is briefly exhilarating.

*The Inlet* is busy and you remember Monday is Canada Day. Still, you manage to find space at the docks among a hubbub of cruising boats. You tie up, pay yet another docking fee, then sit down again to wait. You smoke a cigarette, gradually growing perplexed by the delay, because Matt may show up at your cottage before you have returned, alone among the lions. And, a little closer to the bone of the truth, it has become important to you to be the one who sees him first. You feel uncomfortable realizing this—is it wrong to be attracted to a new man before you've let the other one go?

At last the two couples arrive. Rachel (who is a little like Karen), Gabe (her bespectacled accountant husband), and a couple you've never met before. The new man is dark and cheaply handsome. He looks like a salesman. He's introduced as Kevin but you want to change his name, call him Herb or Larry or Al. His girlfriend (she wears no ring to define their relationship) is tiny and shapely, blonde with round green eyes. She has a permanently startled look, like her flesh was lacquered at birth. Her name is Julie.

You return to the island slowly; there are hairdos to respect. And Rachel is filled with questions about the history of the island, how long you've had a cottage here, isn't it wonderful and the isolation would be marvelous. So you perform your travelogue over the drone of the outboard motor. Then conversation turns to the party. Yes, everyone has arrived. Yes, it's going to be a wonderful weekend. The party, the island, the summer. You sound like a professional emcee at a very amateur event.

In the end you feel dazed. You sense that you're looking down at yourself from some perch of tired knowledge, watching someone who looks like you performing in your stead. It's bad but a little good that part of you has managed to escape and is safe from the rest of the night.

Strangely enough, when Matt arrives, you've gone to the bathroom and are not present to greet him first. By the time you emerge, he's made his way to the kitchen himself to dig a beer out of the refrigerator. You find him standing alone at the edge of the living room.

"Matt!" you say. "I missed you getting here."

He grins. "Did you think I wasn't coming?"

You do not answer him. You are so glad to see his face. He wears a white sports shirt, a black and white bandanna and an already perfect tan. Choker, medicine pouch, bracelets. He has come as Crazy Horse. And you are frankly relieved. It makes him your accomplice in this crime of separation from everyone else at the party. You almost embrace. Nearly. But at the last minute one or both of your decides perhaps you shouldn't. It makes for an awkward nearly. You stand leaning towards one another, tilting, nearly touching. You see yourself standing in the center of the storm of some manifest temptation. Jesus, you finally ask yourself, am I in love with you? But you don't want to answer yourself; it's enough to know it's a question rarely asked if the answer can never be yes.

"Have you met everyone yet?" you ask.

"Actually no. Saw Alan as I passed the patio and he directed me here to the refreshments. That's it."

"Well, when you're ready, I'll introduce you around. I want you to feel at home." Your words sound funny and formal to you, as if they arrive out of some missionary mist.

Later it's confirmed how he doesn't fit in, the way Alan said he wouldn't. He stands outside the preppy youth of Alan and his friends, the *someone else* who cannot stop being Crazy Horse. He's like the piece of grit among the sugar cubes—after they dissolve, he remains behind unchanged. The others no doubt construe this difference to be his fault, but to you it's not something to blame: it's something to burrow inside. The others leave him alone for the most part because they possess a history together, a charter, a code of expected behaviour and opinion, the components of which combine to define their exclusive club. To most of the women, he's an oddity; to a few—Rachel and Susan Gallagher for instance—he's a somewhat appealing one.

By the time the party has assumed full stride, you've been asked a couple of times how you came to be friends with "such an unusual man."

The men don't let him inside the sanctity of their bond. It's as if they've taken some cue from Alan. Matt is the other side of some battle that the party has briefly interrupted. Nor is Matt all that respectful of the club's sensibilities. It matters not at all that he's outnumbered by the political enemy's camp. As you pass within earshot of conversations involving Matt, the words drift out around him, insult wannabes, arguments on the verge.

"Oligopoly," you hear Matt say at one point. Or, "That's just bashing the poor."

Still later, Bobby Gallagher points out somewhat heatedly that *he* himself is a realist. "You," he says to Matt, "are an idealist." He pronounces the word "idealist" like it's an advanced case of the clap.

"Huh," snorts Matt in reply. "Being a realist is just a euphemism for ethical compromise."

As for you, you continue to spend most of your time functioning as your own shadow. One part of you attends the party, mingling, smiling and chatting, while the other is somewhere else, still gazing down at the antics of your dutiful twin. The party begins to shimmer: loud conversation, loud music, laughter and suggestive jokes, all of it otherwordly and frantic. Like walking through gooey cobwebs or feeling the trickle of your own sweat inside a plaster cast. There's one period of marvelous clarity, though. You come out of the cottage onto the terrace at one point, surprised by the night's deep chill. Gradually your party guests have been moving indoors. The terrace now retains only the most stubborn. One oblivious dancing couple—Kevin the salesman and Julie of the lacquered astonishment—glides tremulously to the strains of an insipid ballad you have never cared for. Bobby Gallagher and Derek Connors chat a few yards away. And then there's Matt standing off by himself at the patio wall, gazing in the direction of the beach. You see what he sees, that moonlight has begun to delicately ice the lake.

You walk towards him, then help him look out over the lake, standing there with him in silence.

"Are you all right?" you ask him shortly.

"Sure. How about you?"

"I guess the party's moving indoors."

"Yes. It's gotten cool."

"But what a moon," you say.

He turns. "Would you like to dance?"

"I'd love to," you reply.

As you slip into his arms, you notice the terrace is now empty. He delicately guides you over the cracks between the patio stones. You don't recognize the music in the background but the music doesn't matter. You dance to it in silence. This is Matt's island and your island too. You've laughed here and talked hour after hour. This dance is a celebration of everything you've shared. Neither one of you says a word.

There is but one distraction. As you turn inside the music at some point, you notice Alan at a window inside, talking with someone there obscured by the edge of a drape. Alan gazes down at you, a gaze which evolves into a stare, on its way to becoming a glare. As Alan lifts his glass towards his lips, the gesture does not interrupt the intensity of his look. Then Matt turns you to the music as Alan is about to drink.

When the song ends, you and Matt stop dancing.

"Thanks for inviting me to the party," he says.

"Thanks for coming."

"I should get going."

You understand and nod.

Delicately he leans forward and touches your forehead with his lips. "I'll see you and Carmen down on the beach in a day or so."

"Okay. I'll be there."

He departs then, escapes the patio, almost snatched into the darkness by the time you remember to call out goodnight.

He waves from the cave of the night then vanishes inside it.

Your few minutes of clarity abruptly end. You become two people again. You watch yourself turn to see if Alan is still at the window, but he has vanished too. By the time you enter the cottage, you need five minutes to yourself. You make your way to the bathroom and gratefully slip inside. You stand before the mirror and wonder who you've become. As you wonder, your five minutes turns into ten. Maybe you can stay here even longer, except that someone turns the laughter up, reminding you that you should get back to your guests.

You come around the corner of the living room at the height of their collective hilarity. For a moment or two, no one notices you. You discover Alan, now drunk, is entertaining the troops. And you slip briefly into shock. He has tied one of your mother's kerchiefs (where did he find it?) into a bandanna around his head, donned a necklace and a bracelet borrowed from your jewelry box. With both hands held aloft, the fingers spread in a V, he performs his impression of Matt Bowman for the edification of his friends.

"Power to the people, man," he cries. "Far out. Groovy, man." It's a clumsy imitation, but intense and very mean. When he notices you at last, he considers halting at the line separating cruelty from stupidity. But he cannot bring himself to stop. "It's just poor-bashing, man," he cries before he realizes he's said too much.

It's too late by then. Stupidity has won the day. Both you and Alan know he's found that place of his where he's comfortable being mean.

Peripherally you feel everyone turning and looking at you. Still, incredibly, it takes them a few seconds more to realize you are angry. So the laughter continues a bit as if beckoning you to join in.

But you feel that clarity again, your arrival at the place where you understand yourself. You glide smoothly into the room through the gradually dissipating laughter. Hardly aware of what you're doing, beyond knowing it needs to be done, you pick up someone's half-finished drink—*something* and Coke, the ice cubes tinkling in angst—and throw it in Alan's face. The room falls instantly silent except for the lingering echo of someone's bedraggled "oohh."

Alan gazes at you, stupefied. "Jesus, Nickie," he says.

Two friends who've been standing nearby have already exited stage left and right. It makes Alan look more alone, as if he's suddenly naked.

"You bastard!" you cry.

"Nickie?"

You feel everything is done. You turn your back on him.

The audience defines embarrassment itself. Some of them gape at you in astonishment; others have turned away. The waiting silence possesses an anticipating-a-speech quality, like someone is about to explain the concept of horror. Or bliss. Or something else that hides inside the emotions.

So you think of something to say and decide to go for broke. "I'm sorry," you tell the assembly, "but the party's over now. This is my cottage and I want you all to leave."

This is a development Alan seems to have anticipated even less than the drink still dripping from his face. "Nickie, Jesus," he cries. "I mean, Jesus."

You turn to face him. "Especially you, you ingrate. This is *my* family cottage. I invited *one* friend. *One*. I want you out of here."

"Nickie, for Christ's sake."

You gaze at your guests again. They rise like mourners, begin to drift and float away, bemused by their role in this kind of grief over socially unacceptable death. They gather purses and lonely jackets, all the while avoiding your eyes. You know what collective embarrassment is like. It's the mouldy fur inside a slum refrigerator.

Alan comes forward and roughly grabs your arms, too stupid to know you're no longer willing to be subdued. Even when you shake him off. Even as, all around him, the parade of departing guests tries to leave with a dignity it cannot ultimately manage.

The rest is a little fuzzy, a transmission interrupted by static. Bobby Gallagher's dinghy departs the island with its first load of passengers. Rachel and Gabe the accountant, Salesman Slick and Lacquer Face wait in your boat while Alan tries to plead with you with a forced, strategic calm, saying, "Nickie, please. You're being crazy." You tell him in a menacing voice to get into the fucking boat.

You make the crossing hard throttle; no one will care about the party hairdos now. The group in your boat simply hangs on, still embarrassed perhaps but filled no doubt with horror at the speed of this crossing in the dark. At *The Inlet*, only Rachel communicates. She catches your eye and nods slightly to convey that she understands some of it at least.

From the dock, Alan, now sober, embarks on a speech of his own. "I'm sorry, Nickie. I was drunk. I didn't mean ..."

"... I don't ever want to see you again," you interject over his hapless remarks, from your seat inside the boat. "It's over between you and me, Alan. Don't call or visit. Have I made myself clear?" You would like to be calm but everyone hears what you say and you are grateful for it. You briefly imagine litigation, the witnesses you can call. But this fantasy evaporates: we do not sue for cruelty the way we do for inconvenience.

You leave all of them on the dock, magically cruise back into the channel. You push the throttle forward, ricochet across the water. You stand up on the seat, steer the boat with your foot. It's a careless way to behave, especially after dark, but there's renewal in the way the wind slaps your face and the lake *Red-Seas* itself for you. After you round the point of the island, you notice and then ignore the lights from Bobby Gallagher's *Rook* still moored at the edge of your patch of lake. You beach your boat and hop onto the shore, then stand there a few moments while anger gives way to resolution, resolution to a kind of triumph. You remember yesterday's apocalyptic signs, your sense of catastrophe on the way. It's now a tremendous relief—even triumph—to know the apocalypse was you.

From your vantage point on the shore you can make out the twinkling lights of Matt's *Crow's Nest* in the distance. Your cottage lights shine brightly too but seem to be dying somehow, dimming like a fire you've managed to get under control. When you start up the hill towards your cottage, you veer in the direction of Matt's, tugged along in a daze.

You don't knock at the screen door. Instead you stand there a moment or two, watching him through the mesh. He sits at his dining room table, bent over an open scribbler. Moths buzz around the light blazing brightly over his head, reminding you of you if only you were a butterfly.

"Matt?" You slip inside the cottage.

"Nickie?" He gets up and comes toward you. "I heard the boats. What's going on?"

You press your fingers to his lips. There are questions and answers that do not need to be asked; his "Are you all right?" Your "I've never been better."

The gash of the night is at last complete. You can bleed into each other's arms.

Barry Grills

# PART THREE: JULY, 1996

## MATT

**Monday, July 1**

IT SEEMS LIKE AN ETERNITY since I last sat down to write in this journal. How can forty-eight hours transform itself into what feels like a brief lifetime? How can a mere two days contain so much incident, so much circumstance, inspire so much astonishment? Or am I being melodramatic? Probably. This kind of chronological concentration is a masquerade, of course, another instance of time donning a disguise so that it can creep into the ballroom and dance its peculiar reel with the other components of destiny. Time's elasticity is magnified whenever it is sewn into the baggy pants of human perception. Still, even knowing this to be true, I'm mystified by the way the past two days have been reshaped, compressed and stretched into so much wonder, especially when wonder was something I didn't even appear to require. Or do I exaggerate the importance of what has taken place in the mist of my disorientation? Certainly, as I sit here now, disorientation is what I feel the most.

My pen, while trying to negotiate this page, struggles to overcome a sensory inebriation. I'm drunk on emotion, on passion. The words blur, tend to writhe on the page, incapable so far of an accurate report about the incidents that have taken place since Nicole's abbreviated party. Yet I know, during some future reading of this diary, I'll be grateful for a faithful rendering of the immensity of what has taken place. I try to concentrate. I want to set it down accurately for the time ahead when I may not want to believe it any longer.

It's not simply the incidents themselves I grapple with but the contradictions within those incidents. The tines of my fork cannot separate one flavour from another, cannot disentangle an incident from its apparent paradox. I must dine on the sumptuous feast before me and hope my digestive tract eventually sorts things out. But where to start? At the edges of my plate? Or in the center where the congealed anomalies are the deepest, the most entwined, the most subtly blended?

Nicole is asleep. I can hear the sounds of her slumber magnified by the hush inside the cottage. Each breath creeps gently around the corner at me, stalking me from behind. In its rhythm I hear another anomaly, this one too about love. I hear the inhalation and exhalation of safety and vulnerability. She is trusting but, of necessity, suspicious as well. This tightrope walk between risk and rectitude is the same for everyone, I know. But I've now drawn so close to this woman I can measure the gamble she takes in the fissure of each breath. It's a sweet breath that passes in and out of Nicole's mouth. I know because I have tasted it. I only hope I can keep it safe.

It's getting dark now. Not long ago the sun went down wearing rich purples and mauves, but these colors have faded now against the deep black of approaching night, while I have perched here at my table, delaying the writing of what I must set down. The lake too gradually vanishes, taking on a deeper gray where it gathers along the horizon. I'm fascinated by this transformation because it's all I've had time to notice today about the world outside this cottage. Until this quiet time alone, this drunken now, this near perfect solitude, I've paid no attention to the day. I think it was sunny. I think the air was crisp and dry. I seem to remember it was rather cool. But I didn't truly absorb this information, at least not to the extent that, under oath, I could swear it to be true. Until this moment there's been no other day because Nicole has been my day.

So, okay, Matt, how does it come to be this point in time? How many are the bridges between then and now, between this writing and the one I had only just embarked upon when Nicole slipped into the cottage to interrupt me two nights ago? What I wrote then, the night of the party, bears no resemblance to what I contemplate writing now. In fact, as I glance over my last forlorn entry, I cannot help feeling amused by this provocative understatement. Amused and a little dishonest. After all, are understatements not the icebergs on the oceans of what we say, so we can hide most of what we feel under the surface of our words? Forgivable, I guess, in view of everything that's happened. The last time I wrote in this journal I felt rather sorry for myself. I'd begun to nurse my broken heart, welcoming the temporary bitterness it requires if it is to heal. I admitted to myself that my crush on Nicole Graham was probably no longer a crush at all. It seemed, despite my best efforts to the contrary, that I had fallen in love with her. I wrote that night how crushed I was by my own betrayal of a satisfying solitude.

Nor could anything Nicole did or did not do be blamed. Rather it was her environment that sentenced me to futility, the nature of the world in which she has lived so exclusively of me to this point. I didn't fit, I saw, in the youthfulness of her world, or in its economic comfort. I didn't fit inside its political complacency. I am someone else, I wrote two nights ago, forty-seven and frustrated by the fact that some early important milestones have slipped away from me. Milestones disrobed are often revealed as mistakes. More than this, I'm an outlaw of sorts, always just a mile or two ahead of the relentless posse policing a society I cannot ethically respect.

Still, I felt cheated by the inherent nature of my difference while I stumbled through her party, trying to fit my *l'étranger* inside their exclusive cocoon. There I was, some prehistoric mutation, caught drinking alien booze and thinking alien thoughts and opining alien viewpoints which could not be shared by the inhospitable landscape on which my time machine had foundered. Aware that I was an interloper, I felt foolish and hopeless afterwards, dismayed to realize that I was now at least partially in love with someone who represents—as remarkable as it may seem—a period of modern history that has left me far behind. I even went so far as to view myself as a child molester. And although I knew this metaphor did not strictly apply, I felt thankful for the comparison. It seemed a way to feel a gratifying remorse. I knew it wasn't the child, the victim of my love, Nicole whom I preyed upon. No, somehow it was her times I was trying to bugger. I felt worse than foolish, worse than absurd—I felt quite perverse.

These were the thoughts I was writing when Nicole stumbled into my cottage that night. It all reads so bitterly now, so overcooked and dark. But some of what I said then may contain a grain of truth, perhaps more than I want to admit now that Nicole and I have become lovers.

I hear movement from the bedroom. As I turn, however, it's only Carmen peering through the bedroom doorway, gazing at me in surprise, seemingly as mystified as I am that things between Nicole and me have become what they've become. She lies down again on the rug at the side of my bed, not far from her sleeping mistress. Canine Ben lies a couple of feet away at the end of the bed, having sorted through the romantic developments better than I. Now the cottage sounds grow softer again as if someone has picked them up inside a globe and gently shaken them to watch them drift in snowfall silence towards the waiting bottom.

Here, then, for the record of this journal, is my version of what happened.

How reluctant we were. How cautious. Even after she slipped into my arms, right here at the edge of this dining room table, even after, as she did so, her physical, sexual self inspired my astonishingly eager need. Still, I resisted it, as if whatever remained of Nicole's innocence was somehow dependent on my behaviour. I felt she too was holding back. I didn't know, at that point, how intense had been her evening after I left her party. Whatever the reasons, instead of succumbing in any way to what we might have felt, we withstood our respective needs, toying with those congealed anomalies I now have learned are merely her and me trying sanguinely to become some kind of worthwhile us.

After our embrace that night, I pulled away from her, held her at arm's length examined her beautiful face, the image of which sometimes lies in my belly heavy as lead. It was obvious something very important had taken place, a quarrel, a fight. I had heard the boats departing the island myself, their motors tearing the night apart along its previously peaceful seams. I wondered too if there had been an accident, if someone had been hurt.

"I'm fine," she told me eventually. "Better than fine. Great. Better than great."

And I must admit she looked vibrant. Distressed, yes, but triumphant too, as if her demanding opening night performance, full of controversial drama, had met with critical acclaim.

I sat her down on the couch beside me, hoping to calm her. It wasn't that I wanted her calm. No, I wanted the explanation to be calm so that I could understand it.

"They're gone," she told me then.

"They're gone?"

"I told them all to leave."

"You told them all to leave?"

When she looked at me and grinned, I felt appropriately foolish, echoing the way I was everything she said. Besides, I felt excited myself. I'd imagined a moment or two a few hours before when I too had wanted her guests to leave.

"I threw a drink in Alan's face," she then confessed. She paced back and forth. "I threw a drink in Alan's face!" She nearly clapped her hands to demonstrate her shock and glee.

Astonished, I would have repeated her words yet again but managed to control myself. "Nickie," I said instead. "I need this from the beginning."

"I know. I know. I'm just all wound up. I feel like I've won a lottery." She considered me a moment. "Oh, Matt," was what she said.

I took her into my arms again.

"Oh boy," she said with a chuckle. "You sure know how to hug."

I merely cleared my throat. All my senses were aroused. I noticed I was now erect. Flustered, I pulled away from her and sat down again. "Tell me what happened, will you?" I said to cover my retreat.

It took some time—she kept getting up, then sitting down, occasionally pacing—but eventually she outlined what had happened. At one point, sitting with me on the couch, she took my hand and held it in both of hers. Then, to my surprise, she lifted my fingers to her lips and briefly kissed them. At the time I wasn't even sure she was aware what she had done because she began to talk again immediately afterwards, completing the sentence the touch of her lips had briefly interrupted.

Nor was excitement her only emotion during the telling of the tale. She was anxious too, fretful, perhaps even afraid. Like all provocative actions, the way she had ended the party seemed fraught with inevitable consequence. Or is this just my fundamental belief that society punishes us for the decisions we make, regardless of what we do?

"Are you going to regret this in the morning?" I asked.

She glanced towards the window and smiled a little bit. "No," she replied at last. "I don't intend to feel any more regret, not if I can help it anyway."

We spent two hours reviewing her relationship with Alan, celebrating in a variety of ways the fact that it was over. By the time we were done, I was as convinced as she is that Alan had been wrong for her, apparently from the beginning. I didn't say so, though, afraid of betraying my romantic bias. So mostly I simply listened. I didn't want her to discern that I cared for her too much. I was grateful for her friendship; I didn't want to complicate matters for her.

But she made my self-imposed distance difficult at times. She would suddenly interrupt her litany about Alan to gaze at me and smile. At the time, I simply didn't know what these digressions meant. I was still the man who, while fearing any betrayal of our friendship, believed it was hopeless contemplating anything more. What I had written before her arrival was still fresh on the scribbler's page. I was compelled— each time she seemed to wander to a place where I might reside—to bring the conversation around to Alan again. To save her from me, I believed, *another* man who wasn't right for her. And, if truth be known, to save myself from *her*.

"How will he take it, your splitting up?"

"Lousy."

"He'll make trouble?"

"Yes."

"He loves you," I said carelessly. "In his own way, I guess."

She looked at me with a trace of anger, frustrated, I suppose, that it appeared I hadn't been listening. "Alan doesn't love," she said defiantly. "Alan controls."

I nodded.

"When someone loves, Matt, they let the person go. When

you control, you can't. When you love, the last thing you want to do is be with a person who doesn't love you back. When you control, you just can't leave them alone. You just have to try to change their mind."

"That's true," I had to admit, remembering similar scenarios from my own life.

"Matt? It wasn't what he did. It was simply that he did it."

"I know. Thank you for defending my honor, by the way."

She simply looked at me and gently shook her head, as puzzled by me at that moment as I am sometimes puzzled with myself.

"I need to lie down," she told me then. "What time is it?"

It was four-thirty.

"I need to lie down. It's all coming over me now. I'm exhausted."

"I'll bet."

"Will you lie down with me?"

I nodded, although I wasn't sure exactly what she meant.

Shortly, as we laid on my bed, reluctant, still so wearily reluctant, lying in each other's arms, I thought she fell asleep. I wondered what I should do. Toying with this notion and the disappointment, while I was at it, of doing nothing at all, I felt too restless to sleep despite my exhaustion. Holding Nicole, filled with the wealth of her closeness, I was fretfully wide awake. And what, I wondered fiercely, should I finally admit to her? What should I confess? Plead guilty to love? To lust? To love *and* lust? What?

But Nickie wasn't asleep. Not yet. Without opening her eyes, she murmured, "Are you in love with me?"

I twitched uncomfortably at the possibility she had nimbly read my mind. "What answer gets me in trouble?" I murmured when at last I was able to speak.

Even then, as she answered me, she didn't open her eyes. "The one that isn't true," she said. "The one that's just a lie."

"Yes, I am," I answered quickly before I could change my mind.

"Wonderful," she whispered, again approaching the edge of sleep.

I felt that intense relief that affixes itself to exhaustion when something is going to be all right after all. And so, having admitted what I felt, I too now began to succumb to my powerful fatigue. But her voice brought me back one last time.

"Are you going to want to make love to me, you know, when we're not so tired?"

"Yes, I am," I replied again before I could change my mind.

"Wonderful," she repeated.

At least that's what I heard.

Then, with a sigh that acknowledged our accomplishment, one that spoke for both of us, she burrowed deeper against me and fell asleep.

When I awoke later that morning, I felt imprisoned in that eerie purgatory between what has been real and what has possibly been imagined. What had I dreamed, I wondered, and what, in truth, had been said? Yet, when I turned over and discovered Nicole snoring softly beside me, everything seemed true. We appeared innocent and corrupt both at once; we still wore our clothes, chaste bluejeans and t-shirts, but licentiously rumpled, I decided, from the lovemaking we might have contemplated while we were dreaming in our sleep.

I nearly reached out to touch her tangled hair. Instead, I studied her a while. I was going to have to learn to know her in a different way now. I felt anxious to get started. What we memorize about the person we love stays with us much longer than the person sometimes does. And it was possible all I'd actually have was what I could study now. When Nicole at last awoke, perhaps she would not remember, would want to forget what she'd asked me hours ago on the verge of our sleeping and what I had replied.

Then a powerful hopelessness came over me. Daylight's reality. All of the contrasts between Nicole and me, and in the dissimilar times to which we are so connected, seemed too steep an obstacle for us. And was I not now committed to a solitary life? Had I not come to believe there is nothing missing in my life? What was I doing here believing I needed her? Or perhaps when she awoke she would express a similar conclusion. There was still a chance to interrupt the way we were falling carelessly out of the sky. But I didn't want that. I did but I didn't, the most unforgiving anomaly of all. Wanting something you don't want to want. Wanting is a mirror reflecting back, back and back along a line of reflecting mirrors, transforming the act of wanting into an unsatisfactory infinity. I stopped thinking these things on purpose, gave my head the proverbial shake. The maxim I prefer about love is simpler and less responsible. Give all the love you feel; take all the love you can get. It's living for the moment but sometimes the moment is all you're allowed. I call that moment an ecstasy—when the lie that love is perfect is so briefly well told it seems to be the truth.

Carefully, without disturbing Nicole, I got up and made coffee. As it began to drip into the carafe, I took Canine Ben down to the beach. The air was warm. The lake sparkled in the sunshine. I took off my clothes, waded into the icy water, still far too cold for swimming this early in the summer. Gasping, I made myself swim the edge of the lake until I could stand the chill no longer. Then I got out and stood on the shore to let the sun dry me off. The sun had teeth too which nibbled on my flesh, as sharp with heat as the lake's bite had been cold.

But I didn't feel any clearer, any less mystified, standing naked on the beach. I just kept repeating to myself how I would approach this day—*give all the love you feel, take all the love you can get.*

Nickie's cottage wasn't locked. I freed Carmen from confinement there, watching her do her business, then walking both dogs casually back to *The Crow's Nest.* Back home, I peered around the corner, saw that Nicole was waking up. When she smiled and said, "hi," I responded with a neutral kind of "good morning" which was far less than what I actually wanted to say.

"Coffee?"

"Oh please."

"It's on the way. And I've brought Carmen."

"Thank you," she said as I went to get the coffee.

I heard her making a fuss of Carmen. I glanced at Canine Ben who was taking it in as well. It could have been my imagination, but I thought I saw him shrug. One last time I thought, *give all the love you feel, take all the love you can get.* Then I carried the steaming coffee, one for her and one for me, into the room where Nicole was waiting for me.

She cuddled into me and I put my arm around her. Then we silently sipped our coffee for a few moments. Shortly she reached up and touched my hair.

"Your hair's damp," she said.

"Yes. I swam."

"Yeah?"

I nodded.

"It must have been cold," she said.

I kept wondering who was going to say something first. About last night. About what had been said at the edge of slumber. Not only who would pick up the strand first, but how. I certainly couldn't think of the perfect sentence. Perhaps Nicole wouldn't either. I felt privately amused that Nicole and I were enduring that awkwardness that surrounds *about last night*, the kind traditionally suffered after sex for the first time. Sex Without Awkwardness: was there potential there for a how-to psychology text in reverse? Awkwardness Without Sex: An Evangelical Manual on how to burn your bridges before you even get to them.

"Good coffee," she said while I was lost in this conjecture.

"Thank you," I replied.

"Oh boy," she said with a sigh about what I do not know.

"My sentiments exactly," I managed to reply.

We didn't drink the coffee: we schmoozed and worshipped it. In the intense hush of the bedroom, it sounded like we were snorkelling with straws.

"Is *The Rook* gone?"

"Totally. The horizon's completely empty."

"Good."

We sipped more coffee.

I cleared my throat. "I've been thinking. Are you hungry? We could put a picnic lunch together, some wine—some hair of the dog that bit us—take Carmen and Ben down to the end of the island."

"Yes," she said. "We could, couldn't we?"

"Sounds like a fine idea, if I do say so myself."

"Is that what you want to do, Matt?"

Nervously I glanced at her. "Among other things," I murmured, my throat phlegming up so that I had to clear it again.

And I thought: clogged throats don't happen in the movies. Everybody in the movies knows what the fuck they're supposed to do now when the now eventually arrives.

"I want to spend the day with you," I heard come out of my mouth. "That's one thing I know for sure."

"Me too," she said, thank God.

So that was what we did. We put something to eat and drink together, grabbed an old Hudson's Bay blanket off the couch and set out down the beach, the dogs sniffing and playing and running in front of us while we held hands behind them.

As we strolled along, I felt cheerfully reflective. I remembered holding hands with a girl for the first time when I was fourteen. To my dismay back then, handholding gave me an annoyingly persistent erection. Matt's law of physics: hormones at their most active eat ions, split atoms, overpower electrons, vanquish neutrons. A gathering of hormones is like a black hole—entire solar systems are devoured. I considered this while I held hands with Nickie, remembering when I was fourteen that I had put my free hand in my pocket to hold my noisy penis against my leg. Yesterday, my extra hand carried Aunt Agnes' picnic basket. It had only taken thirty-four years, but my hard-on was now free to yodel in four-part harmony. And I thought: give the singing cowboy something legitimate to howl about, for Christ's sake. After all, I may want Nicole to know my youthful side, but that doesn't mean I want to be twelve.

So I abruptly stopped there on the shore, carefully set the picnic basket down on a dry patch of beach, turned to her, took her into my arms and kissed her. I kissed her the way I'd wanted to kiss her for weeks. Hard and soft, wet and dry, lips and tongue, body fitted to body as tightly as I could manage.

"Okay," I said when we were done. Nothing else. I just said okay.

"Okay," Nicole replied, holding her hand humorously over her forehead in her version of a Victorian faint.

We continued on our way.

We weren't long making love after we spread the blanket on the dunes among the dead trees of the petrified forest. We started kissing again. Our bodies began to grapple with one another, and one of us kicked the picnic basket out of the way. Food seemed a universe away from the galaxy of our appetite.

Our lovemaking was that clumsy state inside the no-man's land of too much anticipation and too much consideration; too much fear of displeasing and the sheer, gasping joy of making love to someone you care for deeply. And so, negotiating her various folds, twitches, sighs and responses, I lost sight of myself—juggling the various selves that are my particular self—until, inevitably, I felt I'd somehow fumbled them all. She came with a long, noisy shudder. I didn't come at all.

"It's been a while," I said and I held her in my arms.

"First time jitters," she said, kissing me. "I had them too."

"Because it's . . ."

". . . important," she finished for me.

Beyond this, we didn't say much. All the various selves that were me in love and lovemaking had finally found two opposing corners where they could toss taunts at one another, like two teenaged gangs defending some worthless urban street corner. On the one hand, I felt wondrous and emotionally fulfilled in a way in which even the best of solitudes cannot achieve. On the other, there were questions, doubts, fears and a resistance which—having the benefit of my past, vast experience—seemed the leading contender in the debate to win all argument. Yet, naked in the hot sunshine, naked with naked Nicole, I hung onto her for dear life. That moment I mentioned earlier—an ecstasy—I milked it for all it was worth.

Eventually we dressed again. It's extremely rare that someone uninvited visits the island—there are other public beaches, other bays and cottages on the mainland, and not many people know about the natural beach blessing the southern edge of our little kingdom. So we dressed against the invasion of the sun rather than any unexpected humans who might be surprised to encounter us nude on these dunes. I watched Nicole dress, less surprised by the lushness of her body than by the fact that I had somehow resisted truly noticing it before. Something else, I suppose, I hadn't wanted to want, that I had hoped to walk away from.

At last we turned to the food we had packed to share here among the dead trees. We fed one another, our fingers on each other's mouths, then inside each other's mouths. We licked and sucked each other's fingers, laughed, sighed and closed our eyes at this kind of provocation.

"Wow," Nicole whispered when we were done. "Just when I thought you were a little old-fashioned."

"Really?" was all I could manage to reply.

"Take me to bed, Matt."

So we left the dunes and came back here where we made love, slept, made more love, then slept and made love some more. While the hours passed and the day's seasons slipped by—afternoon, evening, night, then morning, afternoon and evening again.

Until now. Until, for me, this different kind of important solitude, this intermission between the acts of love and magic that have repeatedly mesmerized me. This intermission between the many jaded questions I have not asked Nicole and cannot ask myself.

Experience makes us cautious. The price for joy is fear of losing it after it is gained.

## NICOLE

EARLY TUESDAY MORNING—relatively early anyway—you and Matt agree to a brief parting, a decision more or less arrived at on principle. Privately, as if a little ashamed of your romantic greed, you've decided you can't live on love alone, although, for a couple of days now, this is exactly what you have done. Conscience versus largesse. Then again, maybe Matt is right. Perhaps the wizened, limping homily about love and what one lives on is nothing more than one of those "social edicts" designed to police society's gluttonous children rather than reflect any reliable cosmic truth.

Still, you need some time to think and, in the thinking, the opportunity to personally savor what has become an emotional feast. If you stay with him much longer, immersed in your romantic celebration, you won't be able to move far enough away from the pattern in the festivities to understand the pattern's design.

Because, yes, there is a pattern. It begins with the ease with which you draw close to him, expands to touching and stroking, growing gently frantic to the point where you want him inside you again, craving his lips and fingers on your skin. Then, after you make more love, the pattern guides you further into another postcard of euphoria that ends only after you fall asleep.

You need time and a little space to hold a mirror up to

yourself, to examine your part in the pattern you live now. You've never made love like this before, so freely, so often, so hungrily, so much the initiator. You need time to savor this difference, to interview yourself, to get to know the astonishing woman you've become in only a couple of days. Space too for one more thing: whether you can live on love alone is not the issue; it's whether, ultimately, you would ever really want to.

Matt feeds you on his bed this morning. Scones with marmalade or peach jam or peanut butter. And coffee. He reclines naked on pillows propped up against the iron bedstead. You sit cross-legged and close to him, your plate stationed on the sheets just inches from your dazed, replete genitals. Depraved? Perhaps. But it's all so new and easy, a partnership which simply happens, *hotdiggitydogging* itself along.

Even when, grinning broadly, he dabs his scone against one of your nipples, then bends to lick it clean, you feel the broad normalcy in his gambit as hungry and sensory. The comfort between you and Matt makes you want to give over somehow, unasked. In fact, you believe you'd give in to some mystical everything if only you knew what *everything* actually is. And that's why you contemplate space, leaving him on his own for several hours. You need to come out of this dizzy spell to briefly consider reality again.

But you don't say anything right away. You can't help feeling a vague risk exists somehow. Just thinking about temporarily ducking out on the dream generates a subtle sense of loss. Ridiculous really. Like if you give up this newfound gift of love and passion, it'll never come back again. Just knowing how unrealistic this kind of trepidation actually is compels you to break away, to suggest an interruption in the action.

"I need to go home, Matt."

"Home?" He looks visibly dismayed.

"Back to my cottage."

"Oh." Then he snorts at his own foolishness. "I thought you meant, you know, leave the island."

And this does as much to restore reality as any private contemplation could achieve. How casual does he think you are about falling in love with him?

Still, you keep this brief annoyance to yourself, subdue it by remembering how insidious the erosion of trust can be when one has suffered being in love before. Matt knows as well as you do how relentless a belief in love can be and how stubborn the disillusionment becomes when love doesn't amount to anything.

No wonder you want to delay the first few misunderstandings between you, put off for as long as possible the ritual transformation of your faith in love into suspicions of inevitable failure. If you're feeling the nudge of caution, it's only logical that Matt is feeling it too. Maybe even moreso. His pride in finally achieving freedom is much stronger than yours and he's been living with it longer. In his case, it isn't only that love has failed him in the past but that he has been happy living a life that, until now, hasn't needed much love at all.

Although you know you'll want to talk about these things in future, you believe it's still too early in the relationship for any discussion now. You've had to be stern about this all weekend long, not only with yourself, but with Matt as well. Each time he prepared to say something cautionary, something which might have questioned what you are doing, you wouldn't let him talk.

"Nickie?" he said a couple of times.

"Not now," you told him, kissing his lips into silence.

Save the future for the future, you reminded yourself more than once. Love's need to barter for forevers will come up inevitably. And that, perhaps, is when it will fall apart.

"And you have to work to do," you say now, cradled by his left arm holding you warmly against his accommodating chest.

"Yes," he admits. "Although it feels like I'm living another life. So much has happened that I didn't expect, that I didn't even imagine. I wonder if I can concentrate. I don't even remember how it was just a few days ago. If you can believe it."

"Well," you add, forcing yourself away from him. "I think we need some time to rest."

You begin to slip into cottage-damp clothing that, while lying on the floor, has mysteriously absorbed the odor of sex pervading the entire room.

He watches you dress in silence. "You know something?" he murmurs at last, as if mostly to himself. "I don't remember noticing, when we were just friends, that you were so, uh, voluptuous."

Bemused by his words, you simply gaze at him, not sure whether or not to believe him, wondering defensively what he means.

"Like I wouldn't *allow* myself to notice it," he adds. "You know? Like it was against the rules somehow?"

You suspect he means this to be gentlemanly but it comes out drenched in Madonna complex. You feel reduced by his words. Slotted, pigeonholed, categorized. Get over it, Matt, you think. There's no way you'll let him love you into a state of androgyny for the sake of some *modernity* ethic. Your tits and ass come with the rest of the package.

It's a tender spot he's grazed. That archaic word *voluptuous*, it's such a stupid word, one your mother used to read in some fifties bodice novel. Back then it was common to narrowly define a woman outside of nature's complex human abstraction. Dyed blondes were cheap, intelligent women wore glasses, delicately pretty girls were destined to be sweet. Voluptuous women were believed to be dumb, perched like idiot gargoyles on the hoods of two-toned cars.

Although you decide to forgive him for falling into stereotypes about women, you mention that he's done so. "I'm going to let your failed attempt at compliment go by," you say, "because I have to go back to my cottage and I don't want to leave with hard feelings. I'm glad you're pleasantly surprised by what shows up when I'm in the nude. But I'm still the same person, I hope, now that my secret identity has been revealed."

"I'm sorry," he says. "It was clumsy. I'm all emotion, no brain."

Abruptly, you change the subject. "I need a bath," you tell him, another reason you are going back to your own cottage. "What about you? What do you do when you need a bath, not having a normal bathroom?"

"I'm forced to swim in the lake," he replies with mock gravity.

"It's cold this early in the season. You said so yourself after your swim the other morning."

Drily, he flexes his biceps. "We Bowmans are a rugged lot, you know."

"I've noticed," you say flirtatiously.

But it's true. Matt Bowman naked also turned out to be a pleasant surprise.

"I guess we've both noticed some things," he muses. "I

thought you were beautiful the first day I met you."

You consider a remark about what a handsome couple you'll make but, in the end, you remain discreetly silent. That fear about signing contracts with the devil of the future. And the unsettling things, of course, that you haven't as yet discussed. Yes, whatever they are, whatever they will be—those contentious quills of self-defense—there can be as much damage in what will be learned as there is in too much rash assumption.

"Can I make you dinner at my place tonight?"

"Yes, you can," he replies.

Although you don't want to ask him this pressing question, you cannot help yourself. "Are you still in love with me?"

"Yes," he says with a grin. "I'm afraid it's gotten much worse."

YOU'D CALL KAREN TO TELL HER what's happened, but you don't want to share the news with her yet. Not for a while, anyway. And that's a first for you. It seems you've always called Karen right away to confess when you've fallen in love (as if telling Karen is one of the footings in the viability of the event).

But this time you want to keep it secret. You don't need the verification. Verification of anything seems blissfully irrelevant. Besides, the secrecy will give you time to go over each kiss like a miser, review each touch, count each caress. And this time you're vaguely fearful that sharing how wonderful you feel will let some of your happiness leak away to where you can't get it back again.

So you bathe, with coffee and cigarettes. You lie back in the tub and decide to just be, like a turtle on a sun-blessed log. Somewhere in the distance of your physical consciousness your body protests its abuse—your lips feel swollen from so much kissing, the insides of your thighs have been scorched from so much enthusiastic carnal friction. Is this some kind of payback for the pleasure you have felt?

You bathe. This time, as the water stings your genitals, you remember the top of Matt's head sparkling with threads of gray, seemingly growing out of your twitching belly while he delicately licked you into wonderful orbit.

You bathe. And you ruminate again about the ease surrounding Matt Bowman. All your winches and wheels and cogs, yours and Matt's, seem to fit very precisely into one another as if you've been oiling their polished metal for years. A few squeaks perhaps but no grinding gears so far. And the other men you've tried to love? The gears would grind nearly from the beginning until, over time, the metal shrieked in protest, then finally broke down and seized.

You bathe, wondering now how the grinding will begin this time, what will be its cause. You wonder what can soon go wrong to force this love machine to a sad and tarnished halt. What, you find yourself wondering, was Matt going to say those times you wouldn't let him speak? Was he detecting something wrong in what you perceived was only right? Did he want to voice some doubt or pose an unsettling question?

You thought you saw it on his face—men get that look. It's an embarrassed dog expression. Their eyes fidget. They hang their heads, either in contrivance or in some legitimate remorse; whatever it takes to convey their affordable morsel of shame. Then they begin by saying your name, slowly stretching out its syllables in an apologetic way. "Nickie, I've been thinking." Or, "Nickie, I'm not sure how to put this." Or, "Nickie, there's something I should tell you." Only so many variations and they all begin with the stretching out of your name, as if they can hold back their desperation until it nearly snaps. Whatever it takes so that what they say doesn't seem the sentencing that, in fact, it always is.

Your wondering is interrupted by the squawky *bweeup* of the cell phone on the towel on the toilet lid an arm's length away.

Preoccupied, you pick it up, pushing the button empowering it. "Hello?"

"Nickie? It's Alan." Static from Planet Earth.

You don't even think about the tactical sequence in doing so before you hang up on him. You think about strategy afterwards, when it's already too late, after you know he'll only call back, that he'll interpret hanging up as a gauntlet you have flung. Because he'll want to fight the duel.

Your mood of quiet reflection evaporates just like that. He'll just call back, some salesman from the carpet cleaning company defining the *real* world. So your belly knots up in apprehension and you kick your foolish ass. Well, St. Nick, you admonish yourself, what the hell did you expect?

A couple of minutes go by. You know Alan too well to be relieved by this delay. Instead, you imagine him in his office sitting at his desk, one hand spread like a tiger's claws on the calendar blotter, the other tapping to one hundred on the telephone pad.

*Bweeup.*

"Alan, please, let's not," you say into the mouthpiece.

"Nickie, don't hang up. Don't hang up, okay?"

You say nothing, but you don't hang up. This conversation is something you must go through. You knew it all along.

"I know you're pissed off, Nickie."

"I'm not pissed off anymore. I just don't want to do this with you. It's over between us. I just want to move on now." And, having said this, you know it to be true.

Alan seems to telephone from some era in your distant past, so much so that he seems hardly to have existed at all. But this feeling of distance cannot last. Even if your brain doesn't know it yet, the knot in your stomach surely does. Your gut appears to be the first vital organ to have battled its way through the cobwebs of your current romantic euphoria.

"What I did at the party," Alan is telling you now. "I'm sorry. It wasn't a very nice thing to do."

"I doesn't matter now," you say. "I don't want to rehash any of this."

He hesitates while he sets your statement aside for later, when he can apply his own interpretation to it. "You were right to be pissed off. I don't know if a drink in the face was warranted, but I can see why you were pissed off."

"I don't care, Alan. I don't care to discuss any of this." You intend to repeat yourself again and again until, at last, he's truly gone.

"Bullshit. Of course you care."

"You're not listening to me. I'd like to go now?"

"Jesus, Nickie. C'mon. What's this I don't care shit?"

"I meant what I said the night of the party. About never wanting to see you again. So I don't care to keep seeing you or pretending we have a future. We're finished, Alan. Permanently. Do you understand?"

"Nickie, c'mon. I've apologized."

"Yes. Thank you. I even forgive you for being you, if that helps. But it changes nothing. I don't want to see you anymore. I'm going now."

"Nickie, that's my phone."

"I'll mail it to you," you say.

"Okay, okay. Don't hang up. Never mind about the phone."

"Alan, there's nothing to talk about anymore."

"Nickie, we've had a serious fight. There's lots to talk about."

"Not really. We're done. I don't want to ever see you anymore. There's nothing else to be said."

"Nickie, c'mon. Just like that?"

"No, you bloody fool. Not just like that. The other night? That was just the last straw."

"C'mon," he cries. "Say something that makes sense. Give me something to work with here."

"All right," you say, apprehension giving way to weariness. Still, this is your chance to be frank and you find yourself bracing for the task. "I don't love you anymore," you admit at last. "It's time we called you and me off and got on with our lives."

He considers your words a moment, letting his anger build. "That's a lot to decide just because I made fun of some jerk down the beach who needs a haircut," he shouts at last.

"Goodbye, Alan."

"Fuck you, Nickie. Okay?"

This time there is a photo finish on the hang up. It's just too close to call on who disconnected first.

Your bath water is cold, not so much chilled by the passage of time but by Alan's interruption. Still, stubbornly, you lie there a time, trying to reclaim the mood Alan's phone call interrupted. In the end, of course, you cannot. You knew it would go this way. You shouldn't be surprised. Nor will this be the end of it. You'd like it to be but you know Alan much too well. He'll harass you for a while because you've slipped outside his control. What is it Matt said? "The drink in the face would be more than enough for me. I'd be gone for good." But Matt and Alan are different. Matt doesn't want to suffer. Alan wants little else—for himself and for you.

Overwhelmed, dejected, resigned, you climb out of the bath

and pull the plug. The afterglow of love you've felt for Matt, the sensation which seemed so private, hopeful and unique swiftly joins the water on its way down the bathtub drain.

The phone rings again while you are finishing the post-party cleanup that you ignored while you stayed with Matt. The refrigerator is filling up with leftovers, the garbage bag with dips and veggies and grapes that spoiled or wilted in the dampness and the heat. You feel a little ashamed of yourself, of the waste the food represents. You reflect about domestic transmigration of souls, whether, when you transcend, you have to clean up after yourself before you go. You are thinking about this in a hiccoughy way when the cellular squawk goes off.

You decide, frustrated and tired, for now to answer it. "Yes?" is all you say.

"You're fucking that bastard down the beach, aren't you, you bitch!"

You take the phone—holding it out in front of you like a maggoty chunk of meat—and walk hurriedly towards the lake. You've hung up on him, you suppose dazedly, but the phone cries out again by the time you gain the beach, *bweeups* two more times before you reach the water's edge. There's a fourth ring but, by then, the device is arcing grandly over the pristine lake and it sounds like a dying duck just before it strikes the waves.

LATER, FROM A PAY PHONE AT *THE INLET,* you make the calls you must to Karen and your parents who have to be informed that you no longer possess a phone. It's a grounding inconvenience offset by the rich freedom you feel in being unencumbered by Alan's phone. Matt has mentioned previously that whatever you possess inevitably possesses you. For your part, it may not be true of everything, but it applies where the phone is concerned.

So you stand at the marina phone kiosk and call your mother first. And you gaze at the holiday sunlight, the holiday boating activity, the tan and sparkle of people on the lake, glad to be on vacation. You feel an advantage over them: you feel like a woman on the lam. Is this what Matt means by the deliverance true divestment can provide? Perhaps that's what he means. It feels this way to you.

"Hello, Dear," your mother says, surprised and pleased to hear your voice.

Together you make your way down the ritual agenda, pleasantries and weather reports and the state of everyone's health, your mother's exasperation with your father, her means of professing love.

Then, "I just wanted to be sure if you and Dad were still coming for the weekend on the thirteenth," you say.

"Yes, we are. Is everything okay?"

"Oh yes," you tell her, although this still feels like a lie. "It's just that you can't call me. Alan's phone . . . has stopped working. I though I'd better let you know."

"Can you get it fixed?"

"It's beyond repair," you reply, the double entendre not eluding you.

"And how is Alan anyway?"

You cock your head and close your eyes, wincing at your moment of hesitation. "Mom, I'm sorry. I really have to go. I just wanted to touch base with you about not having the phone. I didn't want you to be worried. We'll talk when you get here."

"All right, Dear."

"My love to Dad."

"Okay."

And, Jesus, at least that's over.

You gaze back over the channel at your mysterious mirage of an island. You should have stayed inside the dream, the one about you and Matt. Should have stayed with him inside the calm cocoon. Reality has already become a trial, a series of irksome interruptions, a number of irksome compromises, an unhappy reminder that what goes on *out there* doesn't care who you think you've become.

You would've liked to tell your mother that Alan's been shown the door, instead of that crap about the broken telephone. But your courage doesn't always work that way. A number of reasons. Phone calls instead of face-to-face conversations, for one. She would have taken Alan's part, not being able to *hear* as well as she might *see* the distress he's inspired and the ownership he's presumed. Alan makes pretty good money—it would be a factor in her mother's tolerance. His income has been enough to forgive him most things your mother would construe to be minor. She won't like Matt, at least as a romantic partner. He's a writer and doesn't enjoy enough income. And she'll say he's too old for you.

You and Matt talked about parents one morning over coffee. You asked him why he never mentions his.

"It just hasn't come up," he said. "Anyway, my parents don't approve of me."

"Why not?"

"Because I'm not like them very much. We have radically different views of things, you know, values, standards, that sort of thing."

"You mean you have to agree with all their opinions?"

"Of course. Most parents in their generation feel that way."

Then he proceeded to outline his theory about his parents' generation and their peers. He explained that he'd noticed two predominant characteristics. First of all they measure their human achievement almost exclusively in terms of what they amass materially. Secondly, they're inordinately preoccupied by what their peers think of them.

"So we end up, as their sons and daughters, becoming something they've amassed, something, by God, that had better not embarrass them in front of their friends."

"Oh Matt, aren't you being a little harsh?"

He continued undeterred. "On top of that, making their narrow perspective even more rigid is their certainty that they're right. Everything's black or white. They don't have time to consider the grays. It's hard to deal with that kind of implacability. It denies any opportunity to be different, to question status quo values. Their status quo cannot even conceive of the notion that it can be wrong. And someone like me can't argue an opposing point of view. To tell you the truth, I don't know if I'm right about anything. Try opening a debate with an acknowledgment that you don't know if you're right, especially against an opponent who has no idea that he could be wrong."

By this time you were grinning at the vehemence in his point of view.

"Sorry," he said. "It is harsh and I love my folks. But sometimes I get worked up about this. Better to dismiss the whole thing as generation gap, Sixties shit or something. Better,

I guess, to just let it go at that."

"You keep your distance from them," you observed.

"They live near Windsor. I don't get to see them much. We get along fairly well when I do, I guess."

Now, staring out over the sun-drenched channel, you feel some of what he's said is true. You've lied about the telephone because you're delaying the inevitable brush with your mother's implacability. Not only will she apply her assessment of your actions to what you have done, but more than that, she'll expect you to share her view of the situation and adopt it as your own. You feel a little annoyed with your mother, but a little annoyed with Matt as well. As if he's told you about a blemish you haven't noticed yourself, some nasty little zit he saw growing at the corner of your lip. You don't want to know if his generation gap actually exists or not. You just want everyone to try to get along. Sometimes life contains too much philosophy. Sometimes living gets lost in the debate.

"Matt, you don't need your parents' approval now," you told him that day you had this talk.

"That's true," he replied. "But in a way it would have been nice to have it just the same."

You turn back into the kiosk, pick up the telephone receiver again, glance at your calling card on the ledge. You punch in Karen's number, then Bell Canada's, the ones which give you permission.

You aren't surprised when the call is answered by her message machine. In fact you've already prepared what you're going to say. While you wait for the beep at the end of her spiel, you realize how cheerful her voice sounds. This should improve your mood but it doesn't. Cheerful as it is, Karen's message emerges in that real world, that place you somehow forgot about while you and Matt were making so much love.

Mercifully the beep arrives.

"Hi, Sweetie, it's Nick. So much to tell you, hardly know where to start. You can't call me. Alan's precious phone is at the bottom of the lake. I'll call you tomorrow night at eight. If you're not there, I'll suggest another time. Love to Liam and Cindy. Talk to you soon, I hope."

Then you hang up, feeling vaguely relieved she didn't answer, yet vaguely dissatisfied too. Needing at this moment for something to be perfect, everything lets you down. Not a day to make a choice or believe in what you're doing.

A cottager stands not far away, waiting to use the phone. Matt's age. Except that he wears powder-blue shorts and a gray t-shirt with a giant fish on it, a fish with a hook in its mouth. His paunch is immense, so much so that the pool of water from which the fish jumps takes on oceanic proportions. Unable to forgive him somehow, you make him wait while you tuck your calling card into your wallet and your wallet into your bag.

But he doesn't seem to mind. He smiles at you cheerfully as you pass one another going to and from the phone. Then, "Heeey," you hear him say behind you to someone at the other end of the line, just before you move out of earshot on your way to your waiting boat.

## THE MAN AND THE WOMAN

AS A WITNESS ONE HAS HIGH EXPECTATIONS of both love and the month of July. One enjoys being a zookeeper of a sort, in charge of pampered, prowling promise. Love, after all, is a nirvana in which one is compelled to have faith. And because faith has a component of vicarious thrill attached to it, so too does the passion one wishes to see in it.

As for the month of July, it's the true beginning of summer. As such it promises sun-drenched days and starburst nights, and the kind of forgivable freedom one can dabble in briefly with the same vicariousness with which one can imagine the thrill of love.

So it is that one watches as the man and the woman are carried away by the passion of love. And the gilded summer carriage transporting their reckless preoccupation is that warm and sensuous summertime the calendar calls July.

During the first few days of their affair, the man and woman are caught in various scenes of an elaborate collage telling their separate stories, though always within the context of the union that they share. They perform the pleasures of passion, feeling each moment of the thrill while deaf to the conventional soundtrack. They've heard the optimistic composer's wistful jingle thought to musically interpret joy, but one knows the music they hear is an ancient invention. And while the man and the woman fall deeper in love, one oohs and

211

aahs, taking in the ecstasy one, themselves, may never have known or sometimes can no longer remember.

"MATT?" THE WOMAN SAYS ONE MORNING in his arms. "Did you ever imagine that this would happen? You and me? Did you ever think we'd be lying naked in bed in each other's arms, that we'd be together like this?"

She's been feeling gently astonished again about how things between them have come to pass. She enjoys this kind of astonishment, thinks of it as a wonderful mood unique among other moods. So she shares it with the man because it would increase her pleasure even more if he was astonished too.

It's a measure of the power in the feeling of love that it overcomes dismal setting. Her bedroom is nearly dark although morning has been around for hours. On the other side of her bedroom drapes the sky is densely cloudy. The effect in the room is a cloying gray, a pervasive dullness. It is going to rain soon. Even in the bedroom one can smell the scent of impending downpour. Nonetheless, the man and the woman feel tucked inside a den—safe, alone, protected, in hibernation until some other day when the sun deigns to shine again.

For his part, the man still feels astonished too. But his astonishment is already frayed along the edges by what can only be called future considerations. Besides, he's been wearing his surprise longer, has gotten used to it and, in familiarity, already knows it can't remain new or perfect forever. He knows that astonishment—like so many other enticing sensations—either drifts comfortably away like campfire smoke or is driven back by questions which accept no easy answers. He asks these kinds of questions when he cannot help himself, when he and the woman are briefly apart and he can't distract himself with the joy he finds in her company.

So he thinks about what she's asked him, mulling it over for a time. He is the kind of man who wants mostly to be sure exactly what she wants to know.

"You mean before all this started?" he asks at last, in pursuit of his ideal of clarity.

"Yes. Way back at the beginning. I mean, that first day on the beach when we met, did you have any idea at all?"

"No. I thought you were beautiful in an objective kind of

way. I mean I *noticed.* But it was just an observation. I didn't consider, not even for a second, that I'd fall in love with you. And I would never have *ever* imagined you falling in love with me."

"How come?"

"Well, I noticed you were young."

He sighs. She remains young after all, and it is one of those irksome questions about their relationship that compromises the solace in loving her.

"You mean that's it? There I was and so what?"

He chuckles at her outrage. "Well, no, that's not the only thing. Don't forget, Ms. Graham, that I thought I was retired from any meaningful romantic love. I wasn't looking for this kind of thing. And when you're not looking to fall in love, it isn't so easy to imagine it happening with someone you meet along the beach."

"You know," the woman puts in, "that forty-seven is pretty young to retire."

"Except," argues the man, "it has nothing to do with chronological age. It has to do with what you've been through and what you don't think you need any longer."

She snuggles in close to him, holds him tightly, believing in some insistent, unconscious way that she can keep that other man, the one who felt no need, from breaking out again. "So there was nothing in the early days," she says, still slightly disappointed.

"Well no, that isn't true either. As a matter of fact, something rather bizarre happened one morning on the beach." Embarrassed, he grows silent, wondering if it's wise to try to tell her what took place.

"Well, c'mon," the woman says. "Don't leave me hanging."

"I don't want you to think I'm crazy," he says.

"Oh, c'mon, I already know you're crazy, wild and free." She laughs.

Careful not to interrupt their physical closeness, he reaches for a cigarette and an ashtray on the bedside table. He lights the cigarette, takes a drag, exhales.

"Matt, you're doing all this for effect. You've got a melodramatic streak. Do you know that?"

He glances at her and chuckles again. And wonders if she is right.

"Okay," he says at last. "Do you remember the day when Ben and Carmen got tangled up down on the beach? We were trying to get them leashed and we got all snarled. Remember that? It was the second time we met, I think."

"Okay," the woman says, wanting to believe that she remembers.

"It was the day I had banana muffins in the oven."

"Oh yeah, okay. I remember that day."

"All right. *That* day. Anyway, something very strange happened while we were getting untangled."

"I remember now," the woman breaks in. "We almost bumped heads. We were being so polite, so considerate, so intense about being thoughtful."

The man smiles at her, with love mollified by patience, patience mollified by love.

Okay, the woman thinks, what am I supposed to remember beyond getting tangled, beyond the fact you were baking banana muffins? Despite herself she is dismayed that she can't recall anything else, especially when he apparently does so clearly. It isn't that he has any kind of advantage over her. It's just that he possesses this secret incident about her and she'd like a chance to keep it secret too.

"The point is," the man continues, "at that moment, as we were getting untangled, I had the most powerful deja vu kind of sensation I've ever had. I don't know if I can describe it well enough to do it justice, but I felt I had known you before. In fact, it seemed for a very long time, that we weren't really strangers. And I even had this idea, this picture in my mind that we were intimate somehow, that we were lovers. I guess you'd have to say it was this powerful feeling that we were predestined to be connected."

"Yeah?"

"It's true," the man says. "It was so startling and so convincing, it totally blew me away."

"You didn't let it show."

"No. Of course not."

She laughs then. "Would have been tough to explain, I guess."

"No kidding. I hate swooning in public. It looks so clumsy and dramatic. Besides, you would've thought I was making a pass or something."

"Maybe," the woman says, although it's difficult to imagine now, there being only the present to interpret this helpless past. "Anyway," she adds, feeling gleeful, feeling endorsed by the finger of destiny, "so that's when you suspected something was going on, for you at least."

He gazes at her, kisses her on the end of the nose. "Well not exactly," he replies. "If I suspected anything, it was that I should get back to reality. Put yourself in my shoes. There you are, retired from romantic love, forty-seven years old and there's a beautiful woman, much younger than you, standing there on the beach, trusting you because you're not another one of those guys who's going to hit on her. And the thing of it is, you *aren't*. You *are not* one of those guys. Then, bam, this moment comes over you, just obliterates your careful reserve. I mean I still feel a little foolish, even now."

"Well don't," the woman says. "I think it's wonderful."

"*Now* you do. But back then you wouldn't have."

One notices she doesn't say anything to that. If love wants to use the present to redefine the past, well, that's just fine by her. Still, she knows he's probably right. No wonder love is so hard to find, doesn't work out as often as it should. One has to open the door to it, even when there's a chance more riffraff will barge in instead. Anyway, what's the difference now? She feels inspired by what happened to him on the beach that day. It's, yes, a powerful endorsement.

"See?" she tells him then. "You were meant to fall in love with me."

"Well I *guess* I was." He stubs out his cigarette in the ashtray on his chest, puts it back on the bedside table.

One watches them pause for a moment or two inside the gloom of the room, to ruminate over his story and what it means to them.

But soon he wants to know when love first occurred to her. Now that he's confessed he feels released by his deja vu admission, so much so that love seems more possible than he's believed it to be up to this point. Strangely enough, *he's* the one who wants to share astonishment now.

"What about you?" he asks. "What about you back then?"

And she wants to tell him something which explains how it

was for her. But first she turns in his arms and blazes a trail of lazy kisses along the flesh of his chest.

"Well," she says when she is done, her chin on his belly where she can look at him near but far away. "I didn't have a deja vu incident or anything. For me, it was more or less an accumulation of things."

"So nothing happened in the early days," he says, surprised at his disappointment, the vanity lying behind it.

"No," the woman replies, "that's not it. Something was going on, all right, but, like you, I think I was in a state of denial or something."

"Admit it," he suggests. "You thought you and I were inappropriate for one another."

"Oh no you don't, Matt Bowman. That's *your* shtick, not mine. You're the one all hung up about age difference here."

"Who says?" the man retorts, caught having his mind read again.

"I know how you think. I *feel* how you think."

"Okay," the man concedes. "So what was *your* denial?"

"I don't know exactly. Just cynicism generally, I guess. And trying to deal with what I was going to do about Alan."

"Sure."

"But there was something about you back then."

"In the early days?"

"Yes, in the early days."

One observes the woman considering whether or not to confess that she calls him Crazy Horse but, in the end, she decides that she cannot. It's not that he'd mind. It's just it's something she can call him which belongs to her alone. She wants to keep it secret in case, after all is said and done, it's the only thing of her own about him she ultimately gets to keep.

"It was this charisma thing," she tells him instead. "I thought almost from the beginning that you had charisma. And it felt like something only I could see, that only I could appreciate. Like it was supposed to be there for me."

The man smiles, embarrassed. He doesn't believe he possesses charisma. One suspects his enthusiasm for the topic has abruptly begun to wane. Although he's enjoyed this game of shared astonishment, unfortunately he keeps remembering how love tries its best to wither.

"Karen knew, though," the woman tells him, breaking into his disillusionment.

"Karen?"

"Oh yeah. She said, when we were together, you and me, that she felt the ground trembling."

"Aahah," is all he says.

And with that, for both of them, astonishment graciously lapses. The man feels calm but is aware of a sleeping sadness. One can tell he's known for a long time that life cannot be confined in a cage of his design.

But the woman is charmed by the notion of their inevitability. As it begins to rain, she kisses him on the belly again, licks the satin of his skin. Until he reaches down for her, pulling her up towards him so they can make love once more.

SOME NIGHTS THEY LIGHT A FIRE ON THE BEACH and stare fixedly into the flames. The man leans against a fallen tree trunk which washed up on the beach a number of years ago to lie embedded in the sand, forlornly bleached by the elements. The woman leans against him inside his encircling arms, her back to him and her head tucked against his shoulder. Every few moments he kisses the top of her head. Every few moments she snuggles in closer against him, trying to fit herself even more tightly inside the eye of his embrace.

Their bonfire mesmerizes. The reflection of the flames can be seen to dance frantically over their pensive faces. The smoke can be seen to drift aimlessly upwards, then gradually along the shoreline as if hitching a ride with the remorselessness of time. The flames hiss and spit. The smoke smells like an autumn morning, seems the safest of possible havens. On the other side of the fire, the lake is calm and silent, black, resting, reflective. Above them the sky is some slow-motion circus of death-defying twinkles and smoky irregular cloud.

"I want to live like this forever," the woman says, whispering, yet shattering the stillness they've kept worshipful for several minutes.

"Me too," replies the man.

One realizes neither one of them means to be part of a lie. It's just that this moment in their human condition has locked onto their physical world at a time when it is sleeping. You can fit the pieces of peace together, create calm from an elaborate puzzle, forgetting that it just can't remain this way, that the puzzle must be disassembled to be reassembled again.

LATE ONE OF THESE NIGHTS ANOTHER THUNDERSTORM scuffs through their island garden, vandalizing its tranquility. They've been walking their dogs along the beach and are returning to her cottage where they intend to sleep tonight.

The storm has crept up on them, as if lunging out of a closet. The sky explodes with a sudden flash of lightning and a boom of echoing thunder.

"Jesus!" the man cries, startled by the storm's arrival.

They stop on the beach to take in this unexpected development. Carmen runs up to them to cower about their legs. To the man, Carmen and thunderstorms define that integral communion of fear and superstition.

More thunder, more lightning, the first sporadic *splat* of rain.

"C'mon," the woman says, pulling him by the hand.

Laughing, they begin to run, man and woman and dogs, towards the light spraying from the windows of her waiting cottage.

By the time they reach the last incline on which the cottage has been built, the storm is raking the island. A brisk wind comes up to drive sheets of heavy rain into their faces and clothing. They laugh out loud in gaps between the thunder and lightning as they hurry to gain the door. Inside they gaze at one another, amused at how quickly they were soaked.

"Get out of those clothes," the woman says.

While the man strips down, noticing in a detached way, that he has become aroused by the power of the storm, the woman retrieves one of her father's robes, then changes into one of her own. After dressing, they stand at her living room window, watching the storm together, cheering on its temper tantrum, its lightning and thunder performance.

"You know something?" the woman says. "It just struck me that I was in love with you as far back as the night of the other storm. Do you remember that night?"

"Oh yes," he says with a smile. "A wonderful storm. The power went off. And I had all this angst about whether I should walk over here and check on you."

"Why angst?"

"Because I wasn't sure how you'd interpret my concern."

"Amazing," the woman says, shaking her head. "You wouldn't believe what I was up to. I was having a bath when the storm started. So I got into my robe to watch it, intending to go to bed after it was over. But I began to wonder if you'd come over and check on me. And what if you did? So I thought maybe I'd better get dressed. But then I thought how stupid I'd feel if I got dressed and then you didn't show up. So I stayed in my robe."

"And there I was."

"Absolutely. There you were."

He hugs her for a moment.

"God," the woman says. "I felt so stupid. I didn't know whether to get dressed or stay in my robe or which would be best, you showing up or not showing up. See? It was already happening. You and me were already happening."

"You should have come to the door naked, as a kind of compromise."

"Right, Bowman, now *that's* a creative solution."

He just chuckles to himself, enjoying the absurdity in his notion.

"So what did you think of me answering the door in my robe anyway?" She smiles at him, knowing she's being coy but enjoying it anyway.

"Well, I thought you were extremely fetching. And very proper about it all. Right out of Jane Austen. 'So nice to see you this evening, Mr. Bowman.'"

"Hmmm," she muses then, wondering what it would be like to do it all over again, making the corrections in the script being his lover now permits.

The man, not surprisingly, is of a similar mind. "If only I knew then what I know now," he says.

"What would you do?" the woman asks, hungry for revision.

He takes her into his arms, kisses her deeply. He slides his hands inside her robe, strokes her ribs, reaches up to find her breasts. Slowly, slowly for him more than for her, he eases her robe apart. He clutches her buttocks and pulls her tightly against him. At this moment, she feels brand new to him, familiar in essence, but brand new in some quicksilver state of quasi-reality he doesn't recognize.

For her, he's deliciously familiar. She finds more wonder and excitement in his sameness than she would if he was new. She parts his robe and strokes his jutting cock, then steps up on tiptoe to hug it between her thighs.

"Oh shit," the man responds.

They make love without removing their robes, hiding inside their dishevelled garments like they would a wind-tortured tent, standing up against the window ledge, the window ledge holding her in place for him, their hands in each other's hair to give leverage to their thrusting. She comes and he comes grunting at the edge of the window, their robes falling from their shoulders in furious disarray, the lovers outlined sharply in the window where day remains deeply gray in the wake of the abating storm.

SOMETIMES THE WOMAN MUST ACKNOWLEDGE that she's troubled because her lover's a solitary man.

"Do you have any friends?" she asks him one afternoon while they are walking their sunny beach, their dogs gamboling several yards in front of them.

"A few," he answers defensively, conditioned to anticipate that some major inadequacy in him is about to be unearthed and held permanently against him.

She glances at him quickly, noticing the chill in the tone of his voice, conditioned in her turn to recognize defensiveness and defuse it right away.

"It's just that you don't mention anyone. It's one of those things you seem to keep to yourself."

"I suppose," the man admits.

Beyond this, he doesn't know what to say. It's difficult to explain a powerful need to enjoy his own privacy to someone who, whether she knows it or not, will come to understand and implement her own.

So they stroll along in silence underneath diving, crying gulls. They walk in and out of little pools of water, tiny bays and fjords the waves design in the unresisting sand of the shoreline.

"I've reached that age, Nickie," the man tells her shortly,

"when the number of friends shrinks and the depth of the friendships increases."

"So you're saying you don't have many friends but the ones that remain are *good* friends."

"Exactly," he replies. "Tried, tested and true. The ones who've survived the ups and downs."

"Sure."

"Lot of people show up for the ups, disappear when the downs take place."

She knows this to be true, though she can tell he's been through this kind of betrayal more than she has.

"But, yes," he adds a moment later, willing to confess. "I'm more of a loner than you're used to."

She wants him to be reassured. "It's okay, Matt. I wasn't questioning whether that's valid. I was just curious. There's so much past to catch up on. So much to find out about so that I know you better."

"Funny," he murmurs more to himself than to her, "how we need to do that."

"Yes. But I look at you and I wonder. I wonder about all those things and people and events which worked together to create the you I know right now. Know what I mean?"

"Sure. Except that, to me, it's a dangerous process. There's a mysterious line back there somewhere in the past. On this side of it, you get to understand someone. A nice portrait gets painted. On the other side of the line, though, there's nothing but old mistakes and crimes for which we've already served our time. You know, those things it's best not to know about."

"You're saying, too much knowledge about someone we love is a dangerous thing."

"That's it exactly."

"Old lovers, for instance."

"Yes, old lovers, for instance."

Of course old lovers is the main thing, the woman thinks. Still, she believes she has that one worked out.

"I want to know all the bad things about the women you once loved. I don't want to know any good things," she confesses then, making sure to nudge him in a playful way.

"Better," he says, not wanting to have to decide which is good and which is bad, especially where the judgment might be moot, "not to bother with it at all."

She doesn't say anything to this, not sure if she agrees with him or not.

Then she reaches another conclusion which occurs to her on whim. "Maybe," she explains, "we need to contrast ourselves with the past to know that this time it's right."

One discovers then that the man doesn't believe in right, or doesn't want to at any rate, not in the way that *she* seems to believe.

"Maybe," he replies, using his most political word, not lying exactly, but somehow managing to step away from the strike of a venomous truth.

The woman wishes she could tell him how extraordinarily right he is as the man for her to love. But she doesn't say so. She's afraid he'll reply—in some gentle, compassionate way—that she's mistaken, and she in turn will believe she's mistaken too, but in some fierce and outraged way. This sense of right is something to save for later, she decides, when everyone's mind is as certain as their feelings appear to be. Periodically, to the woman, one realizes, this first few days of being in love is like a nagging procrastination.

"So, Bowman," she says then in a good-natured tone she's had to initially manufacture. "Don't you think it's time we went public with this thing? Isn't it time we went out on a date, let the world get a look at us as a couple?"

"Well, Ms. Graham," he replies. "What do you have in mind?"

"Tomorrow, the mainland. Lunch at a cafe. Some shopping. Dinner out. Errands. Necking in public places. Holding the world up to our perusal to see if we can dance to it."

"Okay," he says with a grin, enjoying the agility of her mind.

And she squeezes his hand, leans up to kiss him on the cheek. "Don't worry, Mr. Loner, it's nothing to worry about. It isn't the beginning of the end, it's the end of the beginning."

"Harry Hermit goes to town?"

"And lives to tell the tale."

But one sees the man feeling something going away he nearly thought he could keep.

THE NEXT DAY IT DECIDES TO RAIN. And the day after that.

Because of the rain, they get to stay a little longer inside their island garden and its blessed solitude.

It's a warm rain the first day. Feeling bold, a wilderness boldness, the kind that bays at the moon, the man and woman walk naked with their dogs in the stand of trees and intermittent dunes at the end of the island. There, the dogs run to and fro, not caring what their masters aren't wearing or the new parts of their bodies which jive and boogie strangely as their masters walk.

The rain falls halfheartedly but touches everything, playing a hissing sonata on the leaves of the trees, rinsing out the blonde of the sand, darkening it, then in contrast, turning the man and woman's skins a shiny silver. The couple hold hands in this private drizzle, the sand clinging to the bottoms of their feet. As they stroll naked through the rain, they smell and feel themselves part of the chlorophyll bleeding through the veins of this magical, natural world.

This mood of wilderness provocation, of intense glee in their freedom, continues until and even into the night. They lie on his bed, in a darkness of fox-trotting shadows contrived by a sputtering candle, and make a different kind of love to celebrate their primal need. They lie like commas, one inverted against the other, head buried in each other's sex, the way they might feed on a wilderness kill, until they come only a moment apart with squeals and cries of pleasure.

ON THE MORNING THEY DEPART THE ISLAND for their day on the mainland—the rain now pushed aside by a muggy, myopic sunshine—the man turns to gaze at the island as the woman steers her boat boldly out into the lake.

When the woman notices him gazing back at their sanctuary, she determines it's possible there's a sadness in his eyes.

"Are you okay?" she asks, hoping at this moment he doesn't tell her something she wouldn't want to hear. She's anxious to embark on this mission of bringing the world up to speed on the wonderful couple they've become.

"Sure," he says with a smile, surprised that she has asked. Then, "Strange," he adds, forgetting to explain himself, simply falling silent again.

"What's strange?" she then must ask, calling it out over the roar of the boat's motor.

"I don't know," he says after a moment's hesitation. "I feel like I've been away and now I have to go back. It's like not knowing which is home, which is my real place."

There's more the man would add but he isn't ready yet. He doesn't want to tell her that he's been thinking how much more difficult it will be to leave this island forever now that he's spent this time with her here in a state of love and joy.

The woman feels their homelessness too. But for her it's the poignance of being smack in the center of the rich present; no satisfaction at the past nor any anticipation in the future can pretend to be good enough. She too is silent, considering how difficult it is to explain this small section in the middle of the present, even to someone who's feeling it too. It's like having nearly caught up to perfection to watch it bolt away again, leaving a torn shirttail in your hands to remind you that your quarry got away.

Moments like these are hard on the expectations of witnesses. One wants to ask the cosmos if this scene can be deleted. One asks this in the name of hope and compassion. But more honest witnesses know that this would not be true. More honest witnesses would admit they were merely anxious to get on with spying on love's vicarious thrill.

## NICOLE

BY THE TIME YOU MANEUVER THE BOAT safely into the crowded arrangement of finger docks at *The Inlet*, a mild chop is frosting the channel waters. A south wind has come up during your crossing and it blows hot, muggy and brisk. Your island has always served as a breakwater for this section of the mainland—if the wind comes directly out of the south. As a result, a gentle wave action like the one at the marina this morning is usually all this section of the channel knows.

After he helps you tie up, Matt stands there on the dock and intentionally faces the wind, letting it cleanse his features and blow his hair back along his shoulders. He closes his eyes, looking at this moment more like Crazy Horse than ever, perhaps about to address the spirit world with some grateful incantation.

Instead he says, "Surf'll be up on the other side of the island."

The pensive melancholy you noticed in his mood as you departed the island seems to have vanished. This transformation is so complete you resist breaking the mood. To preserve this moment, you smile and nod at him.

"Used to love those windy days the most when I was a kid," he says. "Used to spend hours riding the waves. Guess I wanted to be driftwood even then."

You've ridden the waves yourself in years gone by when

the lake attacked the summer shore of the island with heavy whitecapped breakers. Standing beside him, you tell him so, although you say nothing about wanting to be driftwood. Still, your separate memories of separate days, now shared somehow with him, are reason enough for the two of you to take time on the gently rocking dock for a brief, warm embrace. It acknowledges the transition you've enjoyed now that you've become lovers. And, to you, it's as if you've brought with you something of what the island has done for you recently on this day's excursion to a vaguely threatening mainland. At this moment, thank goodness, the leap from there to here doesn't seem so dramatic, so painfully irrevocable.

On the way into town with Matt behind the wheel, you consider the advantage his car represents because you don't need to take a cab. So far this summer, on days Alan was not with you on the island, a taxi was the only means to deal with the three miles between *The Inlet* and the shopping you had to do. Remembering taxis is fine, but considering the function Alan once had in your life is not. You slam the door on his memory, slide the bolt which locks it out.

Matt is a cautious driver. He comes to full, deliberate stops at each stop sign or light and carefully checks for oncoming traffic before proceeding. You mention his care behind the wheel.

"Function of age, mostly," he replies.

"Oh c'mon now," you mutter back. "You're not a senior citizen yet."

You're beginning to wish he'd drop this aging business once and for all. It's becoming a pain in the ass. It's like a popular song on the radio that you keep hearing over and over, a melody with some early humourous merit that's now grown tedious and flat.

He notices some of the annoyance in your voice, turns to you with an accommodating smile. "What I mean is I've reached the stage where I can usually avoid having to hurry anywhere. A function of lifestyle would have been a better way to put it. No pressing business lunches, no meetings with the bank. It's rare that I have to be a certain place at a specific time."

Although you know he's proud of this rebellious freedom, you hear a warning at the edges of his words and find yourself wondering if his freedom mission is just another way to romanticize irresponsibility. Or perhaps, away from the island now, he intended to caution you that he's the man he is and intends to stay that way. Or maybe there's no warning in his remarks at all. Maybe it's just your own uncertain perception stage-directing what he says. Regardless of which is which, you feel a chill encroaching on your need for him, what amounts to a vague fear of loss.

You drive along in silence. Only the Escort has anything to say. It vibrates metallically somewhere underneath the floor, a noise which intensifies when he comes to a halt and the engine idles.

"What's that vibration?" you ask, a little apprehensive about the sound.

"Exhaust shield," he replies.

"Can it be fixed?"

He grins at you and shrugs. "Actually I'm waiting for it to fall off."

"Is it serious?"

His grin abruptly subsides. "Not that I'm aware of, Nickie. I can't afford to do any work on this car right now."

"I'm sorry, Matt. I was forgetting that. It just sounds worse than it probably is."

"It does. Believe me. It's been rattling like that for more than a year." He's about to add something else but doesn't.

"What?" you prod.

"I'm not in a position to service cars as preventative maintenance. For me, that reflects luxury. I fix them *if I can* when they stop running and I have to go somewhere."

"I know. You've mentioned this before. It's just the noise. I thought it was serious."

"Anyway," he says gently. "It doesn't matter. This economic thing . . ." and the thought runs out of gas.

"You were right the first time," you tell him. "It doesn't matter."

"In a perfect world, at least," he adds, leaving you behind for a moment to attend some war of ideals alone where you can root for his underdog.

You did, of course, forget. He's told you everything about what he considers his mainstream liabilities and how, ironically, they free up his future for him. Matt will not mislead, refuses to imply, will nurse no flimsy assumption you might want to make about what he should be. All along he's been very clear, not only about what he can and cannot do, but about what he *will* and *will not* do. And he's told you enough of his background to provide at least a spotty historical perspective. The loss of his small communications business when blood clots put him in hospital, the decision to no longer delay on a private life of writing and travel, his acceptance of poverty and solitude to at last do whatever he chooses to do. Perhaps you resist everything he has said because it tends to exclude romantic partnership. Even now, as your love for him grows more intense, partnership has become a fragile thread sewn into the wonder of your feelings.

Damn, damn, damn. Will he every truly understand that wanting to be with him isn't necessarily wanting to tie him down? Or is he unable to consider such a possibility because the last person to swear that oath was lying through her teeth?

You have driven into the busiest part of downtown by now. Traffic is thick and slow, a haltingly diffusing gridlock caused by pleasant weather and the onset of a heavy tourist season. The intensity of the bustling activity belies the size of the town. You gape at the contrast between the island and this scene of hectic confusion. Both of you have rolled down your windows; it's very hot outside. Although it's not yet noon, the sidewalks are crowded with shoppers and gawkers, and their voices can be heard penetrating your silence inside the car. You might be going to a fair or attending a major sporting event, so celebratory is the fanfare outside. You have to remind yourself that you are here only because you needed to pop into town for the day. It's not a movement you want to join.

"I think I'd better grab the first available parking spot," says Matt. "We'll have to hoof it from there."

"Okay," you say, trying to be more cheerful than you really feel. "We've got the entire day."

While Matt eases the car through traffic, it strikes you that the mainland—its people, vehicles and shared shopping errands—is now in direct collision with the isolation of the island, a collision you've never appreciated so well before today. Although your injuries seem minor, it strikes you that Matt has suffered more than you in the wreckage left by the contrast. He cannot be Crazy Horse here. How could anyone be? You feel sad and a little disapproving that the conventional world tends to steamroll over the man you love, diminishing him at this moment, briefly altering what he is to you, inadvertently sneering at his suitability for you.

You're mystified by this, not only by the abruptness of the transition, but by how intensely it saddens you.

"Matt?" You labour to keep the strain out of your voice. "Maybe this wasn't such a good idea today."

He comes to a halt at a red light not far from Tim Horton's, directly behind a BMW with the top down. A perfect BMW couple laughs and talks together in the front seat, as if by appointment of Her Majesty. Unable to move any further for the moment, he can turn and study you.

"Had to happen sooner or later," he says. "First time out. We have to make the adjustment."

"Are you okay?"

"Of course. Are you?"

"Sure. I guess I just miss the island already, the way it's been for you and me."

"Can't stay on the island forever. Even if we wish we could."

Soberly you nod, aware again of some extra ingredient of warning in the pronouncement he's just made.

But before you can contemplate his words further, he suddenly directs the Escort towards an open parking space. He drives directly in, not even attempting to back properly into the spot.

"Safe at last," he says, having claimed this urgent section of asphalt turf.


ALTHOUGH EVENTUALLY THINGS IMPROVE, it takes some time for you to shake off completely your feeling of loss caused by this new sense of incompatibility with your surroundings—especially the way in which it eddies around Matt. It's as if all the reservations he has yet to express to you about the future of your union are being piled up like sandbags in this setting, to hold back the flow of your amorously hopeful stream. Visible now, his doubts threaten to contain the urgent current of your love. What will he eventually say to verify your love's futility?

You feel a petulant need to cry out that it just isn't fair. How can you be wrong about love? How can it be wrong to love Matt when it's been such an easy thing to do? And how can this day conspire to make Matt's unsaid reservations appear so accurate when, to argue with him, you must prove that he is wrong?

It isn't that Matt seems out of place in this hectic world of downtown society. To the contrary, as far as you can see, he fits in very well. He's pleasant, gregarious and warm. It's just that you know he's someone else—most of the time at any rate—that he arrives in this outer world of society only when necessary, for a brief required visit. He's struggled to reach a psychological place which gives him no need to stay. And you're perceived, whether wrongly or rightly, to be part of this world he only visits: the one, beyond your presence, he wishes to resist. And so you must consider—with a persistent, nagging sadness—that you are only a place he's somehow only passing through.

But this conclusion isn't entirely fair either. How can Matt decide arbitrarily that you're from a different world than he is? How can he decide that you'd rather be part of a society he finds quietly malignant when in fact you imagine travelling with him upon your own jointly chosen path? And hasn't he heard of balance? Can he not consider that you might broaden or enhance the journey he intends to make on his own, never mind what society does?

Still, thinking about this, you sit with him at a sidewalk cafe not far from *The Roadhouse*—the restaurant where you saw him sitting alone two months ago not long after you'd met. Both of you are now under a large umbrella, waiting for your sandwiches to arrive. There's no way to bring up the topic of your artificially separate worlds. He hasn't said anything yet to require such a complex response. He hasn't defended the virtue of his poverty, beyond reminding you about the reason he hasn't repaired his car, beyond wearing his jeans on a hot, muggy day because his last pair of shorts fell into tatters a summer or two ago. And he hasn't lacerated society the way you thought he might. There's been nothing negative at all, beyond a wince which flickered over his face when an elderly woman backed up from an outdoor rack of blouses and trod on his foot without apology.

Which means perhaps the fault is yours. Or at least you're over-anticipating the reasons he'll eventually give for being wrong for you. And, like it or not, by the time he does, you worry you'll have recognized the truth in them yourself, making them impossible to dispute.

Or maybe it's just the shock of this crowded mainland station after so many blissful days alone with him on the island. But even assuming this to be the case, somehow he's got the argument covered. *Can't stay on the island forever*, he said, *even if we wish we could.*

But after lunch and over coffee, he eases your worries significantly. He leans close to you and takes both of your hands in his. He draws them slowly to his lips, then gently kisses them. All without a word. But the result for you is the same as it would have been had he delivered a long and eloquent speech. Soon, with astonishing speed, you hardly remember what you were worried about.

After lunch, you comfortably join the throng of tourists on the street. It turns out there's a sidewalk sale taking place. Matt joins you in your half-hearted search for a bargain, although you ultimately don't find one. Still, shopping together is fun. You cut up together, perform for one another, try on sunglasses, even exchange remarks with strangers you encounter along the street. You hold hands, touch shoulders, occasionally kiss one another on the cheek. And your love feels magical again. You delight in how people can see your happiness, translating each passing smile, even the fleeting ones, into an enjoyable endorsement of your predestined function to go through life as a couple.

This is more like it, you decide. This is how you imagined it would be when you suggested coming into town, not the trick-or-treat confusion you conjured up this morning when the mainland seemed so alien. You blame yourself for your early trepidation. How could you have become so apprehensive for hardly any reason at all?

Matt suggests an ice cream cone.

"If we share one," you reply. "I don't need a whole one."

You agree on butter pecan.

You stand on the street corner sharing the cone, taking turns most of the time, licking the ice cream in unison a few times—with a knowing, provocative gaze—so that your tongues can clandestinely touch, resuming your island tryst here on a busy street inside your own little code.

Eventually you have coffee, an excuse to get in out of the heat. The waitress at *Mom's* is elderly, mom from head to toe, guidance and patience and perfect in her *apple-pie-ness*, two red circles of rouge painted like targets on her cheeks. Something has spilled on her name tag, taking out the "e" in Buelah until all that's left is Bu lah above her matronly breast.

She notices you holding hands on the arborite of the restaurant table. "That's so nice," she says in passing.

You remind Matt that your parents are coming for the weekend on the day after tomorrow. "So I have to go to the A & P."

"Okay."

"It isn't much but I need a few things."

"No problem," he says.

There's another potential issue buzzing around you like a fly. Suddenly he takes a swat at it while you happily stir your coffee, unaware the time has arrived. His voice drifts out of some ethereal place where—you decide with a pang of guilt—your own thoughts should have been.

"What are you going to do about me while your parents are on the island?"

"Yes, well," is all you say to have time to explain yourself.

He waits, a droopy grin clinging for its life on the cliff of his face.

"Well, you won't be staying over, Matt."

"Of course not. And you won't be staying at *The Crow's Nest* either."

"No."

"Could be a long couple of days."

"We'll get through it," you say. Then you add with a grin of your own: "But look out on Monday night. I'll tear you limb from limb."

"I'll look forward to being torn."

But he grows pensive after this, and you know another question will be coming at you soon. In fact it arrives while you are deciding whether to head it off or not.

"Are you going to tell your mom and dad about you and me?"

You gaze at him and wonder what you can say to banish

potential hurt. But he's told you he likes your honesty, that he finds it extremely rare. He's made so much of this, the truth has become your only option.

"I don't know," you say.

"Tough one, isn't it?"

You don't know what to say to that. For you, tough doesn't quite cover it. There's the way that he means it's tough, referring to sorting out the tactics. But it's tough for you in another way—whatever reasons you eventually select while deciding not to mention to your astonished parents that Matt is your new romantic interest will develop into reasons that may endorse Matt's own reservations about your future together. The ones he has not mentioned seriously yet, but the ones you know exist.

"I've thought about it, Matt. I've considered it a bit."

"Of course."

"To tell you the truth, I thought I wouldn't premeditate it. I'll know what to do when the time comes."

"Sure. That makes sense. It's less artificial that way."

"Yes. I'm proud of you and me, Matt. I don't want to imply, by strategically making the announcement, that I'm ashamed of what's happened."

"That's always a danger," he admits.

*Bu lah* comes with refills.

"You know what I think about most?" you tell him after she's gone. "I think about what is their business and what's none of their business at all."

He nods, gravely considering your words. "Trouble is, what they think is their business and what *you* think is their business can be two different things entirely."

"I know."

"Our parents never stop being our parents no matter how old we get."

"I know," you say again. "It's a pain in the neck."

"I leave it," Matt says then, "in your capable hands."

But that isn't good enough for you. He's ducking the issue. "Well, what do *you* think?" you ask. "What would *you* prefer?"

"I'd prefer you to use your own best judgment."

"Oh c'mon now. You must have your own feelings. And don't start out with that 'in a perfect world' business."

His grin is broad and affectionate. "In a perfect world," he begins.

"Matt!"

"Okay, okay." He takes a few seconds to compose his thoughts. "You and I both know they won't be happy about this."

"We know no such thing."

"Let me put it another way. You and I both know that I don't fit the mold of what your parents have in mind for you."

You feel a deep impatience now. What century are you from, Bowman? Do parents still arrange marriages, expect to entirely endorse the choices their children make?

"So what's your point?" you demand.

"My point," he says, "is that your instincts are exceptional and you should use your own judgment. Whatever you decide is all right with me. I believe you know what to do. That's all."

"Thank you," you say halfheartedly, feeling cornered by his compliment. "One complication is that they don't know about Alan. In fact, they'll half expect to see him there. One other thing. For the record, I don't give a shit what my parents think."

"Of course you do."

"Not about this, I don't. I'll give them time to absorb the new developments but, beyond that, it's none of their business."

He looks at you thoughtfully. It's a warm expression, perhaps conveying that he's proud of you. But warmth or not, there's something else in the look, something which bothers you. As if, at the bottom of it all, he doesn't actually believe you.

LATER YOU DECIDE ON *THE ROADHOUSE* for dinner. You have, by now, outlasted the bustling crowds which began to drift home by late afternoon. You've been to the A & P where you've flirted in each aisle, gazing over displays of cans of beans with meaningful, lusty glances. Matt has eased the burden of your shopping by transforming the chore into another celebration of your partnership. In the end you don't seem to mind that the groceries you must purchase are not what you would buy, that because your parents are arriving Saturday morning you shop as your mother's surrogate, buying only what *she* would buy. Matt calls this "the woman-mother thing" or "matriarchal imperative."

"What about fathers and sons?"

"The man-father thing," he replies. "Patriarchal imperative."

"Quite the little psychologist, aren't you?"

"Don't know," he says to this. "Still trying to figure it out."

You park the car again in the wasteland left behind downtown by the hundreds of departing tourists. It's just after six and you walk hand-in-hand towards *The Roadhouse*, hungry, a little tired, satisfied, this last celebration the only thing that lies ahead of you before you return to the island and the safety of your shared solitude.

A couple (older than you but younger than Matt) goes by and he asks you what you think of those pouches they and every other tourist wears around their waist.

"I don't know," you say.

"They look like tumors," he mutters. "There should be special hospitals where we can have them surgically removed, a kind of body pouch MASH unit that eradicates them once and for all."

"You've given this a lot of thought, haven't you?"

"Yes I have," he says.

You simply shake your head in mock dismay.

What makes someone look up to see the executioner's axe? How do we anticipate the coming of a storm? What makes us glance in a certain direction to see the very last thing we wished to see? These are questions you'll ask yourself a number of times over the next few days. And there'll be no answer beyond a dull, fatalistic assumption that humans are telepaths, plotting out in advance the incidents we conspire in which will make us unhappy.

Whatever the reason, you choose this moment, barely fifty yards from *The Roadhouse*, to glance into the street. Still holding Matt's hand, closing the gap between this moment in time and your restaurant destination, you notice a familiar car drive by, only casually at first, then, as recognition dawns, with a deep explosion of alarm. You focus on the man behind the wheel and recognize Alan Birken.

No doubt about it.

Your stomach knots up like the joint at each end of a tightrope. You come to a jerky halt on the sidewalk as his car vanishes around a corner. Although it's apparent Alan hasn't seen you, you stand frozen to the spot, trying to conceal your shock.

"What's wrong?" asks Matt.

"Nothing," you reply instinctively.

"Are you sure?"

Lies, you know, are dominoes. They stand on their edges, each one in the shadow of its sibling. And when the truth comes out—as inevitably it must—they topple in an accusatory design revealing your dishonesty. . .

". . . Nickie?"

The first domino has taken its place on its edge and reluctantly you position the second one nearby it, then the third, hurrying to complete a design of temporary untruths you feel will give you time to think.

"Matt, I don't want to go out for dinner. I want to go back to the island. I want to be alone with you again. Is that okay?"

"Of course," he says, relieved that this is all it is. "I just wondered what was wrong."

"Nothing, nothing's wrong. I guess I've just had enough."

"Okay." He turns around with you and you head back towards his car.

You pretend your legs aren't rubbery, that everything's all right. You pretend that lies aren't dominoes because your intentions are noble and good. Most of all, you try to pretend it wasn't Alan behind the wheel of that car.

But it was, you know it was. There is no reason for Alan to be in this small town; he is here to badger you into being with him again. And you feel a nasty desperation. You feel a nasty fear.

## MATT

**Sunday, July 14**

DRIZZLE. THE RAIN LOOKS LIKE A TATTERED CURTAIN from my vantage point in the waning light, moth-eaten and streaked. The silver droplets left behind on the window panes seem resigned to their despair. In the rain, night falls more quickly than usual, taking advantage of the density of the cloud cover to overrun day as it retreats. I envision this surrender as sadly complete, the way day must wave its white flag at the inevitability of night's triumph. I know all of this reflects my mood—chipped, resolute, surrendering in its own right to what cannot be changed.

This rainfall crept up on the island a few hours ago like some sneaky little politician emerging from the back benches, intent on destroying what had been a pleasantly sunny and muggy day. I didn't notice the transition while it was taking place. Instead, after I washed my dinner dishes, there it was—a new bleakness in the sky so surprising it seemed manufactured. Then the rain began to fall a few minutes later.

And so here I am alone with myself again. On the surface everything is so much the same as it used to be before I fell in love with Nicole. Nothing here to mark the difference. Same brand of coffee, same edible oil product to make it taste familiar. I sit at the same spot at this dining room table and a cigarette smolders in the ashtray the way it usually does when I write in this journal. Even Canine Ben succumbs to ritual, lying under the table not far from my feet, his favorite spot when I am working. For him it takes on the security of a den; the table shields him from falling objects, my feet bestow the companionable touch that helps defend him from solitude. All of this is the way it was each night before Nicole came into my life, before we turned to love and lovemaking like a couple of near-drowned, gasping divers.

Oh yes, one more thing remains unchanged. My past. The incidents which cannot reform themselves to satisfy the critical gaze of posterity. The wrong and right of me, my deeds and patterns remain permanent. Any change in them I might be tempted to manufacture would be a mistake of memory or, worse, some kind of crowd-pleasing lie.

There should be comfort in the kind of familiarity I feel at this moment. Like knowing the ocean is always going to be there whether the ship on which I currently sail goes down in a storm or not. Am I the ship or the sea on which it navigates? It's a metaphysical question I'm sure I'll never clearly answer, at least to my satisfaction. But tonight perhaps I'm the sea; my particular sea—whether inland or briny or connected to an ocean I never truly fathom. The various ships which ply my depths must inevitably come and go, caught in my particular current. I come back to this same place time and time again, to the sea that is me with its unchanging coastline of rugged solitude. This is why, I suppose, I survive all those nautical wrecks—the Gwens, the Esthers, the Carolyns and, yes, the Nicoles—to discover that I am still the same sea which I've always sailed upon.

So I should be comforted by this sameness. Yet although it's there—the comfort—there's something about it which limps tonight, which has been bruised by my longing for Nicole.

As this journal has already observed, courtesy of last night's entry, yesterday I felt fine. Worked all day and was pleased with the result—that's what I said when I reported in to these pages last night. It's all there in black and white. Come to think of it, I accomplished a great deal today as well. There's a manuscript growing ever deeper in the carton on the corner of this desk. But tonight I don't feel fine. I haven't seen Nicole since early yesterday morning when she departed *The Crow's Nest* to go home and shower before crossing the channel to pick up her parents at *The Inlet*.

I try to maintain perspective. Nicole's absence is perfectly understandable. She must entertain her parents and deal with my intrusion into *her* particular sameness. But tell that to the mysterious source of my yearning over Nicole and I being apart. Tell it to the starving ghost which lives inside my flesh, the one that wants to haunt me with all that was thrillingly felt just a few short days ago. Tell it to the mean little notion that those feelings have been lost for good. It's folly really. In empirical terms, nothing has actually changed. But the ghost keeps haunting me anyway, a little annoyed that he's not been served his meal of romantic sensation for nearly two full days.

What is it about love that will not learn, that makes it such a poor pupil of the realities of life? Knowing love is often bad for us, we crave it anyway. It's like candy and tooth decay. In the aftermath of passion, a dentist patches our teeth with fillings. Still, we reach for the toffees just the same and a new cavity is born, requiring that it shortly too be filled. Why doesn't love give in, give up? Why doesn't it truly withdraw when it finally perceives that it cannot win? Love is like a search party ten years after the airplane crash, still stumbling around in the bush, looking for someone to rescue. Anyone, by the way—it's not as fussy as it pretends to be. As if the issue isn't the victim it hopes to find but any casual representative of the state of *victimhood*, so that some principle of faith in the search is kept inviolate.

Ah yes. Faith. No doubt the key to the puzzle. I have a personal view of faith. I know it doesn't loiter around in the arcade of the brain. No, it prefers more pastoral settings. Peace and calm where it can walk with you arm in arm, nattering away endlessly about love's necessary function until, out of fatigue more than anything else, you decide what it says makes sense. We have words for this pastoral setting, words like heart or soul, places where whispers boom because of the contrasting calm in their surroundings. Faith can't raise its voice enough to be heard inside the brain—too many flashing lights and sound effects in the mind, too many common ambitions to win the game and defeat our many opponents.

Truth is, I could write about this forever and never uncover anything new. I've tried to sort through it all before. In the end I'm left with shelf after shelf of shiny metaphors lined up like plastic models of old and classic automobiles.

It's my mood, of course. All of these considerations germinate inside my garden patch because I'm feeling sorry for myself. I've become addicted to Nicole and I now suffer my first maddening state of withdrawal. Love dressed up as a drug. Calling it something else doesn't provide any true solution to love's various forms of torture.

Maybe I've always feared how futile Nicole and I are as lovers. Because love itself is futile. Like faith, love doesn't have the courage to play in the arcade either, where all the bad boys hang out. No, like faith, it just stays home to whisper politely about the merits of goodness and agreeable perfections, ignoring the fact the world is too cynical to take real love seriously.

But wait a minute, Matt. You're forgetting your romantic creed. *Give all the love you feel—take all the love you can get.* And, yes, that's cynical too. But at least it's a cynicism which looks you right in the eye, doesn't glance away shiftily like most other cynicism does when the topic rolls around to ethical purities. Besides, I'm old enough to know that you don't go to the grave with answers. Life has merit if you manage nothing more than a couple of intriguing questions.

I imagine Nicole is suffering too. Until this evening, when I finally succumbed to the ache of my own loss exclusively, I spent more time wondering how *she* is making out. She's down the beach with her parents, dealing with the unpleasant fact that, sooner or later, she's got some explaining to do. Maybe she's told them already about the breakup with Alan, and about me, his ready replacement. Yes, maybe they know about her and me, and about her latest attempt at sacrificing innocence on the altar of passionate love. For all I know, while I moan away my loneliness tonight, they've tied her to a chair to talk some sense into her.

Actually, strangely enough, her father was my only human contact today. I ran into him early this morning down on the beach not far from here. We stood there at the water's edge and chatted pleasantly about one thing and another. He asked me how my work was going. I asked him about his summer so far. I could tell, this morning at least, that he had no idea I've been sleeping with his daughter. In fact, Sid was more interested again in whether I'm a fisherman or not.

"I've done it a few times," I replied, "mostly when I was young."

"But not avidly," he prodded.

"No."

He considered this a moment. "Well," he said at last, "I think fishing is just reflection, a place to have a conversation, a way to get to know people."

"That's true," I agreed.

"I thought I'd go out this evening. There's a spot on the other side of the island. I've brought in a bass or two there. And not a bad size either."

I merely nodded, a little embarrassed that he couldn't remember telling me this last time we met. And I was recalling how fishing finally died for me as a worthwhile past-time, when it became analogous to politics. More or less on creative whimsy at some point, I began to imagine voters as schools of silvery fish, hooked by the fatuous bait entrepreneurs cast over the side of our compliant, leaky boat. Since then I think of the comparison often, to the point where fishing itself has become a disconcerting concept.

"Betty doesn't want to go," Sidney was saying then. "She thinks it might rain." Now he glanced at me, shyly I think, like a young man asking for a date. "Wondered if you might want to join me," he managed to suggest at last.

"Tonight? After dinner?"

"Yeah. I know you're not a fisherman. Hell, I don't think I am either."

"I could use a change of scene," I said.

"Well, we'll see what the weather brings. Betty has all these body aches that tell her when it's going to rain. She woke up with them this morning."

"Okay. Either way, I'll be here this evening anyway. I didn't have any other plans."

And that was how we left it.

Now that the rain has arrived, I wonder which it is that keeps him at his own cottage. Likely the rain. But possibly he's grown newly choosey about whom he fishes with. No amorous interlopers or ruthlessly romantic rogues need apply.

This showdown had to arrive sooner or later. Not only Nicole's parents cautioning her about what is wrong with me as a romantic partner, but, shortly afterwards, Nicole recognizing the truth in what they said. The same truth, by the way, I have recognized all along myself, ashamed that I haven't mentioned it to her before this. If, for some reason, Nicole hasn't told her parents that we are lovers, it only puts off until later the validity of their concerns. In fact it may also indicate that she is aware of my failings herself and wants foolishly to delay until those failings cure themselves. Which cannot happen, of course. Failings rarely fail to be failings; that's the failure of failings.

I've listed my personal inadequacies a number of times before. Right here in this journal. It appears I'm about to do it again and perhaps I should, just to stay focused now that the cracks in the relationship are about to show themselves. Perhaps I should type it out and put it under a magnet on the refrigerator, sort of an anti-shopping list. Yes, reminders of things not to purchase when you're considering courting the spectre of romantic love.

I suppose I wrote out this list the first time in this journal when I realized I cared for Nicole and saw no future in the feeling, back then before I had any idea she cared for me in return. Then more recently I made the list again, inspired to do so, as I recall it, by her resistance to hearing me express my concerns directly to her in person.

Tonight I'm not sure why the exercise seems warranted yet again. Unless it's the pain of loneliness seeking the companionship it sometimes finds in the pain of self-abuse. Yes, perhaps that's it. That or moderating the intensity of my yearning for Nicole with a cold showering of my emotions, to slow them down a little so that my brain can catch up to negotiate.

Poor Nicole! She can't win tonight. If she doesn't tell her parents that I'm the man she loves, then I'll be hurt, whether I want to be or should be or not. If she does, then I'll want to discuss what is inappropriate about me as a lover in the future.

I shouldn't have let this happen, this whole romantic thing, because it compromised the woman I cherished as my friend. Then again, to think that her choice is entirely up to me is rather a stupid notion. Besides, it's been a wondrous kind of love, so fine and exciting and warm. It isn't what we've shared or felt together that's the problem. It's just trying to give it some future which seems the hopeless part.

As for my list of circumstantial failings, I know them all by heart. And I know how they are connected to one another and how, as a group, they are connected to the past, those other hapless times I believed I was in love. It's all joined together—this worn garment of my failure—by the threads which define my past. And there's no escaping this. I've learned to see the pattern in the demands a love relationship makes. I know the pattern in the required compromises which must be made so that love develops in a serene way beyond the point of initial passion.

I am, after all, in the autumn of my years, an autumn just begun but autumn just the same. But Nicole is only halfway through her summer. It's not that our seasons collide in any measurable way. Rather, it's what we've learned separately inside our respective seasons which causes the disparity. I've learned much more than Nicole, I fear, about why I do not fit inside a conventional love relationship. And, further, I know exactly why I do not want to fit.

The list . . .

*Age Disparity:* Nicole is thirty-two and I am forty-seven. In fact, I will be forty-eight before she is thirty-three. There are several things wrong with this disparity when one scans the future for possibilities. Sometimes I imagine myself in hospital again, an institution I know far too well, and I imagine Nickie suffering at the hands of some kind of obligatory supportive function. She's too young to have to go through that.

Testifying to this fact is a series of painful memories from a number of years ago. I remember clearly Esther's reaction to my long drawn-out hospital stays when the doctors tried to puzzle out my mysterious propensity for developing blood clots without discernible cause. She would telephone my hospital room from time to time to abuse me about my condition. "If you don't stop this," she would shriek, "I'm going to divorce you."

Although I should have accepted this threat as a satisfactory alternative, I wasn't ready to do so yet. Instead, her threats only added to my misery.

Carolyn too hated my institutionalized vacations. When it became her turn to provide solace and support, she resorted to daily visits which lasted for barely five minutes. She hated hospitals, she said. What she really hated, however, was that my function as a provider appeared to be drawing to a close.

Strangely enough, since I've been on my own, the blood clot malady has departed. And what this tells me, I'm not sure. I can't ignore that I'm in good health now. The blood clots have vanished as mysteriously as they initially appeared.

Age brings its host of physical ailments. Nicole, in her youth, is better off without them. And I'm better off without their potential for inspiring her inevitable but understandable betrayal. Another age factor I fear even mentioning here is that Nicole may one day soon want a child or more than one. She demurs when motherhood comes up even vaguely. My two sons are grown. I cannot even contemplate whether I have the stamina or generosity for a second stab at fatherhood.

*Economics:* I have no money and no reason to expect I ever will. Nor do I intend to pursue wealth at the cost of my creative freedom and physical health. I did so for far too much of my life and know with a profound certainty that I'll never do it again. The contrast between my limited means and the economic security Nicole is used to is astonishingly deep. Once the dust of romantic joy begins to drift away, the carpet underneath will display clearly my economic inadequacy. Love drifts away as it tries to tread such a carpet. And much more quickly too when the partner who has little material ambition refuses to compromise the nobility he perceives in this unpopular approach to life.

Gwen, Esther and Carolyn all had one thing in common— an expectation that I would share their enthusiasm for the middle class. I fed that expectation inadvertently in my anxiousness to please them, only to discover each time I did so that I became spiritually and creatively lost. Nicole's error in our relationship is her timing. She loves me at a point in my history when I will never change my life to please anyone again.

*My Jaded Past:* This one I regret but it exists nonetheless. Bluntly put, the trouble is I don't believe. I have heard the songs of love before, so lyrical at first and then so discordant after the allure of the conventional relationship takes precedence. Even

Gwen, the mother of my children, lied to me. Before we were married, we discussed travel and a free-spirited lifestyle. Yes, she said back then, this was what she wanted too. After the marriage, however, she wanted to buy a house. And she wanted me to stop writing. And she wanted children early instead of a little later on, which was what we had previously agreed upon.

Esther lied as well. She said she would not love me for my functions but in the end it was my functions, primarily economic, which defined my every passing day, until somehow I evaporated as the person I wanted to be, replaced by all the material goals I was expected to accomplish. Carolyn lied too, though in a different, convoluted way, engaging in the same volley in the tennis court of financial security, delivered this time with the backhand instead of the forehand.

No wonder I don't believe. Strange how often people fall in love with someone, then embark on an intensive editing of what attracted them to that particular someone in the first place. It's the most cynical characteristic of love. Cynical because it implies love can have no permanence without this kind of creative tampering in a person's ideals and ambitions. And the tampering gives rise to the impermanence in the end anyway.

When love is going to die, we should just let it die. All the cosmetic operations—the facelifts and tummy tucks—cannot keep it alive. But we keep going on and on. We build a prefabricated shell of love based on conventional ideals. Then, at some point, when we look at ourselves in the mirror, we discover a human husk bearing no resemblance to the person we thought we were. I looked in the mirror numerous times back then and wondered where I'd gone, that other guy, that other person I intended to be. And this is why I do not believe any longer in the future of romantic love. Not even sweet Nicole can pilot her way between the treacherous reefs of what I've learned about love during my long and jaded past.

*Different Destinations:* I imagine, come fall, Nicole will move to Kingston to work with her friend Karen. She has played her piano for me and her music is exquisite. It soars and ebbs, both moods filled with a provocative poignancy. It touches me. Music is her true career. She can build a life around this new opportunity while I, on the other hand, intend to go to the mountains. There I hope to reinforce the sense of freedom I have at last gained for myself. There, I intend to bond with a natural world I once neglected. I must make up for all that time I lost trapped inside a suburbia of questionable ambitions. I must reinvigorate a creative drive I permitted various people to compromise.

There are other items too on my anti-shopping list. My political anger and the solitude it requires and creates. It is a sour note sometimes when I come face to face with society's political complacency. Nicole would find the frequency of this occurrence tedious.

But I hate this list. No matter how carefully considered it is, how reasonable it looks on paper, I fret that it reflects defeat, a loss of faith in the possibility there is someone out there who is entirely right for me. And, as such, the list is merely a masquerade which hides a mood of self-abuse. I call it Matt Bowman's critique of impure reason. Even tonight, having again compiled my list of failings, I don't feel enlightened in any way. I've only grown much sadder. What began as an exercise in clear thinking has managed to evolve into a stupor of self-pity.

As I said a few pages ago, faith doesn't visit well the arcade of the brain. But the brain doesn't visit well the dew-sparkled meadow of amorously hopeful love or the hypothetical ambitions of the battered soul. No, the brain prefers crowds, crowds who view life from the same conventional perspective. The brain, tired of trying to understand the ill-defined pleas of the soul, gives in to the familiar—what is learned, shared, acceptable.

So I am left with the vacuum which results after one has accomplished a very self-defeating exercise. Then I remember how important Nicole has become to me.

Actually I saw her today a great distance away just for a moment or two—from my perch here at *The Crow's Nest*. She was on the beach with her mother, on lounges they had dragged down to the water's edge to better enjoy the day. I stood just outside my cottage at the edge of the hill and I silently begged Nicole to turn and notice me. I urged this telepathic plea hundreds of yards across sand and space, but she didn't turn around. She didn't hear me calling her in such silent faith. Perhaps at that moment she was telling her mother everything and was considering the practical sense in her mother's concerned response. Perhaps love as anything more than blind endless faith or wouldn't-it-be-nice ideal was already dying at that moment as she saw the merit in her mother's advice.

Whatever the distraction, she didn't notice me, didn't turn to see me standing behind her in the distance. After a few moments I slipped away in disappointment.

But infallibly right in my sense that our love is doomed, I think.

I come back to my medicine for solace, my credo: *Give all the love you feel—take all the love you can get.*

Tomorrow, I guess, I should go back to Kingston for a couple of days. To check on things. To make some phone calls. Mostly, though, to regain some kind of perspective. Back in Kingston there is no perfect island setting to suggest that love has a point and a future. Back there, it might be easier for me to reinvoke the provisions of my personal charter, the one which guarantees me peace and solitude if I remain loyal to my chosen mission.

## NICOLE

AT LAST THE MONDAY MORNING you've been longing for all weekend staggers into your life. You embrace its arrival with a provocative but private sigh of relief. Now, at least, the fog which has been obscuring your usual clarity of mind for more than two days can finally begin to lift. All that remains is one last trip across the channel after which you'll deposit your mother and father firmly on the soil of the mainland, then wave a grateful goodbye as they drive away from *The Inlet* and out of the sacristy of your personal tensions.

After this, you want to see Matt. In fact, you want to run across the beach like some actor in a feminine hygiene commercial and throw your arms around his neck. And maybe then, after you've kissed away the chill your bones have absorbed during the two days of your separation, you plan to suggest—not altogether seriously but not altogether fantastically either—that the two of you run away together. Right now, to some other island, some other meadow, some other temperate hideaway where the world must leave you alone.

But Monday morning stutters. Your mother tarries, delaying their departure. She can't find her glasses. Then, after she finds her glasses, she can't locate the photographs of your distant cousin Gabriel's wedding last month, the ones she insisted you see. Then, after what was lost has been found, she turns mysteriously to tidying up sections of the cottage. She moves a number of inconsequential possessions around, this knickknack from an end table over to the window ledge, another one—the totem pole from British Columbia—from the window ledge to the fireplace mantle. She even hangs up one of your t-shirts she finds in the demilitarized zone between the clothes hamper (its destination) and the chair by the dresser (its original posting of duty) where you usually stack the clothing you might wear the next day.

You want to throttle her. What is she doing and why is she doing it?

Occasioned by your stay at the cottage, you've begun to realize this summer that Betty Graham has all the territorial graciousness of the average Siberian tiger. All of this fussiness seems to indicate that she wants her cottage back. If it all could be done again, she'd have you stay somewhere else this summer to contemplate your future. You can bet too that she wants you to stop having problems with Alan, that she wants you to grow up romantically, never mind that the nature of romantic maturity probably eludes her in the same way it eludes everyone else.

The trouble is you have become part of the inconvenience she feels in life's capacity for change. You intuit that your mother wants everything to simply stop. She doesn't want to have to deal with anything new, whether it originates with you or anybody else. All the old information—defining you and life in general—has filled up her canister of data. She has no remaining room for the unexpected. Her world resists change, even when she has to bar all the windows and doors to keep the changes out there from slithering inside her perception.

Life for your mother seems to have reached a paradigm paralysis on this particular milky Monday morning. So much so that even your father's patience, usually as broad as the Sahara, shows signs of wearing out.

"Betty," he complains from the kitchen doorway where he waits for her, knee deep in the puddle of their luggage, "we really have to get going."

"I know, Sid, I know," she answers as she passes.

But she goes into the living room one more time, glancing here and there, insisting that she survey her domain again in case any further last minute adjustments are required.

Biting your tongue for the moment, you wade now too in the pond of their luggage, glancing outside at the sky still stubbornly gray. Although last night's rain has stopped, it looks like it might resume at any moment. At the upper edge of the lake, the horizon is bleeding upwards to assimilate the colorlessness of the massing clouds.

"Mother, please," you cry. "We'll get caught in the rain if you don't hurry up."

Hearing this, she emerges at last from her final patrol, lips pursed in that peculiar expression of defiance she demonstrates whenever she's in this kind of mood. Finally, though, you get her out of the cottage and the three of you carry bags and clumsy suitcases down to the waiting boat.

In the end the weekend wasn't long enough to tell your parents you're seeing Matt romantically. Your news about breaking it off with Alan—even minus the gory details of the party—consumed all the allotted discussion time for your love life. Defending your decision in the face of your mother's rigidity became too much of a drain on your energy resources. The revelation about Matt, you decided, would have to wait. Although you opted not to mention his role in your life this time because you lacked the strength to do it justice, in the end it boiled down to tactical wisdom. If you wanted Matt and you to work out, that would mean picking the right time to get your parents on side. She who confesses and runs away, you thought wryly, lives to confess something else another day.

Ultimately your father seemed to understand better than his wife the decision you had reached about Alan. But your mother, even now, is holding out. Although she'd never admit she feels this way, you realize she's decided there's something wrong with you where love and men are concerned. She wants you to plead guilty to the allegation that you don't want or need a romantic partner at all in the long term because you're simply too independent. Still, even while you know a little of this is true, it was while she was intimating this conclusion that you nearly told her about Matt. But you didn't. Instead you informed her the evening your Mum and Dad arrived that you believe Alan is stalking you.

"Stalking you? What does that mean, Dear? What is this

stalking thing?"

"I think he's stalking me," you replied impatiently, glad to get his particular worry out in the open. "Spying on me, following me."

Then, taking a deep breath, you explained how there are laws against stalking now, how you saw Alan in town last Thursday while you were running errands. "He drove by in his car," you said.

"Maybe he just wants to talk to you," your mother suggested, once you'd convinced her that seeing him in the first place was not some kind of childish hallucination.

"Mom, he's in the area because he intends to harass me. You don't really know him the way I do."

"Oh, Nickie, this is all so *melodramatic.* Sometimes disagreements get blown all out of proportion. Afterwards you look back on them and they just seem silly."

At that point, you felt furious with her for failing to understand and trivializing your concerns now that you'd realized how vulnerable you could be here on the island.

"Alan," your mother insisted, "loves you very much." But you knew this viewpoint was an observation of convenience rather than anything she necessarily believed, that it was inspired by her dogged resistance to change. So round and round her dismissals went until, drained and frustrated at being unable to reach her, you felt explaining your point of view—and even your needs and fears themselves—was a futile exercise.

In the end there you were, stumbling around in an exhausted fog. Missing Matt, wanting but being unable to tell someone sympathetic how much you care for him. Defending yourself for breaking it off with Alan. Failing to convey your fear and anxiety that Alan wasn't going to let it go. Wishing now that you had told Matt that you saw Alan drive by last Thursday, so that at least he could be at your side, a comrade-in-arms. So much to think about and all of it wafting and drifting ever more densely around you, this tiring and confused fog billowing around your brain to the point where you couldn't see your hand in front of your face.

But with your parents departing, you feel the fog beginning to lift. Even when you pull away from the island and pass *The Crow's Nest*—noting that Matt's boat is mysteriously gone—you begin to believe again that everything will be all right. You'll tell your parents about Matt next time you see them. And, by then, Alan will have been dealt with somehow. At that point, everything will make more sense. What your mother perceives as melodrama at this point will have righted itself, replaced by the road you'll take into the next phase of your future.

So you bolt across the channel to avoid the chance of rain, the channel crossing calm because there is no wind.

After you tie up the boat, you help your parents to their car with their things. Then you embrace them one by one, your mother first just before she climbs inside, still in a bit of huff but impatient to get going despite her previous delays. Then you hug your father too. He has that look of chagrined and captive compromise you've seen him exhibit in the past. This time, no doubt, he's caught between being obligated by the solidarity necessary to his marriage and feeling sympathy for his daughter who is temporarily out of favor.

"Don't worry, Nick," he says. "I'll try to talk to her." But his voice sounds subdued and cautious. It doesn't inspire very much confidence.

You wave at them as they drive up the hill away from *The Inlet* but neither one of them appears to notice. By the time their car disappears from view you feel some important point of departure for you has been reached while you weren't paying attention. For one brief, dizzy moment it's exhilarating. You enjoy the rich sensation of being newly sure of yourself. For one brief moment the hatchets of your particular past feel safely buried for good. For one brief moment your future seems to truly belong to you, regardless of how it eventually turns out. For one brief moment you sincerely believe you will never be tempted again to apologize for merely knowing your own mind.

BUT THIS FEELING OF DEFT SELF-ASSURANCE is brutally murdered hardly a moment later as you make your way back to the boat. Like most crimes of psychological origin, it's committed while you aren't looking. Your thoughts are somewhere else. In this case, while you stroll back towards the docks and your waiting boat, your thoughts have returned to Matt and the anticipation you feel of your joyful reunion with him. So it is that you suffer a deep shock, a rush of dismay when

Alan comes around the corner of the marina building and something—intuition, alarm—causes you to turn and notice him. And you see, right away, that he's carrying a life jacket in his hand. It may as well be a gun, the fear and outrage it inspires.

"Nickie," he calls, still several yards away, beginning to hurry towards you.

And you realize he's been watching you for days, even here, even while you were saying goodbye to your parents. He has, for days, been hiding somewhere nearby, waiting for you to be on your own. So you stop for a moment and glare at him, your hands up as if you can push him away.

"Alan! No! You're not welcome here! Leave me alone! Go away! Don't come near me!"

Startled, he stops in his tracks for a moment. The lifejacket is brilliantly orange. He doesn't say anything.

There is, thank goodness, a handful of boaters on the docks and, as if in some rehearsed choreography, they all turn and gaze at you, hearing as one, you hope, the alarm in your voice.

"Don't come near me," you shriek at Alan again. "You have to leave me alone. It's the law," you add for good measure. "Don't come near my boat!"

This last addendum about the law is inspired. It ensures that the people on the dock, converted into witnesses, must turn to look at him. So that Alan, being Alan, so conscious of form and how he appears in front of strangers, must stop in his tracks for fear of looking foolish. He gives the people on the docks an eye-rolling kind of shrug and, in a different way, looks foolish anyway. It strikes you that there's always been a meanness in his foolishness, the meanness that would restrain you despite your entreaties that he let you move on. It would be dangerous to underestimate it, you know.

Temporarily free to escape, you run now the rest of the way to your boat and cast off the lines. Then you hop on board and start the engine. As you hurry out into the channel, you look back once more in alarm to see him still standing where he was, frozen to the spot where you exposed him for the controlling, obsessive bastard he is.

But your relief at having escaped the mainland is modified by the dilemma lying ahead. You are absolutely certain Alan will come after you to try to change your mind. You arrive quickly at this inescapable conclusion as you retreat across the channel, the boat screaming underneath you as if giving vent to its own cry of outrage.

He won't let it go like that on the shore. In fact, you've succeeded only in throwing down another gauntlet. This is how he'll interpret your words a few moments ago. The more vehement your "no," the more likely he is to assume he can still change your mind.

It's crazy really. It's like being caught playing with your toys in a world strictly defined by only *his* imagination. Your frantic mind struggles to understand his immediate intentions. That was a life jacket he was carrying. He's probably rented himself a boat. Shortly he'll come around the point of the island, looking for you, to wheedle and whine and accuse, then to finally justify what he feels is his right to be angry. You'll have to be ready for him. You'll have to come up with an insurmountable strategy to withstand the imaginary righteousness he considers reality.

You round the point of the island, cut back on the throttle. Matt's boat is still nowhere to be seen. Oh Matt, where are you? It feels like high noon on your dusty western street and you're going to have to conduct this gunfight entirely on your own. You allow a joyfully adolescent fantasy to enter your mind, a fantasy in which your boyfriend, Matt, beats up on your enemy outside the doors of the high school. It's an embarrassing little notion but it doesn't alter your need for an ally. Of all the times for Matt to be away, this is probably the worst.

Still, your insistent fear and trepidation are gradually being matched by your growing resolve, by the inspiration created by your anxiety. So you don't beach your boat. Instead you cut the throttle back to barely trolling speed and you begin to patrol your stretch of shoreline like some coast guard vessel on alert. In this way, you wait for Alan to arrive. And with each sentrylike passage back and forth over this stretch of choppy lake, your courage increases to match your fear. Soon self-preservation has become the yardstick measuring your resolve.

PERHAPS TWENTY MINUTES LATER you hear the high-pitched whine of Alan's rowboat motor. Is he trying to creep up on you?

Is that why he comes around the western point of the island rather than around the eastern tip, the route you usually take? Unless, of course, it's Matt. But Matt takes the western route only when a rough wind on the lake demands it. So no, it isn't Matt. God, no, it has to be Alan on his idea of a mission. You've grown prepared for this. Though you don't know what you're going to do when the time comes to do it.

Carefully you ease your boat in his direction, maintaining your trolling speed.

Finally he draws closer and slows his boat down too. Rather idiotically he waves and you almost laugh. It all seems so absurd.

"Nickie?" he calls. "I just want to talk."

"I don't want to talk," you call back. "You don't belong here. Our relationship is over—for me and that means for your too. I don't owe you any more explanation. What you're doing now is stalking. You're breaking the law."

"C'mon, Nickie," he replies as the two boats ease themselves still closer. "What is this 'breaking the law' shit? You're being stupid about this."

As the boats draw within twenty-five feet of one another, the two of you fall silent. The morning's only sound is the barely idling motors.

Your resolve continues to grow. His *aw-shucks* demeanor is his attempt to put you in the wrong. Your fear has all but vanished. It is clear to you now, as you've always anticipated— Alan has crossed the line. You have the right to never see him again. It is your right to come to that decision without any further explanation.

"Are you going to leave the island now?" you demand as the boats move to within five yards of one another. "Are you going to leave me alone?"

"I just want to talk, for Christ's sake."

The boats pass each other by and both of you steer them around again like ill-matched jousting steeds.

"Are you getting out of here?" you shout over the idling motors. "Give me your clear answer, Alan. Please."

"Not until we talk," he replies. "You're being crazy, Nickie. Just one more talk and then you don't have to ever see me again. You owe me *that much* at least."

"How many times do I have to say it?" you cry. "How many times do I have to tell you I don't want to see you anymore? What does it take with you, Alan?"

"You're being crazy," he shouts. "You're not being adult about this. I need you to be adult . . ."

But you ram the throttle full ahead, cutting off the rest of his words. The boat erupts. At a significant speed, you begin to circle his boat as tightly as you can, being careful not to swamp your own craft, a risk you run in the sharpness of your turns.

You can see that he's begun to yell something at you, but the sound gets lost in the wail of the motor propelling you in ever narrowing circles around his rowboat. So he gives up his attempts to shout, more intent on reaching for the gunwales to steady himself as the first seething nest of waves from your wake tosses his small rowboat back and forth like an amusement park ride.

His face is white with anger or terror or some curious mixture of both. Still, you keep narrowing the circle and then, in dismay, watch him stand up to reach for an oar tucked under the seats.

What's he going to do with an oar? Throw it at you?

The questions evaporate unanswered. At that moment, as a new cluster of waves strikes his helpless boat, he loses his balance and pitches face first over the side.

Instantly you cut back on the throttle and give his boat a wider berth. It appears, at least, that he's slipped his outboard into neutral. His boat doesn't go anywhere, simply rocks up and down on the diminishing wake of your maneuver.

Alan surfaces. He was wearing the life jacket when he went over, securely tied in regulation fashion. A moment ago you wished to never see his face again; now you're grateful to see he's unharmed. It's not your intention to drown him—you just want him to get the message that he should go away.

"You crazy fucking bitch!" he screams after his head breaks the lake's surface.

But the invective falls apart amid a bout of coughing. Alan has taken on water. Whatever else he might have wanted to say he keeps in abeyance as he gasps for air.

It's strangely quiet again. It feels as if none of this is truly happening. These circumstances possess the unreality of a dream, a hastily drawn animation, a series of badly presented special effects. Still at trolling speed, you continue to circle, watching him as he swims to his boat and reaches for the gunwales. He treads water for a few moments more, then finds the strength to climb back into his boat.

"You've got to leave me alone now," you tell him again as you circle him.

"You crazy fucking cow," he replies. "Who'd want you anyway? You're such a fucking asshole. You could have killed me."

You're willing to grant him the virtue implied in his words, to let him feel he's successfully climbed to the summit of righteous indignation. You feel giddy with relief, unaffected by his narrow list of invective.

"All my friends say you're just an asshole. And there I was defending you. Well, they're right. You're just one fucking, *fucking* asshole."

And so on. Until, at last, he runs out of material, exhausts his repertoire.

Still circling in silence, you watch him move shakily to the seat by the motor, his white shirt, white shorts, white socks, white sneakers all clinging desperately to his flesh like vacuum-pressed plastic.

Now he starts up again. "How am I supposed to explain this, you stupid bitch?"

Explain what? you wonder, though vaguely, as if dealing ambivalently with a not too challenging cryptogram.

But he fills in the answer himself. "The guy who rented me this boat. He'll think I swamped it, for Christ's sake."

You dare not find this laughable despite his adolescent concern. Who *cares* about the man who rented him the boat? Who cares what his friends think? Cheer up, Alan, you reflect at this moment. Maybe it'll rain. Maybe he'll just think you got caught in the rain. Then everything will be all right.

"I'm going to file a report with the police," you tell him.

"Fuck you. *I'm* the one who's been assaulted."

"I'm going to report you to the police for stalking me. I saw you in town last week, you accosted me at *The Inlet* in front of witnesses and you show up on my island in a boat, all after I've *told* you to stay away from me. That's breaking the law and I'm going to the police."

He gazes at you a moment, stupefied. Still, he must weigh everything you've said, searching for a crack in the mortar of your logic. When at last he fails at this, an expression of defeat slips gradually into his features.

"The police aren't necessary," he says.

"Sorry, can you say that again, please?"

"I said the police aren't necessary." He yells it the second time, knowing damn well you heard him first time around.

"Well, I don't trust you, Alan," you reply calmly. "I'll give a report. If you stay away from me, then I won't seek a restraining order. How's that for resolution?"

"God, you're a fucking asshole. How do women get away with this shit?"

"Do we have a deal or not?"

"Who wants you anyway?" Saying this, he glances up at the sky as if the heavens have the answers you do not wish to provide. When he looks at you again, he's managed to muster up an expression of disdain.

"I must have been nuts to think you were worth it. You're the asshole of the fucking century."

"Whatever you say," you reply. "As long as everybody's satisfied. right? All you have to do is stay permanently away from me. And you can tell your friends whatever you want."

He looks up at you and shivers.

"So we have an understanding? You'll stay out of my life for good?"

He's lost and he knows it. It's over. He puts the motor in gear, turns the throttle to full and bolts by your boat without a further word.

Nonetheless you cruise this part of the lake a few moments longer until he disappears around the point of the island. Then you head towards the shore, not yet trembling over what has transpired, but certain the trembling will come later, that it has to, that the full impact of what you've just been through must show up inevitably. But, for now, you are relatively calm and extremely grateful for it.

Then it begins to rain. You laugh gratefully at the Pyrrhic victory the rain represents for Alan. At least he won't have to explain why he's wet when he returns to *The Inlet*. The fickle

# THE LAST LIGHT SPOKEN

godhead who watches over Alan's particularly narrow heaven has granted him a favor, rescuing him from any further embarrassment and you from his further blame.

BY NIGHTFALL ALAN'S FUNCTION IN YOUR DAY has dissipated to a point of gentle simmer. As a concern he's stepped aside, replaced by your increasing anxiety over Matt's whereabouts. Matt, by the way, you tell yourself several times, is definitely and severely in absentia. Hopefully he's not in some kind of trouble you don't know about yet. You're worried about him and his absence is adding to a bitch of a day.

After the altercation with Alan this morning, the fog that had lifted after your goodbye to your parents returned again for much of the day. The trembling you'd anticipated arrived not long after you returned to the cottage. You just rode it out, paced it away, celebrating your victory. In the end the trembling didn't last long. Instead, the incident with Alan seemed to blend elaborately into the overall fog you'd felt all weekend, another misty confusion to occupy you while you were on your own. It was as if your emotions wouldn't go home. They acted like drunks at a party you wished would come to an end. Each time you suggested they leave, they'd get clumsy on their way out the door, bumping into one another and inviting themselves back in.

Where Alan was concerned you waffled between profound relief and the frequent return of a more familiar anxiety about Alan's need to control your fate. The tremendous relief you felt when you realized Alan would now give up on you—any obsessive need he might have, any call for personal revenge, would be undermined by the risk he ran of further loss of face in your threat to contact the police—kept falling back against uncertainty and doubt. Whenever your vague uncertainty gave way to glee, the glee turned out to be disappointingly fleeting, just another one of those annoying emotional party guests. So you remained lost inside your fog, unable to identify a solution which would lead to clarity. Nothing challenged permanently the sensation that you were lost and adrift.

Eventually only one concern evolved into concrete reality. Where the hell was Matt and what did his absence mean?

By mid-afternoon, despite the periodic but insistent rain,

259

you realized you had to escape the silence of your cottage. Summoning Carmen, the two of you walked down the beach together during a lull in the falling rain, making your way to *The Crow's Nest.* Feeling almost betrayed by her actions, you noticed Carmen had no idea what you were going through. She dashed in and out of the lake, some joyful foil for the intensity of your persistent confusion. Get a grip, Nicole, you thought. Time to get a grip.

At Matt's cottage, you tapped on the door, tried to open it, found it locked. Immediately afterwards, with his boat gone, you felt *stupid* for trying to get in. Still, if he'd left the cottage unlocked, you might have gone inside to wait for him. Maybe you would have brewed coffee or cooked something in time for dinner. Then, when he returned, there would be something warm and inviting waiting for him instead of only your worry and frayed nerves.

But these notions too were just the fog. You had no idea when he was coming back. You hadn't talked to him for more than two days. Just about anything you might do in the interim was largely a waste of time. Trapped inside your unrelenting mist, you wanted to grasp at any straw, as if doing something— any small thing at all—might reshape the course of destiny into a happier, clearer possibility.

It began to rain again. You took Carmen back to your own cottage, not hurrying in the downpour but letting it soak you through. It wasn't that you wanted to be cleansed by the rain. No, you let it fall on you to enhance your view of yourself as someone strong yet forlorn. With your clothes clinging to your shivering skin and your hair plastered against your skull, you imagined yourself as visibly orphaned as you felt you were inside.

Later, though, some of your melancholy began to ease. Gradually, as you got used to it, you found ways to pass the time. You doodled on the piano, you read, you wrestled a little bit with Carmen. You cooked yourself a pleasant dinner, even enjoyed in a quiet way sitting down to eat it.

Now, in the darkness of your bedroom, trying to go to sleep, trying not to listen any longer for the sound of Matt's returning boat, you embrace a rewarding speculation over his unexplained absence. It helps you stop toying with the other possibilities which harassed you much of the day—questions about why you didn't tell Matt you saw Alan last week, about how Matt might have misinterpreted the completeness in your weekend silence while your parents were on the island, questions about how your silence might avow his as-yet-unspoken doubts about the future of your relationship.

Fear brings on sleep, you discover, much more successfully than the burden of potential loss. Loss just sits on your chest like a fifty-pound cancer. Fear, however, demands an expenditure of energy and soon begins to tire you. You secretly blame Matt for not being here when Alan showed up to confront you. And when the resolve in your blame begins to waver because Matt could not have known what Alan was going to do, you rationalize the act of being reasonable with a notion that he should have *intuited* it. If Matt loves you, he should have known—no other reason is required. At least he should have left you word if he was going to be away, shouldn't he? He shouldn't have succumbed to the self-absorption required to take him away, if indeed he left to sulk because of your weekend silence, right? Damn. What a day.

You're in shit, Bowman, you repeat in your mind as you would if you were counting sheep. Even though he had every right to leave the island for his own reasons, it didn't feel good that he had. Weighing these things, your indignation finally lets you sleep.

## THE MAN AND THE WOMAN

ULTIMATELY THE MAN AND THE WOMAN do not see one another again until Wednesday morning. By then, Tuesday has extended the gulf between them. By then, one realizes Tuesday is wasted time, irretrievable and sad.

Tuesday night the woman heard the man's boat finally arrive at the island, but at that point it was almost dark. By then she'd endured another full day of wondering where he was and why he was not here. By the time his motorboat purred into her hearing, she'd grown edgier about his absence, resenting how she'd spent most of her day listening for the sound of his return.

Not all of her angst was directed at him, though. Some of it she showered on herself. By the time of his Tuesday night arrival, she'd spent several hours more considering unhappy speculations about why he had disappeared. And her doubts seemed foolish to her even while they were relentless. She'd wondered countless times, for instance, if he'd lied to her when he said there was no other woman currently involved with him. The unknown void of his past became dark and deeply treacherous to her. Too much imagination over what she didn't know, she thought—too little faith that events could have an innocent reason. She wondered too if he had privately arrived at a decision to terminate their relationship based on *his* perception of the nature of romantic failure, without consulting her for her opinion. This too she thought of as treachery.

By the time he returned, she was frustrated with herself for caring for him so much—for caring for anyone at all—and for carelessly allowing her feelings to lay a foundation on which so much hopeless assumption about their future could be foolishly constructed.

Stubbornly she resisted the urge to go to him, despite her love, despite her need to hear his side of the story. Instead she waited an hour or so for him, hoping he might come to *her*, bearing some comforting explanation about his absence which would make everything all right again. But the man didn't come as evening gave way to a dense and silent night. And because he didn't come, there was no reasonable way to dispel her speculations.

As for the man, he wanted to see her as much as she wanted him to. Yet he felt it was somehow too late for that. Nearly four days had now transpired since they'd parted as happy lovers, four days since they'd enjoyed the easy rhythm of love composed of possibility. Four days seemed far too long a period between then and now to repair the damage to their union. As he beached his boat, carried a small satchel of his things up to *The Crow's Nest* and considered for the umpteenth time how long they had been apart, hopelessness kept him away from her despite the intensity of his yearning.

The possibility that their relationship might easily conclude had no actual reason to exist. Rather it just *felt* to him that something wonderful was now over. Difficult to define within the rational context of his thoughts, the emotional assumption that something was finished remained powerful and strangely compelling. How could he argue with intuition? It would not clearly show itself. Intuition was like a double-talking huckster dodging questions at a meeting. How could he rationally debate something which made no clear statement in the first place? Like arguing with smoke, he thought. There's nothing to hold onto, nothing concrete to wrestle with.

So it was, on Tuesday, the man and the woman remained apart one more night. Wishing one or the other of them would give in to the need to be  together, they remained two cottages apart, deriving the only comfort they could from their separation—trying to sustain a flimsy solace in the stubborn satisfaction that they possessed the required courage to live their lives apart.

And love's witnesses sighed unhappily at this display of inflexibility and hopelessness. The situation reflected an assault on their shared belief, their mutual faith in love. How could this be? one wondered. How could this happen so early in love's ritual recipe, so soon after the joy of love has only just been discovered? How could it fall apart when the *rightness* of the relationship had been demonstrated so clearly before so many appreciative witnesses? This was what one considered on the Tuesday before the man's return.

WEDNESDAY PRESENTS ITSELF IN A WAY entirely oblivious to the couple's mood. The contrast is so complete it tends to make a mockery of the man's gloom and the woman's jitters. The day is warm and sunny, nearly windless. The lake shines like a breathless debutante, one notices, whose moment of maiden voyage has at last arrived. The sky is some perfect cobalt blanket unbroken even by clouds, although a distant vapour trail has sewn a seam across its fabric.

Even the dogs behave in direct contrast to the gulf between their human masters. As they did the first time they met more than two months earlier, the retriever and spaniel race up the beach towards one another, conduct their sniff of greeting, then run in and out of the water, celebrating the opportunity to play together again.

As for the man and the woman—in an unsatisfactory way this time—the scene resembles their first meeting early in May. Inside this similarity they are strangers again. They don't embrace, barely even smile. One watches them walk towards one another with a shy reserve denying the intensity they've known together as lovers. There's a sadness between them which, despite the intimacy in their recent past—perhaps even *because* of it—they must meet again as people who shouldn't touch one another.

"Hi," the woman says from a place she finds to stand along the beach.

"Hi," the man replies, about five yards away.

Although they could rush into the embrace they would both prefer, they stand this way in silence, clinging to the majesty of their respective hurts.

"Are you okay?" the man finally asks the woman.

"Yes. Are you?"

"I guess so," he replies, aware of how dubious he sounds.

She says nothing.

"It seems like such a long time has passed," the man confesses shortly.

His hands are stuffed into his bluejean pockets as if he has found the two pressure points on his body integral to keeping him together, the last two hinges which will prevent him from shattering into a dozen sorry pieces.

"Where have you been?" the woman wants to know.

"Kingston. I checked my apartment, the mail, phone messages. Made some calls."

"You didn't tell me you were going."

"I didn't decide to go until late Sunday."

Although they glance at one another from time to time, often with a great intensity, they mostly stare out at the lake, at the horizon, as if everything they might eventually understand—about themselves and about each other—exists some distance away on the edge of the curve of the world.

"I wish you'd let me know you were going somewhere," the woman says at last. "I was worried."

"I didn't mean for you to be worried, Nickie. And there wasn't a way to get you word, you know, with your parents here. It would've looked kind of funny, me coming over to tell you I was going to be away for a couple of days."

The woman supposes this is true, but she doesn't say anything.

"How did it go anyway? The weekend, I mean."

"Fine."

"Did you tell them anything?"

"About you and me?" though she knows that's what he means.

"Yes. About you and me."

"I didn't get the chance."

The man nods in noble acceptance. "Well it's probably for the best."

The woman, one notices, bites back her agitation. "There were complications," she says.

"Complications? Whaddyuh mean?"

"Alan was here," she says.

And she tells him the Alan story, going backwards with it, telling him first about the incident with the boats, then about his presence at *The Inlet*, finally about how she saw him nearly a week ago while they were running errands in town.

"Shit," the man says after she is done. "Why didn't you tell me? I should've been here. I wouldn't have gone away. I could have waited for another weekend to take care of my business in Kingston. Why the hell didn't you tell me you saw Alan in town?"

"It's not your problem."

"Fine," he says with exaggerated irony. "I don't suppose it is."

"So what are you so grumpy about?"

"I'm grumpy because it *is* my problem. It's *my* problem because it's *your* problem."

She turns to him and shrugs. "I wasn't sure you felt that way."

"Jesus," is all he can manage in his exasperation.

This time their silence is very long. The dogs continue to play. Seagulls pass overhead, squawking. The rest of the day maintains its remorseless doze of contrasting summer perfection.

The man feels guilty that he left her to deal with Alan on her own—whether inadvertently or not. And all the rationalization he has employed to convince himself that he didn't return to Kingston to sulk like a love struck adolescent now begins to fail him. In its place he must privately admit that he was indeed feeling sorry for himself. He must admit his self-indulgence put the woman in harm's way. Bullied by the blows of this guilt and shame, he deflects his responsibility by growing exasperated with her for imposing this kind of guilt on him. Just for a moment he wants to walk away from her and even from love itself, convinced that what he's always known is true, that love is too often too much trouble, regardless of who is involved.

At the same time, one knows the woman can sense the man loves her very much. She should have had more faith in him and told him when she first saw Alan in town. She must face that she kept silent because of her own uncertainty, because she has been enjoying a different and fragile kind of sulk of her own. It all comes down to trust, she knows. Him trusting her, her trusting him, both of them trusting love. But perhaps it's too soon for that. Or perhaps it's just too late.

So they stand there on the beach not far from the water's edge and cling to the justice being meted out by the non-forgiveness in their mood. This lack of forgiveness is easier to understand than why they do not trust. Most witnesses understand, when they're honest with themselves, that being right is an acceptable consolation when they've failed to win first prize, that cuddly teddy bear one believes is human happiness.

The man glances at her and wonders when it all came down to this—not the four days of separation, but the falling in love in the first place. How does it happen, he wonders, when a man is happy on his own, that fate cannot leave him alone? And what kind of emotional weakness demands that he succumb to the powerful temptation of love?

Yet even thinking this, he swallows because she looks beautiful to him. And he wants to keep on loving her, life seeming impossible otherwise. In the end he simply remembers—where love is concerned at least—that questions and answers confuse most human juries by pretending to be each other, prince and pauper, heads or tails, dawn and dusk.

Without knowing it, the woman is close to reading his mind. "If you hadn't wanted this thing between you and me," she says, "it wouldn't have happened, you know."

"I know," he admits.

"So you weren't as perfectly self-contained as you thought you were."

But he doesn't want to give up on the notion that his spiritual journey had achieved its own merit before he met this woman.

"That remains to be seen," he says, not liking how cruel he sounds once the words have escaped his mouth.

"Shit, Matt," is all she says, injured by his remark.

He doesn't like her pain and feels a shared hurt in it. "Nickie," he says, "I'm sorry. I don't know what we're doing. This isn't what I want. Standing here like this. Being so separate. Are you enjoying this?"

"Of course not," the woman snaps.

"Well me neither. So why are we doing it?"

"I guess we have some issues to sort out."

"I guess we do. But . . ." and he gives up for the moment, helpless to explain.

"You're the one," the woman says, "who worries about everything. You're the one who tries to define everything so that it fits inside the future."

"And you don't consider the future?"

"Not as much as you do."

"Maybe not. But I'm still your little secret here. That indicates to me that you have some concerns about the future."

She wonders if this is true. She knows she wanted to tell her parents about Matt, but she just didn't get the opportunity. Or is this nothing but an excuse? She wants to argue his point but feels weary of the debate, all of it, and the distance that now exists between them. She is weary of not touching him, of not feeling the easy togetherness which drew her to him in the first place.

"Maybe," she suggests, "we should let the future take care of itself."

"I know," the man agrees, although it seems easier to say than to act upon.

"We still have months ahead of us, here on the island I mean."

"Nickie, I'm not a good bargain in a practical sense. I mean, as a partner, I'm just . . ."

". . . Stop it!" the woman cries. "Can we just live for now? Talk to me about that at the end of the summer or in September. Okay?"

"Okay," the man replies.

Still, they do not move. Things are better now—they feel a relief distinctly their own—but they do not draw close.

"I'm sorry I went to Kingston without telling you."

"I'm sorry about the weekend," the woman says in turn, "that I ignored you the way I did."

Thoughtfully they nod and look at one another. This moment of hopelessness seems largely circumstantial.

"I'm sorry about what you went through with Alan," the man adds to his list of apologies. "I should have been here for that."

"It's not your fault," she says. "I should have told you he was here when I saw him last week."

"Do you think that's the end of him?"

"Yes, I do."

"Good," the man says. "I kinda wish I'd seen it. The boat battle, you know?"

They still flirt with the horizon rather than move closer together.

"I missed you, Nickie. It quite literally hurt, I missed you so much."

"I missed you too," she says, suddenly smiling broadly, mischievously. "I guess we're just in love."

"Yeah, that appears to be the problem all right."

The woman looks at him, still smiling. She considers telling him that he is the first man she's ever known who seems perfectly right for her, but she wonders if this will remind him of what he believes are his inadequacies. In the end discretion prevails and she keeps this truth to herself, putting it away for some future date when he'll know as well as she does that it's true.

They gaze at one another a moment or two longer.

"Oh, Matt," the woman says at last. "I love you so much."

"I love you so much too."

And the witnesses see a shine appear on their faces, a glistening, the bemused hieroglyphics of love one so often dreams about.

Barry Grills

## PART FOUR: AUGUST, 1996

### NICOLE

BY THE TIME SUNDAY ROLLS AROUND you've told Karen virtually everything that's happened between you and Matt since the beginning of your love affair. And you've related in great detail, amid her gasps and laughs of horror and delight, the closure of your relationship with Alan. Because you have no telephone, except for one brief call from the pay phone at *The Inlet*, Karen has remained substantially in the dark until this weekend. Now, with the O'Shaughnessys in residence for a few days, your discussions take place whenever you're alone together, while Matt, Liam and Cindy are otherwise occupied.

You've walked along the beach together. You've convened in the kitchen while you were preparing dinner, then again while you were cleaning up. You've travelled the dunes, chatted among the dead white trees in Matt's favorite island locale, his "petrified forest." You've gone over some conversational ground two and even three times, weeding it, tilling it, crumbling it in your fingers, yet you still come back to the same topic—the future you don't want to acknowledge as destiny, that same future which nonetheless drifts relentlessly towards you. In fact, you've described the future as a stubborn deputation lobbying the parliament of your present tense—you wish it would make another appointment; you don't want to listen to its threats.

It is now the August holiday weekend and you've become two people again, living your life in some kind of uneasy tandem. One of you is clear and happy to be spending the weekend here on the island with all of your favorite people around you. But the other you—some anxious alter-ego—is haunted by fear of loss, bemused by the way time has begun to speed up. The resolution of what is eventually going to happen between you and Matt is now visible on the horizon.

You seem unable to sever the linkage between these different but connected yous. Although they are distinct, they overlap at the edges and require each other's contribution to fasten you to life, like a nut and bolt which function only when they are threaded together. The love which makes you feel clear and happy is the same love which nags about the future and what could be very well lost to you at some point immediately ahead. Time too has become a ticking crone—summer promises you it will pass. As each summer day concludes, you realize it's been full of many hopeful moments you wish would never end.

You invited Matt to stay the weekend even though he lives right next door to you. With Liam and Karen coming, you wanted to address this technicality of proximity by pretending it wasn't there. If he stayed with you for the weekend, you could briefly be seen as a couple. You could get up with him in the morning and retire with him at night—locked in flesh and spirit to the cycle of each day—the way Liam and Karen get up together and retire together at night, ensconced in that elusive comfort you fear you'll never permanently find. You wanted to enjoy this one brief marriage for the sake of Karen's visit. And you wanted these three days to transpire with neither you nor Matt having to say, "I really must get back" or "I suppose I should be going."

When you invited him, Matt seemed to understand without you having to explain the true purpose behind the invitation. As a matter of fact he said it was a wonderful idea. He liked the notion of pretending he lives this summer much further away than he actually does.

But, since then, there's been a minor blemish in the arrangement. Twice now, he has returned to *The Crow's Nest* for a couple of minutes, to retrieve a summer shirt he did not pack in his bag and, a second time, to find an article in his files about new reasons for high unemployment, something he had clipped earlier in the year for use in his book of essays. He wanted to show it to Liam who is puzzled by the fact his own work is growing scarce.

Plausible reasons, sure enough, to briefly set aside the masquerade that he has come to stay with you for the weekend. But both times it happened you felt an unreasonable tug of disappointment because you wondered if there was something beneath his actions much larger and more sinister than seemed to exist on the surface.

For the most part, though, the weekend has gone extraordinarily well. Matt arrived to "stay" at your cottage early Friday evening, in time to cross the channel with you to meet the O'Shaughnessys at *The Inlet*. It was Liam's idea to come early, to arrive on Friday night. As he explained it, he wanted to make amends for having to postpone a longer stay earlier in the summer—in July, as they'd previously hoped—because he had to work. "After cancelling out on July, I needed to make sure we got away early," he said. "I'm at the mercy of the availability of work. To tell you the truth, I'm getting tired of it."

Since then, everyone has gotten along famously. Laughter and camaraderie have rewarded your times inside the cottage and down at the water's edge. Matt has even charmed Cindy which, for some reason, surprised you a little. Granted, he has children of his own, but the fact they are adults who, as children, only sparingly shared his life, served to convince you somehow that he wouldn't be able to reach a child in the way he apparently can. Then again, it isn't that he's a parent. No, he's more like an uncle. Maybe he was mostly an uncle when it came to growing up with his sons.

Whatever the reason for it, Matt has made Cindy his friend, discussing her school and comrades with her and making sure to include her in everything the weekend has to offer. When he took her with him to show her his cottage, that time he went to get his shirt, you watched them stroll along the beach together, him so large and her so tiny. And the notion of him as husband and father washed over some inexplicable new idea of yourself as wife and mother so that you swallowed at the mercy of a new emotion comprised in equal measure of pain and pleasure.

Liam and Matt have begun to display a compatibility as well. Mostly they've talked about work and politics, how the two past-times are so inextricably connected these days. Matt has watered down his political anger, presumably for Liam's benefit but probably for yours as well. Liam has managed to admit that something is very wrong in Canada these days, the way work is growing scarce. And although he doesn't understand it the way Matt seems to understand, he has concurred in a bemused way that there's too much corporate manipulation of government policy for the good of the average citizen. Somehow the two men meet in the middle ground and are developing their friendship there.

And Karen? Karen likes Matt too. "He's perfect for you, you know," she said during a conspiratorial walk along the beach on Saturday, "whether he's aware of it yet or not."

"He may never be aware of it," you replied, strolling along beside her.

"Oh, Sweetie, give it time," was Karen's suggestion then.

Still, it all keeps coming back to what lies ahead at the end of summer. And it all keeps coming back to the two yous cohabiting your larger you. There's the one that lives for the moment. But there's also the one that cannot help hoping for a longer future devised by the simple fairness in what you believe you need.

"YOU SEE," YOU TELL KAREN Sunday afternoon from your mutually favorite place high on the rocks at the northern edge of the island, " it's like we've made an arrangement to be in love just until the end of September."

Karen takes her time digesting what you say.

In the silence you remember the last time you came to this place to talk with her about love. It seems much longer ago to you than it actually was. Not even two months have passed since but so much was different then. Alan remained to be dealt with. You were still denying the first insistent symptoms of your attraction to Matt. You hadn't yet made your decision to join Karen in Kingston as a partner in her music school. Now, only weeks later, Alan is gone, Matt has become the love of your life and you can't imagine turning down the opportunity to work with Karen.

The fact you've reached your decision to teach music with Karen was efficiently dealt with early Saturday morning. Karen was pleased but her pleasure was modified by the Matt component which might be lurking inside your choice. To you, her caution was understandable. How could she know, despite the joy you so obviously display, that the relationship has a better than even chance of being imminently terminal? So you explained that it was likely Matt would move out west sometime the following spring.

"And you won't want to go with him?"

"He may not even ask me," you replied. "I think he considers this his private spiritual journey."

Karen gazed at you. Private spiritual journeys, in this instance at least, seemed a nebulous ambition, like believing rainbows actually have a place where they touch down.

"What if he did ask you?" she asked. "Would you go?"

"No. I want to work with you. Besides, I'm the one making the career commitment. If anyone can delay or change plans, it's him. No one else is involved in what he plans to do. That's not the case with me. I want to work with you, Karen. So that's that."

Karen nodded thoughtfully. "Why does life have to get so complicated?"

"Doesn't it though? Maybe we all just think too much, people generally. Maybe we've lost touch with our instincts."

Which didn't help a bloody thing. Neither one of you had the patience at that moment for philosophical debate.

Now, a day later, perched together on the rocks high above a choppy channel stirred up by an abnormally balmy north wind, Karen tries to understand what motivates the man you love.

"You know something?" she says at last. "No matter how lofty it all sounds, it's probably just that same old scenario of a man afraid to commit himself."

"To some extent," you admit.

"What did you call it yesterday? A private spiritual journey?"

"That's right."

"Well that's just fancy lingo for not wanting to be tied down by a mere woman."

For the moment you don't reply. It seems a rather harsh interpretation of a speculative conclusion. Your instinct is to defend Matt from her assumptive leap of opinion, based the way it is on over-simplification. But where would you start if you tried to explain the complexity in your situation and the enigma of the man?

"Well," you say at last. "Like you said yesterday, it's early yet."

"But what's this arrangement to break things off at the end of the summer? I mean, what's *that* all about?"

"It's not an arrangement per se," you explain. "I mean, we didn't sit down and make it a rule. It's more like we acknowledged our concerns about the future of the relationship and decided to let them go until the end of the summer."

"Live for the moment until then?"

"I suppose," you say.

"So what are the concerns?"

"There's the separate direction business you know, how he's intent on going to the mountains and I'm intent on working with you."

"Yeah, yeah. What else?"

"I think he's concerned about our age difference."

"Not that great, by the way," says Karen. "It's not like he's going to get the pension next year."

"I know."

"What else? All of these seem to be *his* concerns, by the way."

"That's true."

"Next?"

"Economics. He's very concerned about how little he makes. He lives a pretty poor existence, he says . . ."

". . . Which could change . . ."

". . . And he's adamant that he won't alter his lifestyle to correct the problem. He's going to write and that's it. No nine-to-five anymore."

"I see. Does that bother you?"

You shake your head. "Couldn't care less."

"Doesn't he believe you?"

"Gee, Karen, we haven't really talked about it. Most of what I'm telling you—I mean what his concerns are—I've figured out by myself."

"And you haven't talked about it because it'll spoil the two months you have left. Right?"

Soberly you nod. "You know something, Karen? I think the

whole situation is aggravated by the fact we're on an island."

"How do you mean?"

"I mean, it becomes it's own world. Being in love on this island means you don't have to answer to anyone. The future, even when it's vaguely threatening, stays out there in the distance, something that exists only on the other side of the channel. We tend to enjoy living for the moment here because we can get away with it. But it makes the mainland—the world out there, I guess—a sharper contrast. It exaggerates all the conventional shit the mainland represents. It exaggerates the differences between here and there, between convention and living your life your own way."

"I'm not sure I understand," murmurs Karen.

"Well it's hard to explain. I mean, while the island is intensifying the privacy and solitude we enjoy, the fun of living for the moment, it also intensifies the sense that once we go back to the mainland—to reality, I suppose—the practical demands will be too much for us. We won't survive things like economics and age difference, the separate directions we may want to go, what my parents think, all the practical considerations we're supposed to take into account. So you end up believing, in the practical sense, that you can't accomplish anything more permanent than a torrid island affair."

Karen grins. "So it's torrid, is it?"

"Oh yeah," you readily admit with perhaps a hint of a blush. "But you see what I mean, don't you?"

"You mean the island-mainland thing?"

"Yes."

"I think so," Karen replies. "In a way, you're saying one or both of you doesn't believe you'd have fallen in love anywhere else but on this island. Because, on the mainland, you would've known it was impractical from the beginning."

"Well sort of," you say with a nod.

In fact, you can almost hear Matt describing it in exactly this fashion. After a moment, you tell Karen so.

She responds by shaking her head. "So all of this is Matt's thing, right? You don't feel the same way, do you?"

"No, I don't." Then you add hastily, "I don't think so. But if Matt ever put it the way you just did, I'd have to consider the possibility that he was right."

"Man," says Karen then. "This is so weird."

"But you see," you continue, "that it's not an arrangement to terminate things at the end of the summer. It's more like we share a powerful suspicion that the love affair isn't practical, not in the larger scheme of things. So we've tacitly arrived at the same conclusion—let the thing burn like a comet for the summer and then let it go out before the conventional world *puts* it out."

"Geez," says Karen, unable to hide her frustration. "It's sort of like *love atheism*. You know? I mean, you guys are making one hell of a leap of faith."

"Leap of faith? In what way?"

"Well, like not believing in God. That's what I mean about atheism. It takes as much of a leap of faith to deny God's existence as it does to believe He does. So you guys are making a love leap of faith. Love atheism. This can't work out—we don't believe it has any kind of permanence—so we'll just fuck our brains out for the summer, fall madly in love, then come the end of September, we'll just end it because—as every love atheist knows—the world is going to rain on our parade."

"Interesting way to interpret it," you must admit.

"Well, shit," says a breathless Karen. "Wouldn't it be just as easy to make the leap in the reverse?"

"A big part of me wants to," you confess.

"And Matt?"

"Probably," you reply.

"So what's *the fucking problem*?"

"Maybe it's because we've both been burned so many times before."

"So what?" says Karen, getting to her feet. "Get over it."

"Easier said than done," you reply, annoyed at her brusqueness.

"I'm sorry, Sweetie," says Karen. "I don't mean to sound smug. It's just that I think it's human nature to expect love to last forever, even though it doesn't always manage to. To tell you the truth, I don't know if you guys are really smart and independent about this or really stupid and victimized by your past failures."

"Thanks," you say with a grin.

"Besides," adds Karen. "Whatever will be, will be."

Carefully you nod in agreement.

"Tell me," suggests Karen as you make your way back to the cottage. "Do you really think you wouldn't have fallen for Matt if you hadn't been here on the island?"

"I don't know," you reply. "Proximity is a big factor. And an island proximity is an even bigger factor."

"But he seems exactly right for you."

"I know. I've never known anyone I felt was *more* right."

"Well, I keep coming back to the same point," Karen tells you. "Island or no island, I just don't see the problem. Not really."

"I said it was hard to explain."

"Maybe we're overlooking the obvious," Karen says as your cottage comes into view. "Come the end of September, when you guys go back to the mainland, take the island with you. Wear the island. Wear it like armor."

Her words bring on a rush of sadness. Just then, you feel overwhelmed by your fears. "I wish it was that simple," you tell your friend. "I really wish it was that simple."

THAT NIGHT, THE DAY'S MUGGINESS, which has been intensifying steadily since morning, reaches an oppressive climax. By midnight all of you feel compressed inside the humidity. You grow clammy with sweat, stoop under its unrelenting weight.

After Karen and Liam go to bed, a fan droning and pirouetting on a chair at the foot of their bed, Matt strolls outside to the terrace and takes up a station down at the garden wall where he can peer into the sticky darkness and think a private thought or two. He lights a cigarette and the hot coal dances slowly through the darkness.

For a time you watch him there from a window, now used to the frequency of his periods of reflection. But the pleasure in private observation quickly dissipates. You join him at the terrace wall and light a cigarette of your own.

"Hot," you say behind him.

"Sultry," he replies. "It feels like sex. You know? Juices and fluids and the smell of reproduction. I like nights like these."

You take each other's hand, gazing into the black. Perhaps he's right. Humidity as humanity, sex on the humidex.

It's so still at this moment even the lake has fallen silent. Matt's breathing—connected by this tranquility to your own—is louder than the lake which, in this stillness, cannot find a way to make a sound as it invites itself on shore.

"Nickie," says Matt after a moment, "how do you feel about children? Do you want to have kids someday?"

Although there is no ambush in the tone of his voice—it's a mild, thoughtful question emerging, you assume, mostly from curiosity—you feel nonetheless that it has you surrounded. You grow nervous, imperiled by what you might eventually say wrongly.

"I don't know," you reply, more or less to give yourself more time.

He smokes and waits for you, still staring into this endless night so murky along the horizon.

Your instinct is to tell the truth but part of you toys with tactics, with what the right answer might be. What does he need you to say so that your love has a better chance of survival? Which answer is likely to find its place on his list of practical reasons for why you shouldn't have fallen in love?

"I guess I'd like to someday," you admit at last. "Not for the sake of it. It's just that I used to imagine myself with the right man and the two of us having children together. But it has to be the right man. I don't want to have to care about children on my own. I'm not a single parent type. And I don't want to make due with the wrong man just because my biological clock is ticking."

Thoughtfully, Matt nods.

"Is there some reason that you're asking?"

"Just wondered," he replies.

And you feel a bolt of alarm at his cryptic non-reply. "Jesus, Matt. Did I pass or fail? Right answer or wrong?"

He turns to you immediately, dismayed at the intensity in your voice. And your agitation doesn't relent simply because he's surprised. Matt is an intelligent man but sometimes he's just so stupid. Can't he understand that you need to know clearly exactly what he means?

"Can you help me here?"

"Sorry," he replies. "I was standing here thinking about it, that's all. And I realized that we haven't talked about it. And I just felt I needed to know. I guess it was careless. Bad timing."

You feel cheated by his defensiveness, betrayed by the fact you've had a part in creating it. This happens now and then between you. When he gives you only half of the information, your need for more causes him to back away.

Nonetheless you press on. "What made you think of it, Matt? Cindy?"

"Yeah, I guess so."

"You like her."

"Absolutely. More than that, though, I was just wishing you were the mother of my children."

"Oh, Matt," you say, surprised, taking him in your arms.

You embrace that way for several minutes before moving apart again.

You feel euphoric afterwards, after his words and the embrace they inspired, so electric that you want to promise, right here, right now, to have all his future children, to breed the kind of family you know he's never had. Still, a subtle sadness remains between the two of you. You stand there shoulder to shoulder, bearing it equally. No wonder you hold your tongue. It's just too early yet to make promises you don't know you can keep.

"That was a wonderful thing to say," you tell him. "Thanks for saying that."

"You're welcome," he replies, like he's handed you a tissue so you could blow your nose. "I meant it, Nick, for what it's worth."

Why is there so much sadness surrounding all of your pleasures? Like one is a disclaimer for the other. Like each has to tag along, can't be left behind alone.

Time goes by. The night wears itself like velvet.

"Humid," he murmurs. "Wow."

"Yes."

"Feel like a swim?"

"You mean skinny?"

"Sure."

"Okay."

"Unless you're worried about getting caught. I forget that we have company."

You laugh at his second thoughts. "I couldn't care less," you say. "It's only Karen and Liam."

A few moments later, you pile your clothing on the sand not far from the water's edge. Down here, enveloped by darkness and heat, you tiptoe naked into the inky lake which smells of hot August and feels like newborn crude.

You do not swim at first. You simply crouch in the shallows, buoyant in two feet of lake motionless on the rippled sand beneath your feet. When you embrace, you hold one another tightly, feeling as thick and dense and permanent as this nighttime shoreline does. The lake whispers over the tops of your shoulders, cool and wet, but surprisingly still.

You reach for Matt, not surprised to find him erect. Glad of this, feeling embraced by the caress of the lake, you move in closer, guiding him inside your now contented flesh. You make love like crabs in the water, burrowing into the sand with your feet. You whisper, gasp and stifle a cry in the darkness when, with astonishing haste, you come so powerfully. Matt too. Straining, reaching, spewing. Making love in the primordial soup from which you are reputed to have evolved.

Afterwards you swim, for a moment or two at least, submarining through the lake in silence, trying not to betray the stillness all around you.

On the shore, as you dress, you tell him what Karen said to you earlier that day, about taking the island with you when, at last, you must return to the mainland.

For a long time he doesn't reply. In fact, his silence is so prolonged, you wonder if he has heard you.

"Matt?"

"I wish we could," he says, glancing off somewhere you do not visit well. His world of Crazy Horse, his land of bickering spirits he cannot share with you.

## MATT

**Tuesday, August 6**

I'M GLAD TO BE BACK AT *THE CROW'S NEST*, back at my station at the dining room table, gazing again into the mysterious darkness on the other side of the window, holding this agitated pen and accepting these private few hours for the creative rewards they usually provide. Not that I've been gone very long. Not that I was far away for the weekend. Just down the beach with Nicole and, until last evening, her friends Karen and Liam and their daughter Cindy. But tonight I'm grateful to be alone. I insisted on it and Nicole, for her part, professed that she too needed some time to get things done on her own.

I wanted to get an early start on my work this morning—a holiday weekend can represent a significant interruption when one is finishing a book-length work. But more than that, more than the need to collect my thoughts, I crave some sense of superficial normalcy. I say superficial because nothing has been truly normal since that weekend more than a month ago when Nicole and I became lovers. At any rate, I craved some privacy and solitude because—at this point in my life—these are the states which define my normalcy.

Yet my senses argue with one another. At this moment I miss Nicole with as much intensity as ever, even while I wish to enjoy being alone. It appears, beyond the demands of my work, that I juggle only two arcing balls—my love for Nicole and my equally powerful love for my freedom.

There is, as usual, a pleasant tension in this situation, but the tension, though agreeable at times, is also worrisome. Inevitably I must fumble one of these balls. For now, though, I'm compelled to keep on juggling—sometimes even frantically, afraid of course whichever ball I fumble first will be the one I shouldn't have dropped.

I know what Nicole would say if ever I described this notion to her—this idea of the juggling balls—to explain the persistent tension I feel in determining what is most rewarding for me to love. She would point to the middle ground and remind me about the virtues of balance.

But the middle ground is always the most difficult to travel. She must know this as well as I do. To negotiate the middle ground, you have to be open to every possibility and closed to that view promoted by an antagonistic world, that cynical place deemed impossibility. Easier—for most of us—to move exclusively in either direction, open to every potential or closed to every potential. Most of the time this is what we do. We choose the black or the white even when the void inherent at the edge of each of these options leaves us vaguely disconcerted. I suppose this is because the extreme is always simpler, ordains itself more comfortable. You can hide inside the extreme (the way, in school, we once ducked behind our fellow students to hide from the teacher asking questions about last night's homework assignment). Because we get tired. Because we're so often pushed from the narrow tightrope of the middle ground by the other falling bodies we let inside our hearts.

So what does this mean, Bowman? Is love ultimately impossible? Beyond the yearning, the physical hunger and the moments of blissful comradeship, all destined to wear down gradually like the treads on a rubber tire, is love a remorseless range of cliffs from which we must inevitably plummet? Or can these powerful feelings of caring for someone fit alongside the caring I have learned we must reserve for ourselves?

I don't know. It seems like such a riddle. I envy those who can fall in love and embark on a romantic relationship which takes only from its partner its fair ration of caring. I admire the relationship that does not culminate in the typical, peculiarly possessive arrangement defined by stereotypical role or suffocating ritual.

Both Nicole and I are aware that this island is a paradox. It is, for us, the point of our arrival and the point of our departure. Here love is free and unrestrained. But while it has the freedom to sculpt a miraculous work of emotional art, this time of creative wonder also carves from the block of stone the shape of our potential destruction. While Nicole and I have arrived in this place in a state of convivial freedom, we must eventually depart its atypical isolation, somehow maintaining our status as free individuals when we enter a conventional setting which too often insists we compromise our individuality by adhering to romantic ritual.

I would love to be able to negotiate that difficult, elusive middle ground which is both the island and the mainland, and the unpredictable spaces in between. But that's just it. The middle ground goes on forever, *is* forever, and is difficult to travel for that very reason. It's easier to fall to the right or left where hopes readily terminate or, for that matter, aren't allowed to begin. In the solitude where we crash, at least we can rest and collect ourselves before contemplating the middle ground we've promised ourselves never to explore again.

Even writing about this dilemma is exhausting for me. It doesn't accomplish anything. Any knowledge it bestows is shattered by the possibility I will forget what I have learned. So I gaze out over the black night of the lake through the barrier of the cottage windows and try to escape for now the puzzle of my personal abstraction.

I realized today, quite clearly, that my book of essays will be completed by the end of August, a month ahead of schedule. By rights, this means I should leave at that point, return to the mainland and whatever awaits me there. But I know I'll not depart when the essays are finished. I'll still have reasons to stay.

For one thing, once I leave *The Crow's Nest* this year I can never come back again. I'll need to spend September haunting this island for the thousands of memories it holds, saying goodbye to each one of them the way I might bid so long to dispersing revolutionary comrades after a successful rebellion. Even though the memories will still exist after I'm gone, they'll have no concrete place to board the subway of my future.

Memories, I think, resemble love in that way. When one leaves the place where memories or love are born, a great deal of that love and the clarity in the recollections must remain behind in the location where they took place. Sometimes I like to think this is to give us room for new love and new memories. At other times, I suspect it's license to compound our foolishness by introducing forgetfulness, the machinery of still more painful loss.

But even this reason for staying here is only a matter of philosophy. In truth, I'll remain for the month of September to make more love with Nicole. Yes, to make more love in the broadest meaning of the term. I will delay as long as possible any interruption of this island ecstasy I now share with Nicole. I cannot conceive of abbreviating my stay until the more logical time when this ecstasy must finish. It's much too late to consider a premature denial.

The time to consciously end what has become so wonderful for me has come and gone long ago. If I shouldn't have let this love affair begin, the moment I could have prevented it has long since passed away. Now I have no will to bring this relationship to a close. While we're alone together on this island I must draw on this romantic opium pipe, ignoring while we are here the potential for destruction which lies in my addiction.

I miss Nicole tonight. I miss her along my flesh. It's as if my skin has grown thin and translucent without her skin to wrap myself inside. I'm not sure I've ever loved someone as deeply and persistently as I love her, although this could be a memory trick, a convenient betrayal of the intensity of past carings. Regardless, there exists a worrisome irony: while the love I feel is maddeningly powerful and insistent, it makes me all the more stubborn to be the man that I've become, the one who derives his self-worth from a place on the outside of mainstream society, from within himself instead of through some confining arrangement with his peers. In this way, it's now clear that the passion which draws me so close to Nicole is the passion which pulls me away from her. And the more connected she seems to ritual society the more resistant I become. The more I love her, as time goes by, the more resolved I am to resist her.

She's even become my muse. I credit Nicole for the fact my

work has gone so well. I've brought unusual force and energy to my essays because of the unusual force and energy in my feelings for her. But even this is both good and bad, a rather commonplace dichotomy I tend never to forget: the difficulty in possessing anything is that it's impossible to keep without having it possess us in return. Either we must find a way to accept that everything in life is on loan or live with as little as possible so that, when it is taken away, we only carelessly shrug, accepting the freedom derived from being robbed of what we did not truly value.

Today, shortly after lunch, Nicole left the island to go shopping on the mainland. I saw her depart from my window. I felt an astonishing ache in her going. But I also felt freed by her departure. As soon as she was out of sight I took Canine Ben for a long walk around our island, as if now that she was gone I could spend some time with my waiting mistress, in this case this island I've cared about for so long.

But in the end my island courtesan didn't give me much. After meeting with her a while, I still had no idea what anything truly means or where it can reasonably go. As I walked this island setting, I felt bemused, thick, like I suffered from a head cold. I seemed to have no mind. I found myself on the edge of a battlefield where my warring tribes of emotion seemed bent on the carnage of a state of sensory anarchy. And the ghost of my past—which to some degree has seen this kind of anarchy before—walked the island beside me, catcalling and bitching about the failures my emotions have conceived before, when I was careless in my past.

But walk the island we did, Canine Ben and me.

It was a moderately pleasant day, cooler than on the weekend, sunny by times, cloudy at others. There were plenty of distractions along the way, although these too were normal and common. Soaring, complaining gulls, for instance. Sand flies defying a breeze which was brisk at times off the water. Turtles on the rocks, nervously sunning themselves. Frogs darting into pools of water in a new bog at the southern end of the small woods which this year's heavier rainfall has created.

I found myself trying to inspect the various highlights in the years I've spent on this island—like soldiers on parade. But the rigidity in my intention only diminished the pleasure in the exercise. In the end it was better to just let myself drift like the paraphernalia Ben and I found along the beach, washed up out of the lake when no one was looking, to bob in the shallow waters.

I'm not sure I truly believe or truly have accepted that once the end of September arrives and I return to the mainland I will never come back here again. I don't know what this lack of acceptance means. I only know that the sadness I felt over this fact was more powerful when I first arrived than it is now that August is here. Perhaps aspects of my past are more easily jettisoned than I thought. Or perhaps they are overrun by the potential I feel in my future. Or perhaps I live so comfortably in the present that both past and future have grown increasingly irrelevant. I simply do not know. I'm not sure I *want* to know. I wish my instinct was a butterfly I could briefly catch and examine. But instinct isn't a butterfly. No, it's a shy little voice whispering so softly one isn't always sure whether it has spoken at all.

At any rate, the memories inspired by this island today came upon me at random like beads that have fallen in all directions from a broken piece of string. In the petrified forest, for instance, as I leaned against the blistered white carcass of a tree which, even dead, felt so much like a friend, I remembered being a child digging in the sand, in search of buried treasure. And I remembered pretending to be a warrior stalking cavalry on the dunes. And I remembered, as I grew older, coming here to *think* and *feel* when both those preoccupations had grown up enough to adopt some kind of constructive purpose. I remember how I began to write hopeful profundities in a school scribbler left over from my studies, how, when I read them afterwards, they had become embarrassingly *un*profound.

Then, as Ben and I continued our walk, it struck me with great force that I'd brought more of my mainland life to this island back then than I ever took off the island back to the mainland. Eventually, Nicole aside, this uneven trade of goods should make it easier to leave somehow, to accept never returning. But Nicole and I were born here as a unit of love; maybe I should never leave. Except that I want to. I want to get on with what lies ahead. Perhaps for the very reason that I brought my mainland futility here more often than I took the island's peace back to my stormy mainland.

Yes, as an adult I came to this island in a state of determined retreat. When I returned to the mainland I was somehow renewed, ready to defend my trenches against my various enemies of convention. When I left the island it was to return to the front lines. It strikes me this time that Nicole and I currently live our lives in an opposite way. We fight the battles of love, choice and independence here. We don't retreat. On the mainland then—hoping these battles have been resolved—we will need to rest, to *retreat* into our anticipated separate lives *there*. It remains to be seen—in the wake of choice—whether retreat or war is what we achieve.

The more I toy with these contrasts and the more I build my various comparisons, the more confusing my life seems. I want to be Sgt. Friday so that I can be crisp and clear: "just the facts, Mr. Bowman, just the facts if you can."

Yet there's no escaping what I've learned about the love I knew in my past. I've tried and failed to prolong three previous long-term relationships. I embarked on each of them committed to their permanence. Gwen, the mother of my children, was kind and pleasant and likable. But in the end, although she told me otherwise, she preferred rigidly conventional ambitions, the kind that smother a man like me who draws his breath experientially. Nonetheless, I was committed to the propriety in the edict that the arrangement should continue until death. No wonder there was no one more surprised than me that day I heard myself telling her that I thought the marriage should come to an end.

Time passed after that but nothing in my romantic ambitions changed in any way. I clung to the notion of a permanent romantic partner. When I met Esther, then desperately slept with her, I dressed her up next morning in the outfit of that same permanent romantic partnership I felt inclined to need. And even when it became apparent that she was too volatile for me, too abusive, too out of control, I remained committed for several years based on some kind of principle alone. I remained committed too when I realized we had different moral and economic values. In the end the commitment could not survive, based the way it was on the ideal of permanence instead of on love itself. Inevitably, smothered by conflict, I was compelled to leave again.

Then Carolyn. Carolyn too was not what at first she seemed to be. Initially I thought she was bohemian. But she brought several children to the relationship, several hungry mouths to feed. My commitment yet again to another romantic forever became a commitment to *provide*. And when the commitment finally broke me, temporarily at least, threatening my health and the focus of my personal ambitions, I was left to sort through my twisted wreckage alone, abandoned after my collapse. While I sifted through the salvage I could use for the rest of my future—to discern why I had set so much aside that was vital to my being—I finally realized it was best to live a life entirely alone—what I have come to describe as a *private* life.

Gwen, Esther, Carolyn: three anticipated forevers. Each of them became identical as an object of my romantic commitment, yet all of them were different from one another in the same way that Nicole is no doubt different from them.

From this I must conclude that it is not the woman which represents the flaw in my notion of permanence. No, it is the function of personal sacrifice connected to the conventionality in partnership, interchangeable with each partner. As a solitary goldfish, I get to swim a limitless lake; as a goldfish with a mate, I am aquarium bound, performing repetitious strokes on the other side of society's inflexible glass. I've learned I'll always need my infinite, boundless lake. I've also learned that captivity murders love.

In the end I can't deny that Nicole is probably right for me. But I also can't deny that partnership for people like me usually turns sour. I abhor watching the most passionate state of love being pushed aside by relentless, ritual functions combining to create a potential for despair. If Nicole and I could take back to the mainland what we have found together on this private island, perhaps our partnership could survive. But the mainland insists on conformity and has so many stubborn means of demanding it from us. Nicole and I cannot hide on this island forever from the cruel judgments cooked up on the mainland and its perpetually simmering stew of expectations.

So I'm left to consider only this concept of a brief and carefree ecstasy of finite time and location. I prefer a brief interlude of freedom and wonder that I can share with Nicole.

But it's likely nothing more than this: a period of interlude. In the end I suspect we'll willingly conclude the relationship at the end of our September. To prevent, I think, the joy we've known with one another becoming once again what it has previously become with others: an arrangement, an agreement, a sacrificial rite in which our very natures—hers as well as mine—are fed to the hungry lions of obligation and ritual.

Unless, of course, Nicole is truly different. Unless she understands this unhappy potential for romantic mediocrity as well as I now understand it. Or is this simply the addictive nature of hope? I have perhaps seven weeks to learn if Nicole and I can survive, to decide if what I believe is true: that love ultimately becomes another tail which insists it wag the dog.

## THE MAN AND THE WOMAN

THE WITNESSES ENJOY THE REST OF THEIR AUGUST. The
month feels like angora—thick, soft, warm against their fingers.
The witnesses nudge one another in approval, the way
members of a society often do when they believe warm fuzzies
are a collective experience made all the richer because they're
shared. One knows that criteria are built into a sense of
happiness, and the most powerful comfort of all is knowing that
the terms of the criteria have been previously agreed upon,
having passed the test of prior common approval. It takes a
courageous person to know joy without the reinforcement of
the one's collective definition. Private joy runs the risk of being
thought foolish or indulgent or even, if it persists, a symptom of
madness. One feels public joy is not so careless or so worthy of
derision.

During August one adopts the man and the woman as their
own. One rounds them up and nourishes them inside the pen of
one's romantic mythology. And one watches what one wants to
watch of the couple at play, ignoring all the rest.

One ignores, for instance, that the man and the woman
have begun to love one another with a kind of joyful
desperation in which even pleasure is an arcing pendulum that
waxes and wanes. Time on the island is running out, not only for
the man and the woman, but for the witnesses as well. For
everyone now no touch is too exotic, too comforting or too

engorged with wonder. No meeting of the couple's minds is too wise or too informative. Love erupts like a bountiful Vesuvius. It's as if love has never happened before—to the man, to the woman, to anybody else. And no one would dare mention that this period perhaps reflects a lush hopelessness like the last provocative rapture before the next day's armageddon.

If one notices this desperation and the hopelessness within—as a witness—one doesn't acknowledge it. Instead one renews a faith in perfection, in the ritual hope for the happy ending one fears being denied for oneself. Ultimately one will forget this ending too, regardless of which way it goes. But for witnesses, the fun—as the homily goes—is in simply getting there. One enjoys an oxymoronic approach to life, forgetting to remember, remembering to forget.

ON THIS NIGHT IN PARTICULAR it rains outside in the darkness. The man and the woman can hear it spanking the trees outside her bedroom window. Raindrops pound on her cottage roof like maniacal elfin dancers. To the man, the rain hisses like a giant snake or claps like an enthusiastic crowd. To the woman, it wraps her with her love inside a spiritually knitted blanket. The rain touches her deep in her belly, reminding her that lovers are a link in a chain fastening one event of nature to the next. To her, she and Matt should feel like one of nature's pearls, spiritually inviolate, married to earth and rain and sunshine by a function of mystical predestination captured along the necklace strand worn by Mother Nature.

For his part, the man feels himself a component in this natural order of life too, but he doesn't conceive of pearls or jewels. Instead he's aware of a hushed excitement he might describe as a light shining on his soul. It feels deeply electric, he might say.

There is, though, a sensation that they share—the smug delight that the rain falls in some appreciative endorsement of the stupendous love they've just made. They don't know exactly when the downpour began but they suspect it was as they approached the summit of their gasping pleasure, while they were zealously seeking tongues and sharing saliva, tasting once again the flesh-sweated union now ritual inside each other's embrace.

The man licked all of the woman's body, tasting salt, the

residues of perfumes and creams, even, he suspected, the history of her flesh. He gathered all of this up on his tongue— her sweat, sexual juices and a subtle twitch, her unique vibration of love. Then he spread her out below him, locked his fingers in her fingers, waited an anticipatory moment or two while, as if for the first time, he glanced down at his swollen self hesitating a moment longer, somewhat ashamed to come face to face with so much gratuitous need. He is proud after all that he is a gentle man. He felt reprehensible to encounter so clearly this stallion side of his nature, the greedy, demanding self where full and empty are identical quarrelling twins. At last, though, he found his way inside her without unlocking his hands from hers, just sliding in smoothly without having to take aim, without needing her to wrap him in her fist to steer him in the right direction.

It all seemed so flawless and preordained at that moment. Each layer of his endless quest to be whatever he must be now culminated in his arrival at this vital, sexual moment. His *now* moved into italics the way it never had before. In the place of past and future, there was only the worshipful sensation of the present and what he couldn't help but want. It drove him onwards into this woman, absurdly in search of the better man he might be on the other side.

Yes, it was stupendous lovemaking. For both of them. *By* both of them. Eventually they cried out in a shared and marvelous agony, first her, then him immediately afterwards. They chuckled when they were done, giddy with their accomplishment. Delicate kisses followed. A silent gazing at one another followed the kisses.

Then both of them became aware of the rain and the sound of its applause. It seemed to be their guide sent to lead them safely towards the natural order in life's events. They felt gifted, one realized. They perceived they clenched their fists on the phallus of forever. As if some god intended their presence there after interviewing thousands of angels applying for the position.

But of course this divine sensation did not last—it's too sensory to last, one knows. Now, in its place, a subsiding has begun. Now it rains and their electricity falls away. They're left with the quiet hiss of the rain and the growing fatigue building on their afterwards.

The woman is the first to speak, cuddled against her partner's chest. "I love the rain on the roof," she says. "It's like being safe and approved of."

Without being aware that the other is as mesmerized as they are, they gaze together at the drunken shadows cast along the wall by the flickering flame of a tall black candle standing bravely but crookedly old against a breeze originating through the opening at the bottom of the window.

"Yes," replies the man about the rain he hears on the roof. "I like the sound of it too."

Especially here on the island, he thinks. Everything on the island has always been so much more. Clearer, more profound, more readily discerned.

But he doesn't share this conclusion with her, not this time. He wants to keep even insignificant pieces of knowledge to himself, as if the electric part of his private person must be well insulated sometimes from the electricity he and she have learned to create for each other as lovers.

"I've never enjoyed making love the way I do with you," the woman whispers shortly.

She has arrived at this conclusion many lovemakings ago but has declined to mention it until now, in case he doubts the truth in her words, construes them to be well-smithied bars on the jail he should wisely escape.

But the man doesn't think of it that way. "Me too," he replies instead.

And it's true. He cannot remember himself being quite so sensual before. Still, he remains aware of one drawback in this powerful ease of need: the fact that his newfound sensuality tends to frighten him. Too often now, he believes, it simmers outside his control.

"Matt, do you think it can really stay this way?"

"I don't know," he says. "I like to think it can. It seems like a worthwhile thing to believe in."

"I mean," the woman adds, "it's hard to imagine taking all that we have for granted, letting it slip into habit, letting it get away."

"Yes," he replies, knowing she's sincere but feeling crushed under the weight of his all-too-vast experience, the part of him which still refuses to believe. "I've never understood how or why that happens," he says, "why we get used to something so exotic we shouldn't even be *able* to get used to it."

"Let's not talk about it," the woman says, suddenly filled with trepidation, overhearing caustic conversation from the lips of a cynical future.

Perhaps if they shut up about themselves they can hide from a growing and ill-defined sense of inevitable failure she secretly feels at this moment.

"Okay," the man agrees, feeling somewhat desperate himself, feeling his own failure bearing down on him and how much it resembles hers.

One sees them stop talking for a while to listen to the rain.

But now it sounds merely like falling rain: wet, dismal, distant. It no longer resembles a talisman in a mystical order of events, and it doesn't feel like it connects them to anything at all. That too is slipping away. The roof is no longer a warm and sheltering blanket. No, it's merely shingles, tar and an ever-thickening shield between the electricity they felt a few moments ago and the inevitably-failing fuses they seem destined to become.

"I just don't know what happens," the man muses at this moment, referring to nothing in particular yet incorporating almost everything he's ever managed to learn.

His words are so vague and large they simply dangle there, unable to lumber forward where they can become a specific statement. If he's not careful, he decides, this new wave of unexpected sadness will bring him to the verge of tears.

But the woman is already weeping, resolved to do so silently, not wanting to be caught succumbing to her fears.

He notices it anyway, not from any sound she makes, but because tears reflect the candlelight in the mirror of her cheeks.

So he leans closer and kisses the tears away, wishing there was more he could do to declare their recent epiphany a permanent home. But to accomplish such a feat would take a revelatory explanation which is clearly beyond him. This electricity achieved by humankind defies all his ability to explain. He cannot give her a satisfactory reason why it's born and then dies away. Easier to try to explain the reason he was born, finding some more profound reason than the fundamental hoedown danced by sperm and egg. Easier to outline why his first breath was the only one which wasn't numbered by abusive mortal time. Regretfully, all he possesses is theory and hopeless philosophical inebriation. One recognizes that the man is convinced that any real explanation of the failures in love and other perceived nirvanas exist outside his wisdom.

So the rain falls and the man and woman hold each other, waiting to be all right again, clear and independent, able to endure. They wait to be reconciled to the mystery in human electricity—accepting of the fact that, while it lights up radiantly on occasion, it so eagerly goes out. And they nearly come to the conclusion that love is a galactic nova—while he and she and their witnesses are, at the best of times, only the condition's Earthbound astronomers, condemned merely to observe, deducing something phantasmagorical in what they see.

"CAN I READ SOME OF YOUR BOOK?" she asks him one afternoon while she waits for him to finish in *The Crow's Nest* at the table which is his desk.

He looks up from a sheet or two of manuscript bleeding from every orifice with words and arrowed lines of red, irascible ink. "Of course," he replies.

"You listen to my music," she adds by way of argument.

"Of course you can," he insists.

She's somewhat surprised he's given in so easily. Sometimes, when he's Crazy Horse, when he's his own medicine man—the person he seems to be the most whenever he is working—she believes he'd prefer her to wait for him outside.

At times like these he seems older, not in a chronological way, but in the sense that he is something which has already gotten away, denied her by a glitch in time. She sometimes even wonders if he was lost to her as far back as the very beginning. This realization makes her feel young, childish and foolish, too much of a rookie to know what to do with the wise old fish she's caught in her inexperienced nets.

Except that, most of the time, she's convinced they are well matched. In fact, sometimes she's older than he is. Sometimes she remembers well that he lost his innocence much later in life than she did, a factor which explains why they are of an equal age, where innocence is concerned. She's concluded he was innocent far too long while she was innocent far too briefly. In her mind, they are two strangers who have met casually at a funeral of innocence—at least of innocence's virtue—and now trudge behind its coffin to that peculiar, haunted cemetery where innocence is buried and left forever to decay.

She noticed the residue of his innocence one day in something that he said. Back before they became lovers in the way they are lovers now.

They had taken the dogs up to the northern escarpment. There, amid the rocks and teetering cedars of the island's summit, they sat and smoked and talked, squinting out over the channel at the mainland across the way. Light years away, the mainland seemed that day, *another* place. Perhaps she was already in love and didn't want to admit it yet. Perhaps this was why the mainland seemed so far away from this island ruled by Peter Pan.

"I used to feel the butt of the world's private, cruel, little joke," Matt said that day.

"In what way?"

"I felt unusually innocent, extraordinarily naive. I felt the world knew how stupid I was to believe in all the things I believed in."

"Things like what?"

"Justice, true love, a basic standard of goodness. Even when I say what they are, I want to blush in embarrassment. Like I should rush off to change into *Captain Marvel.*"

She smiled.

"Love especially," he added then. "I had such an innocent idea of it. It was going to be, you know, nice. Worse yet, I thought everyone else wanted it to be nice too. It was like Santa Claus in a way, a kind of ritual game of make believe. Except that I really believed in Santa Claus. The rest of the world was just faking it, you know, sustaining the myth for the edification of children like me. I felt stupid to believe when everyone else was just pretending to believe for the sake of the occasion."

"Geez," she said in some surprise. "And I thought *I* was cynical."

He considered this a moment. "I guess the depth of your disillusionment is directly proportionate to the depth of your initial faith."

"You mean the earlier you become disillusioned, the less

powerful the disillusionment is?"

"Something like that," he said.

Now, during the two or three days in which she reads his collection of essays, the woman glimpses at times the same kind of hopeless innocence in what he has written. He does in fact propose a world more just, committed to a higher standard of fairness. He does perceive a time when the greedy and self-indulgent, who would impede the arrival of this state of fairness, have been erased by civilization like dinosaurs, fossilized, forgotten. As if, ironically, innocence is what one grows *into*, not *out of.*

The essays make her think. About his politics, his *outsiderness*, his apparently inherent resistance to a mating of his soul.

As the man notices her thinking, he wants to demur on some of the points his writing makes. At least a part of him does, the part that drifts towards the easier road or feels his giving in to loving her cannot ever be avoided. Perhaps, he decides, she can rescue him from the persistence of his hope. Maybe it would be good to give up on his idealism once and for all. Maybe he could be happy then in a state of compromise. When he beds down with his ideals, he and they do not get to sleep alone. Disappointment climbs under the covers with them like some lascivious predator, until he doesn't know which lover to embrace: the ideal or her wanton sister, the disappointment stalking her.

He explains all this to the woman.

"Madonna complex," she says. "You want to marry the ideal, feel ashamed when you bed down with the disappointment."

But he simply stares at her, shocked by what she's said.

"Don't take it the wrong way," she says.

"I'm not. I want to dismiss it as cynical but I can't without verifying the truth in the cynicism."

"I didn't mean to do that," the woman says. "It wasn't a snare."

"Well," he counters, "it's checkmate just the same. Cynicism always has lots of answers, lots of friends to back it up. Idealism is always walking by itself, asking the same hopeless question over and over."

"You mean 'Why?'"

"No," the man replies. "The question is 'why not?'"

ALAS, ONE NOTICES THERE'S SOMETHING ELSE that troubles the woman about what lurks inside his writing.

"Matt, is it a problem for you that my family is economically comfortable?" she asks him towards the end of August.

They picnic in the petrified forest, the man's idea. He goes there often now, sometimes with the woman, more often on his own. He comes to this place, when he's on his own, feeling gently tragic, almost noble in a way. Like Hamlet playing the part of Benjamin J. Grimm. He comes to say goodbye. He comes to consider the future and the interloper who's taken part of his future so that she can fuse it to her own. He comes here to sort through questions and answers about where he goes from here. But when he returns to his cottage, the questions and answers have broken up, even multiplied, split like stock market shares. And time still passes steadily. He's fed up with his stubborn muddle and the shrinking opportunities to finally sort it out.

The middle of August has come and gone. It's still summer but it's a summer soiled by its maturity. It even smells older, like potpourri left out too long on the counter. And both of them have remarked with a glum resignation that the sun goes down much earlier now. Indeed, the angle of the sun has changed. Where once it hovered overhead, it now ricochets across the water, and the resulting sparkle is stale and flat. It's just tired. Summer's just getting tired. Some days it appears to have fallen asleep, exhausted at the end of its watch, too soon before autumn can come to relieve it from duty, one recognizes.

"Matt?"

"Sorry," he replies. "Just thinking."

"Did you hear what I asked you?" There's an edge to her voice.

But if she is annoyed, it's because she fears his answer, not because he was off somewhere cavorting with some private daydream.

"I heard you," he says. "Of course not. I wouldn't mind being economically comfortable myself. Why should it be a problem if someone else is?"

"Okay," the woman says doubtfully. "I just wondered."

"I have trouble with rampant greed and self-interest," the man adds, feeling just a little indignant. "That's all through the book. But economic comfort—I'm not talking vast wealth—well, that's not always the same as rampant greed and self-interest."

"Okay," she says again, this time a little surer.

"But," the man adds, "your economic comfort. . ."

". . . My parents' economic comfort. . ."

". . . Okay, your parents' economic comfort tends to remind me how perilously insecure mine is. It reminds me of what a drawback I am in the conventional world." He smiles, intending somehow to soften the blow of what he's said.

"Matt?" his lover says, not the least disarmed. "Are you going to be an asshole about this economic thing forever?"

His smile disintegrates. He feels dark and betrayed. "I hope so," he replies.

They look away from one another while this small world of dunes and white, fossilized tree stumps and hazy, blue sky and distant poplars remains stubbornly the same around them. One notices that they recognize the insignificance of human anger—what does it change? Only fragile human hearts.

The woman endeavours to bring them back from the brink of this quarrel. "Matt, you and I talk so much. It's one of the most rewarding things about being with you. We make love and talk, make love and talk. Sometimes the talking is like making love."

"Yes, it is."

"And," continues the woman, "I've never had a relationship where the talking is so good. Hell, I've had relationships where there wasn't any talking at all."

"I hear a 'but' coming," says the man, resigned to whatever she'll say next.

"But," the woman says with a tentative smile, "we always talk about the past and present, never about the future."

"I think we've been consciously avoiding that," the man admits.

"Yes."

They fall silent again.

Until the woman says, "You talk about everything. You're the most candid man I've ever met."

"I hear another 'but' on the horizon."

"But," and this time she doesn't smile, "I know you're

thinking things you haven't shared with me. Things about you and me and . . ."

". . . The future," he finishes with a kind of theological gravity.

"Yes."

The man doesn't want to talk about it now. Not until he's figured things out on his own. He doesn't want to make another serious mistake. He still reviews often his list of reasons indicting him as a failure to be her permanent lover. He wants to be sure of these inadequacies, their wrongness or their rightness, before he entertains a future with this woman. *This woman*. This woman he loves. This woman he loves *so much*.

"Matt?"

"Yes?"

"I'll want to talk soon," she says.

"Me too, I guess."

"When?"

"At the end of summer?"

"You mean August?"

"Yes. Okay."

"September first," the woman says.

"Okay."

"I love you, Matt, you know."

"I love you too, Nickie. I love you like crazy."

They smile at one another, reprieved. This conversation hasn't turned out as badly as they both suspected it might.

As for the witnesses, they sigh at the apparent joy contained in the couple's mutual smile. Even aware of the sadness at its edges, one believes this sadness seems merely a delicate shading enhancing the central hue.

That's the thing about witnesses. When one gazes at the landscape of love, something painted by someone else, one forgets the various brush strokes it took to create the scene. And one doesn't remember the nervous courage which was required to mix the paints. Or the trembling which resulted when the artist reached for the brush to make that first brave pass—brush and color and faith—over the empty canvas. No, one merely sees the final vista in which one must believe. If love is to be a journey, surely it must have a destination.

## MATT

**Sunday, August 25**
STRANGE HOW PEOPLE FIT INTO A ROOM with one another. Tall, short, tilted, straight up. That's how I see it. A room. Its walls are circumstantial, its passageways labyrinthian. When and how we meet the room's other wanderers is determined by whom we encounter and in which passage we happen to be travelling at the time.

This comes to mind, I suppose, because it occurred to me earlier tonight that Sidney Graham and I might have become close friends, had some of the circumstances surrounding our meeting been different. Maybe if Nicole and I weren't sharing the maze in the intimate way we are. That is, if we weren't wedged inside the potential for a friendship between Sid and me like a sliver jammed between the nail and the flesh of a finger. Or to put it in more candid language, if I was not making so much secret love to his daughter, then perhaps the friendship might have had a chance to develop, at least along more typical lines.

As it stands now, should the relationship between Nicole and me continue, it becomes predetermined that I must move inexorably closer to that strictly defined societal function we call son-in-law, a status possessing its own inherent rituals and set of rules, all of them tending to prevent the kind of friendship I'm talking about. Worse yet, there's every potential for him to see his daughter hurt, should Nicole and I drift away from one another the way it sometimes seems we must, contemplating the way we do setting out in different directions.

If Sid and I had met on the beach a couple of months ago and there had been no Nicole, we might be island buddies by now. We might regularly fish the way we did earlier this evening, regularly meeting on the beach to shoot the shit or finding a shady spot not far from one of our cottages to wax philosophical over a couple of beers. Without Nicole, all of these normal activities might supersede our essential differences— his comfortable economic circumstances and the contrast of my own; his easy adherence to the assumed rightness propounded by the privileged status quo versus my nearly revolutionary fervor to seek significant change. Or, failing that, skulking off into the privacy of my own chosen sunset. I imagine Sid and I would find a comfortable ground at the edge of our insistent contrasts where we could build a friendship. If, that is, I was not in love with his daughter.

But I *am* in love with his daughter. The possibility of Sid and me being buddies exists in the subjunctive case. There most definitely is a Nicole and there's no escaping the fact that I greedily take her to bed with me every chance I get and, in so doing, intrude to some degree on Sidney's emotional territory.

Meanwhile, Nicole and I teeter on the top rung of a rickety stepladder, not knowing whether to take each other's hand and leap into oblivion together or whether to slink back down the steps separately, privately, accepting a separation neither one of us knows for certain we can ultimately truly bear.

Sid and I can never be island buddies, not in any true sense. Come the end of September, I lose *The Crow's Nest* forever. Come the end of September, I either move, as I said, inexorably closer to becoming his son-in-law or assume the role of the man who took advantage of his daughter before finally breaking her heart.

I know what Nicole would say. Nicole would remind me that few encounters in the labyrinth of human relationships are my exclusive responsibility. She'd insist I remember that I cannot control how other people feel. But these conclusions come at the end of our immersion in a period of change, after most of our hurts have eased, not at the beginning. They come when we've admitted we'd prefer to be alone.

So there it is, I guess. Fait accompli. And that's the way it goes. Most of the time, when we figure things out, it's simply just too late. Or is it that I merely feel fatalistic tonight? I'm a half open door half closed—blowing in my own mind's windsock, as near as I can tell.

Although I write in my usual location at the dining room table—and now it's growing very late—I still feel myself to be back there at my station, a couple of hours ago in time. I recall easily the chilly but coincidental comfort of sitting in the front seat of the Graham boat, holding a fishing rod, gazing at my fishing line and a red and white bobber on the choppy surface of the lake while twilight filtered down like silt, piling up all around me. There I was in a sweater and a jacket, remembering that autumn is coming on just over the island horizon now puffing out its chest and sucking in its summery gut.

I dance back and forth between then and now. Here, now, in my *Crow's Nest* den, the lake is dark again, brooding out there in the tolling black on the other side of my windows. While I sat in the boat, though, the lake was rhythmically close, blue at first, then green, then gray as dusk descended. I felt an unusual connection to it. But by the time we beached the boat on the home side of our island, it was nearly dark. I'd already let go of the lake, let it get away from me.

The fishing idea came up this morning during a period of sadness, hurt and disorientation I was surprised I felt.

I was on my way back from the western end of the island with Canine Ben when I noticed Nicole and her parents breakfasting on the terrace at the front of their cottage. Intending to continue on my way, I nonetheless waved at them and all three of them waved back. After a moment, though, Sid stood up and beckoned me in their direction. I had no choice but to walk up the hill to where they sat around their patio table, soiled napkins at the edges of their plates, an uneaten croissant peeking out from under a cloth in a wicker basket in the center of the table.

I felt on the outside of this family scene. Or was it only that it struck me right away, as I gained the terrace, how much I've grown used to Nicole's welcoming embrace? It's absence this morning was an unexpected, hurtful blow.

"Hi, Matt," was all she said, seated at the table, lifting her coffee cup to her lips.

She wore her dark glasses which somehow made things worse. Her voice seemed to originate from some wasteland behind their opaque lenses, like it slithered out of a tunnel entrance to the underworld like a reptile about to sun itself.

"Hi," I managed to say. Then, "great day," I added for good measure.

But I felt tottery and weak. To my dismay, I quite literally ached to hold Nicole in my arms. At that moment I longed for her parents to know how much I love their daughter. I no longer cared, should I crumble in this way, whether it might represent giving in to a choice I would later regret.

But by then Sid was shaking my hand and Nicole's mother was asking me how I had been. Her voice too seemed to originate from some otherworldly source, from behind *her* dark glasses. Nonetheless, despite feeling so unnerved, I kept up my end of the bargain as we continued to exchange pleasantries.

"Would you like a cup of coffee?" Sid remembered to suggest.

"Thank you, no," I said. "I have a pot on at home."

"Matt works on weekends," Nicole explained to her parents.

"Sundays too?" said Sid.

"I'm afraid so," I replied.

I concentrated on smiling at Nickie's parents. I felt like some hastily constructed marionette, legs weak and gangly, midsection twitching with impudent yearning, an artificial smile smeared into place on the features of my face.

And so it went for a couple of minutes until Sidney invited me to go fishing with him this evening.

I told him it would be a pleasure in view of the fact we'd been rained out last time he'd suggested it.

He grinned, I think, at the formal tenor of my acceptance. But over his left shoulder I could see Nicole nodding her approval.

After Sidney and I made arrangements to meet at his boat, I bade them all a pleasant day and stumbled back towards the beach.

My forlornness over having to do without Nicole's embrace

eventually passed but not until I'd regained the safety of my own cottage. Even then, for a time, I had to face the intensity of my yearning and how unexpected it was. I spent much of the morning examining my new distaste for the duplicity Nicole and I preserve when she is visited by her parents.

I felt like a spoiled child. My untoward yearning on the Graham terrace seemed a foolish self-indulgence in view of my role in keeping our love affair secret. I know damn well Nickie would tell her parents about me if she was more certain of what our future holds. So what did I expect?

Although I was over my outrageous pique by the time I met Sidney down at the boat, I nonetheless remained keenly aware of what an interloper I am in the sanctity of his family. I even wondered at one point if Sidney secretly counts on me to keep his daughter safe while she lives on this island alone. If so, I couldn't escape the conclusion that he has been betrayed. Then again, I thought, what nonsense! What an old-fashioned notion! Nicole and I are adults. Whatever betrayal I wish to assume originates in my own mind. Having come to this conclusion, I tried to cut myself some slack.

Why do I do this so much? Why do I spend so much time examining other people's perceptions of who I am and what I do? Is it because the burden of maintaining my own judgment wears me out too easily? And what do we call a point of passage in life when one tires of one's own perception? Is it a state of fatigue caused by defending one's turf? Or is it achievement of a kind of wise acceptance of the probable pointlessness in life's reported meaning? Although I pondered these questions deep and long, I didn't come up with any answers. The questions goofed off at the edges of my thoughts much of the afternoon, in fact until after dinner, without getting anything beneficial done.

Still, I managed to keep my appointment with Sidney. After we cast off his boat, he took us around the western tip of the island.

"I know this spot where they're usually biting," he suggested over the purr of the motor.

"Okay," I said with a nod.

I noticed the care with which he piloted his boat. It exaggerated for me the contrasting recklessness Nicole displays whenever she navigates these waters.

I guess one ends up feeling close to someone with whom one sits in a boat, fishing for a couple of hours. Hemingwayesque bonding, I suppose. Still, it's more than this. Sidney Graham is an agreeable man—I've known this since we met that first morning on the beach way back in June.

This evening we fished for bass. He anchored the boat in a little cove on the north side of the island, just west of Nicole's favorite spot high up on the rocks. When Sid and I first arrived, it was still light enough for me to look up and pick out the ledges near the top of the cliff where Nicole and another me have sometimes sat and talked.

As for the fishing, Sid nestled the boat into a spot of green-blue water bordered on two sides by submerged rocks and moss-covered logs. Here we skewered worms on our hooks, attached bobbers to our lines and cast it all into the lake. Then we stared at the bobbers and talked while a gentle chop clucked against the boat.

"Nick tells me you're almost done your book."

"Yes," I replied.

"Ahead of schedule, she says."

"That's right."

"So you'll be leaving the island early?"

"No," I said. "I don't think so. In view of the cottage sale, you know, this being my last year here, I thought I'd wait it out. I'll go back to Kingston to send out the manuscript and take care of some other business, but then I'll come back here. Just commune with the place as long as I can, I guess."

"So nothing's changed?"

"Changed?"

"In the situation with the cottage."

"No," I replied. "Nothing's changed."

He considered this a moment, taking off a sweat-stained cap, passing a hand through this silver hair, then putting the cap back on.

"It's none of my business but it seems like such a shame." He glanced at me for a moment, assessing, I think, my willingness to hear him out. "It's just that I have this traditional idea of property. The idea that it should be passed on, especially when someone cares about it so much. You're sure you can't come to some kind of arrangement with your aunt?"

"An arrangement?"

"Perhaps she'd hang onto it if you volunteered to use it and look after the upkeep. Didn't you say it was the upkeep that's the problem?"

I noticed his bobber dancing up and down on the surface of the water. Sid seemed oblivious to the fact.

"Are you getting a bite?" I asked him.

He gazed at the bobber but, by then, it floated serenely on the surface, making a liar of me. "I don't think so," he replied.

Fair enough, I thought. I studied my own line.

We returned to the topic of coming to an arrangement with my aunt. I explained it was more complicated than that, not only from her point of view but from mine as well.

"I think *The Crow's Nest* was, for years, something she shared with my Uncle Bart. Now that he's gone, I don't think she has the heart to keep it. On top of that, she only has her pension to live on. I think she wants to put the money from the sale in the bank and add the interest to her income."

"I see," remarked Sid.

"But the thing about my uncle, I think that's the main reason."

"Love's a funny thing," mused my companion at this point. "It's one of those things you aren't always conscious of valuing until you lose it. That's the way it goes for some people, I know."

I glanced in his direction, wondering for a moment what he might know or have discerned about his daughter and me. Was there extra meaning hidden inside his remark, a warning of some kind?

"I know," I said anyway.

And I do know we often get careless about love. I consider this in the silence now, here at my writing table, with dragons snorting darkness just outside my windows. I do know, for some people, a state of loss is exactly how it ends up. Except . . .

"As for me," I explained back then in the boat, while the night and the lake changed color as dusk drew steadily closer, while the boat rocked gently on the chop of the restless lake, while Sid seemed to study his bobber but actually gazed somewhere else, "it gets more complicated."

"While you don't want to lose it," said Sid, "you don't want to make the sacrifices you'd have to make to keep it. Like postponing going out west for a while."

"More or less," I said, hoping we were indeed talking about the cottage and not his idea of something else. "This island is my favorite place in the whole world. But it's mostly a setting with a focus on my past. If I sacrifice the potential in my future to keep it, then my future gets locked into a kind of prerequisite to my past. You see what I mean?"

"I suppose I do," he said.

"I think," I added then, "I'm a different man now than the one I used to be when I considered this island home. I think, when I came here this spring, I'd already decided it was time that I moved on."

"Well," said Sid as he reeled in his line to check on the status of his bait. "It just feels like such a shame. I guess the optimum situation would be not to have to make a choice at all." He gazed at his naked hook, cocked his head at me to make sure I noticed it had been stripped of all its bait, grinned self-deprecatingly, then reached for the cardboard container holding our allotment of worms.

I sensed he had more to say and I waited for him in silence. He didn't speak again until he'd tossed his bobber back into the lake.

"I mean," he said eventually, "that in optimum circumstances you could make some kind of arrangement to buy the cottage from your aunt and go out west as well. That way you'd have this past and future thing worked out. You could play it all by ear. If things didn't work out out west, well you'd have a place to come back to." For a moment I fretted this subject would continue, that he would even suggest some kind of mutually agreeable scheme which would help me buy *The Crow's Nest*. A partnership? A loan? I'd have to turn it down, of course. And I'd have to find acceptable reasons for doing so—acceptable to him, at least. But when at last he spoke, it was on another topic and I felt relieved.

"I guess you know that Nick has decided to work with her friend Karen in Kingston," my companion said.

"Yes, she told me."

"Now that it's a reality, her mother's a little upset. I think, as long as it was only a possibility, she didn't worry about it very much. Now that Nickie's made up her mind, well, you know."

"Sure. She won't be able to see her as often."

He nodded. "Betty has an old-fashioned way of looking at things. She imagines her daughter finding a good man, settling down, having children. Betty wants to be a grandmother, I think. She was pretty disappointed when Nickie broke it off with Alan."

"Well," I said as diplomatically as I could, "times have changed. These days women take their time making up their minds. Just like men, I guess."

"That's true."

"Fifty percent of marriages end up in divorce," I added, not quite sure, after I'd made this point, what I was trying to say.

He glanced at me kindly enough. "It's how you choose to look at it," he said. "That means fifty percent of marriages *don't* end up in divorce."

"I suppose," I admitted, somewhat chagrined to realize I'd never quite considered it this way myself.

What did this my-glass-is-half-empty view reveal about my romantic perspective? Was I now a man who looked under a rock for scorpions more often that at the rock itself?

We fished in silence for a moment or two. The bobbers floated peacefully. So far, I hadn't had a nibble.

"You're divorced yourself, aren't you?"

"Couple of times," I confessed.

"You must be pretty gun shy by now."

"I suppose I am."

He merely nodded.

"I've gotten used to living a private life," I added. "I sometimes wonder if that was what I was supposed to do all along."

I glanced at him with a new nervousness. What did he make of all of this? What did he know? What, if anything, did he suspect? Or were we just conducting a casual exploration of the history of our lives?

"What do you intend to do out west?"

"That's a little hard to say," I replied, knowing I sounded cryptic.

He stepped back an inch or two. "I don't mean to pry."

"No, no," I assured him. "That's okay. I'm really not sure

exactly where I'll be or what I'll be doing. In a way, that's the point of the whole thing. All I know is that I need to spend some time in the mountains. I've been putting this trip off for years and I don't want to postpone it any longer. Beyond that, I suppose I'll do there what I do here."

"Write?"

"Yes. Some freelance work, I hope."

"So it might not be permanent?"

"I'll just take it as it comes."

"Well," he said, "that's what it is to live an unattached life."

"Yes," I replied.

This topic too slipped away from us. We talked of other things afterwards, less personal things—fishing, movies about fishing, golf and a cautious exploration of the world of politics.

We caught no fish. For more than two hours, my bobber floated serenely a few feet from the boat. When at last we agreed it was time we packed it in, neither one of us seemed to mind that the fish had stood us up.

"I'm not sure fishing is always about catching fish," Sid reminded me just before he started the motor to take us home.

I didn't think of it then—even as we beached the boat and shook hands down at the water's edge—but it occurs to me now, as I jot down what I remember of our conversation, that it's quite possible I will never see Sidney Graham again. For one thing, Nicole has mentioned that her parents won't be visiting in September, that this weekend is their last one on the island this year.

But this piece of information is only a technicality. There's another reason to believe Sidney and I have parted company for the last time. As I sit here now, transcribing my remarks this evening, I hear something inescapable in the echo of my voice, namely the certainty it seemed to possess when I was discussing my future plans. "I've gotten used to living a private life," I said. "I just need to spend some time in the mountains."

It was the man I really am who said these things and who knew, when he spoke, that they were true. And Sidney must have realized that they are true as well. I'm glad he doesn't know how much I love his daughter. If he did, he'd probably suggest I have no business doing so. Because she's going to Kingston and I'm going west. Because I'll fit everything I own quite easily into an aging Ford Escort as I make my next trip through life, while Nicole has every reason to begin building something larger than that in a city I feel compelled to escape.

And there's the bottom line which, for a few precious moments in the Graham boat seems inescapable. Nicole and I are headed in different directions because we have different ambitions and objectives.

We'll be discussing these things in a week or so, as we've agreed to do. But I know it won't make any difference. No matter how intensely we love one another, there's no denying that we've made separate and distinct plans to get on with our lives. And neither one of us is willing to compromise. For one thing, both of us have compromised too much already in the early innings of our respective pasts—it's a habit we wish to break. For another, we're not as foolish as we'd like to be.

That's the thing about love. Whatever it is made of on the inside of its foolishness—the ecstasy, the touch, the brilliantly shining light—its skin is compromise, someone giving in or giving up. Which is fine for people who've something left to give, whose skin still has some stretch. But for those of us who've reached the limit of what we have to give there's nothing left to consider beyond Matt Bowman's axiom: *give all the love you feel, take all the love you can get.*

After that, you're on your own. No matter where you're headed, no matter who briefly shares the road with you, when you reach your destination you arrive there on your own.

## PART FIVE: SEPTEMBER, 1996

### NICOLE

AS YOU AND MATT DRIVE INTO KINGSTON on the Saturday of the last holiday weekend of the summer, you notice an increasingly visible mood of disorganized celebration on various streets near the center of the city. Driving a circuitous route towards his apartment, he explains the students who will attend Queen's University in the coming year have picked this weekend to descend on the city. To your surprise, there are hundreds of them, even thousands. And at this point the spirit of celebration, of communion all makes sense. Youth, anticipation, a prevailing mood of careless and unusual freedom—all of these facts and sensations combine to create an atmosphere of casual Mardi Gras which permeates the streets.

Frequently, as you drive through a commercial area of town, you pass boldly lettered signs saying, "Welcome Back" or Welcome Back, Students." They are gently obsequious, these signs, begging for business from behind a mask of hospitality. That's how Matt describes it, anyway. He doesn't approve of all of this, or at least he finds it tiresome, a point of view which grows more obvious the further into the city's center you drive.

You must admit it's persistently inconvenient. As you work your way closer to the downtown core, the streets become choked with moving vans, trailers and an assortment of sport/utility vehicles, some parked at awkward angles on the streets, others piloted recklessly by grinning baseball caps, announced in advance by a crescendoing radio concert of rambunctious rap or grunge. On lawns and porches, often in more than one location on each block, students gather in large, fidgety groups, less with a view to moving anything inside the nearby housing than to stand around outside with bottles of beer, laughing and talking and preening.

"This is the student ghetto," Matt explains at one point while his car idles at a stoplight. "Next spring it'll look like it should be condemned."

"Do you live here?" you ask. "Do you live in the ghetto?"

"On the edges of it, I'm afraid. My apartment had students in it before I rented it. It'll probably have students in it after I leave."

In truth, it feels like a student kind of day to you. With a deep sense of nostalgia, you realize quite clearly that summer is practically over, has slipped away while you weren't looking. And even now—years since you were a student—the link between school and summer's end persists. It's as if school is all that remains to be done when summer begins to wither.

Certainly, this day has an autumn chill about it, a preliminary coolness, easy, slight, infantile. Overhead, perfectly-white clouds stroll across a deep blue park of sky. The sun ducks in and out between them, not so much playfully as in a state of ambivalence, perhaps even out of sorts or moody, confused about where to go and why.

Matt turns onto a narrow side street and, in so doing, interrupts a pair of students passing a football back and forth in the middle of the road. Affably the students move to the sidewalk to let you pass. Up ahead, though, an even larger group occupies the road to flick a frisbee from one to another. And on the right side of the street, two threadbare couches have been set up on the lawn at the edge of the sidewalk. A half dozen young people lounge on the beaten up sofas, sneakered feet stretched out in front of them, bottles or cans of beer in their hands, hooting from the bleachers at the frisbee-tossing students who occupy the street. Gradually, with a ceremoniously rebellious lack of haste, the frisbee klatch moves out of the way to let you pass.

Suddenly you feel it too, a mild annoyance at all this casual good nature. It's like a commercial interruption inserted maddeningly inside the serious drama reflecting true life. The childish goodwill and accompanying insolence seem like a room which must be tidied before going off to war or showing up at surgery. Peering into the hectic activity from your location outside of it, the goings-on appear powerfully self-absorbed and moronically insipid. In your mind, this display is comparable to shopping for and arguing bra sizes at the height of a hurricane.

"I used to have more patience for all of this than I do now," Matt murmurs in a toneless voice, as if his thoughts have popped in on yours for a visit or a meeting.

But when you glance in his direction, he appears extremely far away, merely talking to himself. Alienated by his distance, you don't have the heart to reply. Feeling so separate from him, you begin to view events differently. What appeared to be a meeting of the minds now seems somehow like falling ill; his mood of judgmental influenza is compromising the health of your mood too.

You've visited Kingston before to spend a weekend with Karen and Liam, but this was during the summer or later in the fall. This festive celebration of returning students on the last holiday weekend of the season should provide its own unexpected amusement because it's new and different. You resent that it doesn't. You resent Matt because his mood has overwhelmed yours. And there's that *other* thing: the apprehension you've been feeling which began a few days ago after Matt suggested coming here to spend this time with him.

It was Matt's need to return to Kingston for the weekend. He wanted to check his mail, send out his manuscript, check for telephone messages, make some calls, look after some bills. The two of you could stay at his apartment, he said. The dogs would be allowed in his building and they travel well together in the back of his car where he's folded down the seats. Even now, Carmen and Canine Ben stand quietly just behind you, motionless except for occasional glances out the window at all this mysterious human activity.

On the surface of it, the change of scene seemed like a good idea. Underneath, however, you felt a deep suspicion that this expedition to Kingston reflected Matt's employment of a malignant kind of tactic. Was he bringing you to Kingston to demonstrate in practical terms why you must inevitably fail as lovers? Were you to briefly leave the island to clearly see how ill matched you are on the turf where conventional expectations make it obvious you can't succeed?

You would have mentioned your concerns to him except to do so would make things worse. He would have stood accused of manipulation. He would have feigned surprise and injury, something men manage so very well when they rise to bargain a plea. It flashes across their face, that "Are you crazy?" look. Somehow, with what was already bearing down on you, you simply didn't want to see him look at you in a way that implied any kind of contempt.

So now you know it isn't the students. It isn't their careless invasion of the city you'll similarly invade a month from now yourself that sours your private mood. Not really. No, it's your own sense of apprehension and the inescapable conclusion that the end for you and Matt has possibly—even ghoulishly— stumbled into view.

It's all come down to this weekend. Like it or not, in one way or another, this weekend is going to contain developments you'll remember all your life. You and Matt will make decisions which have a better-than-even chance of tearing your love apart. You can't escape the notion that the next seventy-two hours may represent three of the worst days of your emotional life.

Matt turns right, down another cluttered side street. "You know," he says while he carefully negotiates the roadway, "I think what bugs me is that they're so self-satisfied, that the world is their fucking oyster."

"The careless youth we forget we ever had ourselves?"

"More or less," he admits.

Then he grins in his Crazy Horse way, as if he can deliberately improve his mood, defuse the sulky character of his not-so-silent disapproval.

"Sometimes I think we should just mail them their degree, their American Express card, their Tory membership and their slice of applehood and mother pie, and save ourselves all this trouble. That way, they get what they came for, the status quo is comfortably maintained, and we get some peace and quiet."

"Oh, Matt," you say with a tired little smile, wishing you'd stayed on the island where everything is all right, where politics keeps its distance.

IN HIS APARTMENT, MATT POINTS OUT PROUDLY how many things he doesn't own. Which, you have to admit, is virtually everything. He's already told you several times too many that his is a furnished apartment. But now he pushes this fact to extremes. Taking you on a tour, he opens kitchen cupboards, pointing out the ugly, scratched, chipped, mismatched dishes which he stresses come with the place. In one cupboard, you notice, there are dozens of empty plastic yogurt and margarine containers. These are his he says when you ask him what they're for. He never does explain why he hoards them, what would possess him to keep so many when he has such limited cupboard space. In the end you are reduced to wondering which one of you truly defines themself by what is or is not owned. At this moment, it seems to be him; it isn't you at all.

The apartment, of course, is small. Canine Ben is used to it. He retreats to a den under a table where he lies down and gazes at the rest of you from between his experienced paws. Carmen goes exploring, though somewhat cautiously.

The kitchen is hardly bigger than a closet. You can just get through the doorway, turning sideways to move around a jutting, yellowed refrigerator. The living room is also the dining room. There's a table for two over by the window looking down on a busy street. The rest of the room is furnished by a futon and an antique chair with tape along one arm only partially hiding a vicious tear in its disintegrating fabric.

This room is also his office, you see. There's a medium-sized desk holding a lamp and a telephone jammed into the last corner near the hall. There are books everywhere. They reside on the floor in each open space between the furniture at the edges of a fraying beige carpet gone grimy and faded over time. Some of the books are stacked; some stand on their ends. As you bend yourself in half to glance at a title or two, you realize Matt's is a library designed exclusively for elves. Even this seems an attempt to be reductive, to shrink any potential you might assume exists in the rest of his life. You straighten up again, feeling a hurtful twinge in the small of your back. Can't he get some shelves somewhere to share his titles with you?

The bedroom is the largest room, with a double bed, a

dresser, a bookcase. Track lighting overhead, you discover with some surprise: as if the fixtures have time-travelled back from some mystifying future to be trapped with all the dust bunnies defining the past.

Yes, it's dusty. But underneath the dust it's clean. Even the bathroom. Matt Bowman cleans his toilet and tub. Good for you, you think, gratified to be surprised.

"Is this okay?" he asks after the tour.

"Of course it is," you reply. "You've always made it clear it isn't the Taj Mahal."

Then, hoping to emphasize the point that you are not dismayed, you hug him there in the center of his crowded living room. Inside the embrace everything improves again, at least for a little while. And his books don't seem so tragic teetering shelflessly on the floor.

YOU MAKE LOVE THIS NIGHT like a pair of desperate panthers. You growl and snarl and feed on one another all over the squeaking bed. As if this lovemaking could be the very last, the one you'll have to remember when you can't avoid remembering. Actually you know it need not be the final time for you and Matt. Rather, this lastness is illusory, a black fantasy, a peeking under the lid of Pandora's Box only to discover a prevailing desperation peering back at you.

But this night's lovemaking isn't clearly passion any more, not the comforting need you earlier knew accompanied joy. No, it's something more ravenous than that. Hard cock and bulging breasts and sexual juices everywhere, an atmosphere of frenzied panic. You don't freely celebrate your love, not this time. It's more like trying to catch and reassemble falling pieces of yourselves with cruelly fumbling fingers. Even the embrace following this desperate sexual repair is an attempt to contain your destruction. When you put your arms around him, it's to hold everything together—him, you, most of all the startling, frantic power contained inside your love.

"YOU DON'T LOOK SO GOOD," observes Karen Sunday afternoon across a cafe table from you.

"I'm tired," you reply, which is what you always say when someone mentions you're not yourself.

"Huh," says Karen then. But she glances back down at the scrawl and chaos of her menu, intending to choose some trendy idea of a healthy lunch.

Over her shoulder, traffic and periods of drizzle pass by outside; they're as tired as you are but somehow more relentless.

Both of you order salads, Karen's spinach, yours some fruity concoction attrition forced you to select.

"Matt comes here sometimes," you murmur more or less to yourself. "He told me he drinks coffee in the corner and watches everyone. A change of scene, to get out of his apartment."

"Really? Maybe I saw him here before you two ever met," says Karen distractedly.

Karen remains engrossed, you suspect, by your earlier conversation on the way downtown in Liam's Jeep. How you'll live with them in October until you find an apartment of your own. Matt's a new topic for her today. You must wait for her to catch up.

"It'd be quite a coincidence," you manage to say, although you find her notion of previously seeing Matt less comforting than you'd like.

The cafe reverberates with lunch hour activity and ceremony, stainless steel tapping on porcelain, porcelain clattering on heavy wooden tables. Voices rise, laugh and even occasionally squeal because the students are in evidence here too, the way yesterday they occupied the streets. They display a familiar and self-conscious self-absorption. Yet, here, their preening seems more alien, too much light inside the darkness of this downtown cafe where morbid works of art do their dying tragically along the plaster walls.

But the students perform their song and dance anyway, making a ritual out of having difficulty selecting tables. They sit down, then get up again and move, consider this table for a few moments before moving somewhere else. They remind you of a dog unable to find the best place to lie down. You find all of this annoying, much ado about nothing. And you grow irritable at the melodrama with which they greet a casual acquaintance, as if undying devotion is somehow verified when it is performed with some excess before a captive lunch time crowd.

Matt would notice all of this too, you realize. When did your observations become just an echo of his? Is his Kingston strategy working? Is all of this just a means to show you he doesn't belong, doesn't *want* to belong? Or are you more the same than you have formerly believed—Crazy Horse and Crazy Filly dropping out of the secular world?

"Nick?"

You shrug as if this justifies how far away you've been. "I was just trying to picture Matt in this place before he came to stay on the island. It just doesn't work. It doesn't seem like the kind of place he'd enjoy."

"It's Sunday," Karen replies as if this explains everything.

"That's true." You look around again. "So this is where I'll be living," you say.

"This is it."

"Do you think I'll like it here?"

"Yes," says Karen without hesitation. "Yes, I think you will."

"I think Matt brought me here to show me what's wrong with everything."

"How do you mean?" asks Karen with a frown.

"How he doesn't fit in anymore, how he *can't* fit. How, because of that, he can't ultimately fit with me."

"Whoa," says Karen in consternation. "Back up, will you?"

So you tell her about your suspicions, that Matt invited you here to spend time with him while he ran his errands, but you no longer believe it was simply because he wanted you here with him. You explain how, instead, it feels like he's brought you here to underline the urgency of all his romantic concerns, to magnify the fatuousness he perceives exists in a world he's already rejected.

By now Karen is well aware of the train of suppositions his romantic concerns reflect. Karen supposes what you suppose; you suppose what Matt supposes. She doesn't even mention the great mystery of what his concerns might be. Because no one actually knows exactly what they are. You just suppose you know—age and economic difference, the quicksand role and ritual lurking at the edge of your intended pathway through life together. And Karen supposes she knows what *you* suppose you know. All this supposing is a frustrating kind of mirage—even when all of you acknowledge it exists. Because no one appears to have really seen it, it's based purely on speculation and a religious kind of assumption.

"Do you think Matt loves you?" Karen asks shortly between recklessly balanced forkfuls of spinach, mushrooms and purple onion rings.

"Yes, I do."

"What about you? Do you love him?"

"Absolutely. Like crazy."

Karen sighs. She notices as you push your salad away, most of it uneaten. "I don't get it," she says.

"I don't get it either."

The pair of you order coffee, although Karen hasn't quite finished her salad yet. Your server asks about dessert. In unison, the two of you send him packing.

"So what do you think is going to happen?" Karen asks you afterwards.

"I don't know. I think, come the end of September, we're supposed to call it off."

"Whatever for?"

"Because it's done."

"Done?"

"It doesn't have any future beyond that point."

Karen stares at you in silence. A second later, though, you see her light go on. "Oh, I get it," she says. "Your 'best before' date on the carton of milk."

"Huh?"

"You remember," she says, reaching out to touch your arm. "Earlier this summer. You said something about love having a 'best before' date. You know, best before September thirtieth, for instance. After that, you pour what's left down the sink and go out and buy another quart."

And at last you remember too. You said those things before you even knew you were falling in love with Matt. It wasn't said with Matt in mind at all. At the time, it was your way of disposing of the senselessness of all your *other* romantic disasters. Karen made fun of the idea but you'd been a little more serious when you raised the concept. It seemed boldly honest at the time, a giving in to inescapable fact. Strange now, though, that the possibility of living out the tenets of your careless analogy fills you with fear and sadness. Now that you love someone who seems to believe even more than you do that love indeed does boast a 'best before' date, you want to book-burn the metaphor to extinguish any potential it has to represent an accurate wisdom.

"Love," you tell Karen bitterly, "is so fucking stupid."

"Really?"

"Oh yeah," you add with a flick of your hand. "We don't like it, we don't really want it, we don't enjoy it all that often and, yet, we keep doing it. We keep looking for it."

"Or it keeps finding us," adds Karen with a not-very-welcome beacon for a smile.

"And all this romantic wreckage piles up behind us."

"We think about that too much."

"The wreckage?"

Karen nods.

"Well it's there," you say impatiently. "You have to admit it's back there, garbage on the growing pile of what we never learn."

"So what?"

You don't answer her. Easy for you to say, Karen, you decide in the ensuing silence. You don't have any wreckage. One trip to the dealership and home with a Cadillac. No rust on the model yet. Love just purrs along.

"So what are you going to do?" Karen asks at last.

"We're supposed to talk this weekend."

"Well, that's good." Then, "Isn't it? It's good, isn't it?"

"I don't know."

"You think he'll break it off?"

"No." Then "Maybe," you amend, admitting to an uncertainty you've only this moment clearly felt.

Karen gazes intently at you. "The talk's a good idea, regardless of the outcome. You should know where you stand."

Soberly you nod.

"You know something?" Karen says then. "I think you guys have been on that island too damned long."

"At some point, I may wish we'd stayed there."

"You remember what I said about bringing the island with you?"

"I remember," you reply.

And you do. You liked the spirit in the suggestion. It sounded very wise. But when you passed it onto Matt, the two of you seemed unable to translate its faint emotional hope into a practical course of action. You remember this failure well, perhaps even more clearly than what Karen might have intended.

"It's a wonderful idea," you tell your best friend now. "I'm just not sure it works in reality."

"Why not?"

"I only know that Matt wasn't the same by the time we pulled into Kingston yesterday. Something had come over him. Over *us*, I guess. Because I felt it too."

"Felt what?"

"That he didn't want to live here anymore. Karen, I'm pretty sure that even if he decided to stay in Kingston simply to be with me, in the end I'd lose out anyway. I really don't believe he'd be the same man I knew back on the island."

Sadly Karen nods. "That's a tough one. Does he still want to go out west?"

"Yes. But I want to work here with you. I'm looking forward to it."

"You're not just worried about changing your mind and hurting my feelings, are you? You're not just deciding to work with me because you feel obligated?"

Adamantly you shake your head. "I really want to do this, with or without Matt. Maybe that's the bottom line. Maybe we're headed towards separate places."

"You guys had better talk."

You nod in agreement, suddenly wishing you were in a restaurant where you could smoke, so you could reach out, snare an ashtray, pull it closer to you, and smash your cigarette into the gray residue of *someone else's* charred confusion. In a restaurant where you could have a cigarette, you would enjoy crushing the damned thing out.

"SO WHAT ARE YOU GOING TO DO?" you ask Matt, in bed several hours later.

"I don't know," he replies, reaching for his cigarettes. "Talk, I guess. See what that reveals."

In the darkness, you nod. You've just plunged in, both of you, without subtle preamble of any kind. This is *The Talk*. Who can be surprised? Who needs to come at it softly, timidly, as if unsure whether it's just some social blunder?

"Want a smoke?" Matt asks, giving in to an afterthought.

"Okay."

He does his *Frenchman's Creek* impression, lights both cigarettes at once, then hands you one of them. The first time he did so, your mood was gay and frivolous, the cigarette maneuver seeming a well-executed parody. Now it's something he sometimes does without even thinking about it. Strange, you think at this moment. You know where parody begins, some time after a shift in paradigm. But what comes next? What follows parody? Vacuum? Irony? Cynicism? Do we have to misplace every moment we ever succeed in finding? Besides, both of you are adamant that smoking has to go.

As for you and Matt, no one wants to begin. You smoke your cigarettes in silence. The coals are red fireflies mating back and forth as they travel from your lips to an ugly blue ashtray Matt has positioned on his belly.

You've made love again like last night, with the same wild animal desperation, jungle cries and screeches, jungle lust and fear. It was very good then very bad, this jungle kind of lovemaking, like a chemical delusion. That's been the cycle recently. You start out frantic to taste the good, forget the bad on its underside, its afterword, some long essay of guilt and nagging panic integral to the habit.

Karen told you back last June that love for her was comfortable. Since then, you've enjoyed glimpses of this kind of comfort with Matt, some of them longer and lazier than you might once have expected. But not in bed these days. It's not comfortable there; it's more like a feeding frenzy, a punk piranha party.

"We don't want to do this," Matt murmurs out of the darkness at last.

"You mean talk?"

"Yes. We keep hoping something else will happen. A magic solution. God's searchlight suddenly goes on, burns an answer into our brains."

"Yes. I suppose we do."

More silence.

"I can't talk in the dark," you explain much later as you reach over his cooling flesh for the lamp on a small table on his side of the bed.

When at last you find the switch, you turn on the light and reveal the hideous lamp stand you noticed here hours ago. It's a ceramic rendering of a blue and purple duck, easily the silliest piece of work you've ever seen. If the lamp belongs to Matt, well, you wish somehow it didn't. But, tired of hearing about what he does or doesn't own, you're definitely not going to inquire.

"Is that all right?" you ask as he squints in the lamp's illumination.

"Of course."

"You know," you say, reaching for another cigarette, this time one of your own, "you and I are crazy about one another."

"Yup. I know."

"I'm the best woman you've ever loved."

"Yup."

"And you're the best man I've ever loved."

He nods and says, "All of this is true."

"We work, Matt. We *really* work."

"I'd say so."

When you study him for a moment or two, you know everything you have said is starkly, irrevocably true. Even at this moment, the cords in his neck are beautiful. His eyes. His mouth. At this moment you cannot imagine never seeing him again. It defies reason entirely. It even seems, in some omnipresent way, that you've always known him, that from the moment of your birth you began to move inexorably towards him, that there is and has always been a capital "R" reason for falling in love with Matt. Or is this just romantic excess? Maybe, perhaps, probably. But that's the way it feels sometimes and the feeling belongs to you. It's your property; there shouldn't be any need to defend it.

Yet you and Matt have reached an impasse which is difficult to understand. It's dreamlike and vague, drifting at times like smoke around the two of you. You suppose it represents the rather unextraordinary fork in the road you've reached where one of you must decide to go on along the other person's route. Maybe this bottleneck just seems to be mysterious to conceal how ordinary it is. Maybe you prefer the idea of smoke to the rules surrounding these kinds of forks in the road. Rule number one, of course, is deciding which one of you must ultimately give in.

"Matt, I know what this *isn't* about," you say.

"You do?"

"Yes. I know it *isn't* about age difference and it *isn't* about your economic circumstances. It *isn't* about mistakes we've made in the past. It *isn't* about the romantic wreckage we've accumulated behind us. It *isn't* about all the stuff you sometimes get so noble about either."

"Noble? Whaddyuh mean, 'noble?'"

"The reasons you feel compelled to ride off into the sunset, you know, saving me from inadequate and inappropriate you."

"Oh, c'mon now," he says, failing to muster up an indignation he cannot seriously convey.

"Those are the things it *isn't* about, Matt. They're just the embroidery around the recent decisions you and I have made about how to live our lives."

"What decisions are you referring to specifically?" he asks.

"Mine was a decision to move to Kingston and work with Karen in her music school. Yours was a decision to leave Kingston, to go to the mountains. That's what this is really all about. The other stuff is just the shit that cumulatively brought us to the point where we arrived at our decisions."

He considers what you've said for a very long time. It's one of the reasons you love him so much. No other man has taken you as seriously as Matt Bowman does.

"Well?" you say with a nudge.

Carefully he nods. "I suppose," he replies. "I see what you mean, at any rate."

You press on. "All that other stuff—age, economics—would work out if we were honest with one another and lived by our stated points of view. On their own, if we found the same perspective, they simply wouldn't matter."

"I guess that's true," he says.

"I'm not going to give a shit if you don't make any money. Age difference? That's hardly worth mentioning. It's an idea that should be left in a museum somewhere. What we've learned from loving other people who weren't as right for us as you and I are, well, that just makes it easier to know who we are now. It makes it easier for us to state what we won't do for the sake of the relationship. It's a plus, not a minus."

"You're very convincing," he says at that point, reaching for still another cigarette.

Like a weekly poker night, the air has gone blue with smoke. You extinguish a cigarette; he lights his. The smoking seems eerie and out of whack, a glance at another dimension. Even the ashtray lying on the flesh of his stomach. Somehow these tobacco batons make all of this discussion seem an outer-dimensional symphony conducted by coughing gremlins. It takes on an aspect of dreaming, tripping out, the most embarrassing moment you ever knew in high school. You don't know why exactly. It's just something about him lying there naked with a fucking blue ashtray where his navel should be. And the two of you taking turns to ensure that someone is always smoking.

"Matt?"

"Yes?"

"You see what I mean, don't you?"

"I see what you mean. Some of the stuff dressed up as a problem isn't a problem at all. It's just how we got to this point."

"Exactly," you reply.

"And the real problem is where do we go from here, which one of us changes plans to keep this love affair going."

"I guess," is what you say.

"Nickie," he says, looking very pained, "my whole life, virtually my whole life, I've postponed the rest of my life. To accommodate someone else, someone else's needs. I can't do that anymore."

"I know," you answer quickly, surprised by the anguish in his voice. You stroke his arm; you love him. "I know, Matt. I understand all of that. I'd rather die than do that to you."

"And you?" he says at that point. "It's the same thing for you. You've decided to do something you really want to do. I've no right to ask you to change your mind. And I wouldn't. I can't."

"I know," you say again. "I know."

You lie there together at the edge of the cliff, swooning with acrophobia.

"We're victims of the times," you suggest. "Of time too, for that matter."

"Yes," he murmurs back. "I was thinking that."

"The time part," you add, "well that's reflected by the one

month we have left on the island. But the times?"

"Yes," he agrees. "That's another story."

"I mean," you explain, "not that long ago someone—probably the woman, I'm afraid—probably me, would have compromised. Based on the notion of true love, I would have gone with you, no matter where you were going. It would have simply felt right at the time and that would have been good enough."

"But later," Matt adds when you are done, "you would have become resentful. We'd have worked ourselves into the traditional rut of role and ritual. And then you'd feel all of this regret. Right?"

"Right. The way our parents did, depending on the circumstances, of course. There are lots of parents who regret what they didn't do with their lives. But now, these days, in our generation, we believe we have to know where we're going, each of us, separately. And, for love to work out with someone, we have to be eventually headed towards the same place . . ."

". . . at the same time," adds Matt.

"So what do we do?" you ask

"I don't know," he says.

"God," you say with a groan. "I can't believe I'm discussing this so calmly when my heart is hurting so much."

"Yeah. I know exactly what you mean."

"I used to be so melodramatic," you confess.

"Me too. It was at the height of melodrama that I made all of my mistakes. It took me years to learn that."

"But I hurt, Matt!"

And you do. You want to throw up somewhere and then just leave it behind for everyone to see as a kind of marker, a cairn along the trail, a warning for innocents about the disasters lying ahead. Not just a warning marker either. A cenotaph or plaque denoting your courage, your sacrifice, ensuring that someone understands how—even unwilling to change your plans—you love this man as deeply as you've ever loved anyone.

"I hurt too, Nick," Matt is telling you.

You know he tells the truth. It's in everything he's ever done with you; you know that much for sure. His capacity for pain, like yours, is based on his capacity for vigour. When you decide to gorge yourself on life it's inevitable that you must occasionally get indigestion.

Acknowledging then that both of you hurt, you slide into a sad embrace. In his arms, your eyes begin to tear. But you fight the need to cry, considering it too dramatic. It's a judgment without appeal; somehow you manage not to weep.

"We've still got September," Matt tells you shortly.

"Yes. But I'm going to want to die at the end of September if you and I decide never to see each other again."

"Me too," he admits calmly enough. "But we won't die. We've learned too much for that. In the end the need to see where life takes us next will win out. Both of us are that way. You know why we love each other so much?"

"Why?" you ask, a tired edge in your voice.

"Because we both like the idea that there's something important on the other side of the next hill. We're both too alive to die for love."

All of this seems true and wonderful and so very fucking wise. Except it keeps coming around to the same question. *What happens now?*

"What about September?" is the way you convey this endless question to him.

"Maybe it'll tell us something we haven't figured out yet."

"So we just keep going?"

"What's to be gained otherwise?"

It seems too glib a point of view to have any real merit. But it's what you want to hear. It's agreement in principle to one more month's reprieve, one more island month, just you and Matt and how it's been so perfect. Besides, you can't think of any other alternative anyway, nor do you want to. If this decision is simply procrastination, then fine. One more month of frantic love. You'll take it, embrace it, laugh and cry yourself through it. What happens after that will have to look after itself.

"I guess the thing about life and love," says Matt in the silence of your relief, "is that it's not over until the fat lady sings."

"Until the *what?*"

"Until the fat lady sings. It's an old expression."

"Jesus, Matt," you say. "That's dumb!"

He manages a tired chuckle. It reverberates along your

cheek and jaw.

Both of you are beginning to fall asleep. Someone should turn out the light but for the time being no one does.

*Until the fat lady sings?* Although you want to, you can't leave the damned idea alone. What does she end up singing? What the hell is the name of the song? Yes, for whom does she sing? Does she sing for thee? You slide further down the crevice towards slumber. For whom the fat lady sings. A farewell to girdles. And you drift into the darkness of sleep just as, at the edge of some nonsensical universe, Matt turns out the light.

ON THE WAY BACK TO THE ISLAND the next day, you feel uneasy about last night's conversation, about how smoothly it went, how rationally. An old habit perhaps, this pattern behind your conclusion that you should have had a fight. At the very least, you think you should have found a reason to be annoyed. Men and how confusing they can be . . .

The Escort grinds along the highway, noisy and fragile, its parts banging, shaking and rusting as loudly as they can. The car is in desperate need of an assortment of repairs Matt has already admitted he will never be able to afford.

"How are you going to make it all the way out west in a car like this?" you ask him now as all of you stutter along the highway—you, Matt, Carmen and Canine Ben—the Escort quaking and shivering. And this time the question contains the outrage you never quite managed last night.

"It's all I have, Nickie."

And there it is again, that fucking nobility he injects into his responses.

One thing, you decide. Come the end of September, if that indeed is the end, you aren't going to miss that tone of relentless nobility, of economic martyrdom. You'll miss a hundred wonderful things, maybe even a thousand. But not that endless nobility. If he decides to stay with you, the nobility has got to go. It's a wart on the arse of his personality—the damned thing should finally be lanced.

## THE MAN AND THE WOMAN

AFTER THE WEEKEND IN KINGSTON COMES AND GOES, the witnesses to the future of love writhe on the spit of the man and the woman's collapsing September. As a witness, one turns lazily above the coals of one's romantic expectations, braised this way and that by the couple's relentless ambivalence. Although the man and woman's passion for one another remains clearly evident—there exists, one notices, a joyful celebration of love in many of their times together—one feels a deep confusion whenever the man and woman draw away from one another. One fails to understand the stubborn need for solitude the man and woman demonstrate in between their romantic encounters. Nor does one want to acknowledge the reasons for the couple's apparent acceptance of the end of September as the day their relationship should end. Their reasons, after all, seem large and small, conclusive and inconclusive, lofty but insolent.

So it is that the witnesses feel teased by what they consider shameless shenanigans. Watching what takes place, they spin temperamentally between periods of romantic hope and disappointment. And when disappointment prevails, as a witness one grows stern or even angry, the way one might react towards rebellious children one hasn't yet figured out how to discipline successfully.

This is a characteristic of witnesses in this world—they

possess a punitive streak. Punishment, it would seem, is all they can extend to those individuals among them who wish to behave outside of their prevailing mores. When all else fails— namely a ritual passing on of a clear ideology, an indisputable mythology, and the comfort of mindless solidarity—one tends to feel displeased. One throws up their hands, then ultimately condemns their dissenters with disdain.

Where the man and the woman are concerned, however, it's still too early for condemnation. The witnesses continue to root for them and the ideal of romance with which they wrestle. But this support is a love with parental qualifications. Witnesses are happiest when people love within a context of rules and expectations, to keep the herd inviolate, the required capital "T" at the head of truth. To the witnesses of this world, people who love life more than the *meaning* of life threaten the tiny lifeboat one perceives this planet to be. One grows extremely nervous whenever the lifeboat is rocked, the way anxious people behave in the uppermost gondola of a ferris wheel when it comes to a halt to take on passengers. Once one has given up all other means of restraining passengers who fidget around too much, one must inevitably consider whether or not to throw the passengers overboard.

But drastic alternatives such as these come only after everything else has failed. For now, the witnesses wait, drawing on the reserves of their patience, forgiving their suffering and the sacrilege they overhear at the hands of the man and the woman. In this way, September slowly evaporates while the man and the woman stumble towards some kind of ending the witnesses can believe is actually a beginning.

SOMETIMES, ON THE CUSP OF SUMMER AND FALL, summer steals a little more time from its pre-winter autumnal sibling. Especially in September. Sometimes it's hot, sunny and sultry up to and into October. Not often, but sometimes.

This year, though, summer dies early. In fact, by the time the man and woman return from Kingston, summer is already dead. Instead of extending a gift of sunshine and warmth, September turns cold and rainy. The man and the woman, unable to escape the malice of their climate, both remark how short this summer has been, remembering how late spring was to warm before it gave way at last to June. This autumn seems malevolent. It stands accused of murdering summer, choking it in its crib, shooting it in the back. What else can this be but seasonal fratricide?

This year the September island decays into a filmy, predominant gray. The gray lake bleeds out of a gray horizon, eventually stumbling gray up onto the gray-brown beach. The island is bleached deeply gray and white. Gray trees stoop limply under the weight of their gray-green leaves, standing gray and somehow lonelier among gray-gray rocks and moss. Gray sheets of rain shower the island; gray mists obscure the morning.

Even infinity has only one color—the gray skies overhead are relentless, nothing more than gray distances in the distance, stretching on and on and on. Gray sunsets, dusks and twilights arrive torn and disappointed, like asylum-seekers at some lonely seaport where they can see they are unwelcome. Bad enough that these twilights show up earlier than they did at the height of summer, worse still that they arrive on the island conveying an expression of dazed, emaciated surrender. Gray dusks are like that, like faces from which fear or exhaustion has removed all pigment.

And somehow twilights such as these transform night, make it more intense, longer, deeper, blinder. Night is now so black, so large and complete, it assumes command of everything. "I am night," it says, "verisimilitude in ink."

Woodsmoke too turns gray, leeched of its bluer tones. It rises out of the chimney at each cottage—especially as September wears on—like a nervous afterthought. It drifts from each of the cottages or both of them, depending on who is visiting whom, who is staying away from whom, who needs to be with whom, who wishes to be alone; yes, depending on who has built a fire to ward off the rainy chill either for themselves or for each other. And on days of heavy rainfall, when the clouds drop down to earth, the wood smoke emerges from the chimneys then only seems to tire, unable to rise. On days like these, the gray-white smoke drifts lazily along the beach like some uninspired clam digger saving for tomorrow the foraging to be done today.

WHEN HE'S ALONE, THE MAN makes several attempts to say goodbye to his favorite island. He contrives to visit every square inch of it, intending to acknowledge its due, to express his gratitude for all it has meant to him over the years. But somehow, no matter how stubbornly he works to accomplish this task, it doesn't amount to much of a ceremony in the end. It fails to evoke any actual feeling in him. The ghosts from his long past here on the island tend to hide from him, whether nervous or spoiled or newly irrelevant, he cannot say for sure.

Yet this, he supposes, makes a great deal of sense within the context of how deeply in love he is. As far as he's concerned, the island belongs to the woman now. She seems to be everywhere, no matter where he travels. The island has abdicated its past in favor of the dilemma connected to her function in the present. More and more he begins to suspect the island will not possess a past until he's left it far behind, until he's absolutely sure he'll never return. But for now, the woman has not only altered the setting but his purpose in being here. No wonder he finds it impossible to say goodbye to his past. The past has already departed, replaced, it would seem, by the woman's relentless ownership of what he has nearly become. He feels stupid to persist in delivering his adieus. It's like waving a handkerchief at a passenger on a train when the train is already out of sight: ceremony for ceremony's sake. In the end, goodbye is just something he says so that he can say he did.

But there's something else which empties his farewells of any substance, namely the sense that the island doesn't appear to believe he will never be coming back. Oh, it listens politely enough, seems to nod in reverent acknowledgment when he arrives to shake its hand. But it doesn't really believe him. Each time he tells himself he won't be back, the island exudes a more fundamental familiarity he finds impossible to escape. It conveys in a powerful way its sense of owning a piece of permanence. This largeness fills him with doubt, not only about whether he'll never return after he shortly leaves but about his infinitesimal function in something so complex as destiny. What makes him so certain he won't return? Does saying goodbye mean anything at all if the recipient of his farewells won't accept the salutation? No wonder his ceremonial ablutions seem so hollow to him, a going through the motions at the altar of goodbye.

He explains this to the woman: the goodbyes he tries to bestow, the way they lose their significance in the face of the island's overwhelming familiarity. "It's like the island is smirking at me," he tells her. "It's like it believes I'm only kidding myself."

"I don't know, Matt," is all she says, although she secretly considers the possibility that, indeed, he really is Crazy Horse and, being Crazy Horse, whether he knows this yet or not, there's no such word as goodbye.

Or is this just wishful thinking? How silly she can be sometimes, her thoughts folded into the drawers of her brain like so many ironed shirts by the loyal maid of unwarranted hope. She does her best to smile in amusement and forgiveness of herself.

"What?" inquires the man, noticing her smile and wanting to share in it. Or argue with its cause. Or know beyond a reasonable doubt that he's being mocked.

"Just thinking," the woman replies, "how little there is in life we ever truly figure out."

It's a cautious way to put things; it doesn't matter much. But it keeps the man inside with her, safe from the storm of what might be her more inherent wisdom and its potential to criticize.

WHEN THE WOMAN TAKES TIME TO BE ALONE, she writes music at her piano. The song she composed some time ago about the island storm she shared with the man in June now begs to become a larger work. She begins to refer to it as "my island suite." The storm is still included in the music, defined by crescendoing chords and powerful fortissimos, but she adds many other island moments to the complex composition. An island morning; an island twilight; an island night; the dancing, reflected sunbeams on the lake in early afternoon. And, of course, an island Crazy Horse to seed the entire work with some intriguing explanation for the new emotional clairvoyance she believes this summer has bestowed on her.

After all, the man lurks inside each bar in much the same way she now presides over the new meaning of his island. Whether the suite is about the island or the man she loves so much, she composes it regardless, with an intensity and discipline she hasn't felt for years. She thinks of it as something important to take with her when she crosses to the mainland at the end of September when their island affair is over. And it's occurred to her that the music one creates is not nearly so flimsy, so fragile in the end, as the love one tries to nurse over the course of a creative life.

THEY STILL MAKE LOVE OFTEN throughout September, one sees, although the desperation characterizing it at the end of August has now begun to wane. Without realizing it, they've stopped arguing with what fate has decreed for them. Their lovemaking is calmer now, warmer, although sometimes it turns achingly sad in the wake of their acceptance. It's like being bled by thorns wrapped up in elegant cashmere, a confusing torture which makes palatable the true sympathies pleasure has for pain and pain can hold for pleasure.

They are newly awkward, however, about initiating sex, as if one will accuse the other of giving in to selfishness. As if—should their need to make love not match precisely the other's in timing and intensity—they are seeking to take advantage somehow, gilding some sexual lily. Still, they get through these early moments—the first tentative assumptions of self-indulgence—eventually pushing back this wailing wall of protestant denial intent on wearing their pleasure down. When they break through to the other side, they're unashamed again, absorbed by what they feel and the excitement it provides.

They talk about making love outdoors again, somewhere holy and symbolic. Just one more time, they suggest, in the bosom of Mother Nature. But September deprives them of this; it's simply much too cold. Shortly, privately, they give up on the idea. Neither one of them believes this sexual communion with nature will ever happen again now that fall has established itself so deeply. And their future is so dubious, well, one simply lets such notions drift away. One begins to weave again the threads of one's cocoon.

ONE NIGHT THE MAN CONFESSES he has named their love "an ecstasy."

It's late and cold and dark. They snuggle into each other's

arms—his bed, his room, his cottage, his section of the island. Her leg rests on top of his. He puts both arms around her, though gently and tenderly. She breathes along the flesh of his chest while he breathes into the rich disarray of her hair. He smells sweat, shampoo, saliva and sex. She tastes everything, even the chill inside this room. All sensation gathers at the back of her tongue on the brink of where she swallows.

The woman has decided she can't visit here any longer. The man has begun to pack. He's dismantled his computer, boxed its various components. Most of his clothing is packed. There's another box containing food items—canned goods and condiments mostly—that he'll take back to the mainland, though he's offered these to her for the time after he's gone. He's counted out his remaining days—four—and divided this number into the food and clothing he'll require. Everything else is in a box or a bag or a suitcase in a corner near the cottage windows where, at times, she stands or he stands or both of them stand together to look out over the gray-cold lake. He's even retrieved the plywood sheets he will nail over the windows on the morning when he goes. They're stacked at the corner of the cottage, stained by yesterday's rain.

It came over her earlier tonight, a sadness so mean it kicked her in the belly. Because his things are all packed and ready to go. Because there's an implied anxiousness to depart in the way he's gathered these items together so early, four whole days before he finally goes. So she's decided not to visit *The Crow's Nest* again, not even for morning coffee. Even when they went to bed, still wanting one another the way they always have, her sadness nearly overcame her. Now, after sex, after their mutual accolades of pleasure, it seems impossible that they made love with so much wealth, that its sensations remained so golden when her sadness wouldn't go away.

The man felt his own sadness too while they were making love. He considers it an inherent part of this ecstasy he knows he can never explain, although sometimes he wants to try.

"An ecstasy," she whispers, echoing the words back at him.

"Yes. What's between you and me."

A good word for it, she supposes, although something lurks inside it which is sadly terminal.

"I'd rather remember you and me as an ecstasy than as

something that ultimately withered," he adds at this point.

She understands what he means. Agrees, then disagrees, agrees, then disagrees again.

"Sometimes I wonder," he continues.

But he stops there, doesn't say anything else, no longer remembering what he wonders or, as he begins to remember whether he wans to keep it to himself or keep it *from* himself.

And she decides to be glad that he doesn't continue. "No 'what ifs,' Matt," she says.

She doesn't want to argue them, to even imagine them. They'd change the rules again, 'what ifs' opening windows of opportunity they've spent the entire month believing should be permanently closed.

She's right, the man decides, and he lets the 'what ifs' go. "A friend once told me that you don't necessarily get to be a partner with your soul mate," he says at last instead.

"Do you think we're soul mates, Matt?"

"Yes, I do."

"Some people do," the woman says. "Some people get to partner with their soul mates."

"Yes," agrees the man, "when they're going in the same direction, when everything they want together is essentially the same. When the timing isn't off. When the circumstances are right."

"Matt? I don't want to talk about this any more."

He kisses her on the top of the head. "I'm sorry, Nickie," he says.

"When we talk now," she explains, "about you and me, well, it's like we're picking at a scab."

"I guess that's what it is, all right. It's just that I feel so sad and I want the reasons to be clear again so that the sadness is justified. I want to know I'm supposed to be sad that we couldn't compromise."

"Matt, please shut up." It's just so much blistering blather to her.

He must know this too. She feels him nod in the darkness.

But later she asks, "You'd rather just have an ecstasy than something that gets comfortable?"

"It doesn't get comfortable," he replies. "It just finds a way to shrivel up."

Is this true? she wonders. What about Karen and Liam? What about trust? Is it each other they don't trust or is it love itself they don't trust, the way, to be held onto, love has to be confined, the way, when love is confined, its perpetrators find themselves imprisoned inside a life which perpetually shrinks? What's so bad about buying groceries or watching silly television? What's wrong with going to bed too tired to make love? Nothing or everything?

But she doesn't ask him these questions. She doesn't want a debate. He might convince her or she might convince him. And, in the convincing, one or the other of them would be smothered inside the protective wing of the more persuasive argument.

"You know what's funny?" she says instead.

"What?"

"Kingston's not a very large city."

"I know."

"Until you go out west, we'll probably run into one another. On the street, down at the market, pretending we weren't shopping for something at Wal-Mart, attending some function or other."

"I know."

She sighs. "I just wanted to mention that."

"It's something I've considered," he replies a long time later.

ON THE NIGHT BEFORE THE MAN is to leave the island, the woman has a dream. Although it takes place on the island—here where everything has been so solid and true—the island in the dream begins to quickly fall apart. There are bleachers everywhere not far from the water's edge, and these are jammed with ghostly spectators less alive than mannequins. They do not cheer nor catcall but sit in the stands without moving, without making a sound of any kind. They appear painted into place, conceived by a movie set designer perverse and wise enough to capture imagination and reality at the moment they collide. Yet, inside all of this motionless silence, the woman feels the audience watching her, entertained by her growing terror and the frustration she feels as she fails to save herself.

In the dream Matt runs away from her, scampering down

the beach, perhaps to his waiting boat as yet unseen at the edge of the lake. The beach treats the man and woman differently. While Matt is allowed to flee with ease across the top of the moving sands, for her the beach grows thick and turgid, rising to her ankles, then her calves, reaching for her knees.

Not far away, beyond the eerie bleachers, trees on the crest of the island teeter then collapse in silence. The lake pitches and yaws too, not in waves or whitecaps but as one large beaker of water, first rising, then falling, a horizon gone askew, running amok.

"Quake!" the woman cries. "Earthquake!"

But the dream robs her voice of sound. Although she knows she's screamed these words, they fail to break the silence, strangled the moment they escape her mouth.

And still the audience doesn't move, superimposed like a photograph on the face of this island earthquake. The bleachers are bolted to the quake and ride out all the tremors.

The woman pretends the spectators do not exist except as some lifeless blind pulled down over the window of her reality. She turns her attention to Matt, calling out to him, asking him to wait for her.

"Please," she cries to him. "Just one more minute. Matt?"

Silence.

Except he appears to hear what she cannot, the sounds her words create. He stops running and turns, his face angry and pale. "I told you this would happen," he shouts. "I told you it would." His words thunder along the trembling beach, sounding astonishingly fierce as they penetrate the grisly silence.

"Matt?"

But he gestures with angry inevitability in the general direction of the macabre audience gathered so artificially on the artificial bleachers. "I told you this would happen," he shouts at her again. Then he turns away once more, running across the beach.

The woman would give chase but the sand is much deeper now. It rises to her hips, immobilizing her. She struggles there, crying out in terror.

Then she lurches awake in the silent darkness of her silent bedroom, cold and hot and terrified in a pool of silent sweat.

ON THE MORNING THE WITNESSES watch the man preparing to leave the island, they cannot help recalling the day when the couple first met. Like then, the dogs frolic along the beach again. The man and the woman stand a yard or two apart again with the same reserve they demonstrated that beginning day in May. It's their shy and cautious initial meeting performed all over again. They've returned to where they once began (with each other at least) but pretending to be wiser, more dignified by courage.

As for the day, it's not raining yet. But it will, one knows. The skies are heavy with water, a gray rag above their heads, just waiting for the fist prepared to wring it out.

The woman would like to say so much, anything she can come up with just short of everything. But she knows she cannot. There's something perfect in this flaw, this inevitable failure which clings to the loss she feels like lead in the pit of her stomach. The hurt will not break down, knows no way to sublimate. It simply aches in her guts the way love and failure so often do when they are too large and new to be anything other than overwhelming.

She bends her will to her important task—which is not to ask him if she can go out west with him when he departs in seven months time.

The man too exercises all that he has left, his stubborn determination. Somehow he doesn't promise to wait for her in Kingston until some vague time in the future when she can go to the mountains with him.

The man stares at the horizon, unable to look at her. He loves this woman's pensive face, those moments when she smiles, those times when her face is sleeping, the way it used to laugh. If he turns now and encounters its sadness, he knows he'll give in to everything dressed up as his personal doubt.

"Are you all right?" the woman asks at last.

Now he turns and looks at her. "No, I'm not," he says. "Are *you* all right?"

"I'm awful," she replies.

"Do you think we're being stupid?"

"Part of me does," she admits.

"Yeah," the man says then, turning away from her, "that's how it seems to me."

Both of them think about the various straws they have promised not to clutch. It's been agreed that no phone calls will be made, no letters will be sent, no e-mails will be tossed across a magic cyberland. If they accidentally encounter one another, they've promised to briefly chat as friends, even if the conversation turns shallow and doesn't tell the truth. It's all been settled now, worked out, negotiated like a successful divorce. Once they've stopped being lovers, they intend to behave themselves.

Yet both of them wish they could be two people inside their one true self—one twin set apart in a state of calm, just for their own use; the other taking up an agreeable residence inside their lover's skin so that they're never apart, so that loss is somehow defeated, so that the pain of solitude, of being so unique, can be interrupted once and for all by undiluted periods of romantic recess.

"Nickie?" the man says then, his hands jammed into his pockets. "Everything between you and me was true. It was all really me."

"I know that," she responds impatiently.

Redundancy. It makes as little difference to her at this moment that everything was true as it does that she believes it was. Stupid of him to bring up something so obvious when they've loved this fact into their awareness until they could take it entirely for granted.

"I just wanted to be sure that you knew that," he explains, wishing all of this sounded better or more, hearing instead a tone in his voice he would construe to be pathetic if it came from someone else.

"I know it," she says with a sigh. "So are you all ready?"

He nods. "Everything's in the boat."

"And *The Crow's Nest?*"

"Boarded up," he says. "I can't look at it though. I feel it up there on the hill behind me. But I can't turn around and look at it."

"I don't know if I could either, if I were you."

"And you leave this weekend?" the man says at that point, afraid again just then that he'll perhaps give in.

"Yes. Karen and Liam are coming."

But they know these details already. There's nothing more

to be said. It can't be explained any better. They're driving large moments of chitchat into the wound time has become for them.

"You'd better get going," the woman says after they have stood there painfully and pointlessly for a couple of minutes more.

"Nickie?"

But this is all he says. His next words will be foolish again. Whatever they were going to be—and he doesn't really know—they're better left unsaid.

"See yuh, Crazy Horse."

Then she turns away, whistling for Carmen to follow her.

The man doesn't hear what she says over a hurtful roaring in his ears. Except that he'll probably recall it later and wonder what she meant. He watches her depart. He nearly hurries after her. But he forces himself to remain where he is, rooted to this small section of beach, standing there alone with his dog and what seems inescapable about the nature of his future.

The woman walks quickly down the beach but begins to accelerate. Now that she is going, she really wants to be gone. So she breaks into a trot, then speeds up into a run, listening for the footsteps she'd love to hear behind her—the man catching up to her and, yes, catching up to *them*.

But his footsteps never arrive. By the time she reaches her cottage, she has only heard her own.

## THE ENDINGS

**Monday, September 30**

I DON'T KNOW WHAT TO SAY ABOUT WHAT I'VE DONE, now that the final occasion has arrived to write in this journal of my summer on the island. My thoughts have been dazed all day by the sadness I feel. Hurting this much, I know this isn't an appropriate day to reach accurate conclusions. It's too early yet to do anything other than suffer. Tomorrow or the next day or the next day after that is time enough to carry on. Until then I must recover from this prevailing sense of loss. I know I'll get through it—most of us usually do. I've suffered this way before, then climbed finally out of the morass. It gradually eases—the pain we feel when love doesn't work out—and in a day or two I'll probably understand again what was inherently right about my resolve to leave Nicole behind.

But for now it's all too painful. For the purposes of this journal, it's best to simply report what happened when I left the island for good. If I am to make sense of it later, I'll appreciate the details I jot down now. At some point I'll need such evidence to help me justify my actions.

Not that it'll be easy—so much of this disheartening day took place inside a haze of emotional pain. I nearly changed my mind at least a dozen times, even knowing to do so would have reflected only habit, a decision to overlook the compromises in my past, an emotional forgetfulness about the decisions I have

347

made to lead a private life. The temptation to go back, to prolong this affair with Nicole, tempted me many times.

Believing in possibilities that are ultimately bad for me is, yes, definitely a habit. I suppose we live in patterns like these—deeply worn and rutted psychological mazes—enabling us to make the same mistakes over and over again because we're used to them and they seem to give us comfort. If we're not strong, we succumb to all the familiar temptations which intruded on our lives so destructively in our past. It goes back to being young, when we didn't know how to resist the various forces manipulating us.

Today I came up with the required strength to be true to my intentions but I feel broken by the effort. Sometimes, even now, I feel a yearning so desperate and deep for the happiness I knew with Nicole that I wonder if I will manage.

I anticipated this yearning. I anticipated its deviousness. I have understood for quite some time how yearning manifests itself—converting our decisions into dubious mistakes, into errors in judgment or a failure to have faith. I know very well these days what yearning tries to do to make someone like me change his mind. It throws spiteful accusations at the most exposed sections of my fortifications, the doubtful places along my lines of committed resolution.

Yet, even knowing how yearning can deceive, how many times did I nearly succumb? And why are these the times I remember most clearly? That last few minutes on the beach, for instance, that empty and foolish last moment when Nicole and I stood there face-to-face with the inevitability of our parting. I remember with stark clarity how Nicole and I wondered if we were being stupid. I almost said, "Yes, I think we are," but in the end, with tremendous resolve, I managed to say something else. Or did I ask the question? It's so hard to remember who said what to whom and how the words actually sounded.

And then, when she began to run across the beach, returning to her cottage, the temptation for me to capitulate grew even worse. This time I felt her pain more clearly than my own and I was nearly overwhelmed by my cruelty. I suppose it struck me clearly at that moment that it was me—rather than ill-luck, ill-timing, the incompatibility of our circumstances—who was chiefly responsible for hurting her. So I nearly ran after her. Indeed, I took a step or two, intent on rescuing her or maybe both of us. Yet, before I could make such a guilty mistake, I planted my feet in the colorless sand and managed not to back down.

The oddest temptation to change my mind came, strangely enough, only moments before I left *The Inlet* behind the wheel of my car. Standing on the dock with Gord Mahaffey, I felt tempted to believe I would become a man like him if I didn't go back to Nicole. Looking back on it now, I suppose this too was the artful manipulation of my yearning trying to transform the solitary nature of my future plans into a vow of loneliness. Freedom? my yearning sniggered. More like a monastic oath. Without Nicole, my yearning warned, it was more likely I'd conclude life bitterly and shabbily. Without Nicole, I'd be left with only the lonely, accurate point behind the principles guiding me.

Something Mahaffey said, I suppose, something he did, something perhaps about the way he has always behaved triggered my concerns. Then a long moment later I remembered once again that, yes, yearning deals in doubts, eats away at our judgment, tries to cheat us of our resolve.

"Well I guess that's it," I said at last, standing on the dock with him.

Soberly Mahaffey nodded, the spell broken. He was no longer yearning's device but a man with his own excuses for being forced to be alive.

We didn't say goodbye. We parted in silence.

The drive back to Kingston is the most difficult period to remember as I try to recall it now. As an exercise in function, I know only that it took place, but I don't remember the details of the drive itself, how I arrived here from there during the fog of the inbetween. I was too absorbed with my sadness, with Nicole and what it means to me now that she is gone.

Most of all, I kept recalling the way she ran down the beach this morning, the way I didn't follow her. I felt ashamed and hopeless. At one point these feelings became so powerful I nearly turned the car around to drive all the way back to her. But the impracticality of the idea grew clearer in my mind— dealing with Mahaffey again, renting another boat, trying to explain, all of these logistical factors exposing what was, in reality, inappropriate whimsy.

And while these sensible reservations grew stronger, the pain of my shame and the recollection inspiring it gradually eased. I slowly realized there would be nothing new to say to her, should I return with a change of heart, save for fatuous romantic clichés which would not address the true nature of our joint misfortune based mostly on ill-timing. And whatever I might contrive to say would be far too hollow to reflect the love that we enjoyed, even while the words would fail to overcome the fact that, as lovers, we cannot last.

By then it had begun to rain, a drizzle beading on the windshield. My wipers beat out a laconic rhythm matching beat for beat the ache in my heart.

Still I kept coming back in my thoughts to the clichés of romance, how they fail to address or make permanent the near perfection of our summer. All ecstasies, I believe, are designed to come to an end. This, I'm afraid, is virtually a given. And the question then becomes which way you would have them die. Murdered early in mercy? Or gradually passing away over time, decaying, disintegrating, evaporating in ever benumbing pain? It's a choice for love not all of us wish to consider. I like to think I see the justice in the quick kill of dying love but there's always room for doubt. I too wish there really was a state we could rightly call forever.

Nonetheless, the animosity of this debate—between withering death or a premeditated crash in a burst of searing flames—transported me to Kingston in a congress of stubborn argument, escorted, I suppose, by the proud pain defining my loss.

I don't remember at all unpacking the car in the rain. I only know that I did. Instead I remember most the cruel sameness of my apartment. Sameness has an odor—stale, dusty, decrepit. It lurked in every room. It drooled decay from every corner where it skulked inside the gloom.

So I took Ben outside with me and sat in a white plastic chair on the porch. There I watched hundreds of cars go by and smoked half a package of cigarettes.

I felt angry with myself, smoking until my throat was raw purely to punish myself. The island and *The Crow's Nest* now seemed a component in my loss. No wonder I was angry. How many times had I explored the island during the past few weeks, trying to conjure up the kind of goodbye that would alleviate the power of the island's hold on me? Now, here I was, missing it desperately, crushed that circumstances had decreed that it be lost to me forever. And, separate from the island in the way I was now separate from Nicole, I realized again how one had become another in my injured perception—the island and Nicole, promise and departure, faith and faithlessness.

I suffered there on the porch while cars hissed by on the rain-drenched street, while rain dribbled from the roof, encroaching on my solitude. My summer in every way now seemed a great mistake. Before this summer, the island had already assumed an acceptable place in the recovering injuries of my past. Going back to say goodbye had only opened the wound.

As for Nicole? How could I have permitted us to become lovers when I knew we had no future? Or is this just what we can't help doing, with circumstance our accomplice?

I knew I had no answers to questions of this kind. We do whatever we do inside whatever is done to us. There's no explanation for this beyond living life itself and bringing to this process a fundamental passion.

Still, I sat there at the edge of the rain with my version of an ending, an ending more triumphant for Nicole and me. I sat there constructing it, reworking it, transported from the porch and the falling rain to a better place and time. This was an ending I could accept, embrace, enjoy. I think about it now, as I write this last entry of my summer, the ending I would choose to insert into reality for myself, if such an omnipotence was permitted me.

It happens in the mountains, in some small town out west. It's summer again and I climb a hill downtown. I round a corner and there she is, several yards away. She's stopped to glance in a shop window at leather goods, I think. I freeze along the sidewalk, not quite sure at first this woman is truly Nicole, afraid, I guess, to hope it is. How many months have I been looking for her on the other side of every corner I have ever turned?

But this time it's her; it really, truly is. So I begin to hurry in her direction and at that moment, perhaps sensing my proximity, she turns. She looks at me, not recognizing me for an instant. Then when she does, she smiles. And I am smiling. And we hurry towards one another along the virtually empty sidewalk. And we embrace.

Inside this embrace it's now clear we've learned how vital we are, together and apart. Here, with mountains gleaming in the distance, we've found the appropriate place to build a future we can share. We are aware of all of this as we embrace along the sidewalk in this town without a name somewhere in the mountains. And everything is now all right. She is real, has flesh, is the woman that I love. She hasn't compromised; she's only changed her mind. At last, we've found a matching time and place, a starting point from which we can continue on as a couple.

I keep thinking about this ending and the hope it represents. For now, the ending isn't likely. Hope is foolish, after all, but, like it or not, we seem to be stuck with it. I guess hope is like love itself—imbecilically, it just never quite gives in. Hope and love mesmerize us with the notion that we can have our cake and eat it too. There's no resisting love nor its collaborator hope, even when we know most loving cannot last in the way we want it to. Despite our various resolutions to keep ourselves from disappointment, love overwhelms them all. Love never changes face when it gets together with hope. It remains what it's always been: a chance to turn on a light illuminating the room containing our ancient darkness.

So the journal of my summer ends on a practical note. If not for the meeting I must attend tomorrow in Toronto at the offices of *Bartlett & Strong*, I might have remained a few days longer on the island with Nicole. What then would have happened? Would anything have changed? Would I have found a wisdom in love I haven't discovered before? Unlikely, I suspect.

In the end we do what we must do. I'll take a train to Toronto and meet with my new publisher. She might notice that I am pale, even ask me what is wrong. And I'll tell her vaguely that I don't feel up to snuff, perhaps the victim of a virus of some kind. And we'll do the work required of us. I won't tell her I'm deeply in love and that love doesn't very often work out. She may know this fact already. Or maybe she does not. What Lynn

Danby knows about love isn't the issue. Tomorrow life will be lived in a much smaller way than that. I'll rise to this occasion, then continue on alone.

YOUR DAYS TROOP BY LIKE BATTLE-WEARY SOLDIERS after Matt Bowman leaves the island. Each is different from the other yet wears the same tattered uniform.

That first day, Matt doesn't come back. You believe for a time that he might, until the rain begins to fall. Somehow, after the rains come, his return grows more improbable. The rain seems to slam the door in the face of every reasonable possibility.

For now, you don't cry at your loss or over the ache of what has failed. You sit down at your piano instead and work the persistent rain into your growing island suite. Four raindrops to the bar, a plaintive kind of dirge. The rain, your mood, the pain, pianissimo.

Mid-afternoon finds you weary, too tired to think, too exhausted to understand anything, least of all something as incoherent as love. What is love anyway? Just some spoiled sibling, a raging siren? Strange how loudly it shrieks without saying anything. So that you can't make out the words in the din of its endless screams.

You nap and wake up crying. But this overdue, silent weeping only makes you angry. It feels like a surrender of sorts, a retreat from a hard-won position of resignation.

The night falls, bringing with it deeper silence and restlessness. Night, you, the island: three agitated, silent comrades. You pass a couple of hours, prowling your mutual cage. Later, though, you endure another bout of powerful fatigue. Strangely enough, despite a nimbly dancing anxiety, it's easy to fall asleep. You've been falling most of the day and sleep lets you fall some more.

Tuesday is a better day. The sun shines and at least one minor explanation of one minor little point holds the promise of understanding. Knowing Matt has left for Toronto on business reflects knowing where he is in a way which justifies why he isn't here. So much so that you forget to hope to see him, stop listening for his return, expect no hazy reversals in the state of your misfortune.

Wednesday is better too because you nurse a powerful anger, a little of it directed at yourself, most of it aimed at the man you love. Your anger with yourself is over how you let yourself fall victim once again. How could you have allowed yourself to fall so deeply in love when, in truth, you knew you didn't want to? In your experience, love has always harvested fierce nettles. Why did this time seem like it would be different?

As for Matt? Why would he embark on something he probably knew he couldn't finish? Why would he love you as much as he does, then give you up just short of conceiving of a practical solution to the impediments in your relationship? The answers to these questions lurk just outside the asking. Place and time and circumstance intruded, if Matt was to be believed. You were too young and he was too old; you too economically safe and him too carelessly impoverished; your potential for motherhood arriving at a parental depot on the heels of his vanishing fatherhood. Your independent need to go to Kingston, his passion to go out west. His politics of intensity, the intensity of his politics, and your apparent apathy and impatience with his persistent outrage. Then, for both of you, that powerful state of romantic damage. Who would obligate whom, who would win control, who would stop loving first when the disappointments grew too numerous?

All of these issues make sense, then make no sense at all. They give in to inevitability in a perpetuating way. It's like donating to the food bank and, in doing so, inadvertently endorsing the injustices that make the food bank exist. Still, you own only your own perception. His perspective, life's paradigms, the world's view—how can you truly know what they see which you do not? The only vision you have with which to see is the same one you've always had.

You renew your anticipation of Matt's magical return on Wednesday because it dawns a beautiful day. Sunny, crisp, blue, blonde and green, the colors so many promises wear when they go to their audience at court. On Wednesday you stroll along the beach with Carmen, finding Matt-patterns in your behaviour to duplicate, occasionally nearly certain that he will have solved your mutual predicament by now and show up to tell you how.

Yet, by the end of the day when Matt has not returned, you aren't in fact surprised. He can't have solved the puzzle he more sternly maintains exists. He is going one place, you are going another, he would say. Better that neither one of you feels compelled to merely tag along.

On Thursday you are stronger, more accepting of these desperate truths. Love doesn't conquer all, the way romantics maintain it does. Love is like a cheetah, shortly out of wind. Or, like a demagogue, it goes on violent purges, then backs away again. It's a brief period of heady conquest, then an exhausted retreat back to where it first began. After all the passion it generates has lain waste the human heart, the victims soon discover love's borders remain unchanged.

Still, being stronger this day, you manage to complete the bulk of your packing. And you begin to look ahead happily to tomorrow evening when the O'Shaughnessys arrive. There is life after love as any damn fool knows, and some of it is rich and deeply satisfying, you observe with a shaky defiance. There may even be another man more suitable than Matt Bowman, not quite so Crazy Horse but more dedicated to the value of wanting to be with you. Whatever you feel now in the middle of this emotional wasteland, you know love isn't done with you, nor you with it. If love is done with anyone, Matt Bowman is his name. Because that's the way he wants it, the way he wanted it all along.

"Nickie?" Karen calls from the kitchen on Saturday.

You do not answer. You would, except you're nearly overcome by a new wave of desolation as you stand alone in the empty cottage living room, ready to depart. Everything is now completely done. You stand alone and nearly naked inside the finality of it all.

The room has turned deeply dusk. Liam has boarded up the cottage windows and the day—gone gray again outside—is barely able to penetrate whatever leaky cracks and shrunken portals are available to its intrusion. There are sheets over all the furniture now. Carmen lies at your feet, clinging more than usual to you so that the two of you seem a particularly exposed unit amid the ghostly furniture, the forming dust and the deep twilight of the room.

It's all over now, you know. Summer, your stay at the cottage, this place. The conclusion is overwhelming, time getting away from you, blaming you the way time does for not making the most of it. Odd that this expected ending shows up so strangely unexpected.

Yet here you are, obligated to continue. You feel, just for a moment, like you're the only being required to be alive in a tragic universe which has already passed away.

"Nickie?" Karen's voice slips into the room just a second or two ahead of Karen herself.

And you stand there in the twilight, still unable to reply.

"Are you okay?" asks Karen.

At this, you turn to her. "I'm okay," you begin to say, but your voice crumbles in the middle. "I will be," you amend. "It just all feels so finished."

"Oh, Sweetie."

The two of you embrace in the middle of the room while Carmen moves safely out of the vicinity of this inexplicable human contact. Noticing Carmen's withdrawal, you wish you could be more like a dog yourself, simpler, more frequently puzzled, not understanding so much in the nearly complete way you seem to understand it now.

"It's hard," says Karen then.

You feel the words against your shoulder more than you hear the sound of them. Nonetheless, what she says is true; you know that, yes, it's hard.

"It's just that sense that everything's over," you try to explain again.

"I know."

"I mean," you add carefully, "summer, Matt, this place. I really love it here."

"I know. And you'll love it in the future. It'll all come back by then."

"I suppose I will," you say.

You end the embrace. You smile apologetically for succumbing to your grief. Karen smiles apologetically, perhaps for having no grief to call her own.

"I'm okay," you tell her. "I know, fundamentally, that everything's all right."

"Of course it is," says Karen.

"I just felt all alone in here, inside all of this closure."

"Sure."

"I'm okay," you say.

"You're sure?"

Solemnly you nod. "I'm sure," you tell your friend.

"Everything's ready," says Karen then. "The boat's loaded."

"Cindy? Liam?"

Karen smiles gently. "Dispatched to the boat to wait. I kinda thought this morning might be a little rough."

"I'm okay," you say.

Still, people are waiting for you. You feel ashamed and disappointed that your strength has given way. Last night you felt repaired, at least most of the time. There was laughter now and then. You and Karen and Liam and Cindy, a happy family of sorts. And the worst of the remaining packing was done. But last night nothing seemed truly over somehow, at least not in any permanent way. Whatever completion there was in preparing to go seemed largely ceremonial. Today, though, it's really finished, all the things which had to be done. It's the bitter blow of something someone somewhere would perhaps consider the shocking truth.

No wonder you are shaken. It comes at you all at once. Everything you felt was wonderful has slipped entirely into the past. It challenges your belief in possibility, briefly undermines your hope.

"Let's get out of here," you say to Karen. "It'll be better if we get going."

"Okay," your friend replies.

And it's true. You begin to feel better in the boat. Liam is at the wheel and you're grateful for it. As he pilots all of you around the island, amid the jumble of your things, you gaze in silence at the shore and wonder when you'll return. Liam drives slowly, perhaps to give you this opportunity to regain your composure, perhaps because Karen told him to. Indeed this cauterizing of your wounds, though painful for the present, remains essential to your recovery. You believe this to be true in spite of the nagging pain.

How hard it must have been for Matt, you surmise, leaving this place believing he can never return, this island where he has lived so much more than you. But then you suppose this is his punishment for giving in so easily.

You gaze at his ill-fated *Crow's Nest*, clinging in flimsy desperation to the top of the hill in the distance. Maybe, you begin to decide, his aunt will not be able to sell the place—not this fall, at least, not next spring, not until you and Matt and love itself have had more time to sober up. And wouldn't that be something, the two of you able to return to this island, pick which cottage in which to reside? Yes, wouldn't it be wonderful if everything worked out this way?

But you catch yourself at this point, disconcerted to find yourself counting maybes again. There are too many to count. Although it's true some of them must survive—a simple law of multiples—you believe you'll be relieved when most of them have slipped away.

Liam navigates the crowded boat around the tip of the island until the mainland is in view. You're dismayed at the relief you feel that the mainland is still there, astonished that seeing it this time reminds you, not of what has been lost, but of the possibilities remaining. Some of your possibilities still mingle with loving Matt, but the most important triumph is that some of them do not. Still, you feel a powerful, new encouragement about what potentially lies ahead. What is it Matt said about a month ago now, about nothing being over until it's over? What was it? Some silly homily about a fat lady singing?

Now Liam guns the motor and the mainland looms much closer while the island backs away.

You must have said something out loud while you were thinking these various thoughts, while the mainland moved much closer and the island turned away. Because, when you glance at Karen, you catch her watching you querulously. To convey you are all right, you exchange a warm and pleasant smile with her.

"I'll bet," says Karen then over the drone of the outboard motor, "everything works out great in Kingston."

Gratefully, you nod, not feeling so alone. "I hope so," you reply in the face of her reassuring smile.

THE WITNESSES STAND THEIR GROUND. One locks a collective fist around the ideal of romance and holds fast until the knuckles turn white. One gathers everyone into a huddle, deriving strength from numbers, entwining arms, holding on to one another, shaping the world into the ceramic teacup one understands it to be. Together one pushes. Together one pulls. One watches with a shared gaze, exercising a communal will. And emerging from this solitary strategic communion is a populist perception one can apply to the man and the woman, pushing the couple into the ideal mythology one wishes to sustain.

One imagines turning back time, say approximately five days. So the man navigates the lake and its channel in a gloom so complete and confining it distorts his perspective of time itself. On the open side of the island, the lake has turned white, indistinguishable against the pale foreboding of the sky, so much so that lake and sky become one. The vista of the open water is not a vista at all—it's a scene from which all color has been washed away.

Not until he steers his small, aluminum boat around the tip of the island into the channel itself does the empty canvas display even the faintest of pastel images. The mainland shows itself. It appears on the horizon like a jagged scar in the pale flesh of the lake and the rain-soaked clouds.

The channel is calm, registering barely a ripple. But the man clenches his teeth and holds on tightly anyway, one hand twitching on the throttle of the outboard motor, the other holding fast to the damp gunwale of the boat. The cold, aluminum craft seems singularly corporeal, the only sensory reality inside so much painful pallor, stinking of gasoline and clunking hollowly whenever he moves his foot. The day's gloom surrounds him entirely, matching the gloom building inside his spirit, clogging his heart and much of his mind. Time, reality, conscious thought, and what he manages or fails to observe are shuffled like a tarot deck, then dealt into the gray hopelessness his future has become. It's time which suffers most and more clearly breaks down. The crossing seems to pass in only a second, yet takes a lifetime as well.

Does Canine Ben assume his usual position in the bow, forelegs up on the seat, head erect, his ears blown back in the breeze? The man supposes he does but he can't say for sure— not enough time during this crossing to have noticed, too much time in the crossing to really have cared. The gloom of the day and inside his spirits is just too much for him, the worst kind of inebriation. His mind and heart collapse into a torpor constructed by his sadness, until his body functions entirely on its own, disconnected from any conscious command. And while his body accomplishes its normal tasks, his soul staggers through this most recent doleful universe, this most recent windswept desert, this new Serengeti of loss in the endless exploration by which life is usually defined.

Snidely he considers the riddle of it all. *Why did the soul cross the windswept desert? To get to the other side.* And on the other side? Destiny serves dinner again, experimenting this time with another poisonous recipe, a pinch of arsenic, a tablespoon of nightshade, a cup of whimsical hemlock, all of this concoction ladled out of the pot by a state of seemingly endless confusion. Gastronomic futility, he decides. But we feed ourselves anyway. There's no alternative more bitter or final.

All of this the man considers in painful dribs and drabs while his boat crosses this endless channel. Fragments are all he can consider, so drunk and exhausted is he by the weight of his sadness.

Most of all he keeps remembering something the woman said a few days ago. "Kingston's a very small city. We'll probably run into one another."

The man thought so too at the time of her observation. But now it doesn't seem likely. He revises his opinion. Kingston's not *that* small. Its cracks are large enough that a man can fall through them should he wish to. You don't just run into people because you've decided to change your mind. Not if destiny has become involved. Destiny has a nasty sense of humour; all of its jokes are best defined by the tenets of Murphy's Law. *The likelihood of running into the person you love*—the person you miss more than any other—*is in inverse ratio to the intensity of the love you feel. No good caring will go unpunished. If you can lose someone, you will.* All of Murphy's propositions seem to fit the fatal nature of love with only the slightest of alterations.

So the question becomes, as the mainland approaches, what happens if he fails somehow to encounter the woman again? What if they go all the wrong places at all the wrong times? Nonsense, really. Another hallucination of passivity. If the pain of loss drives him to it, he'll find a way to track her down.

But left in the hands of happenstance, there is no definitive answer to the initial question, which may be the reason he asks it so often as he navigates the channel home. Sometimes it comes out of his mouth out loud; sometimes he repeats it in silence. Either way, he toys with the mouse of the question like a particularly sadistic cat. It becomes a skip in his record, echoing over and over, "What if? What if?" All the way across the channel, for the second and the year the journey seems to take.

*The Inlet* too assumes some measure of the gloom. A portion of his awareness notices most of the summer boats have already been lifted out of the water. The finger docks float nearly empty. Almost everyone has gone home, leaving him tragically behind. The contrast between now and summer is so profound, so complete, he feels like an apparition just arrived from the other side as he guides his small boat into an empty berth.

Still, he goes through all the motions. His body ties up the boat, then reaches for one small piece of luggage. His body climbs out of the boat, staggering a moment at the edge of the dock, then regaining its equilibrium. His body calls for the dog, then follows it up to the waiting Escort. His fingers find his keys in the front left-hand pocket of his jeans, the way they always have. They unlock, then open the car door. They snap, finger and thumb together, in the direction of the dog. He hears his voice emerge outside his body. "C'mon, Ben," is all it says. And the retriever leaps into the car. His body opens the trunk, positioning the small bag he has been carrying deep inside the seemingly cavernous hatchback immediately behind the front seat.

In this way his body conducts its ritual of departure, systematically unloading the boat, stacking the various items on the dock so they can be carried one by one to the waiting car. His body functions without assistance from the rest of him, dragging his thoughts and hopelessness behind it like injured, bleeding entrails over the dock, the grass and asphalt, some forlorn and permanent wound. At this moment he's convinced he understands the true nature of despair. It's a drunken binge of sadness and loss, a long weekend spent in melancholic excess.

Gord Mahaffey, the marina's proprietor, appears on the dock as his customer returns for the final plastic bag, the final container of what belonged to him during his tragic summer. It sags on the wooden slats at their feet, some kind of fretting orphan last to be adopted.

"So that's it," Mahaffey says. "Going home."

"That's it," the man replies.

He wonders if they're supposed to shake hands. But Mahaffey keeps his hands inside the pockets of his navy blue wind breaker until the other man forgets that he has wondered. There's an oil stain on Mahaffey's jacket, not far from the name of his marina business, just down from the shoulder. It assumes an extra reality somehow, wedged like an arrow into the bulls eye of Bowman's sombre, dreamlike state.

For a time both men stare out over the channel at the island in the distance.

"Good summer?" Matt Bowman's body remembers to inquire.

"As good as could be expected," he thinks Mahaffey replies.

They stand there, both of them apparently waiting for something to happen even while they know it will not.

"I paid you for the boat, didn't I?" the customer asks at last.

At this moment he can't remember, isn't certain of anything. He doesn't feel himself to be in any way the man he was that eternity ago when he first arrived at the marina to cross over to the island.

Mahaffey turns to him, perplexed, wondering if he is crazy perhaps, or maybe considering if he can charge him twice for the boat he used all summer.

"Of course I did," Bowman says then, answering his own question. "It's been a long summer, I guess."

"They're *all* long," mutters Mahaffey, "even when they're too short."

And, at this moment, compelled by a powerful need to relent, a relenting as large and complete as any he can remember, Matt Bowman glances once more at the other man beside him on the dock. And he wonders about Mahaffey anew; what past exists for him? How did he evolve into the sour lemon he's become over the passing years? Is this the kind of man Matt himself must inevitably become? Is this the man he's going to be out of carelessness or lack of attention, out of ignoring opportunity?

Mahaffey, he notices, gazes intently across the channel at

the island on the other side. And Bowman wonders if the island reminds Mahaffey of some place where *he* once lived, some place that *he* gave up. Hard to tell for sure because his face is too distracting. Lined and freckled, shaded by a two-day beard, there's something careless on his upper lip, the residue from some unextraordinary bodily function gone socially awry.

Embarrassed, one sees Matt Bowman turn away. One realizes, for some reason he'll never fully understand, it's at this moment that he decides. The powerfully coercive oracle of what he might one day become cries out its prophecy from the shambles of Mahaffey's face.

"Look," says Bowman then. "I have to go back to the island. I forgot something."

"What?"

"I have to go back. It'll only take me a few minutes."

Mahaffey, in the terse, nearly angry way he deals with even a minor surprise, cocks his thumb towards the waiting Escort. "What about the dog?"

"He'll be fine. I'll be back in a few minutes." Bowman is already climbing into the boat.

Mahaffey notices the last bag sitting mutely on the dock. "Take that with you," he says. "I can't guarantee it'll still be here when you get back."

Without a word, Bowman reaches for the bag. He unties the boat, pulls the cord, starts the motor. "Be right back," he cries over the outboard's roar. "Keep an eye on Ben for me."

Mahaffey just shrugs.

For Bowman, everything grows clearer as he recrosses the gray-pale channel. Full throttle, that's clear. Nicole, that seems very clear. Or else he's entered a more enjoyable state of drunkenness, the celebratory kind which hope sometimes inspires, faking clarity inside its haze of inebriation.

The woman has been standing on the terrace, aware in the same way as the man that gloom moves in everywhere, claiming and undermining the value of entire neighborhoods. She drinks coffee. It goes down uneasily to sour in the lump of her stomach. But she consumes it anyway, to be doing something stubborn, to be exercising her will. She's dazed that this day has at last arrived and neither she nor the man have found a way to change their minds. Yet, somehow, nothing feels finished exactly.

There's a pending in the air. Or is this just the quiet electricity of faith, of being perpetually alive?

It hasn't even been a half hour or so since the man departed the island. Two hours from now she might truly believe the two of them are finished but, for now, it's simply too soon for this. This is the way it is with hope. It evaporates very slowly. Besides, it's the most persistent of habits, virtually an addiction, one knows.

Then, as if in response to the force of her unbending will, she hears the sound of the man's boat rounding the tip of the island. Still, she remains where she is, unwilling to be fooled. She stays put to be certain it's him, to be certain he's coming back because it's her he wants to see.

She watches his boat purr into view. It turns in towards the island, not down near his cottage but moving in her direction. And she begins to realize that he's probably come back, that probably everything has been solved. There is magic after all, the kind much more sensational than the trickery of sleight of hand. And she runs happily down the hill from the terrace, then across the waiting beach.

He beaches the boat, nearly stumbling in his haste to leap onto the shore. One gasps as they embrace.

"Nickie," he says, breathless and flushed. He's now so neon with excitement he seems to be alight, humming and burning against the day's insistent dullness.

"Matt?"

"I can't do this," he says. "You know I can't."

"I can't either," the woman replies.

"We'll work something out," he tells her breathlessly, his words splashing out of his mouth, forming verbal rainbows. "There's time to think of something, work out what we can do."

"Yes," she agrees. "We'll work something out."

"I love you, Nickie. That's the most important thing."

"And I love you, Matt."

"I'll come back on the weekend. I'll help you and Liam and Karen pack up." He takes a brief, ecstatic breath. "We can do this," he concludes.

"Yes."

They embrace some more. They kiss. They say all those things that witnesses like to hear until the words rain down like wedding bouquet petals, the color of witness crimson, the color of witness gold, the white of witness purity.

The witnesses applaud. They are sentimental, after all, and do not notice the hallmark clichés in the scripts one reads or writes. Sentimentality is fine for the people of this world, they know, for the majority of lovers and wanderers who don't acknowledge how sentimentality reduces important experience to the emotionally familiar. After all, familiarity is all there is, where witnesses are concerned. It's how one gives testimony, alters the details of what one has seen to suit the expectations of the court. Familiarity is even more powerful, the witnesses know, than the gravitational pull of life one is foolish to defy.

"I have to go," says the man at last, easing out of her embrace. "Ben's waiting in the car."

"Okay."

"I love you, Nickie. I'll see you on the weekend."

He leaps back into the boat. He uses the oar to push it away from shore. The motor roars into life. He waves, he smiles, he blows the woman a kiss.

Then, shortly, he's gone again.

After all of this, the woman lingers at the edge of the water until long after the boat has disappeared. Then, shining out of the irrelevant gloom, she turns around at last to walk up the familiar hill towards her waiting cottage.

After she has gone, the witnesses draw the curtain, satisfied with what has transpired, with what will continue on—endorsed—from here.

## ABOUT THE AUTHOR

Barry Grills is a former chair of The Writers' Union of Canada and the Book and Periodical Council. His short stories have appeared in various literary magazines and anthologies, including *Best Canadian Stories*. His critically acclaimed memoir, *Every Wolf's Howl*, won an Alberta Book Award for its publisher, Freehand Books. His first Fluid Grouse Enterprises book, *Roadkill*, was a finalist in both the Next Generation Indie Book Awards and the Whistler Independent Book Awards. He is also the author of three musical biographies on the lives and careers of Anne Murray, Alanis Morissette and Céline Dion. His work on an updated version of Dion's life, co-authored with Jim Brown, was the source for a CBC television movie. In 2019, he was appointed a life member of The Writers' Union of Canada. He currently lives and works in North Bay, Ontario, Canada.

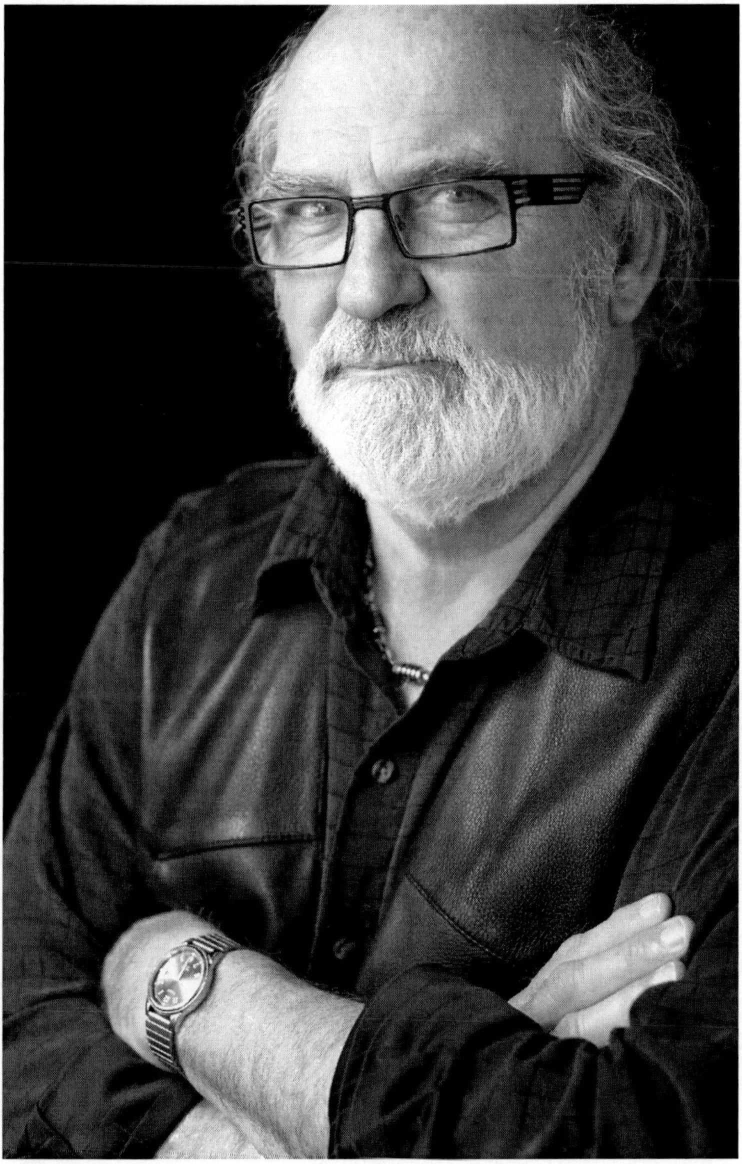

Manufactured by Amazon.ca
Acheson, AB